Praise for Jo Nesbo and COCKROACHES

"With his labyrinthine, shiver-inducing plots, full-blooded char-acterizations and uncanny sense of mood and place, Nesbo is simply a master storyteller."   *Winnipeg Free Press*

"Once you read a Nesbo novel, you're hooked on this author."
                                                The Chronicle Herald

"*Cockroaches* will thrill Harry Hole addicts."
                                        Northamptonshire Telegraph

"Jo Nesbo is my favorite thriller writer and Harry Hole my new hero."   Michael Connelly

"Maddeningly addictive."   *Vanity Fair*

"For those with a Stieg Larsson–shaped hole on their bedside table, fellow Scandinavian Jo Nesbo's star has been rising for some time."   *The Guardian*

"Nesbo forged something new from the cliché of the dyspeptic alcoholic copper, making Harry Hole the most successful Nordic crime export since Henning Mankell's Kurt Wallander. [In *Cockroaches*] the complex narrative and large dramatis personae are handled with steely authority."   *The Independent*

"Nesbo has a terrific feel for character, and Hole carves a place of distinction for himself in a crowded field."   *Booklist*

Jo Nesbo

COCKROACHES

TRANSLATED FROM THE NORWEGIAN BY DON BARTLETT

Vintage Canada

VINTAGE CANADA EDITION, 2014

Copyright © 1998 Jo Nesbo
English translation copyright © 2013 Don Bartlett
Published by arrangement with Harvill Secker, one of the
publishers in the Random House Group Ltd.

Published in Canada by Vintage Canada, a division of Random House of Canada Limited,
Toronto, in 2014. Originally published in hardcover in Canada by Random House Canada,
a division of Random House of Canada Limited, in 2013, and simultaneously in the United
Kingdom by Harvill Secker an imprint of the Random House Group Limited, London.
Distributed in Canada by Random House of Canada Limited.

Vintage Canada with colophon is a registered trademark.

www.randomhouse.ca

Library and Archives Canada Cataloguing in Publication

Nesbø, Jo, 1960–
The cockroaches / Jo Nesbø ; translated by Don Bartlett.

(The Harry Hole series ; 2)
Translation of: Kakerlakkene.

ISBN 978-0-307-36029-8

I. Bartlett, Don II. Title. III. Series: Nesbø, Jo, 1960– . Harry Hole mystery series ; 2.

PT8951.24.E83K3513 2014   839.82'374   C2012-908391-7

Typeset in Scala by Palimpsest Book Production Limited, Falkirk, Stirlingshire

Cover photograph: Dinodia; Glow Images

Printed and bound in the United States of America

2 4 6 8 9 7 5 3 1

Among Norwegians living in Thailand there is a rumour circulating that one of their ambassadors, who died as a result of a car accident in Bangkok, was actually murdered under extremely mysterious circumstances. There is no evidence to support this, but it makes for a good story.

No persons or events mentioned in this book should be confused with real persons or events. Reality is far too strange for that.

Bangkok, 23 February 1998

PART ONE

1

Tuesday 7 January

THE TRAFFIC LIGHTS CHANGED TO green, and the roar from lorries, cars, motorbikes and tuk-tuks rose higher and higher until Dim could see the glass in Robinson's department store vibrating. Then the queues started moving and the shop window displaying the long, red silk dress was lost behind them in the darkness.

She took a taxi. Not a packed bus or a tuk-tuk riddled with rust but a taxi with air conditioning and a driver who kept his mouth shut. She leaned back against the headrest and tried to enjoy the ride. No problem. A moped shot past and a girl on the pillion clinging to a red T-shirt with a visor helmet gave them a vacant look. Hold on tight, Dim thought.

On Rama IV Road the driver pulled in behind a lorry spewing exhaust fumes so thick and black she couldn't see the number plate. After passing through the air-conditioning system the exhaust was chilled and almost odourless. Almost. She wafted her hand discreetly to show her reaction, and the driver glanced in his mirror and moved into the outside lane. No problem.

This was how her life had always been. On the farm where she had grown up she had been one of six girls. Six too many, according to her father. She had been seven years old when they stood coughing in the yellow dust and waving as the cart carrying her eldest sister trundled down the country road alongside the brown canal water. Her sister had been given clean clothes, a train ticket to Bangkok and an address in Patpong written on the back of a business card, and she had cried like a waterfall, even though Dim had waved so hard it felt as if her hand would fall off. Her mother had patted her on the head and said it wasn't easy, but it wasn't that bad, either. At least her sister wouldn't have to wander from farm to farm as a *kwai*, as her mother had done before she got married. Besides, Miss Wong had promised she would take good care of her. Her father had nodded, spat betel juice from between black teeth and added that the *farangs* in the bars would pay well for fresh girls.

Dim hadn't understood what her mother meant by *kwai*, but she wasn't going to ask. She knew, of course, that a *kwai* was a bull. Like most people on the farms around them, they couldn't afford a bull, so they hired one of the ones that circulated the district when the rice paddy had to be ploughed. It was only later she found out that the girl who accompanied the bull was also called a *kwai* as her services formed part of the deal. That was the tradition. She hoped she would meet a farmer who would have her before she got too old.

When Dim was fifteen her father had called her name as he waded across the paddy field with the sun behind him and his hat in hand. She hadn't answered at once; she had straightened up and looked hard at the green ridges around the small farm, closed her eyes and listened to the sound of the trumpeter bird in the leaves and inhaled the smell of eucalyptus and rubber trees. She had realised it was her turn.

For the first year they had lived four girls to a room and shared everything: bed, food and clothes. The last of these was especially important, for without nice clothes you wouldn't get the best customers. She had taught herself to dance, taught herself to smile, taught herself to see which men only wanted to buy drinks and which wanted to buy sex. Her father had already agreed with Miss Wong that the money was to be sent home, so she didn't see much of it during the first few years, but Miss Wong was content and as time went by she kept more back for Dim.

Miss Wong had reason to be content. Dim worked hard, and the customers bought drinks. Miss Wong should be pleased she was still there because a couple of times it had been a close-run thing. A Japanese man had wanted to marry Dim, but withdrew his offer when she demanded money for the plane ticket. An American had taken her along to Phuket, postponed his journey home and bought her a diamond ring. She had pawned it the day after he left.

Some paid badly and told her to get lost if she complained; others reported her to Miss Wong if she didn't comply with everything they wanted her to do. They didn't understand that once they had bought her time from the bar Miss Wong had her money and Dim was her own boss. Her own boss. She thought about the red dress in the shop window. Her mother had been right: it wasn't easy, but it wasn't that bad, either.

And she had managed to retain her innocent smile and happy laughter. They liked that. Perhaps that was why she had been offered the job Wang Lee had advertised in *Thai Rath* under the heading of GRO, or Guest Relation Officer. Wang Lee was a small, dark-skinned Chinese man, who ran a motel some way out on Sukhumvit Road, and the customers were mainly foreigners with special requests but not so special that she couldn't meet them. To tell the truth, she liked what she did better than dancing for hours in the bar. Besides, Wang Lee paid well. The sole disadvantage was that it took such a long time to get there from her apartment in Banglamphu.

The damn traffic! It had come to a standstill again, and she told the driver she would get out, even though it meant crossing six lanes of cars to reach the motel on the far side of the road. The air wrapped itself around her like a hot, wet towel as she left the taxi. She searched for a gap, holding her hand in front of her mouth, aware that it made no difference, that there was no other air to breathe in Bangkok, but at least she was spared the smell.

She slipped between vehicles, had to sidestep a pickup with the flatbed full of boys whistling, and she almost had her heel straps taken off by a kamikaze Toyota. Then she was across.

Wang Lee looked up as she entered the deserted reception area.

'Quiet evening?' she said.

He nodded his displeasure. There had been a few of them over the last year.

'Have you eaten?'

'Yes,' she lied. He meant well, but she was not in the mood for the watery noodles he boiled up in the back room.

'You'll have to wait,' he said. 'The *farang* wanted to have a sleep first. He'll ring when he's ready.'

She groaned. 'You know I have to be back in the bar before midnight, Lee.'

He looked at his watch. 'Give him an hour.'

She shrugged and sat down. If it had been a year ago he would probably have thrown her out for speaking like that, but now he needed all the income he could get. Of course, she could go, but then the long journey would have been wasted. Also, she owed Lee a favour; she had worked for worse pimps.

After stubbing out the third cigarette she rinsed her mouth with Lee's bitter Chinese tea and rose for a final check of her make-up in the mirror over the counter.

'I'll go and wake him,' she said.

'Mm. Have you got the skates?'

She lifted her bag.

Her heels crunched on the gravel of the empty drive between the low motel rooms. Room 120 was right at the back, she couldn't see a car outside, but there was a light in the window. So perhaps he had woken up. A little breeze lifted her short skirt, but failed to cool her. She longed for a monsoon, for rain. Just as after a few weeks of flooding, muddy streets and mildew on her washing she would long for the dry, windless months.

She tapped the door lightly with her knuckles and put on her bashful smile with the question 'What's your name?' already on her lips. No one answered. She tapped again and looked at her watch. She could probably haggle a few hundred baht off the price of the dress, even if it was Robinson's. She turned the door handle and discovered to her surprise that the door was unlocked.

He was lying prone on the bed, and her first impression was that he was asleep. Then she saw the glint of the knife's blue glass handle sticking out of the loud yellow jacket. It's hard to say which of all the thoughts racing through her brain appeared first, but one of them was definitely that the trip to Banglamphu had been wasted anyway. Then she finally gained control of her vocal cords. The scream, however, was drowned out by a resounding blast on a lorry's horn as it avoided an inattentive tuk-tuk on Sukhumvit Road.

2

Wednesday 8 January

'NATIONAL THEATRE,' A SLEEPY, NASAL voice announced over the speakers before the tram doors flipped open and Dagfinn Torhus stepped out into the cold, damp darkness. The air stung his freshly shaved cheeks, and in the glow from Oslo's frugal neon lighting he could see frozen breath streaming from his mouth.

It was early January, and he knew it would be better later in the winter when the fjord was frozen over and the air became drier. He started to walk up Drammensveien towards the Ministry of Foreign Affairs. A couple of solitary taxis passed him; otherwise the streets were as good as deserted. The Gjensidig clock shone red against the black winter sky above the building opposite, informing him it was only six.

Outside the door he took out his entrance card. 'Post: Director' it said above a photo of a ten-years-younger Dagfinn Torhus staring into the camera, chin jutting, gaze determined, from behind steel-rimmed glasses. He swiped the card, tapped in the code and pushed open the heavy glass door in Victoria Terrasse.

Not all doors had opened as easily since he came here as a twenty-five-year-old almost thirty years ago. At the Diplomatic

School, the Foreign Office institute for aspiring officials, he had not exactly melted into his surroundings with his broad Østerdal accent and rural ways, as one of the posh Bærum boys in his year's intake had pointed out. The other aspirants had been students of politics, economics and law with parents who were academics, politicians or themselves members of the FO aristocracy to which they were seeking admission. He was a farmer's son with qualifications from the Agricultural High School in Ås. Not that it bothered him much, but he knew that real friends were important for his career. As Dagfinn was trying to learn the social codes, he compensated by grafting even harder. Whatever the differences, they all shared the fact that they had only vague notions of where they wanted to go in life and the knowledge that only one direction counted: up.

Torhus sighed and nodded to the security guard, who pushed his newspapers and an envelope under the glass window.

'Any other . . .?'

The guard shook his head.

'First to arrive as always, Torhus. The envelope's from Communications. It was delivered last night.'

Torhus watched the floor numbers flash by as the lift raised him higher in the building. He had this idea that every floor represented a certain period in his career, and so it was subject to review every morning.

The first floor was the first two years on the diplomatic course, the long, non-committal discussions about politics and history and the French lessons he had hauled himself through by the bootstraps.

The second floor was the placement. He had been stationed in Canberra for two years, then Mexico City for three. Wonderful cities, for that matter, no, he couldn't complain. True, he had put London and New York as his first two choices, but these were prestigious postings that everyone else had also applied for, so he had made up his mind not to regard them as a defeat.

On the third floor he was back in Norway without the generous foreign benefits and housing supplements which had allowed him to live a life of insouciance and plenty. He had met Berit, she had become pregnant, and when it had been time to apply for a new foreign posting number two was already on the way. Berit was from the same region as he was and chatted to her mother every day. He had decided to wait a little and opted to work like a Trojan, writing kilometre-long reports on bilateral trade with developing countries, composing speeches for the Minister of Foreign Affairs and reaping acknowledgement as he made his way up the building. Nowhere else in the state system is competition as fierce as at the Foreign Office, where the hierarchy is so obvious. Dagfinn Torhus had gone to the office like a soldier to the Front, kept his head down, back covered and fired whenever he had someone in his sights. A few pats on the shoulder came his way, he knew he had been 'noticed' and had tried to explain to Berit that he could probably get Paris or London, but for the first time in their hitherto humdrum marriage she had put her foot down. He had given in.

His upwardly mobile trend had vanished almost without a trace, and suddenly one morning in the bathroom mirror he saw a director shunted into the sidings, a moderately influential bureaucrat who would never manage the leap to the fifth floor, not with him being ten years or so from retirement age. Unless he pulled off a sensational coup, of course. But while that kind of stunt could lead to promotion, it could just as easily lead to the boot.

Nevertheless, he continued as before, trying to keep his nose in front of the others'. He was first in the office every morning so that he could read the newspapers and faxes in peace and quiet, and already had his conclusions to hand at morning meetings by the time the others sat rubbing sleep out of their eyes. It was as though striving had entered his bloodstream.

He unlocked his office door and hesitated for a moment before switching on the light. That, too, had a history. Unfortunately it had leaked out, and he knew it had attained legendary status in Ministry circles. Many years ago the then American ambassador in Oslo had rung Torhus early one morning and asked what he thought about President Carter's remarks the previous night. Torhus had just come in the office door; he hadn't read the newspapers or the faxes and was lost for an answer. Needless to say, that had ruined his day. And it was to get worse. The next morning the ambassador had rung as he was opening the newspaper and asked how the events of the night would affect the situation in the Middle East. The following morning the same thing happened. Torhus, undermined by doubts and lack of information, had stuttered an incoherent response.

He had started to arrive at the office even earlier, but the ambassador appeared to have a sixth sense, for every morning the telephone rang just as he was settling into his chair.

It was only when he discovered that the ambassador was staying at the small Aker Hotel, directly opposite the Foreign Office, that he worked out the connection. The ambassador, who everyone knew liked to get up early, had of course noticed that the light in Torhus's office came on before the others and wanted to tease the zealous diplomat. Torhus had gone out and bought a head lamp, and the next morning he had read all the newspapers and faxes before switching on the office light. He did this for almost three weeks before the ambassador gave up.

At this moment, however, Dagfinn Torhus couldn't give a damn about the fun-loving ambassador. He had opened the envelope from Communications, and on the decoded paper copy of the cryptofax stamped TOP SECRET there was a message that caused him to spill coffee over the notes strewn around his desk. The short text left a lot to the imagination, but the essence was basically this: Norway's ambassador in Thailand, Atle Molnes, had been found with a knife in his back in a Bangkok brothel.

Torhus read the fax once more before putting it down.

Atle Molnes, former Christian Democrat politician, former chairman of the Finance Committee, was now a former everything else as well. It was so incredible that he was forced to glance over at Aker Hotel to see if anyone was standing behind the curtains. Reasonably enough, the sender was the Norwegian Embassy in Bangkok. Torhus swore. Why did this have to happen now of all times, in Bangkok of all places? Should he inform Secretary of State Askildsen first? No, he would find out soon enough. Torhus looked at his watch and lifted the telephone receiver to call the Minister of Foreign Affairs.

Bjarne Møller tapped gently on the door and opened it. The voices in the meeting room fell quiet, and the faces turned towards him.

'This is Bjarne Møller, head of Crime Squad,' said the Police Commissioner, motioning him to take a seat. 'Møller, this is Secretary of State Bjørn Askildsen from the Prime Minister's office and HR Director Dagfinn Torhus from the Ministry of Foreign Affairs.'

Møller nodded, pulled out a chair and tried to manoeuvre his unbelievably long legs under the large, oval oak table. He thought he had seen Askildsen's sleek young face on TV. The Prime Minister's office? It had to be serious trouble.

'Great you could make it at such short notice,' the Secretary of State said, rolling his *rrr*s and drumming the table nervously with his fingers. 'Commissioner, could you give a brief résumé of what we've been discussing.'

Møller had received a call from the Police Commissioner twenty minutes before. Without any explanation, she had given him fifteen minutes to make his way to the Ministry of Foreign Affairs.

'Atle Molnes has been found dead, probably murdered, in Bangkok,' the Police Commissioner began.

Møller saw Director Torhus roll his eyes behind his steel-rimmed glasses, and after he had been given the rest of the story he understood his reaction. You would definitely have to be a policeman to state that a man who had been found with a knife protruding from one side of his spine, through a lung and into the heart, had 'probably' been murdered.

'He was found in a hotel room by a woman—'

'In a brothel,' the man with the steel glasses interrupted. 'By a prostitute.'

'I've had a chat with my colleague in Bangkok,' the Police Commissioner said. 'A fair-minded man. He's promised to keep a lid on the matter for a while.'

Møller's first instinct had been to ask why they should wait before going public with the murder. Immediate press coverage often produced tip-offs for the police, as people's memories were clear and the evidence was still fresh. But something told him this question would be regarded as very naive. Instead he asked how long they counted on being able to keep a lid on this sort of matter.

'Long enough for us to establish a palatable version of events, I hope,' the Secretary of State said. 'The present one won't do, you see.'

The present one? So the real version had been considered and rejected. As a relatively new *politiavdelingssjef* – or PAS – Møller had so far been spared any dealings with politicians, but he knew the higher up the service you went, the harder it was to keep them at arm's length.

'I appreciate that the present version is uncomfortable, but what do you mean by it "won't do"?'

The Police Commissioner gave Møller an admonitory look.

The Secretary of State looked unimpressed. 'We haven't got much time, Møller, but let me give you a swift course in practical politics. Everything I say now is of course strictly confidential.'

Askildsen instinctively adjusted the knot of his tie, a movement Møller recognised from his television interviews. 'Well, for the first time in post-war history we have a centre party with a reasonable chance of survival. Not because there is any parliamentary basis for it, but because the Prime Minister happens to be on the way to becoming one of the country's least unpopular politicians.'

The Police Commissioner and the Director from the Ministry of Foreign Affairs smiled.

'However, his popularity rests on the same fragile foundation that is the stock-in-trade for all politicians: trust. The most important thing is not to be likeable or charismatic, it is to enjoy trust. Do you know why Gro Harlem Brundtland was such a popular prime minister, Møller?'

Møller had no idea.

'Not because she was a charmer, but because people were confident that she was the person she claimed to be. Trust, that's the key word.'

The others around the table nodded. This was clearly part of the core curriculum.

'Now, Ambassador Molnes and our current Prime Minister were closely connected, through friendship as well as their political careers. They studied together, rose up through the party ranks together, battled through the modernisation of the youth movement and even shared a flat when they were both elected to Storting at a very young age. Molnes voluntarily stepped out of the limelight when they were joint heirs apparent in the party. He gave the Prime Minister his full support and hence we were spared an agonising party duel. All this obviously means that the Prime Minister owed Molnes a debt of gratitude.'

Askildsen moistened his lips and looked out of the window.

'In other words, Ambassador Molnes didn't have any diplomatic training and wouldn't have got to Bangkok if the Prime Minister hadn't pulled strings. Perhaps this sounds like cronyism, but it's an acceptable form of it, introduced and given general currency by the Socialist Party. Reiulf Steen didn't have any Foreign Office experience when he was made ambassador in Chile.'

The eyes refocused on Møller, a playful glint dancing inside somewhere.

'I'm sure I don't need to emphasise how this could damage trust in the Prime Minister if it comes out that a friend and party comrade, whom he appointed himself, was caught in flagrante in a brothel. And murdered into the bargain.'

The Secretary of State motioned to the Police Commissioner to continue, but Møller couldn't restrain himself.

'Who hasn't got a pal who's been to a brothel?'

Askildsen's smile curled at the edges.

The Foreign Office Director with the steel glasses coughed. 'You've been told what you need to know, Møller. Please leave the judgements to us. What we need is someone to ensure that the investigation of this matter does not take . . . an unfortunate turn. Naturally, we all want the murderer, or murderers, to be apprehended, but the circumstances surrounding the murder should remain under wraps until further notice. For the good of the country. Do you understand?'

Møller looked down at his hands. For the good of the country. Bloody hell. They had never been much good at doing what they were told in his family. His father had never risen through the police ranks.

'Experience tells us that the truth tends to be hard to conceal, herr Torhus.'

'Indeed. I'll take responsibility for this operation on behalf of the Foreign Office. As you appreciate, this is a somewhat delicate matter which will demand close cooperation with the Thai police. As the embassy is involved we have some leeway – diplomatic immunity and all that – but we're walking a tightrope here. Therefore, we wish to send someone with honed investigative skills and experience of international police work and who can produce results.'

He stopped and looked at Møller, who was wondering why he felt an instinctive lack of goodwill towards the diplomat with the aggressive chin.

'We could put together a team with—'

'No team, Møller. Too conspicuous. Besides, your Commissioner thinks that a whole division would hardly be conducive to good relations with the local police. One man.'

'One man?'

'The Commissioner has already suggested a name, and we consider it a good suggestion. Now we'd like to hear your opinion of him. According to conversations the Police Commissioner has had with his colleague in Sydney, he did remarkable work down there last winter in connection with the Inger Holter murder.'

'I read the story in the papers,' Askildsen said. 'Impressive stuff. Surely he has to be our man?'

Bjarne Møller swallowed. So the Police Commissioner had suggested they should send Harry Hole to Bangkok. He had been summoned to assure them that Hole was the best the force had to offer, the perfect man for the job.

He glanced round the table. Politics, power and influence. This was a game he couldn't begin to understand, but he realised that in some way or other it would work out in his favour, that whatever he said now would have consequences for his career. The Police Commissioner had stuck her neck out by suggesting a name. Probably one of the others had then asked to have Hole's qualifications endorsed by his immediate superiors. He looked at his boss and tried to interpret her expression. Of course, everything might turn out fine with Hole. And if he advised them not to send him, would that not cast the Commissioner in an unfortunate light? He would be asked to suggest an alternative and then *his* head would be the one on the block if the officer concerned messed up.

Møller looked at the painting above the Police Commissioner: Trygve Lie, the UN Secretary General, gazed down at him imperiously. A politician as well. Through the windows he saw the roofs of the apartment buildings in the low winter light, Akershus fortress and a weathercock shivering in the icy gusts on top of the Continental Hotel.

Bjarne Møller knew he was a competent police officer, but this was a different game, and he didn't know the rules. What would his father have advised him to do? Well, Officer Møller had never had to deal with politics, but he had known what was important if he was to be taken at all seriously and had forbidden his son to start Police College until he had completed the first part of a law course. He had done as his father said, and after the graduation ceremony his father had kept clearing his throat, overcome with emotion, while slapping his son on the back until he'd had to ask him to stop.

'A great suggestion,' Bjarne Møller heard himself say in a loud, clear voice.

'Good,' Torhus said. 'The reason we wanted an opinion so quickly is that, of course, all this is urgent. He'll have to drop everything he's working on; he's leaving tomorrow.'

Well, perhaps it's just the sort of job Harry needs right now, Møller hoped.

'Sorry we have to deprive you of such an important man,' Askildsen said.

PAS Bjarne Møller had to stop himself bursting into laughter.

3

Wednesday 8 January

THEY FOUND HIM AT SCHRØDER'S in Waldemar Thranes gate, a venerable old watering hole located at the crossroads where Oslo East meets Oslo West. It was more old than venerable, to be honest. The venerable part was largely down to the authorities' decision to put a preservation order on the smoke-filled brown rooms. But the order did not include the clientele: old boozers, a hunted and extinction-threatened bunch; eternal students; and jaded charmers long past their sell-by date.

The two officers spotted their man sitting under a painting of Aker Church as the draught from the door allowed a brief glimpse through the curtain of smoke. His blond hair was cropped so short the bristles stood up straight and the three-day beard on the lean, marked face had a streak of grey even though he could hardly be older than his mid-thirties. He sat alone, straight-backed, wearing his reefer jacket, as if about to leave any minute. As if the beer in front of him on the table was not a source of pleasure but a job that had to be done.

'They said we would find you here,' said the older of the two and sat down opposite him. 'I'm Waaler.'

'See the guy sitting in the corner?' Hole said without looking up.

Waaler turned and saw a scrawny old man gazing into his glass of red wine while rocking backwards and forwards. He seemed to be freezing cold.

'They call him the last Mohican.'

Hole raised his head and beamed. His eyes were like blue-and-white marbles behind a network of red veins, and they focused on Waaler's shirt.

'Merchant seaman,' he said, his diction meticulous. 'Used to be lots of them here a few years back apparently, but now there are hardly any left. He was torpedoed twice during the war. He thinks he's immortal. Last week, after closing time, I found him sleeping in a snowdrift down in Glückstadsgata. The streets were empty, it was pitch black and minus eighteen. When I'd shaken some life into him he just looked at me and told me to go to hell.' He laughed.

'Listen, Hole—'

'I went over to his table last night and asked if he remembered what had happened – I mean, that I'd saved him from freezing to death. Do you know what he said?'

'Møller wants to see you, Hole.'

'He said he was immortal. "I can put up with being an unwanted merchant seaman in this shit country," he said. "But it's a sorry business when even St Peter doesn't want anything to do with me." Did you hear? "Even St Peter"—'

'We've got orders to take you to the station.'

Another beer landed on the table in front of Hole with a thud.

'Let's settle up now, Rita,' he said.

'Two hundred and eighty,' she answered without needing to check her slips of paper.

'Jesus Christ,' mumbled the younger officer.

'That's fine, Rita.'

'Oh, thanks.' She was gone.

'Best service in town,' Harry explained. 'Sometimes she can spot you even when you haven't been waving both arms in the air.'

The skin on Waaler's forehead tightened and a blood vessel appeared, like a blue, knobbly worm.

'We haven't got the time to sit here and listen to your drunken ramblings, Hole. I suggest you give the last beer a miss . . .'

Hole had already put the glass carefully to his lips and started drinking.

Waaler leaned forward and tried to keep his voice low. 'I know about you, Hole. And I don't like you. I think you should have been booted out of the force years ago. Guys like you make people lose respect for the police. But that's not why we're here now. We've come to take you with us. The PAS is a nice man. Perhaps he'll give you another chance.'

Hole belched and Waaler leaned back.

'Another chance to do what?'

'To show what you can do,' the younger officer said with a boyish smile.

'I'll show you what I can do.' Hole smiled, put the glass to his mouth and tipped his head back.

'Pack it in, Hole!' Waaler's cheeks flushed as they watched Hole's Adam's apple rise and fall beneath his unshaven chin.

'Happy?' Hole asked, putting the empty glass down in front of him.

'Our job—'

'I couldn't give a shit about your job.' Hole buttoned up his reefer jacket. 'If Møller wants something he can ring me or wait until I'm at work tomorrow. Now I'm going home and I hope I won't see your faces for the next twelve hours. Gentlemen . . .' Harry raised himself to his full 192 centimetres and lurched to the side.

'You arrogant prick,' Waaler said, rocking back in his chair. 'You bloody loser. If only the reporters who wrote about you after Australia had known you haven't got the balls—'

'The balls to do what, Waaler?' Hole was still smiling. 'Lock up drunken sixteen-year-olds because they've got Mohicans?'

The younger officer glanced at Waaler. Rumours had been doing the rounds at Police College last year that some young punks had been hauled in for drinking beer in public places and beaten in the cells with oranges packed in wet towels.

'You've never understood *esprit de corps*, Hole,' Waaler said. 'You just think about yourself. Everyone knows who was driving the car in Vinderen and why a good policeman smashed his skull against a fence post. Because you're a drunk, Hole, and you drove while under the influence. You should be bloody glad the force swept the facts under the carpet. Had they not been concerned about the family and the force's reputation—'

The younger officer accompanying Waaler was learning something new every day. This afternoon, for example, he learned it was very stupid to rock on a chair while insulting someone, because you are totally defenceless if the insulted party steps over and lands a straight right between the eyes. As customers often fell over at Schrøder's there was no more than a couple of seconds' silence before the buzz of conversation resumed.

He helped Waaler to his feet as he glimpsed the tails of Hole's jacket disappearing through the door. 'Wow, not bad after eight beers, eh?' he said, but shut up when he met Waaler's gaze.

Harry's legs strode out casually along the icy pavement of Dovregata. His knuckles didn't hurt; it would be early tomorrow morning before either pain or regret came knocking.

He didn't drink during working hours. Though he had done it before, and Dr Aune contended that every new relapse started where the old one finished.

The white-haired, roly-poly Peter Ustinov clone had laughed so much his double chin shook as Harry explained to him that he was keeping away from his old foe Jim Beam and confining himself to beer. Because he didn't like beer much.

'You've been in a mess, and the moment you open the bottle you're there again. There's no halfway house, Harry.'

Well. He was struggling home on two legs, generally managing to undress himself and getting himself to work the next day. It hadn't always been like that. Harry called it a halfway house. He just needed a few knockout drops to sleep, that was all.

A woman said hello from under a black fur hat as she passed. Was it someone he knew? Last year lots of people had said hello, particularly after the interview on TV when Anne Grosvold had asked him how it felt to shoot a serial killer.

'Well, better than sitting here and answering questions like that one,' he had said with a crooked smile, and it had been the hit of the spring, the most repeated quote this side of one politician's defence of an agricultural policy: 'Sheep are nice animals.'

Harry inserted the key into the lock of his flat in Sofies gate. Why he had moved to Bislett escaped him. Perhaps it had been because his neighbours in Tøyen had started looking at him strangely and keeping their distance, which at first he had construed as showing respect.

Fine, the neighbours here left him in peace, though they would appear in the corridor to check everything was OK if, on rare occasions, he should slip on a step and roll back down to the nearest landing.

The backward rolls hadn't started until October, after he had hit a brick wall over Sis's case. Then the air had been knocked out of him and he had started dreaming again. And he knew only one way to keep the dreams at arm's length.

He had tried to pull himself together, take Sis to the cabin in

Rauland, but she had become very withdrawn since the assault, and she didn't laugh as easily as before. So he had rung his father a couple of times, although the conversations hadn't been very long, just long enough to indicate that his dad wanted to be left in peace.

Harry closed the door to his flat, shouted that he was home and nodded with satisfaction when there was no answer. Monsters come in all shapes and sizes, but so long as they weren't waiting for him in the kitchen when he came home there was a chance he would have an undisturbed night's sleep.

4

Thursday 9 January

THE COLD SNAP CAME SO suddenly that when Harry stepped out of the door he involuntarily gasped for breath. He looked up at the reddening sky between the houses and opened his mouth to release the taste of gall and Colgate.

In Holbergs plass he caught the tram rattling down Welhavensgate. He found a seat and opened the *Aftenposten*. Another paedophilia case. There had been three of them over recent months, all Norwegians caught red-handed in Thailand.

The leader reminded readers of the Prime Minister's promise during his election campaign that he would intensify investigation of sexual crimes, including those involving Norwegians abroad, and demanded to know when the public would see any results.

Secretary of State Bjørn Askildsen, from the Prime Minister's office, commented that they were working with the Thai government to further investigative powers.

'This is urgent!' the *Aftenposten* editor wrote. 'People expect to see some action. It's not right that a Christian minister can permit this outrage to continue.'

∗   ∗   ∗

'Come in!'

Harry opened the door and looked straight into Bjarne Møller's yawning mouth. He was leaning back in his chair with his long legs sticking out from under the desk.

'There you are. I was expecting you yesterday, Harry.'

'So I was told.' Harry sat down. 'I don't work when I'm drunk. Or vice versa. It's a kind of principle I have.' This was intended to sound ironic.

'A police officer is a police officer twenty-four hours a day, Harry, sober or not. I had to persuade Waaler not to report you, you know.'

Harry shrugged, indicating that he'd said all he had to say on the subject.

'OK, Harry, we won't discuss that now. I've got a job for you. A job which in my opinion you don't deserve, but which I'm going to give you anyway.'

'Would it make you happy if I said I don't want it?'

'Cut the Philip Marlowe stuff, Harry. It doesn't suit you,' Møller replied brusquely. Harry smirked. He knew the PAS liked him. 'I haven't even told you what it is.'

'I assume from the fact that you send a car to get me in my free time it's not to put me on traffic duty.'

'Exactly, so why don't you let me finish?'

Harry gave a brief, dry chuckle and leaned forward in his chair. 'Can we speak our minds, PAS?'

What mind? Møller almost asked, but limited himself to a nod.

'I'm not the man for important assignments right now, boss. I suppose you've seen how things are going at the moment. Or how things are *not* going. Or barely going. I do my job, the routine stuff, try not to get in anyone's way and clock in and out in a sober condition. I'd give the job to one of the other boys if I were you.'

Møller sighed, laboriously drew up his legs and got to his feet.

'Can I speak *my* mind, Harry? Had it been up to me, someone else would have got the job. But they want you. So it would be a great favour to me, Harry . . .'

Harry looked up warily. Bjarne Møller had helped him out of enough scrapes over the last year for him to know that it was just a question of time before he had to start repaying the debt.

'Hang on! Who are *they*?'

'People in high positions. People who can make my life hell if they don't get what they want.'

'And what will I get to take on the job?'

Møller knitted his brows as fiercely as he could, but he had always found it difficult to muster a stern expression on his open, boyish face.

'What do *you* get? You get your salary. For the duration. For Christ's sake, what do *you* get!'

'Ah, I'm in the picture now, boss. Some of those high-up people reckon that officer who cleared up the case in Sydney last year must be one hell of a guy, and it's your job to make him toe the line. Am I wrong?'

'Harry, please don't push this one too far.'

'I'm not wrong. I wasn't wrong yesterday when I saw Waaler's face, either. That's why I've already slept on it and this is my suggestion: I'm a good boy, I turn up for work, and when I've finished, you give me two detectives full-time for two months and complete access to all our data.'

'What are you talking about?'

'You know what I'm talking about.'

'If this is about your sister's rape case, I'm afraid I have to say no, Harry. The case was closed, once and for all, remember?'

'I remember, boss. I remember the report in which it was stated she had Down's syndrome and that therefore it was not inconceivable that she'd made up the rape to hide the fact that she'd become pregnant by a casual acquaintance. Yes, indeed, I do remember.'

'There was no concrete—'

'She wasn't hiding anything. Jesus Christ, man, I went to her flat in Sogn and in the bathroom I saw her bra in the laundry basket, drenched with blood. He had threatened to cut off her nipples. She was terrified. She thinks everyone is like she is, and when this guy dressed in a suit bought her a meal and asked if she fancied seeing a film in his hotel room she just thought he was being nice. And even if she had remembered the room number, it would have been hoovered, cleaned and the bed changed more than twenty times since she was raped. There wouldn't be much concrete evidence.'

'No one remembered any bloodstained sheets—'

'I've worked in hotels, Møller. You'd be surprised how many bloodstained sheets you change over a couple of weeks. People bleed all the bloody time.'

Møller vigorously shook his head. 'Sorry. You had your chance to prove it, Harry.'

'It wasn't enough, boss. It wasn't enough.'

'It's never enough. But you have to draw a line somewhere. With our resources—'

'Well, give me a free hand. For a month.'

Møller suddenly raised his head with one eye closed. Harry knew he'd been rumbled.

'You cunning bastard. You've wanted the job all the time, haven't you? You just had to do a bit of bartering first.'

Harry stuck out his lower lip and waggled his head from side to side. Møller looked out of the window. Then he sighed.

'OK, Harry. I'll see what I can do. But if you mess up I'll have to make a couple of decisions I know some people on the force think I should have made a long time ago. And you know what that means, don't you?'

'Boot up the arse, boss,' Harry smiled. 'What's the job?'

'I hope your summer suit is dry-cleaned and you can remember where you last put your passport. Your plane goes in twelve hours to a faraway destination.'

'The further the better, PAS.'

Harry was sitting on a chair by the door in the cramped flat in Sogn. His sister was sitting by the window watching the snowflakes in the light from the street lamp below. She sniffed a couple of times. Since she had her back to him Harry couldn't see whether it was because of a cold or his imminent departure. She had lived in sheltered housing for two years now and was managing well under the circumstances. After the rape and the abortion Harry had taken along some clothes and a toilet bag and moved in, but it wasn't long before she told him enough was enough. She was a big girl now.

'I'll be back soon, Sis.'

'When?'

She was sitting so close to the window that condensation formed into a rose whenever she spoke.

Harry sat behind her and placed a hand on her back. He could feel from the gentle tremble that she was about to cry.

'When I've caught the baddies I'll be straight back home.'

'Is it . . .?'

'No, it's not him. I'll catch him afterwards. Have you talked to Dad today?'

She shook her head. He sighed.

'If he doesn't ring I want you to ring him. Can you do that for me, Sis?'

'Pappa never says anything,' she whispered.

'Pappa's sad because Mamma died, Sis.'

'But it's so long ago.'

'That's why it's time we got him talking again, Sis, and you'll have to help me. Will you do that? Will you do that, Sis?'

She turned without a word, put her arms around him and buried her head in his neck.

He stroked her hair and could feel his shirt getting wet.

The suitcase was packed. Harry had rung Ståle Aune and told him he was flying to Bangkok on business. He hadn't had a lot to say and Harry didn't quite know why he had rung him. Perhaps because it was good to tell someone who might wonder where he was? Harry didn't think it was a great idea to ring the bar staff at Schrøder's.

'Take the vitamin B shots I gave you,' Aune said.

'Why's that?'

'Makes life easier if you want to be sober. New environment, Harry. It could be a good start, you know.'

'I'll think about it.'

'Thinking's not enough, Harry.'

'I know. That's why I don't need to take the shots.'

One of the boys from the hostel further up the street was leaning against the wall and shivering in a tight denim jacket while puffing away at a fag as Harry eased his suitcase into the boot of the taxi.

'Going away?'

'Yep.'

'South?'

'Bangkok.'

'Alone?'

'Yep.'

'Say no more.'

He gave Harry a thumbs up and winked.

Harry took the ticket from the woman behind the check-in desk and turned.

'Harry Hole?' The man with the steel-rimmed glasses eyed him with a sad smile.

'And you are?'

'Dagfinn Torhus from the Ministry of Foreign Affairs. We'd like to wish you luck. And assure ourselves that you've understood the . . . delicacy of this assignment. After all, everything has moved with such haste.'

'Thank you for the thought. I've understood that it is my job to find a murderer without making too much of a splash. Møller has given me instructions.'

'Good. Discretion is vital. Don't trust anyone. Not even officials who claim to be working for the Ministry. They might turn out to be from, well, for example, *Dagbladet*.'

Torhus opened his mouth as if to laugh, but Harry could see he was serious.

'*Dagbladet* journalists don't wear the Ministry badge on their lapel, herr Torhus. Or a jacket in January. By the way, I've seen from the papers that you're my contact in the Ministry.'

Torhus nodded, mostly to himself. Then he jutted out his chin and lowered his voice by half a tone.

'Your plane goes soon, so I won't hold you up much longer. Just listen to what I have to say.'

He removed his hands from his jacket pockets and folded them in front of him.

'How old are you, Hole? Thirty-three? Thirty-four? You still have a career in front of you. I've been doing a bit of digging, you see. You're talented and it's obvious people high up like you. And protect you. That can carry on for as long as things go well. But it won't take much for you to land flat on your arse and you could easily drag your pals down with you. And then you'll find that your so-called friends are suddenly over the hills and far away. So try to stay on your feet, Hole. For everyone's sake. This is well-meant advice from an old ice skater.' He smiled with his mouth, but his eyes were studying Harry closely. 'You know what, Hole. I always have such a depressing sense of something finishing when I come to Fornebu Airport. Something finishing and something new starting.'

'Really?' Harry said, wondering if he had time for a beer at the bar before the gate closed. 'Well, now and then that can be good. A renewal, I mean.'

'Let's hope so,' Torhus said. 'Let us hope so.'

PART TWO

5

Friday 10 January

HARRY HOLE STRAIGHTENED HIS SUNGLASSES and looked down the row of taxis outside Don Mueang International Airport. He felt like he had entered a bathroom and someone had just turned on a scalding hot shower. He knew the secret to tackling high humidity was to ignore it. Let the sweat pour down you and think about something else. The light was worse. It pierced the cheap, dark plastic glasses through to his shiny alcoholic eyes, and cranked up the headache that until then had only been rumbling in his temples.

'Meter taxi or 250 baht, sir?'

Harry tried to concentrate on what the taxi driver was saying. The trip had been hell. The bookshop at the airport in Zurich sold only German books, and they had shown *Free Willy 2* on the plane.

'Meter's fine,' Harry said.

A garrulous Dane next to him had chosen to turn a blind eye to the fact that he was plastered and had showered him with advice about how to avoid being cheated in Thailand, clearly an inexhaustible subject of conversation. He must have been of the opinion that Norwegians were charmingly naive people whom it was every Dane's duty to save from con tricks.

'You have to haggle over everything,' he'd said. 'That's the idea, you know.'

'And what if I don't?'

'You'll ruin it for us.'

'Pardon?'

'You'll be helping to raise prices, to make Thailand more expensive for everyone else.'

Harry had studied the man, who was wearing a beige Marlboro shirt and new leather sandals, and decided to drink some more.

'Surasak Road III,' Harry said and the driver smiled, put the suitcase in the boot and held the door open for Harry, who crawled in and noticed the wheel was on the right-hand side.

'In Norway we complain about the English insisting on driving on the left,' he said as they drove onto the motorway. 'But recently I heard more people in the world drive on the left than on the right. Do you know why?'

The driver glanced at the mirror with an even broader smile.

'Surasak Road, yes?'

'Because they drive on the left in China,' Harry mumbled and was glad the motorway cut through the misty skyscraper landscape like a straight, grey arrow. He could sense that a couple of sudden bends would be enough to release the Swissair omelette onto the rear seat.

'Why isn't the meter running?'

'Surasak Road, five hundred baht, yes?'

Harry leaned back in the seat and looked up at the sky. Well, he looked up, for there was no sky to be seen, just a hazy vault lit by a sun he couldn't see, either. Bangkok, the City of Angels. The angels wore masks, cut the air with a knife and tried to remember what colour the sky had been in earlier times.

He must have fallen asleep because when he opened his eyes the car wasn't moving. He hitched himself up on the seat and saw they were surrounded by vehicles. Small, open shops and workshops lay cheek by jowl along pavements milling with people who all seemed to know where they were going. And they were in a hurry to get there. The driver had opened a window and a cacophony of urban sounds merged with the radio. There was a smell of exhaust and sweat in the boiling hot car.

'Traffic jam?'

The driver shook his head with a smile.

Harry's teeth crunched. What was it he had read somewhere, that all the lead you inhale ends up in the brain sooner or later? And it makes you lose your memory. Or did it make you psychotic?

As if by a miracle the traffic suddenly began to move again, and motorbikes and mopeds swarmed around them like angry insects and launched themselves at crossroads with utter contempt for life and limb. Harry counted four fully-fledged near misses.

'Incredible there are no accidents,' Harry said to fill the silence.

The driver looked in the mirror and smiled. 'There are accidents. Many.'

By the time they finally arrived at the police station in Surasak Road, Harry had already made up his mind: he didn't like this city. He wanted to hold his breath, do the job and get on the first and not necessarily best plane back to Oslo.

At the police station Harry was greeted by a young officer who introduced himself as Nho. He had a slim body, short hair and an open, friendly face. Harry knew that in a few years the expression would change.

The lift was full and stank; it was like being thrust into a bag of sweaty sports clothes. Harry towered two heads above the others. One person looked up at the tall Norwegian and laughed, impressed. Another asked Nho a question and then said to Harry:

'Ah, Norway. That's . . . that's . . . what's his name now? . . . please help me.'

Harry smiled and tried to splay his hands apologetically, but there wasn't room.

'Yes, yes, very famous!' the man insisted.

'Ibsen?' Harry essayed. 'Nansen?'

'No, no, more famous!'

'Hamsun? Grieg?'

'No, no.'

The man gave them a stern look as they got out on the fourth.

'Welcome to Bangkok, Harry.'

The Chief of Police was small and swarthy and had clearly decided to demonstrate that people knew how to greet in Western fashion in Thailand. He squeezed Harry's hand and shook it enthusiastically with a beaming smile.

'Sorry we couldn't collect you from the airport, but the traffic in Bangkok . . .' He indicated the window behind him. 'It's not far on the map, but . . .'

'I know what you mean, sir,' Harry said. 'The embassy said the same thing.'

They faced each other in the ensuing silence. The Chief smiled. There was a knock at the door.

'Come in!'

A shaven head poked round the door.

'Come in, Crumley. The Norwegian detective has arrived.'

'Ah, the detective.'

The head acquired a body, and Harry had to blink twice to assure himself that he wasn't seeing things. Crumley was broad-shouldered and almost as tall as Harry; the hairless skull had pronounced jaw muscles and two intensely blue eyes above a thin, straight mouth. The uniform was a pale blue shirt, a large pair of Nike trainers and a skirt.

'Liz Crumley, an inspector in Homicide,' the Chief said.

'They say you're one hell of a homicide investigator, Harry,' she said in a broad American accent. She stood opposite him with her hands on her hips.

'Well, I don't know about that exactly . . .'

'No? You must be pretty good if they sent you halfway round the globe, don't you think?'

'Suppose so.'

Harry half closed his eyes. What he needed least of all now was an over-assertive woman.

'I'm here to help. *If* I can help.' He forced a smile.

'Then it might be time to sober up, huh, Harry?'

The Chief burst into loud, reedy laughter behind her.

'They're like that,' she said, loud and clear, as though the Chief wasn't present. 'They'll do whatever they can to make sure no one loses face. Right now he's trying to save your face. By pretending I'm joking. But I'm not joking. I'm in charge of Homicide here, and if I don't like something I say so. It's considered bad manners in this country, but I've been doing it for ten years.'

Harry closed his eyes fully.

'I can see from the colour of your face that you think this is embarrassing, Harry, but I have no use for drunken investigators, as I'm sure you know. Come back tomorrow. I'll find someone to take you to your apartment.'

Harry shook his head and cleared his throat. 'Fear of flying.'

'Pardon me?'

'I'm frightened of flying. G&Ts help. And my face is red because the booze is beginning to evaporate through the pores of my skin.'

Liz Crumley regarded him at length. Then she scratched her shiny head.

'Sorry to hear that, Detective. How's the jet lag?'

'Wide awake.'

'Good. You're just in time for a quick update from Forensics, and then we'll drop by your apartment on the way to the crime scene.'

'This is your office,' Crumley pointed on the way past.

'Someone's sitting there,' Harry said.

'Not there. There.'

'There?'

He identified the chair pressed into a long table with people sitting side by side. On the table in front of the chair there was just enough room for a notepad and a phone.

'I'll see if I can sort something else out if your stay turns into a long one.'

'I really hope it doesn't,' Harry mumbled.

The inspector summoned her troops to the meeting room. The 'troops' were, to be more precise: Nho; Sunthorn, a baby-faced, serious-looking young man; and Rangsan, the oldest detective in the department.

Rangsan sat apparently immersed in his newspaper, but interjected with occasional comments in Thai, which Crumley jotted down carefully in her little black book.

'OK,' Crumley said, closing the book. 'The five of us will try to crack this case. Since we have a Norwegian colleague with us all communication from now on will take place in English. Rangsan's our contact with Forensics. Go ahead.'

Rangsan painstakingly folded the newspaper and cleared his throat. He had thinning hair, a pair of glasses, which were attached to a cord, perched on the end of his nose, and he reminded Harry of a jaded teacher regarding his surroundings with a slightly condescending, sarcastic gaze.

'I spoke to Supawadee at Forensics. Not surprisingly, they found a whole load of fingerprints in the hotel room, but none that belonged to the dead man.'

The other prints had not been identified.

'And this won't be easy,' Rangsan added. 'Even if the motel doesn't have much of a clientele there must be prints from at least a hundred people in there.'

'Did they find any prints on the door handle?' Harry asked.

'Too many, I'm afraid. And no complete ones.'

Crumley put her Nike-clad feet on the table.

'Molnes probably went straight to bed; there was no reason for him to waltz around leaving prints everywhere. There are at least two people who touched the door handle after the murderer: Dim, the prostitute, and Wang, the motel owner.'

She nodded to Rangsan, who picked up the newspaper again.

'The autopsy reveals what we assumed, that the ambassador was killed by the knife. It punctured the left lung before piercing the heart and filling the pericardium with blood.'

'Cardiac tamponade,' Harry said.

'I beg your pardon.'

'That's what it's called. It's like putting cotton wool in a bell. The heart can't beat and it suffocates in its own blood.'

Crumley grimaced.

'OK, let's leave the forensic report for the time being and go see the real thing. Harry, we'll let you settle in and then we'll pick you up on the way to the motel.'

In the crowded lift down he heard a voice he recognised.

'I've got it now, I've got it now! Solskjær! Solskjær!'

Harry craned his head and smiled in affirmation.

So he was the world's most famous Norwegian. A football player who was a second-choice striker in an English industrial town beat all the explorers, painters and writers. On reflection, Harry concluded that the man was probably right.

The flat he had been given by the embassy was in a fashionable complex opposite the Shangri-La Hotel. It was tiny and spartan, but it had a bathroom, a fan by the bed and a view of the Chao Phraya River, which flowed past, broad and brown. Harry stood by the window. Long, narrow wooden boats criss-crossed the river and whipped up filthy water behind the propellers mounted on long poles. On the far bank, new hotels and department stores towered over an indefinable mass of white-brick houses. It was hard to get any impression of the size of the city because it disappeared in a golden-brown haze when you tried to delve beyond a few blocks, but Harry presumed it was big. Very big. He pushed up a window and a roar rose to meet him. He had lost the airline earplugs in the lift, and only now did he hear how deafening the noise of this city was. He could see Crumley's patrol car like a little matchbox toy next to the pavement far below. He opened a can of hot beer he had taken with him off the plane and confirmed to his pleasure that Singha was not as bad as Norwegian beer. Now the rest of the day seemed more bearable.

6

Friday 10 January

THE INSPECTOR LEANED ON THE horn. Literally. She pressed her bosom against the wheel of the big Toyota Jeep and the horn sounded.

'That's not the Thai way of doing it,' she laughed. 'Anyway, it doesn't work. If you honk your horn they don't let you pass. It has something to do with Buddhism. But I can't resist. What the hell, I'm from the States.'

She leaned against the wheel again as motorists around them made a show of looking away.

'So he's still in the hotel room?' Harry asked, stifling a yawn.

'Orders from highest level. As a rule we do an autopsy as fast as possible and cremate them the day after. But they wanted you to see first. Don't ask me why.'

'I'm one hell of an investigator, or have you forgotten all that?'

She squinted at him from the corner of her eye, then swerved out into a gap and put her foot down.

'Don't get too cute. It's not how you might think, that everyone here will reckon you're a hell of a guy because you're a *farang*, it's more the opposite.'

'*Farang?*'

'Honky. Gringo. Half derogatory, half neutral, all depending how you play it. Just remember, there's nothing wrong with the Thais' self-esteem even if they treat you politely. Fortunately for you, Sunthorn and Nho are on duty today, and I'm sure you'll manage to impress them. I hope so for your sake. If you make a fool of yourself you could have big problems working with the department.'

'I had the impression you were in charge of that department'

'That's what I think.'

They had joined the motorway and, ignoring the engine's protests, she pressed the accelerator to the floor. It had already begun to get dark, and in the west a cherry-red sun was going down between the skyscrapers.

'At least pollution creates beautiful sunsets,' Crumley said in answer to his thoughts.

'Tell me about the prostitution here,' Harry said.

'It's about as bad as the traffic.'

'I've seen. But what counts here, how does it work? Is it traditional street prostitution with pimps, regular brothels with a madam, or are the prostitutes freelancers? Do they go to bars, do they strip, do they advertise in the paper, or do they pick up clients in the shopping malls?'

'All of that and then some. If it hasn't been tried in Bangkok it hasn't been tried. But most of them work in go-go bars where they dance and try to persuade clients to buy drinks. And of course they get a percentage. The bar owner has no responsibility for the girls beyond giving them a place to market themselves, and in return the girls agree to stay in the bar until it closes. If a client wants to take one of the girls, he has to buy her freedom for the rest of the evening. The bar owner gets the money, but most of the time the girl is happy to avoid spending the evening writhing around onstage.'

'Sounds like a great deal for the bar owner.'

'Whatever the girl earns after her time has been bought goes right into her own pocket.'

'Did the girl who found the ambassador work in a bar like that?'

'Yup. She works in one of the King Crown bars in Patpong. We also know the motel owner runs a kind of call-girl ring for foreigners with special proclivities. But getting her to talk is pretty tough because in Thailand prostitution is actually illegal. So far all she's said is that she was staying at the motel and went in the wrong door.'

Liz explained that Atle Molnes had probably rung the woman when he arrived at the motel, but the receptionist, who was synonymous with the owner, denied point-blank having anything to do with the matter over and above renting a room.

'Here we are.'

She pulled up in front of a low, white-brick building.

'The best brothels in Bangkok seem to have a weakness for Greek names,' she commented acidly and got out. Harry looked up at a large neon sign proclaiming that the motel was called Olympussy. The 'm' flashed sporadically while the 'l' had given up for good and lent the place a tristesse that reminded Harry of suburban Norwegian grill bars.

The motel was identical to the American variety with a series of double rooms around a courtyard and a parking space outside each room. There was a veranda alongside the wall where guests could sit in grey, water-damaged cane chairs.

'Nice place.'

'You may not believe it, but when it appeared during the Vietnam War it was one of the liveliest places in town. Built for horny US soldiers on R&R.'

'R&R?'

'Rest and recuperation. Popularly known as I&I: intercourse and intoxication. They flew them in from Saigon on a two-day furlough.

The sex industry in this country wouldn't be what it is today without the US military. One of the streets here is even officially called Soi Cowboy.'

'So why didn't they stay there? This is almost rural.'

'The soldiers who were most homesick preferred to fuck in the all-American way – that is, in an automobile or a motel room. That's why they built this. They could rent American cars from the parking lot. They even had American beer in the minibars.'

'Wow, how do you know all this?'

'My mother told me.'

Harry turned to her, but even though the functioning letters in Olympussy cast a bluish neon light over her skull it was too dark to discern her expression. She pulled a cap over her head before going into the reception area.

The motel room was furnished simply, but the filthy grey carpet hinted at better days. Harry shivered. Not because of the yellow suit that made any further identification of the corpse superfluous – only members of the Christian Democratic Party and the Progress Party would voluntarily wear such suits. Nor because of the knife with the oriental ornamentation that had pinned the suit to the ambassador's back and caused the unflattering bulge to the shoulders of the jacket. The reason was quite simply that the room was freezing cold. Crumley had explained that as the shelf life for bodies in this climate was very short and they had been told they would have to wait at least forty-eight hours for the Norwegian detective, they had put the air conditioning on full, to ten degrees, and set the fan on max.

Nevertheless, the flies were persistent, and a swarm of them rose as Nho and Sunthorn carefully rolled the body onto its back. Atle Molnes's glazed eyes stared down his nose as though trying to see the tips of his Ecco shoes. The boyish fringe made the ambassador appear younger than his fifty-two years. It flopped down, sun-bleached, as though there were still life in it.

'Wife and teenage daughter,' Harry said. 'Has either of them been here to see him?'

'No. We informed the Norwegian Embassy, and they said they would pass on the message to the family. So far we've only been told not to let anyone in.'

'Anyone from the embassy?'

'The chargé d'affaires. Can't remember her name.'

'Tonje Wiig?'

'That's it. She was hard-faced right up to the moment we turned over the body to have him identified.'

Harry studied the ambassador. Had he been a good-looking man? A man who, apart from the dreadful suit and a couple of rolls of fat around his stomach, could make the heart of a young, female chargé d'affaires beat faster? The suntanned skin had taken on a sallow hue and the blue tongue seemed to be trying to force its way between the teeth.

Harry sat down on a chair and had a look around. When a person dies their appearance changes quickly, and he had seen more than enough corpses to know that he didn't get much from staring at them. Atle Molnes had taken with him any secrets his personality might have revealed and all that remained was an empty, abandoned husk.

Harry pushed the chair closer to the bed. The two young officers leaned over him.

'What can you see?' Crumley asked.

'I see a Norwegian lech who happened to be the ambassador and therefore has to have his reputation protected for king and country.'

She glanced up in surprise, and examined Harry more closely.

'No matter how good the a/c you can't cover the stench,' he

said. 'But that's my problem. As for this guy here . . .' Harry grasped the ambassador's jaw. 'Rigor mortis. He's rigid, but the rigidity has begun to give, which is normal after three days. His tongue's blue, but the knife would suggest not from suffocation. Has to be checked.'

'*Has* been,' Crumley said. 'The ambassador had been drinking red wine.'

Harry mumbled something.

'Molnes left his office at lunchtime,' she continued, 'and when the woman found him it was nearly 11 p.m. Our doctor says he died somewhere between 4 and 10 p.m., so that narrows it down a bit.'

'Between four and ten? That's six hours.'

'Correct, Detective.' Crumley crossed her arms.

'Well.' Harry looked up at her. 'In Oslo we usually determine the time of death with a margin of twenty minutes either way for bodies that have been found after a few hours.'

'That's because you live at the North Pole. Here, at thirty-five degrees, a body's temperature doesn't fall much. The time is worked out according to rigor mortis, and so it's fairly approximate.'

'What about livor mortis? There should be discoloration after around three hours.'

'Sorry. As you can see, the ambassador liked sunbathing, so we can't tell.'

Harry ran his index finger up the suit material where the knife had entered. A grey, Vaseline-like deposit gathered on his nail.

'What's this?'

'The weapon was obviously greased. Samples have been sent for analysis.'

Harry rifled through the pockets and pulled out a worn, brown wallet. It contained a 500-baht note, a Ministry ID card and a photo of a smiling girl in what appeared to be a hospital bed.

'Did you find anything else on him?'

'Zip.' Crumley had removed her cap to waft away the flies. 'We checked what he had and left it alone.'

Harry loosened the belt, pulled down the trousers and turned him on his stomach again. Then he pulled up the jacket and shirt. 'Look. Some of the blood ran down his back.' He lifted the elastic of the Dovre underpants. 'And down between his buttocks. Which means he wasn't stabbed while lying in bed. He was standing. By measuring how far the blade went in and determining the angle we can work out the murderer's height.'

'Assuming the murderer was standing on the same level as the victim when he or she struck,' Crumley added. 'The victim could also have been stabbed while he was on the floor and the blood ran down when he was moved to the bed.'

'Then there would have been blood on the carpet,' Harry said, pulling up the trousers, fastening the belt, turning and looking Liz in the eye. 'And you wouldn't have needed to speculate, you would have known for certain. Your forensics people would have found fibres from the carpet all over his suit, wouldn't they.'

Her gaze didn't deviate, but Harry knew he had exposed her little test. She nodded, and he turned back to the corpse.

'One victimological detail might confirm he was expecting a female visitor.'

'Yes?'

'See the belt? It was fastened two notches up from the worn line before I loosened it. Middle-aged men with burgeoning waistlines often pull their stomachs in when they meet younger women.'

It was hard to say whether they were impressed. The officers shifted from one foot to the other and their stony young faces betrayed nothing. Crumley bit off a chunk of nail and spat it out between pursed lips.

'So here's the minibar.' Harry opened the door of the little fridge.

Singha, Johnnie Walker and Canadian Club miniatures, a bottle of white wine. Nothing appeared to have been touched.

'What else have we got?' Harry turned to the two young officers.

They exchanged glances and then one pointed out the car in the drive.

'The car.'

They went outside, where there was a dark blue Mercedes of recent vintage bearing diplomatic plates. One of the police officers opened the driver's door.

'Key?' Harry asked.

'It was in the jacket pocket of . . .' The officer nodded towards the motel room.

'Fingerprints?'

The young man gave his superior a resigned look. She coughed.

'Obviously we've checked the key for prints, Hole.'

'I wasn't asking *if* you'd taken prints, but what you found.'

'His. Otherwise we'd have told you at the outset.'

Harry bit his tongue.

The seats and floor of the Mercedes were strewn with rubbish. Harry noticed some magazines, cassettes, empty cigarette packets, a Coke can and a pair of sandals.

'What else have you found?'

Nho took out a list and read it out.

'Stop,' Harry said. 'Could you repeat the last item?'

'Coupons for betting on horse races, sir.'

'The ambassador obviously liked to gamble now and then,' Crumley said. 'Popular sport in Thailand.'

'And what's this?'

Harry had leaned over the driver's side and picked up a small capsule partly buried under the carpet between the seat adjuster and the floor mat.

The officer looked down at his list, but had to give up.

'Liquid Ecstasy comes in capsules like that,' said Crumley, who had stepped closer to see.

'Ecstasy?' Harry shook his head. 'Middle-aged Christian Democrats might fuck around, but they do *not* take E.'

'We'll have to get it checked out,' Crumley said. Harry could see from her face that she wasn't best pleased to have missed the capsule.

'Let's have a look in the back,' he said.

The boot was as clean and tidy as the inside was messy.

'A man of orderly habits,' Harry said. 'The women of the family reigned supreme inside the car, but he didn't let them touch the boot.'

A well-equipped toolbox glinted in the light from Crumley's torch. It was spotless; only plaster on the tip of a screwdriver revealed that it had been used.

'Bit more victimology, folks. My guess is Molnes was not a practical man. This toolbox has never been near a car engine. At most, the screwdriver has been used to hang up a family photo.'

A mosquito applauded by his ear. Harry hit out and felt his wet skin was cold to the touch. The heat hadn't abated even if the sun had gone down. Now the wind had dropped and it felt as if moisture was trickling from the ground beneath their feet and condensing the air so that it was almost drinkable.

Beside the spare tyre was the jack, apparently also unused, and a thin, brown leather case of the kind you expect to find in a diplomat's car.

'What's in the case?' Harry asked.

'It's locked,' Crumley said. 'Because the car is, officially speaking, embassy territory and therefore not under our jurisdiction we haven't attempted to open it. But now that Norway is represented maybe we can . . .'

'Sorry, I don't have diplomatic status,' Harry said, lifting the case out of the boot and placing it on the ground. 'But I can state that the case is no longer on Norwegian territory, so I would suggest you open it while I go to reception and speak to the motel owner.'

Harry sauntered across the car park. His feet were swollen after the flight, a drop of sweat rolled down the inside of his shirt, tickling him, and he was desperate for a drink. Apart from that, it didn't feel too bad to be on a serious case again. It was a long time since his last job. He noticed that the 'm' had gone out.

Wang Lee, Manager said the business card the man behind the counter passed Harry, presumably a gentle hint that he should try again another day. The bony man in the flowery shirt had sleep in the corners of his eyes and looked as if he definitely did not want anything to do with Harry right now. He had started to flick through a pile of papers and grunted when he glanced up to see Harry still standing there.

'I can see you're a busy man,' Harry said. 'So I suggest we do this as quickly as possible. I know I'm a foreigner and I'm not from your country—'

'Not Thai. Chinese,' he heard, accompanied by another grunt.

'Well, then, you're also a foreigner. The point is—'

From behind the counter came a couple of gasps which might have been scornful laughter. The motel owner had at any rate opened his mouth.

'Not foreigner. Chinese. We make Thailand work. No Chinese, no business.'

'Fine. You're a businessman, Wang. So let me make you a business deal. You run a brothel here and you can flick through papers as much as you like, but that's how it is.'

Wang shook his head firmly. 'No prostitutes. Motel. Rent rooms.'

'Relax, I'm only interested in the murder, it's not my job to lock up pimps. Unless I do it off my own bat. Hence the business deal. Here in Thailand no one checks people like you out, there are simply too many of you. Reporting you to the police isn't enough, either. I'm guessing you can pay a few baht in a brown envelope to avoid being bothered by that kind of thing. That's why you're not particularly afraid of us.'

The motel owner repeated the head-shaking.

'No money. Illegal.'

Harry smiled. 'Last time I looked, Thailand was third in the world corruption table. Please be nice and don't treat me like an idiot.'

Harry ensured his voice was lowered. Threats generally work best when delivered in a neutral key.

'Your problem, and mine, however, is that the guy who was found in the motel room is a diplomat from my country. If I have to report back that we suspect he died in a brothel it suddenly becomes a political issue and your friends in the police cannot help you. The authorities will feel obliged to close this place and haul you off to prison. To show goodwill, to show they're maintaining law and order, right?'

It was impossible to see from the expressionless face whether he had hit the nail on the head or not.

'On the other hand, if I report back that the woman had arranged to meet the man, and the motel was a random choice . . .'

The man looked at Harry. He blinked, pinching his eyes as if he had a speck of dust in them. Then he turned, pulled aside a curtain that hid a door opening and waved for Harry to follow. Behind the curtain was a little room with a table and two chairs, and the man motioned Harry to sit down. He put a cup in front of Harry and poured from a teapot. There was such a strong aroma of peppermint that it made his eyes smart.

'None of girls want to work so long as body's there,' Wang said. 'How quickly can you move it?'

Businessmen are businessmen the world over, Harry thought, lighting a cigarette.

'Depends how quickly we can get to the bottom of what went on here.'

'The man came here about nine at night and said he wanted room. He flicked through menu and said he wanted Dim, he just needed rest first. Told me to say when she was here. I said he had to pay hourly rate anyway. He said fine and took key.'

'The menu?'

The man passed him something which did indeed resemble a menu. Harry leafed through. There were pictures of young Thai girls in nurse uniforms, in fishnet stockings, in tight leather corsets with a whip, in schoolgirl uniforms and plaits, and even in police uniforms. Beneath the pictures, under the heading VITAL STATISTICS was each girl's age, price and background. Harry noticed that all of them claimed they were between eighteen and twenty-two. Prices ranged from one to three thousand baht and almost all the girls had apparently completed a language course and worked as nurses.

'Was he alone?' Harry asked.

'Yes.'

'No one else in the car?'

Wang shook his head.

'How can you be so sure of that? The Mercedes has tinted windows and you were sitting in here.'

'I usually go out and check. Perhaps he has friend with him. Then they have to pay for double room.'

'I see. Double room, double price?'

'Not double price.' Wang showed his teeth again. 'Cheaper to share.'

'What happened then?'

'Don't know. Man drove car to number 120, where he is now. It's at back, so I can't see it in darkness. I called Dim and she came and waited. After a while I sent her in to him.'

'And how was Dim dressed? As a tram conductor?'

'No, no, no.' Wang flipped through to the back page of the menu and proudly showed the photo of a young Thai girl wearing a short dress covered in silver sequins, white skates and a big smile. She was curtsying with her ankles crossed and her arms to the sides, as though she had just performed a successful free programme. Her face was dotted with red freckles.

'And that's supposed to be . . .?' Harry said in disbelief, reading the name under the photo.

'Yes, yes, right. Tonya Harding. The one who killed other American girl, pretty one.'

'I don't think she actually—'

'Dim can be her too if you like . . .'

'No, thank you,' Harry said.

'It's very popular. Especially with Americans. She can cry, if you like.' Wang ran fingers down his cheeks.

'She found him in the room with a knife in his back. What happened after that?'

'Dim ran here screaming.'

'Wearing skates?'

Wang gave Harry a reproachful look. 'Skates come on after panties come off.'

Harry could appreciate the practical side of the arrangement and waved him to carry on.

'Nothing more to tell, Officer. We went to room and looked again, then I locked door and rang police.'

'So, according to Dim the door was not locked when she got there. Did she say anything about it being ajar or was it just unlocked?'

Wang shrugged his shoulders. 'Door was closed but not locked. Is that important?'

'You never know. Did you see anyone else near the room that evening?'

Wang shook his head.

'And where's the guest book?' Harry asked. He was getting tired now.

The motel owner's head shot up. 'No guest book.'

Harry watched him in silence.

'No guest book,' Wang repeated. 'Why do I need one? No one will come if they register their names and addresses.'

'I'm not stupid, Wang. No one thinks they're being registered, but you keep a list. Just in case. VIPs drop by now and then and it could be good to slap a guest book on the table if you have any trouble one day, right?'

The motel owner blinked like a frog.

'Don't be difficult now, Wang. People who had nothing to do with the murder have nothing to fear. Especially public figures. Word of honour. Now. Book, please.'

It was a little notebook, and Harry scanned the closely written pages covered in Thai characters.

'One of the others will come and copy this,' he said.

The three officers were waiting by the Mercedes. The headlamps were on and they illuminated the briefcase, which was lying open on the patio.

'Did you find anything?'

'Looks like the ambassador had unusual sexual predilections.'

'I know. Tonya Harding. I call *that* kinky.'

'When can we talk to Dim?'

'We'll get hold of her tomorrow. She's working tonight.'

Harry stopped in front of the briefcase. Details of the black-and-white photographs came to the fore in the yellow light from

56

the headlamps. He froze. Of course he had heard about it, he had even read reports and talked with Vice Squad colleagues about it, but it was the first time Harry had *seen* a child being screwed by an adult.

7

Friday 10 January

THEY DROVE UP SUKHUMVIT ROAD where three-star hotels, luxury villas and wooden and tin shacks stood cheek by jowl. Harry didn't see any of this; his gaze appeared to be fixed on a point straight in front of him.

'Traffic's better now,' Crumley said.

'Yeah.'

She smiled without showing her teeth. 'Sorry, in Bangkok we talk about the traffic the way other places talk about the weather. You don't have to live here for long to figure out why. The weather's the same from now until May. Depending on the monsoon it starts raining sometime in late summer. And then it pours for three months. All there is to say about the weather is that it's hot. We tell each other that all year round, but it's not the most interesting topic of conversation.'

'Mm.'

'The traffic, on the other hand, determines our everyday lives in Bangkok more than any goddamn typhoons. I never know how long it's going to take me to get to work. Could be forty minutes, could be four hours. Ten years ago it took twenty-five minutes.'

'So what's happened?'

'Growth. The last twenty years have been one long economic boom. This is where the jobs are, and people flood in from the rural areas. More people travelling to work every morning, more mouths to feed and more demand for transport. The politicians promise us new roads and then just rub their hands with glee at how well things are going.'

'Nothing wrong with good times surely?'

'It's not that I begrudge people TVs in their bamboo huts, but it's happened so damn fast. And if you ask me, growth for growth's sake is the logic of a cancer cell. Sometimes I'm almost glad we hit the wall last year. You can already feel its effect on the traffic.'

'You mean it's been worse than this?'

'Of course. Look there . . .'

Crumley pointed to a gigantic car park where hundreds of cement mixers stood in lines.

'A year ago that parking lot was almost empty, but now no one is building any more, so the fleet has been mothballed, as you can see. And people only go to shopping malls because they have air conditioning, they don't actually shop.'

They drove in silence for a while.

'Who do you think is behind this shit?' Harry asked.

'Currency speculators.'

He looked at her, uncomprehending. 'I'm talking about the photos.'

'Oh.' She glanced at him. 'You didn't like that, did you.'

He shrugged. 'I'm an intolerant person. I can't help thinking about the death penalty.'

The inspector checked her watch. 'We pass a restaurant on the way to your apartment. What do you say to a crash course in traditional Thai food?'

'OK. But you didn't answer my question.'

'Who's behind the photos? Harry, there are probably more

perverts in Thailand per square inch than in the whole world, people who have come here because we have a sex industry that meets all needs. And I do mean *all* needs. How the hell should I know who's behind a few pictures?'

Harry grimaced and rolled his head from side to side. 'I was just asking. Wasn't there some row a couple of years ago about an ambassador who was a paedophile?'

'Yeah, we busted a child sex ring involving a number of embassy people, among them the Australian ambassador. Very embarrassing.'

'Not for the police though?'

'Are you crazy? For us it was like winning the soccer World Cup and an Oscar at the same time. The Prime Minister sent his congratulations, the Minister for Tourism was in ecstasy and medals rained down on us. That has a big impact on the credibility of the force, you know.'

'So what about making a start there?'

'I don't know. First up, everyone who was involved with the ring is either behind bars or has been deported. Second, I'm not convinced the photos have anything to do with the murder.'

Crumley turned into a car park where an attendant pointed to an impossible gap between two cars. She pressed a button and the electronics buzzed as the large windows on both sides of the vehicle were lowered. Then she put the car in reverse and put her foot on the accelerator.

'I don't think . . .' Harry started to say, but the inspector had already parked. The side mirrors quivered.

'How do we get out?' he asked.

'It's not good to worry so much, Detective.'

Using both arms she swung herself through the window, placed one foot on the windscreen and jumped down in front of the Jeep. With a great deal of difficulty Harry succeeded in performing the same feat.

'You'll learn,' she said and started walking. 'Bangkok is cramped.'

'And what about the radio?' Harry looked back at the invitingly open windows. 'Do you reckon it'll be there when we get back?'

She flashed her police badge to the attendant, who straightened up with a jolt.

'Yes.'

'No fingerprints on the knife,' Crumley said with a satisfied smack of her lips. *Sôm-tam*, a kind of green papaya salad, didn't taste as weird as Harry had imagined. In fact, it was good. And spicy.

She sucked the foam off the beer with a loud slurp. He looked round at the other customers, but no one seemed to notice, probably because she was drowned out by a polka-playing string orchestra on the stage at the back of the restaurant, which in turn was drowned out by the traffic. Harry decided he would drink two beers. Then stop. He could buy a six-pack on the way to the flat.

'Ornamentation on the handle. Anything there?'

'Nho thought the knife might be from the north, from the mountain tribes in Chiang Rai province or around there. Something to do with the inset pieces of coloured glass. He wasn't sure, but in any case it wasn't the standard kind of knife you can buy in shops here, so we're sending it to an art history professor at Benchamabophit Museum tomorrow. He knows all there is to know about old knives.'

Liz waved, and the waiter came and ladled some steaming coconut soup from a tureen.

'Watch out for the little white guys. And the little red ones. They'll burn you up,' she said, pointing with a spoon. 'Oh, and the green ones, too.'

Harry stared with scepticism at the different substances floating round in his bowl.

'Is there anything here I *can* eat?'

'The galanga roots are OK.'

'Have you got any theories?' Harry asked in a loud voice to drown her slurping.

'About who the murderer could be? Yes, of course. Lots. Firstly, it could be the prostitute. Or the motel owner. Or both.'

'And what would the motive be?'

'Money.'

'There was five hundred baht in Molnes's wallet.'

'If he took out his wallet in reception and Wang saw he had a bit of money, which is pretty likely, the temptation may have been too much for him. Wang wouldn't have known that the man was a diplomat and that there would be such a big stink.'

Crumley held her fork up in the air and leaned forward excitedly.

'They wait until the ambassador's in the room, knock on the door and stab him with the knife when he turns his back. He falls forward on the bed, they empty his wallet, but leave the five hundred so it won't look like robbery. Then they wait three hours and call the police. And Wang is bound to have a friend in the force who'll make sure everything runs smoothly. No motive, no suspect, everyone keen to sweep an incident involving prostitution under the carpet. Next case.'

Harry's eyes suddenly bulged out of his head. He grabbed the glass of beer and put it to his mouth.

Crumley smiled. 'One of the red ones?'

He got his breath back.

'Not a bad theory, Inspector, but there's a flaw,' he gasped in a throaty voice.

She frowned. 'What's that?'

'Wang keeps a private guest book, probably crammed with names of politicians and civil servants. Each visit is logged along with the date and time. To have some defence, if anyone should make a fuss about his establishment. But when there's a visitor whose face he doesn't recognise he can hardly ask for their ID. So what he does is join the guest outside under the pretext of making sure there's no one else in the car, right, to find out who he is.'

'Now I don't follow you.'

'He writes down the number plate, OK? Then he checks it afterwards against the register. When he saw the blue plates on the Mercedes he knew at once Molnes was a diplomat.'

Crumley studied him thoughtfully. Then she swung round to the adjacent table with her eyes open wide. The couple jumped in their chairs and busily concentrated on their food.

She scratched her leg with a fork.

'It hasn't rained for three months,' she said.

'Sorry?'

She waved a hand for the bill.

'What's that got to do with the case?' Harry asked.

'Not a lot,' she said.

It was almost three in the morning. The noise from the city was muted by the regular hum of the fan on the bedside table. Nevertheless, Harry could hear the odd heavy lorry driving over Taksin Bridge and the roar of a solitary riverboat setting off from one of the piers on the Chao Phraya.

As he'd unlocked the door to the flat he had seen a red flashing light on the telephone and after pressing a few buttons he'd listened to two messages. The first was from the Norwegian Embassy. Tonje Wiig, the chargé d'affaires, had a very nasal voice and sounded as if she was either from Oslo West or had a strong desire to live there. She told Harry to present himself at the embassy the next day at ten, but then changed the time to twelve as she discovered she had a meeting at a quarter past ten.

The other message was from Bjarne Møller. He wished Harry luck, no more than that. It sounded as if he didn't like talking to answerphones.

Harry lay on the bed blinking into the darkness. He hadn't bought the six-pack after all. And the B12 shots were still in his suitcase. After bar-hopping in Sydney he had taken to his bed with no feeling in his legs, but one vitamin shot and he had got up like Lazarus. He sighed. When was it he had actually decided? When he was told about the job in Bangkok? No, it was before that. Several weeks ago he had set a deadline: Sis's birthday. God knows why he had taken the decision. Perhaps he was just sick of not being present. Days came and went without him noticing. Something like that. He was tired of the discussion about why old Bardolph didn't want to drink now. When Harry took a decision it was unshakeable; it was inexorable and final. No compromises, no prevarication. 'I can stop any day I like.' How often had he heard men at Schrøder's trying to convince themselves that they weren't long-term full-blooded alkies? He was as full-blooded as any of them, but he was the only one he knew who could actually stop whenever he wanted. The birthday wasn't for a few weeks, but as Aune had been right about this trip being a good starting point Harry had even brought it forward. Harry groaned and rolled over onto his side.

He wondered what Sis was doing, if she had dared to venture out in the evenings. If she had rung Dad as she had promised. And if she had, if he'd managed to talk to her, beyond answering with a yes or a no.

Three o'clock passed, and even though it was only nine in Norway he hadn't slept much over the last thirty-six hours and ought to have fallen asleep without a problem. However, every time he closed his eyes he had the image of a naked Thai boy illuminated by headlamps on his retina, so he preferred to keep them open for a while longer. Perhaps he should have bought the six-pack after all. When he did finally drop off, the morning rush hour over Taksin Bridge had already started.

8

Saturday 11 January

ON THE SEVENTEENTH FLOOR, BEHIND an oak door and two security checkpoints, Harry found a metal sign bearing the Norwegian lion. The receptionist, a young, graceful Thai woman with a small mouth, even smaller nose and two velvety brown eyes in a round face, bore a deep frown as she studied his ID card. Then she lifted the telephone, whispered three syllables and put it back down.

'Miss Wiig's office is the second on the right, sir,' she said with such a beaming smile Harry considered falling in love on the spot.

'Come in,' Harry heard, after knocking on the door. Inside, Tonje Wiig was bent over a large teak desk, obviously busy making notes. She looked up, put on a light smile, raised a lean body dressed in a white silk suit from her chair and walked towards him with an outstretched hand.

Tonje Wiig was the opposite of the receptionist. A nose, mouth and eyes fought for room in a long face, and the nose appeared to carry the day. It was like a big tuber, but at least ensured there was a bit of space between her large, heavily made-up eyes. Not that Miss Wiig was ugly, no, some men might even claim the face had a certain classical beauty.

'So nice that you're finally here, Officer. Shame that it's in such sad circumstances.'

Harry had barely touched her bony fingers before they were withdrawn.

'We'd very much like to put this case behind us as fast as possible,' she said, rubbing one nostril carefully so as not to smudge her make-up.

'I appreciate that.'

'These have been difficult days for us, and it might sound heartless, but the world goes on and so do we. Some people believe that all we do is attend cocktail parties and enjoy ourselves, but nothing could be further from the truth, I can tell you. At this very moment I have eight Norwegians in hospital and six in prison, four of them for possession of narcotics. Have you seen the prisons here? Dreadful. *Verdens Gang* rings every day. It turns out that on top of everything else one of them is pregnant. And last month in Pattaya, a Norwegian man died after being thrown out of a window. Second time in a year. Terrible fuss.'

She shook her head in despair.

'And if someone loses their passport do you think they have travel insurance or money for a new ticket home? No, we have to take care of everything. So, as you know, it's important we get things moving here.'

'It's my understanding that you're in charge now that the ambassador is dead.'

'I am the chargé d'affaires, yes.'

'How long will it be before a new ambassador is appointed?'

'Not long, I hope. Usually it takes a month or two.'

'They're not concerned that you're left shouldering all the responsibility?'

Tonje Wiig gave a wry smile. 'That wasn't what I meant. In fact I worked here as the chargé d'affaires for six months before they

66

sent Molnes. I'm just saying I hope there will be a permanent arrangement as soon as possible.'

'So you're counting on becoming the new ambassador.'

'Well.' She smiled mirthlessly. 'That wouldn't be unnatural. But you never know with the Ministry of Foreign Affairs, I'm afraid.'

A shadow stole in and a cup appeared in front of Harry.

'Do you drink *chaa ráwn*?' Tonje Wiig asked.

'I don't know.'

'Oh, my apologies,' she laughed. 'I forget so quickly that others are new here. Black Thai tea. I have afternoon tea here, you see. Even though, strictly speaking, it should be after two o'clock according to English tradition.'

Harry said yes, and the next time he looked down someone had filled his cup.

'I thought that kind of tradition died with the colonialists.'

'Thailand has never been a colony,' she smiled. 'Neither of England nor of France, as its neighbours were. The Thais are very proud of that. A bit too proud, if you ask me. A bit of English influence never hurt anyone.'

Harry picked up a notepad and asked if the ambassador might conceivably have been embroiled in anything dubious.

'Dubious, Hole?'

He explained in concise terms what he meant by 'dubious', that in seventy per cent of murders the victim was involved in something illegal.

'Illegal? Molnes?' She shook her head energetically. 'He isn't . . . wasn't the type.'

'Do you know if he could have had any enemies?'

'Can't imagine he would. He was very well liked. Why do you ask? Surely this can't be an assassination?'

'We know very little at the moment, so we're keeping all lines of inquiry open.'

Tonje Wiig explained that Molnes had gone straight to a meeting after lunch on the Tuesday he died. He hadn't said where, but this was not unusual.

'He always had his mobile phone with him, so we could get in touch if something came up.'

Harry asked to see his office. Tonje Wiig had to unlock two further doors, installed 'for security reasons'. The room was untouched, as Harry had requested before he left Oslo, and it was a mess of papers, files and souvenirs which hadn't been put on shelves or hung on walls yet.

The Norwegian royal couple peered down majestically at them over the piles of paper and out of the window overlooking a green space that Wiig told him was Queen Sirikit Park.

Harry found a calendar, but there weren't many notes on it. He checked the day of the murder. Man U, it said – Manchester United, unless he was much mistaken. Perhaps a football match he wanted to see, Harry thought, dutifully going through some drawers, but he soon realised one man searching the ambassador's office without knowing what he was looking for was a hopeless task.

'I can't see his mobile phone,' Harry said.

'As I mentioned – he always carried it with him.'

'We didn't find a mobile at the crime scene. And I don't think the murderer was a thief.'

Tonje Wiig shrugged. 'Perhaps some of your Thai colleagues "confiscated" it?'

Harry chose not to respond and instead asked if anyone had rung him at the embassy on the day in question. She was doubtful, but promised to look into it. Harry had a last look around the room.

'Who was the last person to see Molnes in the embassy?'

She tried to recall. 'It must have been Sanphet, the chauffeur. He and the ambassador were very good friends. He's taken this badly, so I gave him a few days off.'

'Why wasn't he driving the ambassador on the day of the murder, if he's a chauffeur?'

She shrugged again. 'I wondered the same. The ambassador didn't like driving in Bangkok on his own.'

'Mm. What can you tell me about the chauffeur?'

'Sanphet? He's been here for as long as anyone can remember. He's never been to Norway, but he can reel off all the towns. And the kings. Yes, and he loves Grieg. I don't know if he has a record player at home, but I think he has all the records. He's such a sweet old man.'

She angled her head and revealed her gums.

Harry asked if she knew where he could find Hilde Molnes.

'She's at home. Dreadfully upset, I'm afraid. I think I would advise you to wait a bit before you talk to her.'

'Thank you for your advice, frøken Wiig, but waiting is a luxury we cannot afford. Would you be so kind as to ring her and tell her I'm on my way?'

'I understand. Sorry.'

'Where are you from, frøken Wiig?'

Tonje Wiig looked at him in surprise. Then she gave a strained chuckle. 'Is this supposed to be an interrogation, Hole?'

Harry didn't answer.

'If you absolutely have to know, I grew up in Fredrikstad.'

'That's what I thought I could hear,' he said with a wink.

The spry woman in reception was leaning back in her chair and holding a bottle of perfume to her nose. When Harry discreetly cleared his throat she gave a start and laughed in embarrassment with her eyes full of water.

'Sorry, the air in Bangkok is very bad,' she explained.

'I've noticed. Could you give me the chauffeur's telephone number?'

She shook her head and snorted. 'He hasn't got a telephone.'

'OK. Has he got a place to live?'

It was meant as a joke, but he could see from her face that she didn't appreciate it. She wrote down the address and gave him a tiny parting smile.

9

Saturday 11 January

A SERVANT WAS STANDING AT the door as Harry walked up the drive to the ambassador's residence. He led Harry through two large rooms, tastefully furnished in cane and teak, to the terrace door, which opened onto the garden behind the house. The orchids sparkled in yellow and blue, and butterflies fluttered past like coloured paper under large willow trees offering shade. They found the ambassador's wife, Hilde Molnes, by an hourglass-shaped swimming pool. She was sitting in a wicker chair wearing a pink robe, a matching drink on the table in front of her, and sunglasses which covered half her face.

'You must be Detective Hole,' she said in a Sunnmøre accent. 'Tonje said you were on your way. A drink, Detective?'

'No, thank you.'

'Oh, you must. It's important to drink in this heat, you know. Think of your liquid levels even if you aren't thirsty. Here you can dehydrate before your body tells you.'

She removed her sunglasses, and Harry saw, as he had guessed from her raven-black hair and dark skin, that she had brown eyes. They were lively but red-rimmed. Grief or the preprandial drink, Harry thought. Or both.

He estimated her age at mid-forties, but she was well kept. A middle-aged, slightly faded beauty from the upper-middle classes. He had seen them before.

He sat down in the other wicker chair, which wrapped itself around his body as if it had known he was coming.

'In that case I'll have a glass of water, fru Molnes.'

She informed the servant and sent him off.

'Have you been told that you can go and see your husband now?'

'Yes. Thank you,' she said. Harry noticed a curt undertone. 'Now they let me see him. A man I've been married to for twenty years.'

The brown eyes had turned black, and Harry reflected that it was probably true that lots of shipwrecked Portuguese and Spanish sailors had drifted ashore on the Sunnmøre coast.

'I'm obliged to ask you some questions,' he said.

'Then you'd better do it now while the gin's still working.'

She swung a slim, suntanned leg over her knee.

Harry took out a notepad. Not that he needed any notes, but it meant he wouldn't have to look at her while she answered. As a rule it made talking to next of kin easier.

She told him that her husband had left home in the morning and had not mentioned anything about coming home late, but it was not unusual for something to crop up. When it was ten in the evening and she still hadn't heard from him she had tried calling, but she didn't get an answer from either the office or his mobile phone. Nevertheless, she hadn't been worried. Just after midnight Tonje Wiig had called and said her husband had been found dead in a motel room.

Harry studied Hilde Molnes's face. She spoke with a firm voice and without any dramatic gestures.

Tonje Wiig had given Hilde Molnes the impression they didn't know what the cause of death was yet. The next day the embassy had informed her that he had been murdered, but as regards the cause of death instructions from Oslo imposed absolute silence on all of them. That included Hilde Molnes, even though she was not employed by the embassy, because all Norwegian citizens can be forced to maintain silence if state security considerations demand it. She said the latter with deep sarcasm and raised her glass to a *skål*.

Harry just nodded and took notes. He asked if she was sure he hadn't left his mobile phone at home, to which she answered she was. On an impulse he asked what kind of mobile phone he had and she replied that she wasn't sure, but thought it was Finnish.

She couldn't help him with the name of anyone who might have had a motive for wishing the ambassador dead.

He drummed his pencil on the pad.

'Did your husband like children?'

'Oh yes, a lot!' Hilde Molnes burst out, and for the first time he could hear a quiver in her voice. 'You know, Atle was the world's kindest father.'

Harry had to look down at the pad again. There had been something in her eyes that revealed she had sussed the double-edged nature of his question. He was nearly sure she didn't know anything, but he also knew it was his unfortunate task to have to take the next step and ask her straight out if she knew the ambassador had child pornography in his possession.

He ran a hand across his face. He felt like a surgeon with a scalpel in his hand, unable to perform the first incision. He could never get over his sensitivity when it came to matters unpleasant, when innocent people had to put up with having their nearest and dearest thrust into the limelight, having details they hadn't wanted to know hurled in their faces.

Hilde Molnes spoke first.

'He loved children so much we considered adopting a little girl.' She had tears in her eyes now. 'A poor little refugee from Burma.

Yes, at the embassy they are so careful to say Myanmar not to offend anyone, but I'm so old I say Burma.'

She forced a dry chuckle through the tears and composed herself. Harry looked away. A red hummingbird hovered quietly in front of the orchids, like a little model helicopter.

That was it, he decided. She knows nothing. If it had any relevance to the case he would take it up later. And if it didn't he would spare her.

Harry asked how long they had known each other, and she told him how they had met when Atle Molnes was a newly qualified political science graduate, a bachelor home for Christmas in Ørsta. The Molnes family was very wealthy, owned two furniture factories, and the young heir would have been a good catch for any young girl in the region, so there was no shortage of competition.

'I was just Hilde Melle from Melle Farm, but I was the most attractive,' she said with the same dry chuckle. A pained expression crossed her face and she put the glass to her lips.

Harry had no problem visualising the widow as a pure, young beauty.

Especially as that very image had just materialised at the open patio door.

'Runa, my love, there you are! This young man is Harry Hole. He's a Norwegian police officer and is going to help us find out what happened to Dad.'

The daughter barely dignified them with a glance and headed for the opposite side of the pool without answering. She had her mother's dark complexion and hair, and Harry estimated the long-limbed, slim body in the bathing costume to be about seventeen years old. He should have known her age; it had been in the report he was given before leaving.

She would have been a perfect beauty, like her mother, had it not been for one detail the report had not included. By the time she had rounded the pool and taken three slow, elegant steps along the diving board, bringing her legs together and soaring into the air, Harry already had a lump in his stomach. From her right shoulder protruded a thin stump of an arm that lent her body a strangely asymmetrical form, like a plane with a wing shot off, as it whirled around in a somersault with a twist. A splash was all that was heard as she broke the green surface and was lost from view.

'Runa's a diver,' Hilde Molnes said quite unnecessarily.

He still had his gaze fixed on where she had disappeared when a figure appeared by the pool ladder on the other side. She climbed up the rungs and he saw her rippling back, the sun glittering in the droplets on her skin and making her wet black hair gleam. The withered arm hung down like a chicken wing. Her exit was as soundless as her entrance and dive; she vanished through the patio door without a word.

'She probably didn't know you were here,' Hilde Molnes said apologetically. 'She doesn't like strangers seeing her without her prosthesis, you see.'

'I understand. How has she taken the news?'

'Who knows.' Hilde Molnes looked pensively towards where Runa had gone. 'She's at that age where she tells me nothing. Nor anyone else for that matter.' She raised her glass. 'I'm afraid Runa is a bit of a special girl.'

Harry got up, thanked her for the information and said she would be hearing from him. Hilde Molnes pointed out that he hadn't drunk any water; he bowed and asked her to keep it for him until the next time. It struck him that this was perhaps a little inappropriate, but she laughed anyway and drained her glass as he left.

As he walked towards the gate, a red open-top Porsche rolled up the drive. He just caught a blond fringe above a pair of Ray-Bans and a grey Armani suit before the car passed him and parked in the shade by the house.

10
Saturday 11 January

INSPECTOR CRUMLEY WAS OUT WHEN Harry returned to the police station, but Nho gave him a thumbs up and said 'Roger' when Harry politely asked him to contact the telecommunications company and check all the conversations to and from the ambassador's mobile phone on the day of the murder.

It was almost five o'clock when Harry finally got hold of the inspector. As it was late she suggested they head to a riverboat to see the canals, 'so as to get the sightseeing over and done with'.

At the River Pier they were offered one of the long boats for six hundred baht, but the price soon fell to three hundred after Crumley had tongue-lashed him in Thai.

They headed down the Chao Phraya before turning into one of the narrow canals. Wooden shacks looking as if they might collapse at any moment clung to poles in the river, and the smell of food, sewage and petrol drifted past in waves. Harry had a sense they were passing through the sitting rooms of the people who lived there. Only lines of green potted plants prevented them from looking straight in, but no one seemed particularly bothered; on the contrary, they waved and smiled.

Three boys in shorts sitting on a pier, wet after emerging from the brown water, called after them. Crumley shook a good-natured fist at them and the boatman laughed.

'What did they shout?' Harry asked.

She pointed to her head. '*Mâe chii*. It means mother, priest or nun. Nuns in Thailand shave their heads. If I wore a white gown I'd probably be treated with more respect,' she said.

'Oh yes? It seems as if you have enough respect. Your people—'

'That's because I respect them,' she interrupted. 'And because I'm good at my job.' She cleared her throat and spat over the railing. 'But maybe that surprises you because I'm a woman?'

'I didn't say that.'

'Foreigners are often surprised when they realise women can get ahead in this country. It isn't as macho as it seems here. In fact, it's more of a problem that I'm a foreigner.'

A light breeze created a cooling draught in the humid air; from a clump of trees came the chirping song of grasshoppers and they stared at the same blood-red sun as the evening before.

'What made you move here?'

Harry had a sense he might have crossed an invisible red line, but he ignored it.

'My mother's Thai,' she said after a pause. 'Dad was stationed in Saigon during the Vietnam War and met her here in Bangkok in 1967.' She laughed and put a cushion behind her back. 'Mom swears she got pregnant the first night they were together.'

'With you?'

She nodded. 'After the capitulation he took us to the States, to Fort Lauderdale, where he served as a lieutenant colonel. When we came back here my mother found out he'd been married when they met. He'd written home and arranged the divorce when he discovered Mom was pregnant.' She shook her head. 'He had every opportunity to run away and leave us in Bangkok if he'd wanted to. Perhaps he did want to, deep down. Who knows.'

'You didn't ask him?'

'It's not the kind of question you necessarily want an honest answer to, is it. I would never have got a real answer from him anyway. He was just like that.'

'Was?'

'Yes, he's dead.' She turned to him. 'Does it bother you, me talking about my family?'

Harry bit into a cigarette filter. 'Not at all.'

'Running away was never really an option for my father. He had a thing about responsibility. When I was eleven I was allowed to take a kitten from some neighbours in Fort Lauderdale. After a lot of fuss Dad said yes on the condition that I looked after it. Two weeks later I'd lost interest and asked if I could give it back. Then Dad took me and the kitten down to the garage. 'You can't run away from responsibility,' he said. 'That's how civilisations crumble.' Then he took his service rifle and fired a bullet through the kitten's head. Afterwards I had to get soap and water and scrub the garage floor. That was how he was. That was why . . .' She removed her sunglasses, took a corner of her shirt, wiped them and squinted into the setting sun. 'That was why he could never accept the US withdrawal from Vietnam. Mom and I moved here when I was eighteen.'

Harry nodded. 'I can imagine it wasn't so easy for your mother to go to an American military base after the war.'

'The base wasn't so bad. Other Americans, however, the ones who hadn't been there but had lost a son or a sweetheart in Vietnam, they hated us. For them anyone with slanted eyes was Charlie.'

A man in a suit sat smoking a cigar by a fire-ravaged shack.

'And then you went to Police College, became a detective and shaved off your hair?'

'Not in that order. And I didn't shave off my hair. It fell out one week when I was seventeen. A rare form of alopecia. But practical in this climate.'

She stroked her head with one hand and gave a weary smile. She had no eyebrows, no eyelashes, nothing.

Another boat came up alongside them. It was loaded to the gunnels with straw hats, and an old woman pointed to their heads and then the hats. Crumley smiled politely and said a few words. Before the woman shoved off she leaned over to Harry and gave him a white flower. She indicated Crumley and laughed.

'What's thank you in Thai?'

'*Khop khun khráp,*' Crumley said.

'Right. You tell her that.'

They glided past a temple, a *wat,* close to the canal, and could hear the mumbling of the monks coming from the open door. People were sitting on the steps outside praying with folded hands.

'What are they praying for?' he asked.

'I don't know. Peace. Love. A better life, here or in the sweet hereafter. The same things that people want everywhere.'

'I don't think Atle Molnes was waiting for a prostitute. I think he was waiting for someone else.'

They glided on, and the monks' mumbling faded behind them.

'Who?'

'No idea.'

'Why do you think that?'

'He only had enough money to rent the room, so I wouldn't mind betting he had no intention of paying for a prostitute's services. But he had no business being at the motel unless he was going to meet someone, right? The door wasn't locked when they found him, according to Wang. Isn't that a bit odd? If you close a hotel door it locks automatically. He must have consciously pressed the button on the handle so that it would remain open. There was no reason for the murderer to press it in. I suppose he or she wasn't aware they were leaving a door unlocked. So why did Molnes do that? Most people who frequent such establishments would prefer to have the door locked when they were asleep, don't you think?'

She wagged her head from side to side. 'Maybe he was afraid he wouldn't hear the person he was waiting for.'

'Exactly. And there was no reason to leave the door open for Tonya Harding because the agreement with the receptionist was that he would ring first. Right?'

In his excitement Harry had shifted to one side and the boatman shouted at him to sit in the middle so that they didn't tip over.

'I think he wanted to keep the name of the person he was meeting hidden. That was probably why they were getting together in a motel outside town. A suitable place for a secret meeting, a place where there was no official guest book.'

'Hm. Are you thinking about the photos.'

'It's impossible not to, isn't it.'

'You can buy that kind of thing anywhere in Bangkok.'

'He might have gone a step further. We might be talking child prostitution.'

'Maybe. But apart from those photos, which really are everywhere in this city, we have no leads.'

They had come a long way up the river. The inspector pointed at a house at the end of a large garden.

'A Norwegian guy lives there,' she said.

'How do you know?'

'There was a real stink in the papers when he built that house. As you can see, it resembles a temple. The Buddhists were outraged that a "heathen" would live there, they called it a blasphemy. To make matters worse, it turned out he'd built it using materials from a Burmese temple in disputed border territory. The situation was a little tense at the time; there were several shootings, so people moved out. The Norwegian bought the temple for next to nothing and since everything in northern Burmese temples is constructed with teak he dismantled the whole shebang and moved it to Bangkok.'

'Strange,' Harry said. 'What's his name?'

'Ove Klipra. He's one of the biggest building contractors in Bangkok. I guess you'll hear more about him if you're here for a while.'

She ordered the boatman to turn around.

'Do you like takeout?'

Harry looked down at the noodle soup in the plastic bowl. The white pieces were like pale, skinny versions of spaghetti and it made him nervous that the soup moved in unexpected places when he wound the noodles onto the chopsticks.

Rangsan came in to announce that Tonya Harding had reported in for fingerprinting.

'You can talk to her now if you like. And one more thing: Supawadee said they're checking the capsule from the car now. The result should be in tomorrow. They've given us top priority.'

'Say hello and cop con crap,' Harry answered.

'Say what?'

'Say thank you.'

Harry smiled sheepishly and Liz spluttered so much she sent rice flying.

11

Saturday 11 January

HARRY COULDN'T PUT A FIGURE on the number of prostitutes he had interviewed in a room like this, but it was not small. They seemed to be attracted to murder cases like flies round a cowpat. Not because they were necessarily involved, but because they invariably had a story to tell.

He had heard them laughing, cursing and crying, he had become friends with them, he had fallen out with them, had struck deals with them, broken promises, been spat at and slapped. Nevertheless, there was something about these women's fates, the circumstances that had formed them, which he thought he recognised and could understand. What he couldn't understand was their irrepressible optimism: that despite having seen into the deepest recesses of the human soul they never seemed to lose their faith in the goodness around them. He knew enough police officers who were incapable of the same.

That was why Harry patted Dim on the shoulder and gave her a cigarette before they started. Not because he thought it would achieve anything, but because she looked as if she needed it.

She had a flinty stare and a determined jaw that told you she was not easily frightened, but right now she was sitting at a plastic table, fidgeting nervously and looking as if she might burst into tears at any minute.

'*Pen yangai?*' he asked. How are you? Liz had taught him these two words in Thai before he entered the interview room.

Nho translated the answer. She slept badly at night and didn't want to work at the motel any more.

Harry sat down opposite her, rested his arms on the table and tried to catch her eye. Her shoulders lowered a fraction, but she still turned away from him with her arms crossed.

They went through what had happened point by point, but she had nothing new to add. She confirmed that the motel-room door had been closed but not locked. She hadn't seen a mobile phone. And hadn't seen anyone who didn't work at the motel when she arrived or when she left.

When Harry mentioned the Mercedes and whether she had noticed the diplomatic plates she shook her head. She hadn't seen a car. They were getting nowhere, and in the end Harry lit a cigarette and asked, almost casually, who she thought could have done it. Nho translated and Harry saw from her face that he had hit the bull's eye.

'What did she say?'

'She says the knife is from Khun Sa.'

'What does that mean?'

'Haven't you heard about Khun Sa?' Nho shot him a sceptical look.

Harry shook his head.

'Khun Sa is the most powerful heroin dealer in history. Along with the governments in Indochina and the CIA he has controlled opium trafficking in the golden triangle since the fifties. That was how the Americans got the money for their operations in the region. The guy had his own army in the jungle up there.

It slowly dawned on Harry that he had heard about Asia's Escobar.

'Khun Sa surrendered to the Burmese authorities two years ago and was placed under house arrest, albeit in one of the most luxurious houses. They say he finances the new hotels in Burma, and some people think he's still the leader of the opium mafia in the north. Khun Sa means she thinks it's the mafia. That's why she's scared.'

Harry studied her thoughtfully before nodding to Nho.

'Let her go,' he said.

Nho translated and Dim looked surprised. She turned and met Harry's gaze before putting the palms of her hands together at face height and bowing. Harry realised she had assumed they would arrest her for prostitution.

Harry smiled back. She leaned over the table.

'You like ice-skating, mister?'

'Khun Sa? CIA?'

The telephone line from Oslo crackled, and the echo meant that Harry heard himself talking across Torhus from the Ministry of Foreign Affairs.

'Excuse me, Hole, but are you suffering from heatstroke? A man has been found with a knife in his back, a knife which could have been bought anywhere in northern Thailand. We tell you to tread carefully and you're telling me you're thinking of trying to crack organised crime in South-East Asia?'

'No.' Harry put his feet on the desk. 'I'm not thinking of doing anything about it, Torhus. I'm just saying that an expert from some museum or other says it's a rare knife that's very hard to get hold of. The police here say it could be a warning from an opium mafia to keep away, but I don't think so. If the mafia wanted to tell us something there are more direct methods than sacrificing an antique knife.'

'So what are you going on about?'

'I'm saying that's the way the clues are pointing right now. But the Chief of Police here totally freaked out when I mentioned opium. It turns out this area is in utter chaos. The Chief had no intention of opening a can of worms, as it were. So I thought, to start with, I would rule out some possible theories. Such as the ambassador being involved in criminality. In child pornography, for example.'

The line went quiet at the other end.

'There is no reason to believe . . .' Torhus started, but the rest was drowned in interference.

'Repeat that please.'

'There's no reason to believe that Molnes was a paedophile, if that's what you're referring to.'

'Eh? There's no reason to believe? You're not talking to the press now, Torhus. I have to know these things in order to make any progress.'

There was another pause, and for a moment Harry thought the connection had gone. Then Torhus's voice was back, and even on a bad line from the other side of the globe Harry could feel the cold.

'I'll tell you all you need to know, Hole. All you need to know, Hole, is you have to tie things up. I don't give a shit what the ambassador has been involved in – as far as I'm concerned he could be a heroin smuggler and a pederast, so long as neither the press nor anyone else gets a sniff of it. If there is any further scandal, regardless of what it is, you will be held personally responsible. Have I made myself clear, Hole, or do you need to know more?'

Torhus hadn't even paused to draw breath.

Harry kicked the desk, making the phone and his colleagues beside him jump.

'I hear you loud and clear,' Harry said between clenched teeth. 'But you listen to me now.' Harry paused to take a deep breath. A beer, just *one* beer. He put a cigarette between his lips and tried to dispel the thought. 'If Molnes is mixed up in anything he is hardly likely to be the only Norwegian who is. I very much doubt he'd have had key contacts in the Thai underworld in the short time he'd been here. Did you read about the Norwegian they caught with boys in a hotel room in Pattaya? The police down here like that sort of thing. They get good coverage and paedophiles are easier to catch than the heroin gangs. Suppose the Thai police can already smell an easy catch, but they wait until this case is formally closed and I've gone home. Norwegian newspapers will send a pack of reporters and before you know it the ambassador's name has cropped up. If we can catch these men now while we have an agreement with the Thai police that this is all hush-hush, perhaps we can avoid a scandal of that nature.'

Harry could hear the Director was getting the picture.

'What do you want?'

'I've been here for just over twenty-four hours and I can tell this case is going nowhere, and that's because there's a cover-up. I want to know what you're not telling me. What you've got on Molnes and what he was involved in.'

'You know what you need to know. There's no more. Is that so hard to grasp?' Torhus groaned. 'What are you actually trying to achieve, Hole? I thought you would be just as keen as we are to get this wrapped up quickly.'

'I'm a police officer, and I'm trying to do my job, Torhus.'

Torhus laughed. 'Very moving, Hole. But remember I know a couple of things about you, so I don't buy your I'm-only-an-honest-cop spiel.'

Harry coughed down the receiver and heard the echoes return like muffled gunshots. He mumbled something.

'What?'

'I said this is a bad line. Give it some thought, Torhus, and ring me when you have something to tell me.'

*   *   *

Harry woke up with a start, jumped out of bed and just reached the bathroom before vomiting. He sat on the toilet; it was coming out of both ends now. The sweat was pouring off him, even though he felt cold in the room.

Coming off the booze was worse last time, he told himself. It'll get better. A lot better, he hoped.

He had injected himself in the buttock with vitamin B before going to bed, and it had stung like hell. He was reminded of Vera, a prostitute in Oslo, who had been on heroin for fifteen years. Once she had told him she still fainted when she inserted the needle.

He saw something move in the gloom, on the sink, a couple of antennae swinging to and fro. A cockroach. It was the size of a thumb and had an orange stripe on its back. He had never seen one like this before, but that was perhaps not so peculiar – he had read there were more than three thousand different types of cockroach. He had also read that they hide when they hear the vibrations of someone approaching and that for every cockroach you can see there are at least ten hiding. That meant they were everywhere. How much does a cockroach weigh? Ten grams? If there were more than a hundred of them in cracks and behind tables that would mean there was at least a kilo of cockroaches in the room. He shivered. It was cold comfort knowing they were more frightened than he was. Sometimes he had the feeling alcohol had done him more *good* than harm. He closed his eyes and tried not to think.

12

Sunday 12 January

IN THE END THEY HAD parked and begun to search for the address on foot. Nho had tried to explain the ingenious system of addresses in Bangkok, with main streets and numbered side streets known as *sois*. The problem was that houses didn't follow in numerical order as new houses were given the next free number wherever they were in the street.

They walked through narrow alleyways where pavements served as extensions of living rooms with people reading newspapers, sewing on treadle machines, cooking or taking an afternoon nap. Some girls in school uniforms shouted after them and giggled, and Nho pointed to Harry and answered something or other. The girls howled with laughter and held their hands to their mouths.

Nho talked to a woman sitting behind a sewing machine and she pointed to a door. They knocked and after a while it was opened by a man wearing khaki shorts and an open shirt. Harry put him at about sixty, but only his eyes and wrinkles revealed his age. There were wisps of grey in his smooth, black combed-back hair and the lean, sinewy body could have belonged to a thirty-year-old.

Nho said a few words, and the man nodded while looking at

Harry. Then the man apologised and was gone again. After a minute he returned, now wearing an ironed, white short-sleeved shirt and long trousers.

He had brought two chairs with him, which he placed on the pavement. In surprisingly good English he offered one to Harry while sitting down on the other. Nho remained standing beside them and rejected Harry's signal that he could sit on the step with a faint shake of the head.

'Harry Hole, Mr Sanphet. I'm from the Norwegian police. I'd like to ask you some questions about Molnes.'

'You mean *Ambassador* Molnes.'

Harry looked at the man. He was sitting as straight as a poker with his brown, freckled hands in his lap.

'Of course. Ambassador Molnes. You've been a chauffeur at the Norwegian Embassy for almost thirty years, I understand.'

Sanphet closed his eyes by way of confirmation.

'And you respected the ambassador?'

'Ambassador Molnes was a great man. A great man with a big heart. And brain.'

He tapped his forehead with one finger and gave Harry an admonitory look.

Harry shivered as a bead of sweat rolled down his spine and inside his trousers. He looked around for some shade where they could move their chairs, but the sun was high and the houses in this street were low.

'We've come to you because you knew the ambassador's habits best, you knew where he went and who he met. And because you clearly got on well with him on a personal level. What happened on the day he died?'

Sitting quite calmly, Sanphet told them how the ambassador had left without saying where he was going, just that he wanted to drive himself, which was very unusual during working hours as the chauffeur had no other duties. He had waited in the embassy until five and then he had gone home.

'You live alone?'

'My wife died in a traffic accident fourteen years ago.'

Something told Harry he could give him the exact number of months and days as well. They had no children.

'Where did you drive the ambassador?'

'To other embassies. To meetings. To Norwegians' houses.'

'Which Norwegians?'

'All sorts. People from Statoil, Hydro, Jotun and Statskonsult.'

He pronounced the Norwegian names perfectly.

'Do you know any of these?' Harry asked, passing him a list. 'These are people the ambassador was in touch with on his mobile phone on the day he died. We got this from the telephone company.'

Sanphet took out a pair of glasses, but still had to hold the piece of paper at arm's length as he read aloud: '11.10. Bangkok Betting Service.'

He peered over his glasses.

'The ambassador liked a flutter on the horses.' And added with a smile: 'Sometimes he won.'

Nho shifted his feet.

'What's Worachak Road?'

'A call from a public phone box. Please carry on.'

'11.55. The Norwegian Embassy.'

'The odd thing is we rang the embassy this morning and no one can recall speaking to him on the phone that day, not even the receptionist.'

Sanphet shrugged, and Harry waved him on.

'12.50. Ove Klipra. You've heard of him, I suppose?'

'May have.'

'He's one of Bangkok's richest men. I read in the paper he's just sold a hydroelectric power station in Laos. He lives in a temple,'

Sanphet muttered. 'He and the ambassador knew each other from before. They were from the same part of the country. Have you heard of Ålesund? The ambassador invited . . .'

He raised his arms in resignation. Not a subject worth talking about now. He went back to the list.

'13.15. Jens Brekke.'

'Who's he?'

'Currency broker. He came to Barclays Thailand from Den norske Bank a few years ago.'

'OK.'

'17.55. Mangkon Road?'

'Another call from a public phone box.'

There were no more names on the list. Harry cursed to himself. He didn't quite know what he had expected, but the chauffeur hadn't told him anything at all he didn't already know from talking to Tonje Wiig on the phone an hour earlier.

'Do you suffer from asthma, Mr Sanphet?'

'Asthma? No. Why?'

'We found a capsule in the car. We asked the lab to check it out. Don't be alarmed, Mr Sanphet. It's purely routine. It turned out to be for asthma. But no one in the Molnes family suffers from asthma. Do you know who it could belong to?'

Sanphet shook his head.

Harry pulled his chair closer to the chauffeur. He wasn't used to carrying out interviews in the street, and he had a sense everyone sitting in the narrow alleyway was eavesdropping. He lowered his voice.

'With all due respect, you're lying. I saw the receptionist at the embassy taking asthma medication with my own eyes, Mr Sanphet. You sit in the embassy half the day, you've been there for thirty years and I imagine no one can change a toilet roll without your knowing. Are you claiming you didn't know she had asthma?'

Sanphet looked at him with cold, calm eyes.

'I'm saying I don't know who might have left asthma medication in the *car*, sir. Lots of people in Bangkok have asthma, and some of them must have been in the ambassador's car. Miss Ao is, as far as I know, not one of them.'

Harry watched him. How could he sit there without a drop of sweat on his brow while the sun shimmered in the sky like a brass cymbal? Harry glanced down at his notepad as if his next question were written there.

'Did he ever drive children in the car?'

'Excuse me?'

'Did you pick up children sometimes, drive him to schools, nurseries or anything similar? Do you understand?'

Sanphet didn't bat an eyelid, but his back straightened.

'I do understand. The ambassador was not one of *them*,' he said.

'How do you know?'

A man looked up from his newspaper, and Harry became aware he had raised his voice. Sanphet bowed.

Harry felt stupid. Stupid, wretched and sweaty. In that order.

'I'm sorry,' he said. 'I didn't mean to offend you.'

The old chauffeur looked past him, pretending he hadn't heard.

'We have to go now.' Harry got up. 'I heard you like Grieg, so I brought you this.' He held up a cassette. 'It's Grieg's symphony in C minor. It was first performed in 1981, so I thought you may not have it. Everyone who loves Grieg should have it. Please take it.'

Sanphet got up, accepted it with surprise and stood looking at it.

'Goodbye,' Harry said, making a clumsy but well-meant *wai* greeting and motioning to Nho that they were going.

'Wait,' the chauffeur said. His eyes were still fixed on the cassette. 'The ambassador was a good man. But he wasn't a happy man. He had one weakness. I don't want to sully his memory, but he lost more than he won on horses.'

'Most do,' Harry said.

'Not five million baht.'

Harry tried to calculate in his head. Nho came to his rescue.

'A hundred thousand dollars.'

Harry whistled. 'Well, well, if he could afford that then—'

'He couldn't afford it,' Sanphet said. 'He borrowed money from some loan sharks in Bangkok. They rang him several times over the last few weeks.' He looked at Harry. It was difficult to interpret his expression. 'Personally, I believe a man has to settle gambling debts, but if someone killed him for the money I think they should be punished.'

'So the ambassador wasn't a happy man?'

'He didn't have an easy life.'

Harry remembered something. 'Does Man U mean anything to you?'

The chauffeur's expression clouded over.

'It was on the ambassador's calendar for the day of the murder. I checked the TV guide and no one was showing Manchester United that day.'

'Oh, Manchester United,' Sanphet smiled. 'That's Klipra. The ambassador called him Mr Man U. He flies to England to see games and has bought loads of shares in the club. A very peculiar person.'

'We'll see. I'll have a chat with him later.'

'If you can get hold of him.'

'What do you mean?'

'You don't get hold of Klipra. He gets hold of you.'

That's all we need, Harry thought. A caricature.

'The gambling debts radically change the picture,' Nho said, back in the car.

'Maybe,' Harry said. 'A hundred thousand dollars is a lot of cash, but is it enough?'

'People are murdered in Bangkok for less than that,' Nho said. 'Much less. Believe me.'

'It's not the loan sharks I'm thinking about, it's Atle Molnes. The guy comes from a very wealthy family. He should be able to pay, at least if it was a matter of life and death. There's something not right here. What do you think about Mr Sanphet?'

'He was lying when he talked about Miss Ao.'

'Oh? What makes you say that?'

Nho didn't answer, just smiled secretively and tapped his temple.

'What are you trying to tell me, Nho? That you know when people are lying?'

'I learned it from my mother. During the Vietnam War she lived as a poker player on Soi Cowboy.'

'Rubbish. I know police officers who have questioned people all their lives, and they all say the same: you can't learn to see through a good liar.'

'It's a matter of having eyes in your head. You can see it in small things. Such as when you didn't open your mouth properly when you said everyone who loves Grieg should have a copy of the cassette.'

Harry could feel the heat rising in his cheeks. 'The cassette happened to be in my Walkman. An Australian policeman told me about Grieg's symphony in C minor. I bought the cassette in memory of him.'

'It worked anyway.'

Nho swerved from the path of a lorry bearing down on them.

'Bloody hell!' Harry didn't even have time to be afraid. 'He was in the wrong lane!'

Nho shrugged. 'He was bigger than me.'

Harry looked at his watch. 'We have to pop into the station, and I've got a funeral to go to.' He thought with dread of the hot jacket hanging in the cupboard outside the 'office'.

'I hope there's air conditioning in the church. By the way, how come we had to sit in the street in the baking sun? Why didn't the old boy invite us into the shade?'

'Pride,' Nho said.

'Pride?'

'He lives in a small room which has precious little to do with the car he drives and the place he works. He didn't want to invite us in because it would have been unpleasant, not just for him but also for us.'

'Strange man.'

'This is Thailand,' Nho said. 'I wouldn't invite you into my place, either. I would serve you tea on the steps.'

He made a sudden right turn and a couple of the three-wheeled tuk-tuks swerved in horror. Harry instinctively put out his hands in front of him.

'I'm—'

'—bigger than they are. Thanks, Nho, I think I've got the principle.'

13

Sunday 12 January

'HE'S GONE UP IN SMOKE now,' Harry's neighbour said, crossing himself. He was a powerful-looking man with a deep tan and light blue eyes, reminding Harry of stained wood and faded denim. His silk shirt was open at the neck, around which hung a thick gold chain that gleamed in the sun, matt and thick. His nose was covered with a fine network of blood vessels, and his brown skull shone like a billiard ball beneath the thinning hair. Roald Bork had lively eyes which at close range made him seem younger than his seventy years.

He talked. Loudly and apparently uninhibited by the fact that they were at a funeral. His Nordland dialect sang beneath the vaulted ceiling, but no one turned with a reproving stare.

When they were outside the crematorium, Harry introduced himself.

'Well now, so I had a policeman standing next to me all the time without me knowing. Good job I didn't say anything. It could have cost me.'

He laughed a reverberating laugh and held out a dry, leathery old-man's hand. 'Bork, on the lowest pension.' The irony didn't reach his eyes.

'Tonje Wiig said you were a kind of spiritual leader for the Norwegian community here.'

'Then I might have to disappoint you. As you see, I'm a decrepit old man, no shepherd. Besides, I've moved to the periphery, in both a literal and metaphorical sense.'

'Oh yes?'

'To the den of iniquity, Thailand's Sodom.'

'Pattaya?'

'Correct. There are a few other Norwegians living there who I try to keep in order.'

'Let me get straight to the point, Bork. We've been trying to contact Ove Klipra, but all we got was a gatekeeper who says he doesn't know where Klipra is or when he'll be returning.'

Bork chuckled. 'That sounds like Klipra all right.'

'I've been told he prefers to make contact himself, but we're in the middle of a murder investigation here and I don't have a lot of time. I gather you're a close friend of Klipra's, a kind of link to the outside world?'

Bork angled his head. 'I'm no adjutant, if that's what you mean. But you're right insomuch as I mediate contacts. Klipra doesn't like speaking to people he doesn't know.'

'Was it you who arranged the contact between Klipra and the ambassador?'

'Initially it was. But Klipra liked the ambassador, so they spent a lot of time together. The ambassador was also from Sunnmøre, although he was from the country and not a real Ålesund lad like Klipra.'

'Odd he's not here today then?'

'Klipra travels all the time. He hasn't answered his phone for a few days, so I would guess he's out seeing to his businesses in Vietnam or Laos and doesn't even know the ambassador is dead. This case hasn't exactly hit the headlines.'

'It generally doesn't when a man dies of heart failure,' Harry said.

'So that's why the Norwegian police are here, is it?' Bork asked, drying the sweat from his neck with a large white handkerchief.

'Routine when an ambassador dies abroad,' Harry said, jotting down the telephone number of the police station on the back of a business card.

'Here's a number where you can reach me if Klipra should turn up.'

Bork studied the card, appeared to be on the point of saying something, but changed his mind, put the card in his breast pocket and nodded.

'I've got your number then,' he said, shook hands and walked over to an old Land Rover. Behind him, half mounted on the pavement, came a glint from recently washed red paintwork. It was the same Porsche Harry had seen pull up in front of the Molneses' house.

Tonje Wiig strolled over to him. 'Was Bork able to help you?'

'Not this time round.'

'What did he say about Klipra? Did he know where he was?'

'He didn't know anything.'

She didn't make a move to go, and Harry had a vague sense that she was waiting for more. In a moment of paranoia he saw the flinty glare of the diplomat at Fornebu Airport – 'No scandals, OK?' Could she have been told to keep an eye on Harry and let Director Torhus know if he went too far? He looked at her and immediately rejected the idea.

'Who owns the red Porsche?' he asked.

'Porsche?'

'There. I thought Østfold girls knew all the makes of car before they were sixteen?'

Tonje Wiig ignored the comment and put on her sunglasses. 'It's Jens's car.'

'Jens Brekke?'

'Yes. He's over there.'

Harry turned. On the steps stood Hilde Molnes, dressed in dramatic black silk robes with a serious-looking Sanphet in a dark suit. Behind them stood a younger, fair-haired man. Harry had noticed him in the church. He wore a waistcoat under his suit, despite the thermometer showing thirty-five degrees. His eyes were concealed behind a pair of expensive-looking sunglasses, and he was speaking in a low voice with a woman, also dressed in black. Harry stared at her, and as though she had felt his eyes on her she turned towards him. He hadn't recognised Runa Molnes at once, and now he could see why. The singular asymmetry was gone. She was taller than the others on the steps. Her gaze was brief and betrayed no feelings, apart from boredom.

Harry excused himself, walked up the steps and offered Hilde his condolences. Her hand was limp and passive in his. She looked at him through glazed eyes, and the smell of strong perfume camouflaged the gin.

Then he turned to Runa. She shielded her eyes from the sun and squinted up as though she had only just noticed him.

'Hi,' she said. 'At last someone who is taller than me in this country of pygmies. Aren't you the detective who came to our house?'

There was an aggressive undertone to her voice, a teenager's forced self-confidence. *Her* handshake was firm and strong. Harry's eyes automatically sought the other hand. A wax prosthesis protruded from the black sleeve.

'Detective?'

Jens Brekke was speaking.

He had removed his sunglasses and was squinting. An untidy blond fringe fell in front of almost transparent blue irises. His round face still had a boy's puppy fat, but the wrinkles around his eyes suggested he had passed thirty at least. The Armani suit had been exchanged for a classic Del Georgio and the hand-sewn Bally shoes were like black mirrors, but there was something about his appearance that reminded Harry of a rude twelve-year-old dressed as an adult. He introduced himself.

'I'm here from the Norwegian police to make some routine inquiries.'

'I see. Is that normal?'

'You spoke to the ambassador on the day he died, didn't you?'

Brekke gazed at Harry in surprise. 'That's right. How did you know?'

'We found his mobile phone. Your number was one of the last five he rang. He called at quarter past one.'

Harry studied Brekke carefully, but his face registered no uncertainty or confusion.

'Can we have a chat?'

'Drop by,' Brekke said, conjuring up a business card between index and middle fingers.

'At home or at work?'

'I sleep at home.'

It was impossible to *see* the little smile playing around the corners of his mouth, but Harry knew it was there nevertheless. As though talking to a detective was just something exciting, something a little out of the ordinary.

'If you'll excuse me?'

Brekke whispered a few words in Runa's ear, nodded to Hilde and jogged down to his Porsche. The place was thinning out; Sanphet accompanied Hilde Molnes to the embassy car and Harry was left standing next to Runa.

'There's a gathering at the embassy,' he said.

'I know. Mum doesn't feel like going.'

'Right. You've probably got family staying.'

'No,' she said.

Harry watched Sanphet close the door after Hilde Molnes and walk round the car.

'Well, you can take a taxi with me, if you'd like.'

Harry could feel his earlobes flush when he heard how that sounded. He had meant to say 'if you'd like to go'.

She glanced up at him. Her eyes were black and he didn't know what they were saying.

'I wouldn't.' She started to walk towards the embassy car.

Spirits were low and no one said much. Tonje Wiig had invited Harry to the gathering, and they stood in a corner twirling their glasses. Tonje was well down her second Martini. Harry had asked for water, but instead he had been given a sticky, sweet orange drink.

'So you have family at home, Harry?'

'Some,' Harry said, unsure what the sudden change of topic meant.

'Me too,' she said. 'Parents, brother and sister. A couple of aunts and uncles, no grandparents. That's it. And you?'

'Something similar.'

Miss Ao wound her way past them with a tray of drinks. She was wearing a simple, traditional Thai dress with a long slit down the side. He followed her with his eyes. It wasn't difficult to imagine how the ambassador might have fallen for the temptation.

At the other end of the room, in front of a large map of the world, stood a man rocking on his heels, his legs wide. He was straight-backed, broad-shouldered and his silver-grey hair was cropped like Harry's. His eyes were hooded, his jaw was set and his hands were folded behind his back. There was a smell of military from a long way off.

'Who's that?'

'Ivar Løken. The ambassador called him simply LM.'

'Løken? Funny. He wasn't on the list of employees I was given by Oslo. What does he do?'

'Good question.' She giggled and sipped her drink. 'Sorry, Harry – is it all right if I call you Harry? – I must be a bit tipsy. I've had so much work and so little sleep over the last few days. He came here last year, just after Molnes. To put it bluntly, he belongs to the part of the Ministry that's going nowhere.'

'What does that mean?'

'His career has ended in a cul-de-sac. He came from some job in Defence, but at some point there were a couple too many "buts" by his name.'

'Buts?'

'Haven't you heard the way Ministry people talk about one another? "He's a good diplomat, *but* he drinks, *but* he likes women too much" and so on. What comes after the "buts" is a lot more important than what comes before; it determines how far you can get in the department. That's why there are so many sanctimonious mediocrities at the top.'

'So what's his "but" and why is he here?'

'To be honest, I don't know. He has meetings and writes the odd report for Oslo, but we don't see much of him. I think he likes to be left alone. Now and then he goes off on trips to Vietnam, Laos or Cambodia with a tent, malaria pills and a rucksack full of photographic equipment. You know the type, don't you?'

'Maybe. What kind of reports does he write?'

'Don't know. The ambassador deals with all that.'

'Don't know? There aren't that many of you at the embassy. Is it Intelligence?'

'To what end?'

'Well, Bangkok is a hub for all of Asia.'

She looked at him and smiled wistfully. 'I wish we did such exciting things. But I think the Ministry is letting him stay here for long and generally loyal service to king and country. Besides, I'm bound by an oath of confidentiality.'

She giggled again and laid a hand on Harry's arm. 'Let's talk about something else, shall we?'

Harry talked about something else and then went to find another drink. The human body consists of sixty per cent water and he had the feeling that during the day most of his had evaporated up towards the blue-grey sky.

He found Miss Ao standing with Sanphet at the back of the room. Sanphet gave him a measured nod.

'Any water?' Harry asked.

Miss Ao passed him a glass.

'What does LM stand for?'

Sanphet raised an eyebrow. 'Are you thinking of Mr Løken?'

'I am.'

'Why don't you ask him yourself?'

'In case it's something you call him behind his back.'

Sanphet grinned. 'L stands for "living" and M for "morphine". It's an old nickname he acquired working for the UN in Vietnam at the end of the war.'

'Vietnam?'

Sanphet nodded unobtrusively and Miss Ao was gone.

'Løken was with a Vietnamese unit in a landing zone waiting to be picked up by a helicopter when they were attacked by a Vietcong patrol. It was a bloodbath and Løken was one of those hit. He got a bullet right through a muscle in his neck. The Americans had withdrawn their soldiers from Vietnam, but they still had medical orderlies there. They ran around in the elephant grass from soldier to soldier giving first aid. They wrote on the injured men's helmets in chalk, a kind of makeshift medical chart. If they wrote D it meant the person was dead, so that those who followed didn't waste any time examining them. L meant the patient was living, and if they wrote M it meant they'd given them morphine. They did that to prevent anyone from being given several shots and dying of an overdose.'

Sanphet nodded towards Løken.

'When they found him he'd already lost consciousness, so they didn't give him any morphine, just wrote an L on his helmet and loaded him onto the helicopter with the others. When he was woken by his own screams of pain he didn't understand where he was at first. But when he moved the corpse lying on top of him and saw a man with a white armband injecting one of the others he understood and screamed for morphine. An orderly tapped his helmet and said, "Sorry, buddy, you're already pumped up to the eyeballs." Løken couldn't believe it and tore off his helmet, where, sure enough, there was an L and an M. However, the thing was, it wasn't his helmet. He looked back at the soldier who had just been injected in the arm. He saw the helmet with an L on, recognised the screwed-up pack of cigarettes under the strap and the UN badge and realised what had happened. The guy had swapped their helmets to get another shot of morphine. He screamed, but his cries of agony were drowned out by the roar of the engine as they took off. Løken lay screaming for half an hour before they reached the golf course.'

'Golf course?'

'The camp. That's what we called it.'

'So you were there, too?'

Sanphet nodded.

'That's why you know the story so well?'

'I was a voluntary medical worker and I received them.'

'What happened?'

'Løken's standing over there. The other guy never woke up again.'

'Overdose?'

'Well, he didn't die of a shot to the stomach.'

Harry shook his head. 'And now you and Løken are working in the same place.'

'By coincidence.'

'What are the odds of that happening?'

'It's a small world,' Sanphet said.

'LM,' Harry said, then drank up, mumbled he needed more water and went looking for Miss Ao.

'Do you miss the ambassador?' he asked when he found her in the kitchen. She was folding serviettes around the glasses and securing them with elastic bands.

She looked at him in surprise and nodded.

Harry held the empty glass between his hands.

'How long had you been lovers?'

He saw her pretty little mouth open, form an answer, which her brain had not yet prepared, and close and open again, like a goldfish. When the anger reached her eyes and he half expected her to slap him, it died again. Instead her eyes filled with tears.

'I'm sorry,' Harry said without sounding sorry.

'You—'

'I'm sorry, but we have to ask these questions.'

'But I . . .' She cleared her throat, raised and lowered her shoulders, as though shaking off an evil thought. 'The ambassador was married. And I—'

'You're also married?'

'No, but . . .'

Harry took her arm lightly and led her away from the kitchen door. She turned to him, the anger in her eyes returning.

'Listen, Miss Ao, the ambassador was found in a motel. You know what that means. It means you weren't the only one he was fucking.'

He watched her to see what effect the words would have.

'We're investigating a murder here. You have no reason to feel any loyalty for this man, do you understand?'

She was whimpering and he became aware he was shaking her arm. He let go. She looked at him. Her pupils were big and black.

'Are you afraid? Is that what it is?'

Her chest rose and fell.

'Would it help if I promise that none of this needs to come out unless you were mixed up in the murder?'

'We were not lovers!'

Harry stared at her, but all he could see was two black pupils.

'OK. What's a young girl like you doing in a married ambassador's car? Apart from taking her asthma medication?'

Harry put the empty glass on the tray and left. It was an idiotic thing to say, but Harry was willing to do idiotic things to make something happen. Anything.

14

Sunday 12 January

ELIZABETH DOROTHEA CRUMLEY WAS IN a bad mood.

'Shit! It's been five days. A foreigner has been knifed in the back at a motel, and we have no fingerprints, no suspects, not one goddamn clue. Just receptionists, Tonya Harding, motel owners and now the mafia. Anything I've forgotten?'

'Loan sharks,' said Rangsan from behind the *Bangkok Post*.

'Loan sharks *are* the mafia,' the inspector said.

'Not the loan shark Molnes used,' Rangsan said.

'What do you mean?'

Rangsan put down the newspaper. 'Harry, you said the chauffeur thought the ambassador owed money to some loan sharks. What does a loan shark do when the debtor is dead? He tries to collect the debts from the family, doesn't he.'

Liz looked sceptical.

'Some people are still caught up with the notion of family honour, and loan sharks are businessmen. Of course they'll try to get their money back wherever they can.'

'That sounds really far-fetched,' Liz said, wrinkling her nose.

Rangsan picked up the paper again. 'Nonetheless, I found the

Thai Indo Travellers number three times on the list of incoming calls to the Molnes family over the last three days.'

Liz whistled softly, and there were nods around the table.

'What?' said Harry, realising there was something he hadn't picked up.

'Thai Indo Travellers is a travel agency on the outside,' Liz explained. 'But on the first floor they run their real business – lending money to people who can't get loans anywhere else. Their interest rates are high and they have a very effective way of making people pay up. We've been keeping an eye on them for some time.'

'Ever make anything on them stick?'

'We could have if we'd tried hard enough. But we think their competitors are worse. Thai Indo Travellers has managed to operate alongside the mafia and as far as we know they don't even pay protection. If they killed the ambassador it would be the first time they've killed anyone to our knowledge.'

'Perhaps it was time to set an example,' Nho said.

'Kill a man first and then ring the family to collect the money. Doesn't that sound a bit back to front?' Harry said.

'Why? Those who need a warning about what happens to bad debtors have been warned,' Rangsan said, slowly turning a page. 'If they get the money as well, that's a bonus.'

'Fine,' Liz said. 'Nho and Harry, you make a courtesy visit to the loan sharks. One more thing, I've just been talking to Forensics. They're totally mystified by the grease we found around the knife wound on Molnes's suit. They claim it's organic and that it has to be from some animal. OK, I think that's everything. Good luck.'

Rangsan caught up with Harry and Nho as they headed towards the lift.

'Be careful. These are rough guys. I've heard they use propellers on bad debtors.'

'Propellers?'

'They take them out in a boat, tie them to a pole in the river, put the engine in reverse and lift the propeller shaft out of the water as they slowly glide past. Can you visualise that?'

Harry visualised it.

'A couple of years ago we found a guy who'd died of a heart attack. His face had been pulled off, literally. The idea was that he would have to walk around town as a warning and deterrent to other debtors. But it must have been too much of a strain on his heart when he heard the engine starting up and saw the propeller coming.'

Nho nodded. 'Not good. Better to pay.'

AMAZING THAILAND it said in big letters over the multicoloured image of Thai dancers. The poster hung on the wall of the tiny travel agency in Sampeng Lane in Chinatown. Apart from Harry, Nho, and a man and a woman behind desks, the spartan room was empty. The man wore glasses with such thick lenses that he seemed to be looking at them from the inside of a goldfish bowl.

Nho had just shown him his police ID.

'What did he say?'

'The police are always welcome. We can have special prices on his trips.'

'Ask for a free trip upstairs.'

Nho said a couple of words and the man lifted a telephone receiver.

'Mr Sorensen just has to finish drinking his tea,' he said in English.

Harry was about to say something but a reproving glance from Nho changed his mind. They both sat down to wait. After a couple of minutes Harry pointed to the inactive fan on the ceiling. Goldfish Bowl smiled and shook his head.

'Kaput.'

Harry could feel his scalp itching. After a couple more minutes the telephone rang and the man asked them to follow him. At the bottom of the stairs he motioned that they should take off their shoes. Harry thought of his sweaty tennis socks with holes in and considered it was best for all concerned if he kept his shoes on, but Nho slowly shook his head. Cursing, Harry flipped off his shoes and trudged upstairs.

Goldfish Bowl knocked on a door, it was flung open and Harry stepped back two paces. A mountain of flesh and muscle filled the doorway. The mountain had two small slits for eyes, a drooping black moustache and his head was shaven, apart from a limp pigtail. His head looked like a discoloured bowling ball; the torso had no neck or shoulders, only a bulging mass that started at his ears and descended to a couple of arms which were so fat it was as if they had been screwed on. Harry had never seen such a large human in all his life.

The man turned and waddled ahead of them into the room.

'His name's Woo,' Nho whispered. 'Freelance goon. Very bad reputation.'

'My God. He looks like a terrible imitation of a Hollywood bad guy.'

'Chinese from Manchuria. They're famous for being very . . .'

The shutters in front of the windows were closed, and in the darkened room Harry could discern the outline of a man sitting behind a large desk. A fan whirred on the ceiling and a stuffed tiger's head snarled at them from the wall. An open balcony door gave the impression the outside traffic was passing through the room, and a third person sat by the doorway. Woo squeezed himself into the last remaining chair. Harry and Nho took up a position in the middle of the floor.

'How can I help you, gentlemen?'

The voice from behind the desk was deep, the pronunciation

British, the tones almost Oxford. He raised his hand and a ring glinted. Nho looked at Harry.

'Erm, we're from the police, Mr Sorensen . . .'

'I know.'

'You lent money to Atle Molnes, the Norwegian ambassador. You rang his wife after his death. Why? To try and force her to pay his debts?'

'We have no unsettled debts with any ambassador. Besides, we don't deal with that kind of loan, Mr . . .'

'Hole. You're lying, Mr Sorensen.'

'What did you say, Mr Hole?' Sorensen had leaned forward. His facial features were Thai, but his skin and hair were as white as snow and his eyes blue.

Nho caught Harry's sleeve, but he pulled his arm away and held Sorensen's gaze. He knew he'd put his neck on the block, had taken a threatening stance and that Mr Sorensen would lose face now if he conceded anything. Those were the rules of the game. But Harry was standing there in threadbare socks, sweating like a pig and absolutely sick of face, tact and diplomacy.

'You're in Chinatown now, Mr Hole, not in *farang* land. I have no argument with the Chief of Police in Bangkok. I suggest you have a chat with him before you say another word, then I promise you we'll forget this embarrassing scene.'

'Usually the police read the Miranda rights to the criminal, not vice versa.'

Mr Sorensen's teeth shone white between moist, red lips. 'Oh, yes. "You have the right to remain silent," and so on. Well, this time it was vice versa. Woo, show them out. Gentlemen.'

'Your activities here can't stand the light of day and neither can you, Mr Sorensen. If I were you I would go straight out and buy some sunscreen with a high protection factor. They don't sell it in prison exercise yards.'

Sorensen's voice went a touch deeper. 'Don't provoke me, Mr Hole. I'm afraid my sojourns abroad have caused me to lose my legendary Thai patience.'

'After a couple of years behind bars you'll soon have it back.'

'Show Mr Hole *out*, Woo.'

The massive body moved with astonishing speed. Harry caught the acrid smell of curry, and before he could lift an arm he was swept off the ground and clasped like a teddy bear someone had just won at the fair. Harry tried to wriggle loose, but the iron grip tightened every time he released air from his lungs, just like a boa constrictor constricts its victim's supply of air. Everything went black and the sound of traffic became louder. Then finally he was free and hovering in the air. When he opened his eyes he knew he had been unconscious, as though he had been dreaming for a second. He saw a sign covered in Chinese symbols, a bundle of wires between two telegraph poles, a greyish-white sky and a face looking down on him. Then sound returned, and he could hear a stream of words cascading from the face's mouth. He pointed to the balcony and then to the roof of the tuk-tuk which had been left with a nasty sag.

'How are you, Harry?' Nho waved away the tuk-tuk driver.

Harry peered down at himself. His back hurt and there was something immeasurably sad about bedraggled sports socks on dirty, grey tarmac.

'Well, I wouldn't have been allowed into Schrøder's like this. Have you got my shoes?'

Harry could have sworn Nho was biting his tongue to restrain a grin.

'Sorensen told me to bring an arrest warrant next time,' Nho said once they were back in the car. 'Now we've got them for violence against a civil servant anyway.'

Harry ran his finger down a long cut on his calf. 'We haven't got *them*, we've got the goon. But perhaps he can tell us something. What is it about you Thais and heights? According to Tonje Wiig I'm the third Norwegian to be thrown out of a house this week.'

'An old mafia modus operandi. They'd rather do that than plug someone with lead. If the police find a guy beneath a window they cannot rule out the possibility that he might have fallen accidentally. Some money changes hands, the case is shelved without anyone being directly criticised and everyone's happy. Bullet holes complicate matters.'

They stopped at the lights. A wrinkled old Chinese woman sat on a carpet grinning. Her face blurred in the quivering blue air.

15

Sunday 12 January

'WHAT'S A PAEDOPHILE?'

Ståle Aune sighed deeply on the other end of the line.

'Paedophile? That's one hell of an opener. The short answer is it's a person who is sexually attracted to minors.'

'And the slightly more in-depth answer?'

'There's a lot we don't know about the phenomenon, but if you spoke to a sexologist he would probably make a distinction between preference-conditioned and situation-conditioned paedophiles. The classic figure with a bag of sweeties in the park is the preference-conditioned. His paedophile interests usually begin in his teens, not necessarily with any external conflict. He identifies with the child, adapts his behaviour to the child's age and can on occasion assume a pseudo-parental role. The sexual activity is usually carefully planned and for him sex is an attempt to solve his life problems. Am I being paid for this?'

'And the situation-conditioned?'

'A more diffuse group. They're primarily more sexually interested in other adults, and the child tends to be a substitute for someone the paedophile is in conflict with.'

'Tell me more about the guy with the bag of sweeties. How's he wired?'

'Well, as a rule, paedophiles have low self-esteem and a so-called fragile sexuality. That is, they are uncertain of themselves, they can't take on adult sexuality and they feel like failures. They think they can only control the situation if they live out their desires with children.'

'And it's all down to nature and nurture, the usual spiel?'

'It's not unusual for abusers to have been sexually abused themselves as children.'

'How do you recognise them?'

'Sorry, Harry, but it doesn't work like that. They don't really stand out at all. They're usually men who live alone and have a poor social network. They might have a damaged sexual identity, but they can function perfectly well in other areas of life.'

'I see. So you can't tell.'

'Shame creates clever camouflage artists. Most paedophiles have lifelong training in concealing their predilections from others, so the only thing I can say is that there are a lot more out there than the police arrest for abuse.'

'Ten for every one caught.'

'What did you say?'

'Nothing. Thanks, Ståle. By the way, I've put a cork in the bottle.'

'Oh. How many days?'

'About forty-eight hours.'

'Hard?'

'Well, at least the monsters are staying under the bed. I thought it would be worse.'

'You've only just started. Remember, you'll have some bad days.'

'Is there anything else but bad days?'

It was dark, and the taxi driver passed him a small colour brochure when he asked to be driven to Patpong.

'Massage, sir? Good massage. I'll drive you.'

In the sparse light he saw pictures of girls smiling at him, as pure and innocent as a Thai Airways advertisement.

'No thanks, I just want to eat.' Harry returned the brochure even though his battered back thought it sounded an excellent suggestion. When, out of curiosity, Harry asked what kind of massage, the taxi driver made an international sign that left no room for interpretation.

It was Liz who had recommended Le Boucheron in Patpong, and the food looked really good, it was just that Harry didn't have the appetite. He smiled apologetically at the waitress who took away his plate, and he gave a generous tip so they wouldn't think he was dissatisfied. Then he went out into the hysterical street life of Patpong. Soi 1 was closed to traffic, but it was even more crowded with people surging up and down, like a seething river, alongside stalls and bars. Music boomed out of every orifice in the wall, sweaty men and women on the pavements were on the lookout for action, and the smells of humanity, sewage and food vied for supremacy. A curtain was pulled aside as he passed and inside he saw girls dancing clad in the obligatory G-strings and high-heeled shoes.

'No cover charge, ninety baht for drinks,' someone shouted in his ear. He continued walking, but it was like standing still because the same was repeated all the way down the overpopulated street.

He felt a pulse beating in his stomach and couldn't decide if it was the music, his heart or the dull din from one of the machines pounding piles night and day into Bangkok's new motorway over Silom Road.

At one bar a girl in a loud, red silk dress caught his gaze and pointed to the chair beside her. Harry walked on, feeling almost drunk. He heard a roar from another bar with a TV hanging from one corner and it was clear some team or other had scored. Two

Englishmen with pink necks clinked glasses and sang '*I'm forever blowing bubbles . . .*'

'Come in, blondie.'

A tall, slim woman fluttered her eyelashes at him, pushed out a pair of large, firm breasts and crossed her legs so that the skintight trousers left nothing to the imagination.

'She's *katoy*,' a voice said in Norwegian, and Harry turned.

It was Jens Brekke. A petite Thai woman in a tight leather skirt was hanging from his arm.

'It's fantastic really, all that: the curves, breasts and a vagina. In fact, some men prefer a *katoy* to the genuine item. And why not?' Brekke bared a set of white teeth in his brown childlike face. 'The only problem of course is that surgically created vaginas do not have the same self-cleansing properties as those belonging to real women. The day they can do that I'll consider a *katoy* myself. What's your opinion, Officer?'

Harry glanced at the tall woman who had turned her back on them with a loud sniff when she heard the word *katoy*.

'Well, the thought hadn't struck me that any of the women here might not be women.'

'It's easy to fool the untrained eye, but you can tell by the Adam's apple and generally it's not possible to remove that. Also, they tend to be a head too tall, a touch too provocatively dressed and slightly too aggressively flirtatious. And much too good-looking. That's what gives them away ultimately. They can't control themselves; they always have to go that bit too far.'

He left the sentence hanging in the air, as though he were hinting at something, but if he was, Harry didn't know what.

'By the way, Officer, have you been overdoing things yourself? I can see you're limping.'

'Exaggerated faith in Western conversational styles. It'll pass.'

'Which? The faith or the injury?'

Brekke watched Harry with the same unseen smile that had been there after the funeral. As though it were a game he wanted Harry to join in. Harry was not in a ludic mood.

'Both, I hope. I was on my way home.'

'Already?' The neon light shone on Brekke's moist forehead.

'Look forward to seeing you in better shape tomorrow then, Officer.'

On Surawong Road Harry flagged down a taxi.

'Massage, sir?'

PART THREE

16

Monday 13 January

WHEN NHO PICKED HARRY UP outside River Garden, his high-rise apartment block, the sun had only just risen and was shining gently down on him between the low houses.

They found Barclays Thailand before eight o'clock and a smiling car-park attendant with a Jimi Hendrix hairstyle and headphones let them into the car park beneath the building. Nho eventually spotted a solitary free slot for guests between the BMWs and Mercedes by the lifts.

Nho preferred to wait in the car as his Norwegian was limited to 'takk', thank you, which Harry had taught him to say in a coffee break. Liz had half teased that 'takk' was always the first word a white man tried to teach natives.

Nho was uncomfortable in the neighbourhood; all the expensive cars attracted thieves, he said. And even if the car park was equipped with CCTV he didn't quite trust car-park attendants who clicked their fingers to an invisible beat while opening the barrier.

Harry took the lift up to the ninth floor and entered the reception area of Barclays Thailand. He introduced himself and looked at the clock. He had half expected to have to wait for Brekke, but a woman accompanied him back into the lift, swiped a card and pressed P which, she explained, stood for penthouse. Then she darted back out and Harry rose heavenwards.

As the lift doors slid open he saw Brekke standing in the middle of a glowing brown parquet floor, leaning against a large mahogany table with one phone to his ear and another on his shoulder. The rest of the room was glass. Walls, ceiling, coffee table, even the chairs.

'Talk later, Tom. Make sure you're not gobbled up today. And, as I said, don't touch the rupiah.'

He smiled in apology to Harry, shifted the other phone up to his ear, glanced at the ticker on the computer screen and uttered a brief 'yes' before ringing off.

'What was that?' Harry asked.

'That was my job.'

'Which is?'

'Right now securing a dollar loan for a customer.'

'Big sums involved?' Harry surveyed Bangkok, which lay half hidden in the mist beneath them.

'Depends what you compare it with. An average Norwegian local council budget, I imagine. Did you have a good time last night?'

Before Harry could answer, one of the phones buzzed and Brekke pressed a button on the intercom.

'Take a message, Shena, will you? I'm busy.' He released the button without waiting for confirmation.

'Busy?'

Brekke laughed. 'Don't you read the newspapers? All the Asian currencies are on the slide. Everyone's pissing their pants and busting a gut to buy dollars. Banks and brokerage companies are shutting down every other day and people have started jumping out of windows.'

'But not you?' Harry said, absent-mindedly rubbing his spine.

'Me? I'm a broker, vulture family.'

He flapped his arms a few times and bared his teeth. 'We earn money whatever happens so long as there is action and people are dealing. Showtime is a good time and right now it's showtime 24/7.'

'So you're the croupier in this game?'

'Yes! Well said. Have to remember that one. And the other idiots are the gamblers.'

'Idiots?'

'Certainly.'

'I thought these traders were relatively smart.'

'Smart, yes, but still absolute idiots. It's an eternal paradox, but the smarter they become, the keener they are to speculate in the currency markets. They're the ones who ought to know better than anyone else that it's impossible to earn money on the roulette in the long term. I'm pretty stupid myself, but at least I know that.'

'So you never have a punt on this roulette, Brekke?'

'I do place the occasional bet.'

'Does that make you one of the idiots?'

Brekke proffered a box of cigars, but Harry declined.

'Wise man. They taste awful. I smoke them because I think I have to. Because I can afford it.' He shook his head and put a cigar in his mouth. 'Did you see *Casino*, Officer? The one with Robert De Niro and Sharon Stone?'

Harry nodded.

'Do you remember the scene where Joe Pesci talks about this guy who is the only person he knows who can earn money from gambling? But what he does isn't gambling, it's betting. Horse racing, basketball games and so on. That's quite different from roulette.'

Brekke pulled out a glass chair for Harry and sat down opposite him.

'Gambling is about luck, but betting isn't. Betting is about two things: psychology and information. The smartest person wins. Take this guy in *Casino*. He spends all his time gathering information, about the horses' pedigrees, what they've been doing in training earlier in the week, what feed they have been given, how much the jockey weighed when he got up in the morning – all the info the others can't be bothered with or are unable to get or absorb. Then he pools it, works out the odds and watches what the other gamblers do. If the odds for a horse are too high, he bets on it, whether he thinks it will win or not. And overall he's the one who wins. And the others lose.'

'So simple?'

Brekke held up a hand in defence and glanced at his watch. 'I knew that a Japanese investor from Asahi Bank was going to Patpong last night. In the end I found him in Soi 4. I primed him with info and pumped him for more until three in the morning, then I let him have my woman and went home. I came to work at six and have been buying baht ever since. He'll soon be at work and he'll have baht worth four billion kroner. Then I'll sell again.'

'Sounds like a lot of money, but it also sounds almost illegal.'

'Almost, Harry. Only almost.' Brekke was excited now, like a boy showing off a new toy. 'It's not a question of morality. If you're a target striker in a football team you'll always be in a semi-offside position. Rules are there to be bent.'

'And those who bend the rules furthest win?'

'When Maradona scored with his hand people accepted that as part of the game. Anything the ref doesn't see is fine.'

Brekke held up a finger.

'Nevertheless, you can't get away from the fact that this is about odds. You lose once in a while, but if you play with the odds in your favour you earn money in the long run.'

Brekke grimaced and stubbed out his cigar.

'Today this Japanese investor has determined what I'm going to do, but do you know what the best feeling is? It's when you run the game. For example, before the US inflation figures are published you can spread a rumour that Greenspan said at a private lunch the rate has to go up. You can confuse the enemy. That's how you scoop the big wins. Hell, it's better than sex.'

He laughed and stamped the floor in his excitement.

'The currency market is the mother of all markets, Harry. It's Formula One. It's as exhilarating as it is deadly. I know it's perverse, but I'm one of those control freaks who like to know that it's their own fault if they kill themselves at the wheel.'

Harry looked around. A mad professor in a glass room.

'And if you get caught speeding?'

'As long as I'm earning money and I stay inside my limits, everyone's happy. What's more, it makes me top earner in the firm. Do you see this office? The boss of Barclays Thailand used to sit here. You might be wondering why a lousy broker like me is here. It's because there's only one thing that counts in a brokerage company: how much money you earn. Everything else is decoration. Bosses, too. They're only administrators who are dependent on those of us in the market to keep their jobs and salaries. My boss has now moved to a comfortable office on the floor below because I threatened to go to a competitor with all my clients if I didn't get a better bonus agreement. And this office.'

He undid his waistcoat and hung it over his chair.

'Enough about me. How can I help you, Harry?'

'I was wondering what you and the ambassador spoke about on the phone the day he died.'

'He rang me to have our meeting confirmed. Which I did.'

'And then?'

'He came here at four, as we had arranged. Five past, maybe. Shena in reception has the precise time. He arrived first and registered.'

'What did you talk about?'

'Money. He had some money he wanted to invest.' Not a muscle in his face revealed that he was lying. 'We sat here until five. Then I accompanied him down to where he had parked in the underground car park.'

'He was parked where we are now?'

'If you've got the guest's space, yes.'

'And that's the last you saw of him?'

'Right.'

'Thanks. That was all,' Harry said.

'Wow, that was a long trip for very little.'

'As I said, this is all routine.'

'Of course. He died of a heart attack. Wasn't that it?' Jens Brekke asked with a half-smile on his lips.

'Looks like it,' Harry said.

'I'm a friend of the family,' Jens said. 'No one is saying anything, but I get the picture. Just so you know.'

As Harry got up, the lift door opened and the receptionist came in with a tray on which were two glasses and two bottles.

'Some water before you go, Harry? I have it flown in once a month.'

He filled the glasses with Farris mineral water from Larvik.

'By the way, Harry, the time you gave for the conversation yesterday was wrong.'

He opened a door in the wall, and Harry saw what looked like an ATM. Brekke tapped in some numbers.

'It was 13.13, not 13.15. It may not be important, but I thought you might like to have it absolutely accurate.'

'We were given the time by the telecommunications company. What makes you think your time is more accurate?'

'Mine *is* right.' A flash of white teeth. 'This device records all my conversations. It cost half a million kroner and has a satellite-controlled clock. Believe me: it's accurate.'

Harry raised his eyebrows. 'Who on earth pays half a million for a tape recorder?'

'More people than you imagine. Most currency brokers, among others. If you have an argument with a client about whether you said buy or sell on the phone, half a million is soon chickenfeed. The recorder automatically adds a digital time code on this special tape.'

He held up something that looked like a VHS cassette.

'The time code cannot be tampered with and when a conversation has been recorded you can't change the recording without destroying the time code. The only thing you can do is hide the tape, but then others would find out that tapes are missing for the period in question. The reason we're so thorough is that the tapes would be valid evidence in a court case.'

'Does that mean you have a recording of your conversation with Molnes?'

'Of course.'

'Could we . . .?'

'Just a moment.'

It was peculiar to hear the very much alive voice of a person you had seen lying dead with a knife in his back.

'Four o'clock then,' the ambassador said.

It sounded toneless, almost sad. Then he rang off.

17

Monday 13 January

'HOW'S YOUR BACK?' LIZ ASKED with concern when Harry limped into the office for the morning meeting.

'Better,' he lied, straddling a chair.

Nho gave him a cigarette, but Rangsan coughed behind his newspaper and Harry refrained from lighting up.

'I have some news that might put you in a good mood,' Liz said.

'I *am* in a good mood.'

'First of all, we've decided to bring in Woo. See what we can get out of him if we threaten him with three years for assaulting a police officer in the execution of his duty. Mr Sorensen claims he hasn't seen Woo. He works freelance, apparently. We don't have an address for him, but we know he usually eats at a restaurant next to Ratchadamnoen Stadium, the boxing arena. Those matches mean huge bets, and the loan sharks hang around there to find new customers and keep an eye on debts that still haven't been settled. The other piece of good news is that Sunthorn has been making inquiries at hotels suspected of running escort agencies. The ambassador apparently frequented one of them – they remembered the car because of the diplomatic plates. They say he had a woman with him.'

'Fine.'

Liz was a bit disappointed by Harry's lukewarm reaction.

'Fine?'

'He took Miss Ao to the hotel and gave her one there. So what? She wouldn't invite him home, would she. As far as I can see, all we can learn from that is that Hilde Molnes has a motive to kill her husband. Or Miss Ao's partner, if she has one.'

'And Miss Ao may have a motive if Molnes was about to drop her,' Nho said.

'Lots of good suggestions,' Liz said. 'Where do we start?'

'Checking alibis,' the answer came from behind the newspaper.

In the meeting room at the embassy Miss Ao looked up at Harry and Nho with eyes red from crying. She had denied visiting any hotels point-blank, said she lived with her sister and mother, but she had been out on the night of the murder. She hadn't been with anyone, she'd said, and came home very late, sometime after midnight. It was when Nho had tried to make her tell them where she had been that the tears started.

'It's better if you tell us now, Miss Ao,' Harry said, closing the blinds to the hall. 'You've already lied to us once. Now this is serious. You say you were out on the night of the murder but you didn't meet anyone who could testify where you were.'

'My mother and sister—'

'Can testify that you returned home after midnight. That doesn't help you, Miss Ao.'

Tears ran down the sweet doll face. Harry sighed.

'We'll have to take you with us,' he said. 'Unless you change your mind and tell us where you were.'

She shook her head, and Harry and Nho exchanged glances. Nho shrugged and took her arm, but she held her head against the table, sobbing. At that moment there was a light tap at the door. Harry opened it a fraction. Sanphet was outside.

'Sanphet, we—'

The chauffeur put a finger to his lips. 'I know,' he whispered and beckoned Harry out.

Harry closed the door behind him. 'Yes?'

'You're questioning Miss Ao. You're wondering where she was at the time of the murder.'

Harry didn't answer. Sanphet cleared his throat and straightened his back.

'I lied. Miss Ao was in the ambassador's car.'

'Uh-huh?' Harry said, caught off guard.

'Several times.'

'So you knew about her and the ambassador?'

'Not the ambassador.'

It took a couple of seconds before Harry clicked, and he stared at the old man in disbelief.

'You, Sanphet? You and Miss Ao?'

'It's a long story, and I'm afraid you won't understand everything.' He gave Harry a searching gaze. 'Miss Ao was with me the night the ambassador died. She would never say because it could cost both of us our jobs. Fraternising between employees is not allowed.'

Harry ran a hand across his head.

'I know what you're thinking, Officer. That I'm an old man and she's a young girl.'

'Well, I'm afraid I don't understand completely, Sanphet.'

Sanphet half smiled. 'Her mother and I were lovers a long, long time ago, long before she had Ao. In Thailand there is something called *phîi*. You might translate it as "seniority", an older person being higher in the hierarchy than a younger person. But it means more than that. It also means the older person has responsibility for them. Miss Ao got the job at the embassy at my recommendation, and she is an affectionate, grateful woman.'

'Grateful?' Harry queried without restraint. 'How old was she . . .?' He paused. 'What does her mother say?'

Sanphet smiled sadly. 'She's the same age as me and understands. I'm only borrowing Ao for a little time. Until she finds the man she will start a family with. It's not so unusual . . .'

Harry released his breath with a groan. 'So you're her alibi? And you know it wasn't Miss Ao the ambassador took to the hotel he frequented?'

'If the ambassador went to a hotel, it was not with Ao.'

Harry raised a finger. 'You've already lied once and I could have arrested you for obstructing the police while investigating a murder. If there is anything else you have to tell me, say it now.'

The old, brown eyes looked at Harry without blinking. 'I liked herr Molnes. He was a friend. I hope the person who killed him will be punished. And no one else.'

Harry was about to say something, but bit his tongue.

18

Monday 13 January

THE SUN HAD TURNED DEEP burgundy with orange stripes. It hung above Bangkok's grey skyline, like a new planet that had appeared in the firmament unannounced.

'This is Ratchadamnoen Stadium,' Liz said as the Toyota containing Harry, Nho and Sunthorn pulled up by the grey-brick building. A couple of miserable-looking ticket touts brightened up, but Liz waved them away. 'It might not seem very impressive, but this is Bangkok's version of the Theatre of Dreams. Here everyone has a chance to be God if they have quick enough feet and hands. Hi, Ricki!'

One of the guards came over to the car, and Liz switched on the charm to a degree Harry would not have credited her with. After a brisk torrent of words and laughter, she turned smiling to the others.

'Let's get Woo arrested as fast as we can. I've just wangled ringside seats for me and the tourist. Ivan's boxing seventh this evening. Could be fun.'

The restaurant was of the basic variety – plastic, flies and one solitary fan to blow the food smells from the kitchen into the rest of the room. Portraits of the Thai royal family hung above the counter.

Only a few tables were occupied, and there was no Woo to be seen. Nho and Sunthorn sat at a table by the door while Liz and Harry sat at the back. Harry ordered a spring roll and, for safety's sake, a disinfecting Coke.

'Rick was my trainer when I did Thai boxing,' Liz explained. 'I weighed almost twice as much as the boys I sparred with, was three heads taller and got beaten up every time. They imbibe boxing with their mother's milk here. But they didn't like being hit by a woman, they said. Not that I noticed anything.'

'What is it with the King stuff?' Harry asked, pointing. 'I see his picture everywhere.'

'Well, a nation needs heroes. The royal family wasn't particularly popular until the Second World War when the King managed to ally himself first with the Japanese and then, when they were on the defensive, with the Americans. He saved the nation from a bloodbath.'

Harry raised his Coke to the portrait. 'He sounds like a cool dude.'

'You have to understand: there are two things you don't joke about in Thailand—'

'The royal family and Buddha. Yes, thanks, I've been told.'

The door opened.

'Well, hello,' Liz whispered and raised her non-existent eyebrows. 'Normally they seem smaller in real life.'

Harry didn't turn. The plan was to wait until Woo had had his food served. A man with chopsticks in his hands takes longer to pull out a weapon.

'He's sitting down,' Liz said. 'Man, he should be locked up for his appearance alone. But we can count ourselves lucky if we manage to hold him long enough to ask a few questions.'

'What do you mean? The guy hurled a policeman from a first-floor window.'

'I know, but I wouldn't get your hopes up. Woo "the Cook" is not just anyone. He works for one of the families, and they have good lawyers. We figure he's liquidated at least a dozen people, maimed ten times as many and still his jack shit on his record.'

'The Cook?' Harry set about the scalding hot spring roll that had arrived at the table.

'He got the nickname a couple of years back. We had one of Woo's victims on our hands; I got the case and was present when they started the autopsy. It had been on the slab for a few days and was so bloated with gas that it looked like a black and blue football. The gas is toxic, so the pathologist sent us out of the room, and he wore a gas mask before perforating the stomach. I was watching from the window in the door. The skin flapped when he opened the body and you could see the green tinge of gas as it poured out.'

Harry put the spring roll back on the plate with a wounded expression, though Liz didn't notice.

'But the shock was that he was teeming with life inside. The pathologist backed up against the wall as the black creatures crawled out of the stomach, down onto the floor and darted off into nooks and crannies.' She formed horns with her index fingers against her forehead. 'Devil beetles.'

'Beetles?' Harry pulled a face. 'I didn't think they entered bodies.'

'The dead man had a plastic tube in his mouth when we found him.'

'He . . .'

'In Chinatown grilled beetles are a delicacy. Woo had force-fed the poor guy.'

'And skipped the grilling?' Harry pushed away the plate.

'Amazing creatures, insects,' Liz said. 'I mean, how did the beetles survive in the stomach, with the toxic gas and everything?'

'I'd prefer not to think about it.'

'Too spicy?'

It took Harry a second to realise that she meant the food. He had pushed the plate to the edge of the table.

'You'll get used to it, Harry. You just have to take it step by step. You should take a couple of recipes with you to impress your girl-friend in the kitchen when you get home.'

Harry coughed.

'Or your mother,' Liz said.

Harry shook his head. 'Sorry, don't have one of them, either.'

'I'm the one who should apologise,' she said, and the conversation died. Woo's food was on its way.

She pulled out a black service pistol from her hip holster and released the safety catch.

'Smith & Wesson 650,' Harry said. 'Heavy-duty.'

'Stay behind me,' Liz said, getting up.

Woo didn't bat an eyelid when he looked up and stared into the muzzle of the inspector's gun. He held the chopsticks in his left hand; the right hand was hidden in his lap. Liz barked something in Thai, but he didn't seem to hear. Without moving his head, his eyes wandered around the room, registered Nho and Sunthorn before stopping by Harry. A faint smile crossed his lips.

Liz shouted again, and Harry felt the skin on his neck tingle. The hammer of the gun rose, and Woo's right hand appeared on the table. Empty. Harry heard Liz breathe out between her teeth. Woo's gaze still rested on Harry while Nho and Sunthorn attached the handcuffs. As they led him out it looked like a little circus procession with one muscleman and two dwarfs.

Liz put her gun back in its holster. 'I don't think he likes you,' she said, indicating the chopsticks which had been stuffed into the rice bowl and pointed upwards.

'Really?'

'It's an old Thai symbol for wishing you dead.'

'He'll have to wait his turn.' Harry remembered he needed to ask to borrow a gun.

'Let's see if we can get some action before the night is over,' Liz said.

On their way into the arena they were met by screams from on ecstatic crowd and a trio of men banging and whistling like a school band on acid.

Two boxers wearing colourful headbands and rags tied around both arms had just entered the ring.

'That's our guy Ivan in the blue shorts,' Liz said. Outside the stadium she had relieved Harry of all the notes he had in his pocket and given them to a bookie.

They found their seats in the front row, behind the referee, and Liz smacked her lips with pleasure. She exchanged a few words with her neighbour.

'As I thought,' she said. 'We haven't missed anything. If you want to see really good fights you have to go on Tuesdays. Or Thursdays at Lumphini. Otherwise there are lots of . . . well, you know.'

'Bouillon matches.'

'What?'

'Bouillon matches. That's what we call them in Norwegian. When two bad skaters are racing against each other.'

'Bouillon?'

'Hot soup. That's when you go and get some.'

Liz's eyes became two sparkling narrow slits when she laughed. Harry had discovered he liked to see and hear her laugh.

The two boxers had removed their headbands, walked around the ring and performed a kind of ritual by resting their heads against the corner posts, kneeling and then doing some simple dance steps.

'It's called *ran muay*,' Liz said. 'He's dancing in honour of his personal *kru*, guru and guardian angel of Thai boxing.'

The music stopped and Ivan went to his corner, where he and the trainer leaned towards each other and put their palms together.

'They're praying,' Liz said.

'Does he need to?' Harry asked, worried. He'd had quite a bundle of notes in his pocket.

'Not if he lives up to his name.'

'Ivan?'

'All boxers get to choose their names. Ivan called himself after Ivan Hippolyte, a Dutchman who won a fight at Lumphini Stadium in 1995.'

'Only one?'

'He's the only foreigner to win at Lumphini. Ever.'

Harry turned to see if her expression came with a wink, but at that moment the gong sounded and the fight started.

The boxers approached each other with caution, keeping a healthy distance and circling. One swing was easily parried and a counter-kick met thin air. The music increased in volume, as did the cheers from the crowd.

'They're just cranking up the temperature,' Liz shouted.

Then they were at each other. Lightning speed, a whirl of legs and arms. Things happened so fast that Harry didn't see much, but Liz groaned. Ivan was already bleeding from the nose.

'He got an elbow chop,' she said.

'Elbow? Didn't the ref see?'

Liz smiled. 'It's not illegal to use your elbows. More like the opposite. Hits with your hands and feet get you points, but it's generally elbows and knees that get you a knockout.'

'So their kicking techniques aren't up to karate standards.'

'I'd be careful there, Harry. A few years ago Hong Kong sent its five best kung-fu champions to Bangkok to see which style was more effective. The warm-up and the ceremonies took more than an hour, but the five bouts lasted only six and a half minutes. There were five ambulances on the way to the hospital. Guess who was in them?'

'Well, no danger of that this evening.' Harry yawned demonstratively. 'This is— Bloody hell!'

Ivan had grabbed his opponent by the neck and in one swift movement brought the man's head down while his right knee catapulted up. The opponent fell backwards, but managed to wind his arms around the ropes so that he was hanging directly in front of Liz and Harry. Blood was spurting out and splashing the canvas as if a pipe had sprung a leak somewhere. Harry heard people behind him shouting in protest and discovered it was because he had stood up. Liz pulled him back down.

'Wow!' she shouted. 'Did you see how fast Ivan was? I said he was fun, didn't I.'

The boxer in the red shorts had turned his head to one side, so Harry took in his profile. He could see the skin around his eye move as it filled with blood from inside. It was like watching an air bed being pumped up.

Harry had a strange, nauseous déjà vu feeling as Ivan moved towards his helpless adversary who was no longer aware he was in a boxing ring. Ivan took his time, studied his opponent a bit like a gourmand wondering whether to start by tearing off a chicken wing or a thigh. In the background, between the boxers, Harry could see the referee. He was watching with his head angled and his arms by his sides. Harry could tell he wasn't going to do anything, and he felt his heart beating against his ribs. The three-man band no longer sounded like a Norwegian Independence Day procession, it was out of control and blowing and banging in ecstasy.

Stop, Harry thought, and at that moment heard his own voice: 'Hit him!'

Ivan hit him.

Harry didn't follow the countdown. He didn't see the referee raise Ivan's hand in the air or the victor's *wai* to all four corners of the ring. He was staring at the cracked, wet cement floor in front of his feet where a little insect was struggling to flee from a drop of blood. Caught in a series of events and coincidences, wading in blood up to the knees. He was back in another country, another time, and only came to when a hand hit him between the shoulder blades.

'We won!' Liz yelled in his ear.

They were queuing to get their money from the bookmaker when Harry heard a familiar voice speaking Norwegian.

'Something tells me our officer has bet wisely and not just trusted his luck. In which case, congratulations.'

'Well,' Harry said, turning, 'Inspector Crumley claims to be an expert, so perhaps that's not so far from the truth.'

He introduced the inspector to Jens Brekke.

'And did you bet as well?' Liz asked.

'A friend of mine tipped me off that Ivan's opponent had a bit of a cold. Strange what a huge effect that can have, eh, Miss Crumley?' Brekke beamed and turned to Harry. 'I wonder if you could help me out of a fix, Hole. I've brought Molnes's daughter with me and should drive her home, but one of my most important clients in the US has called, and I have to go back to the office. It's chaos, the dollar's going through the roof and he's got to get rid of a couple of busloads of baht.'

Harry looked in the direction where Brekke had nodded. Leaning against a wall, in a long-sleeved Adidas T-shirt, half hidden behind the crowds hurrying out of the stadium, stood Runa Molnes. Her arms were crossed and she was looking away.

'When I spotted you I remembered that Hilde Molnes had said

you were staying in the embassy's apartment down by the river. It won't be such a big detour if you share a taxi. I promised her mother . . .'

Brekke waggled a hand to indicate that this kind of maternal concern was of course exaggerated, but nevertheless it would be best if the promise was kept.

Harry looked at his watch.

'Of course he can,' Liz said. 'Poor girl. It's no surprise that her mother's a bit on edge at the moment.'

'Of course,' Harry said, forcing a smile.

'Great,' Brekke said. 'Oh, one more thing. Could you pick up my winnings as well? That should cover the taxi. If there's anything left, I suppose there's a police fund for widows or something.'

He gave Liz a receipt and was gone. Her eyes widened when she saw the figures.

'The question is: Are there are enough widows?' she said.

19

Monday 13 January

RUNA MOLNES DID NOT SEEM particularly pleased to be accompanied home.

'Thanks, I can manage,' she said. 'Bangkok is about as dangerous as Ørsta village on a Monday night.'

Harry, who had never been to Ørsta on a Monday night, hailed a taxi and held the door open for her. She clambered in reluctantly, mumbled an address and stared out of the window.

'I told him to drive to River Garden,' she said after a while. 'That's where you get out, isn't it?'

'I think the instructions were that you get dropped first, frøken Molnes.'

'Frøken?' She laughed and looked at him with her mother's black eyes. The eyebrows, which were growing together, gave her an elfin appearance. 'You sound like my aunt. How old are you anyway?'

'You're as old as you feel,' Harry said. 'So I reckon I'm about sixty.'

She looked at him with curiosity now.

'I'm thirsty,' she said suddenly. 'If you buy me a drink you can take me to my door afterwards.'

Harry leaned forward, and started to give the driver Molnes's address.

'Forget it,' she said. 'I'll insist on River Garden and he'll think you're trying it on. Do you want a scene?'

Harry tapped the driver on the shoulder, and Runa began to scream and the driver jumped on the brakes, banging Harry's head against the ceiling. The driver turned, Runa inhaled to scream again and Harry held up his hands in surrender.

'OK, OK. Where then? Patpong's on the way, I suppose.'

'Patpong?' She rolled her eyes. 'You *are* old. Only dirty old men and tourists go there. We're going to Siam Square.'

She exchanged a few words with the driver in what to Harry's ears sounded like flawless Thai.

'Have you got a girlfriend?' she asked when she had a beer brought to the table, also after threatening a scene.

They were in a large, outdoor restaurant at the top of a broad, monument-like set of stairs packed with young people – students, Harry presumed – sitting and watching the slow-moving traffic and one another. She had cast a suspicious glance at Harry's orange juice, but apparently, with her background, she was used to teetotallers. Or perhaps not. Harry had a feeling that not all the unwritten party rules had been observed in the Molnes family.

'No,' Harry answered, and added: 'Why the hell does everyone ask me that?'

'Why the hell, eh?' She wriggled on her chair. 'I suppose it's usually girls who ask, is it?'

He chuckled. 'Are you trying to embarrass me? Tell me about your boyfriends.'

'Which one?' She kept her left hand hidden in her lap and raised her beer glass with her right. With a smile playing on her lips, she leaned back and fixed him with her eyes.

'I'm not a virgin, if that's what you think.'

Harry almost spat a mouthful of juice over the table.

'Why should I be?' she said, putting the glass to her lips.

Yes, why should you be? Harry thought.

'Are you shocked?' She put the beer glass down and assumed a serious expression.

'Why should I be?' It sounded like an echo, and he hastened to add: 'I believe I made my debut at about your age.'

'Yes, but not when you were thirteen,' she said.

Harry breathed in, considered her comment carefully and slowly released air through his teeth. He would be happy to drop this subject now. 'Really? And how old was he?'

'That's a secret.' She had her teasing expression back. 'Tell me why you don't have a girlfriend.'

He paused for a moment before speaking, an impulse, perhaps to see if he could reciprocate the shock tactics. And tell her that the two women he could say, in all honesty, he had loved were both dead. One by her own hand, the other by a murderer's.

'It's a long story,' he said. 'I lost them.'

'Them? Are there several? I suppose that's why they dumped you, was it? Two-timing?'

Harry could hear the childish excitement and laughter in her voice. He was unable to bring himself to ask what kind of relationship she had with Jens Brekke.

'No,' he said. 'I just didn't pay enough attention.'

'Now you look serious.'

'Sorry.'

They sat in silence. She fiddled with the label on the beer bottle. Glanced at Harry. As if trying to make up her mind. The label came off.

'Come on,' she said, taking his hand. 'I'll show you something.'

They went down the steps, between the students, along the pavement and up a narrow footbridge over the broad avenue. In the middle they stopped.

'Look,' she said. 'Isn't that beautiful?'

He watched the traffic streaming towards and then away from them. The road stretched as far as the eye could see, and the lights from the lorries, buses, cars, motorbikes and tuk-tuks were like a river of lava thickening into one yellow stripe at the furthest end.

'It looks like a snake twisting and turning with a luminous pattern on its back, doesn't it?'

She leaned over the railing. 'Do you know what's strange? People in Bangkok would happily kill for the little I have in my pockets at this moment. And yet I've never been afraid here. In Norway we always went up to our mountain cabin at the weekend. I know the cabin and all the paths blindfold. And every holiday we went to Ørsta where everyone knows everyone and shoplifting is front-page news. And yet this is where I feel safest. Here where I'm surrounded by people on all sides and I don't know any of them. Isn't that strange?'

Harry was unsure how to reply.

'If I could choose I'd live here for the rest of my life. And then I'd come up here at least once a week and just stand here watching.'

'Watching the traffic?'

'Yes, I love the traffic.' She turned abruptly to him. Her eyes were shining. 'Don't you?'

Harry shook his head. She turned back to the road.

'Shame. Guess how many cars there are on the roads of Bangkok now? Three million. And the number increases by a thousand every day. A driver in Bangkok spends between two and three hours in a car every day. Have you heard about Comfort 100? You can buy it at petrol stations. It's a bag to pee in when you're stuck in a queue. Do you think Eskimos have a word for traffic? Or Maoris?'

Harry shrugged.

'Think of all they're missing,' she said. 'Those people who live in places where they can't be surrounded by crowds like here. Hold your arm up . . .' She held his hand and lifted it.

'Can you feel it? The vibration? It's the energy from everyone around us. It's in the air. If you're dying and you think no one can save you, just go out and stretch your arms into the air and absorb some of the energy. You can have eternal life. It's true!'

Her eyes were glowing, her whole face was glowing, and she laid Harry's hand against her cheek.

'I can feel you're going to live a long life. Immensely long. Even longer than me.'

'Don't say that,' Harry said. Her skin burned against his palm. 'That's bad luck.'

'Better bad luck than no luck, Pappa used to say.'

He retracted his hand.

'Don't you want eternal life?' she whispered.

He blinked and knew that his brain had taken a snap of them there and then, on a footbridge with people hurrying past in both directions and a shimmering sea serpent below. Just like you take snaps of places you visit because you know you won't be there long. He had done it before, one night in mid-jump at Frogner Lido, another night in Sydney when a red mane of hair blew backwards in the wind, and on a cold February afternoon at Fornebu Airport when Sis was waiting for him among the press photographers and the storm of camera flashes. He knew that whatever happened he would always be able to access the snaps, they would never fade; on the contrary, they would have more consistency and substance over the years.

At that moment he felt a drop on his face. And then another. He looked up in amazement.

'I was told there was no rain before May,' he said.

'Mango showers,' Runa said, turning her face to the sky. 'We get them sometimes. It means the mangoes are ripe. Soon it'll pelt down. Come on . . .'

Harry was falling asleep. The noise was no longer so obtrusive, and he had started to notice that there was a kind of rhythm to the traffic, a kind of predictability. The first night he would wake up to the sound of horns honking. In a few nights he would probably wake up if he *couldn't* hear any horns honking. The racket of a broken silencer didn't come from nowhere, it had a place in the apparent chaos. It just took a little time to adjust to it, like learning to find your sea legs on a boat.

He had arranged to meet Runa at a cafe by the university the next day to ask some questions about her father. Her hair had still been dripping when she got out of the taxi.

For the first time in a long while he dreamt about Birgitta. The hair sticking to her pale skin. But she smiled and was alive.

20

Tuesday 14 January

IT TOOK THE LAWYER FOUR hours to have Woo released from custody.

'Dr Ling. He works for Sorensen,' Liz said at the morning meeting and sighed. 'Nho only had time to ask Woo where he was on the day of the murder, then it was over.'

'And what did the mobile lie detector get out of the answer?' Harry asked.

'Nothing,' Nho said. 'He wasn't interested in telling us anything.'

'Nothing? Shit, and there was me thinking you Thais were handy with water torture and electric shocks. So now there's a giant psychopath out there who wishes me dead.'

'Could somebody please give me some good news?' Liz said.

A newspaper crackled.

'I rang the Maradiz Hotel again. The first person I spoke to said there was a *farang* who used to go there with a woman from the embassy. This guy said the woman was white and they spoke to each other in a language which he thought might have been German or Dutch.'

'Norwegian,' Harry said.

'I tried to get a description of the two, but they weren't very clear.'

Liz sighed. 'Sunthorn, drive over with some photos and see if they can identify the ambassador and his wife.'

Harry wrinkled his nose. 'Man and wife have a love nest for two hundred dollars a day a few kilometres from where they live? Isn't that a bit perverse?'

'According to the man I spoke to today, they stayed there at weekends,' Rangsan said. 'I've got a few dates.'

'I would bet yesterday's winnings it wasn't his wife,' Harry said.

'Maybe not,' Liz said. 'Anyway, it probably won't get us very far.'

She concluded the meeting by telling the rest of the team to spend the day doing neglected paperwork on cases which were dropped when the murder of the Norwegian ambassador was given top priority.

'So we're back to square one?' Harry asked, after the others had left.

'We've been there the whole time,' Liz said. 'Perhaps you'll get what you Norwegians want.'

'What we want?'

'I talked to our Chief of Police this morning. He had spoken to a Mr Torhus in Norway yesterday, who wanted to know how long this was going to take. The Norwegian authorities asked for some clarification this week if we didn't have anything concrete. The Chief told him this was a Thai investigation and we didn't shelve murder cases just like that. But later on he received a call from our Ministry of Justice. Good job we got the sightseeing done while there was time, Harry. Looks like you'll be going home on Friday. Unless, as they said, something concrete turns up.'

*   *   *

'Harry!'

Tonje Wiig met him in reception, her cheeks flushed and a smile so red he suspected she had put on some lipstick before she came out.

'We must have some tea,' she said. 'Ao!'

Miss Ao had stared at him in dumb fear when he arrived, and even though he'd hastened to say his visit had nothing to do with her, he noticed her eyes, like an antelope by a watering hole, always drinking within sight of lions. She turned her back on them and left them alone.

'Nice-looking girl,' Tonje said, with a searching glance at Harry.

'Lovely,' he said. 'Young.'

Tonje appeared content with the answer and led him into her office.

'I tried to ring you last night,' she said, 'but you obviously weren't at home.'

Harry could see she wanted him to ask why she had rung, but he refrained. Miss Ao came in with the tea, and he waited until she had gone.

'I need some information,' he said.

'Yes?'

'Since you were the chargé d'affaires when the ambassador was away I assume you kept track of his absences.'

'Naturally.'

He read out four dates to her, which she checked against her calendar. The ambassador had been to Chiang Mai three times and to Vietnam once. Harry slowly took notes as he prepared for the follow-up.

'Did the ambassador know any Norwegian women in Bangkok apart from his wife?'

'No . . .' Tonje said. 'Not as far as I know. Well, apart from me, that is.'

Harry waited until she had put down her cup before asking: 'What would you say if I said I think you were having a relationship with the ambassador?'

Tonje Wiig's chin dropped. She was a credit to Norwegian dental care.

'Oh, golly gosh!' she said. So free of irony that Harry could only assume 'golly gosh' still existed in some women's vocabulary. He cleared his throat.

'I think you and the ambassador spent the dates we just noted at the Maradiz Hotel, and if so I would like you to account for your relationship and tell me where you were the day he died.'

It was surprising that someone as pale as Tonje Wiig could turn even whiter.

'Should I talk to a lawyer?' she said at length.

'Not unless you have something to hide.'

He saw a tear had formed in the corner of her eye.

'I have nothing to hide,' she said.

'In which case, you should talk to me.'

She carefully dabbed her eye so as not to smudge her mascara. 'Sometimes I felt like killing him, Officer.'

Harry noted the change in the form of address and waited patiently.

'So much so that I was almost glad when I heard he was dead.'

He could hear that her tongue was loosening. It was important not to say or do anything stupid to stem the flow now. One confession seldom comes alone.

'Because he didn't want to leave his wife?'

'No!' She shook her head. 'You don't understand. Because he ruined everything for me! Everything that . . .'

The first sob was so bitter that Harry knew he had struck something. Then she pulled herself together and dried both eyes

'This was a political appointment. He wasn't remotely qualified for the job. They sent him here in great haste, as though they couldn't get him out of Norway fast enough. There had already been signals I would be the candidate for the post but I had to give the keys to the ambassador's office to someone who didn't know the difference between a chargé and an attaché. And we never had any kind of relationship. That would have been an absolutely absurd notion to me. Can't you see that?'

'What happened then?'

'When I was sent for, to identify him, I suddenly forgot about all the appointment business – I was getting a new chance. Instead I remembered what a nice, clever man he had been. He was!'

She said it as if Harry had protested.

'Even though he wasn't much good as an ambassador, in my opinion. There are some things which are more important than a job and a career. Perhaps I shouldn't even apply for the post. We'll have to see. There's so much to think about. Yes, no, I won't say anything definite now.'

She sniffed a couple of times and seemed to have recovered. 'It's very unusual for a chargé d'affaires to be appointed as an ambassador at the same embassy, you know. To my knowledge, it's never happened.'

She pulled out a mirror and checked her make-up, and said, apparently to herself: 'But there's a first time for everything, I suppose.'

Once Harry was in the taxi on his way back to the police station he decided to leave Tonje Wiig off his list of suspects. Partly because she had been convincing, partly because she could prove she had been somewhere else on the dates the ambassador had spent at the Maradiz Hotel. Tonje had also confirmed there were not a great many Norwegian women resident in Bangkok to choose from.

Therefore it came as a blow to the solar plexus to suddenly have to think the unthinkable. Because it simply wasn't so unthinkable.

The girl who came through the glass door at the Hard Rock Cafe was a different girl from the one he had seen in the garden and at the funeral, the one with the turned-off, introverted body language and the bad-tempered, defiant expression. Runa's face opened into a beam when she spotted him sitting with an empty bottle of Coke and a newspaper in front of him. She was wearing a short-sleeved, blue flowery dress. Like a practised illusionist her prosthesis was hardly noticeable.

'You're early,' she said with delight.

'It's difficult to get the times right with the traffic,' he said. 'I didn't want to be late.'

She grabbed a seat and ordered an iced tea.

'Yesterday. Your mother—'

'Was asleep,' she said curtly. So curt that Harry guessed it was meant as a warning. But he didn't have time to beat around the bush any more.

'Drunk, you mean?'

She looked up at him. The happy smile had evaporated.

'Was it my mother you wanted to talk about?'

'Among other things. What was your parents' relationship like?'

'Why don't you ask her?'

'Because I think you're worse at lying,' he answered honestly.

'Oh yes? In that case they got on like a house on fire.' She had the defiant expression back.

'That bad, eh?'

She squirmed.

'Sorry, Runa, but this is my job.'

She shrugged. 'My mother and I don't get on so well. But Pappa and I were great friends. I think she was jealous.'

'Of whom?'

'Of both of us. Of him. I don't know.'

'Why of him?'

'He didn't seem to need her. She was so much air to him . . .'

Harry couldn't believe what he was about to ask. But he had seen so many terrible things over the years. He paused. 'Did your father sometimes take you to a hotel, Runa? The Maradiz Hotel, for example.'

He saw the astonishment on her face.

'What do you mean? Why would he?'

He stared down at the newspaper on the table, but forced himself to lift his gaze.

'What?' she burst out, stirring the spoon in her cup vigorously and making the tea slop over. 'You say the weirdest things. What are you getting at?'

'Well, Runa, I know this is difficult, but I think your father has done things he would have regretted.'

'Pappa? Pappa always regretted. He regretted and shouldered the blame and complained . . . but the witch wouldn't leave him in peace. She hounded him all the time, you're not this and you're not that and you've dragged me here and so on. She thought I didn't hear, but I did. Every word. She wasn't made to live with a eunuch, she was a full-blooded woman. I told him he should leave, but he stuck it out. For my sake. He didn't say that, but I knew that was why.'

'What I'm trying to say,' he said, lowering his head to catch her eyes, 'is that your father didn't have the same sexual feelings as some others.'

'Is that why you're so bloody stressed? Because you think I didn't know my father was gay?'

Harry resisted the impulse to drop his jaw. 'What do you mean by gay exactly?' he asked.

'Poof. Homo. Faggot. Bender. Buttfucker. I'm the result of the few shags the witch managed to get off Pappa. He thought she was disgusting.'

'Did he *say* that?'

'He was far too decent to say something like that. But I knew. I was his best friend. He said *that*. Now and then it seemed as if I was his *only* friend. 'You and horses are the only things I like,' he said to me once. Me and horses. That's a good one, eh? I think he had a lover – a guy – when he was a student, before he met my mother. But the guy left him, didn't want to acknowledge the relationship. Fair enough. Pappa didn't want to, either. It was a long time ago. Things were different then.'

She said that with the unshakeable confidence of a teenager. Harry lifted the Coke to his mouth and sipped slowly. He had to gain time. This hadn't developed in the way he had anticipated.

'Do you want to know who was at the Maradiz Hotel?' she asked. 'Mum and her lover.'

21
Tuesday 14 January

WHITE, FROZEN BRANCHES SPREAD THEIR fingers towards the pale winter sky over the Palace Gardens. Dagfinn Torhus stood by the window and watched a man run shivering up Haakon VIIs gate with his head buried between his shoulders. The telephone rang. Torhus saw from the clock that it was lunchtime. He followed the man until he was out of sight by the Metro station, then he lifted the receiver and said his name. There was a hissing and crackling until the voice reached him.

'I'll give you one more chance, Torhus. If you don't take it I'll make sure the Ministry advertises your job faster than you can say "Norwegian police intentionally misled by Foreign Office Director". Or "Norwegian ambassador victim of gay murder". Both make for passable headlines, don't you think?'

Torhus sat down. 'Where are you, Hole?' he asked, for lack of anything better to say.

'I've just had a long conversation with my boss at Crime Squad. I've asked him in fifteen different ways what on earth this Atle Molnes was doing in Bangkok. All I've uncovered so far suggests he's the least likely ambassador this side of the outspoken Reiulf

Steen. I was unable to lance the boil, but I was able to confirm that there is one. He's sworn to secrecy, I suppose, so he referred me to you. Same question as before. What don't I know that you do? For your information, I'm sitting here with a fax machine beside me and the numbers of *Verdens Gang*, *Aftenposten* and *Dagbladet* newspapers.'

Torhus's voice brought the winter cold all the way to Bangkok. 'They won't print unsupported claims from an alcoholic policeman, Hole.'

'If it's an alcoholic *celebrity* policeman they will.'

Torhus didn't answer.

'By the way, I think they're going to cover the case in *Sunnmørsposten* as well.'

'You've taken the oath of confidentiality,' Torhus said in a subdued tone. 'You'll be prosecuted.'

Hole laughed. 'Rock and a hard place, eh? Knowing what I know and not following it up would be a dereliction of duty. That's punishable too, you know. For some reason I have the feeling I have less to lose than you if confidentiality is broken.'

'What guarantee—' Torhus started, but was interrupted by crackling on the line. 'Hello?'

'I'm here.'

'What guarantee do I have that you'll keep what I say to yourself?'

'None.' The echo made it sound as if he had emphasised his answer three times.

Silence.

'Trust me,' Harry said.

Torhus snorted. 'Why should I?'

'Because you've got no choice.'

The Director saw from the clock that he was going to be late for lunch. The roast beef on rye in the canteen was probably already gone, but that didn't matter much, he had lost his appetite.

'This must not get out,' he said. 'And I mean that in all seriousness.'

'The intention isn't that it will get out.'

'OK, Hole. How many scandals involving the Christian Democratic Party have you heard about?'

'Not many.'

'Exactly. For years the Christian Democrats had been this cosy little party no one had bothered about much. While the press was digging up stuff on the power elite in the Socialist Party and the weirdos in the Progress Party, the Christian Democrat MPs were largely allowed to lead their lives without much scrutiny. With the change of government that was no longer possible. When there was a reshuffle it soon became clear that Atle Molnes, despite his undoubted competence and long experience of Storting, would not be considered as a minister. Rooting around in his private life would entail a risk that a Christian party with personal values on its agenda could not take. The party can't reject the ordination of homosexual priests and at the same time have homosexual ministers. I believe even Molnes could see that. But when the names of the new government were presented there were several reactions in the press. Why wasn't Atle Molnes included? After he stepped aside some time ago to give the Prime Minister room as party leader most observers saw him as a number two, or at least a three or four. Questions were asked and the homosexuality rumours which had first arisen when he resigned as a candidate for party leader were rekindled. Now of course we know that there are many MPs who are gay, so why the fuss, one might ask. Well, the interesting thing about this case, apart from the fact that the man was a Christian Democrat, is that he was a close friend of the Prime Minister; they had studied together, even shared a bedsit. And it was just a matter of time before the press got hold of it. Molnes wasn't in the government, but still it was becoming a personal strain on the PM. Everyone knew the PM and Molnes had been each other's most important political supporters right from the start, and who would believe him if he said he'd been unaware of Molnes's sexual inclinations all those years? What about all the voters who had supported the PM because of the party's clear views on civil partnerships and other depravity, when he himself nurtured a viper in his bosom, to be a bit biblical? How would that help to create trust? The PM's personal popularity had so far been one of the most important guarantees for a minority government to continue, and what they least needed was a scandal. It was obvious they had to get Molnes out of the country as swiftly as possible. It was decided that a post as an ambassador abroad would be best because then you couldn't accuse the PM of pushing a party colleague with long and faithful service into the cold. That was the point at which I was contacted. We moved fast. The ambassador post in Bangkok still hadn't been formally appointed and that would put him far enough away for the press to leave him in peace.'

'Jesus Christ,' Harry said after a pause.

'Agreed,' Torhus said.

'Did you know his wife had a lover?'

Torhus chuckled quietly. 'No, but you'd have had to give me very good odds if I was betting she *didn't* have one.'

'Why?'

'First of all, because I assume homosexual husbands would turn a blind eye to that kind of thing. Secondly, there is something in the culture of the Ministry that seems to encourage extra-marital affairs. Indeed, sometimes new marriages spring up from them. Here at the Ministry you can barely move in the corridors for bumping into ex-spouses, or lovers, ex or current. The service is notorious for its inbreeding. We're worse than the bloody Norwegian Broadcasting Company.'

Torhus continued to chuckle.

'The lover isn't from the Ministry,' Harry said. 'There's a Norwegian who's a kind of local Gekko here, a big-time currency broker. Jens Brekke. I thought at first he was involved with the daughter, but it turns out it's Hilde Molnes. They met almost as soon as the family arrived and according to the daughter it's more than the odd roll in the hay. In fact, it's quite serious and the daughter reckons they're going to move in together sooner or later.'

'News to me.'

'At least that gives the wife a possible motive. And the lover.'

'Because Molnes was an obstruction?'

'No, on the contrary. According to the daughter, Hilde Molnes refused to let go of her husband. After he pared down his political aspirations I suppose the cover his marriage afforded wasn't so important any more. She must have used visiting rights to her daughter as blackmail. Isn't that what usually happens? No, the motive is probably even less noble. The Molnes family owns half of Ørsta.'

'Exactly.'

'I asked Crime Squad to check if there was a will and what Atle was sitting on in terms of family shares and other assets.'

'Well, this isn't my field, Hole, but aren't you making things a bit complicated now? It could quite simply have been a nutter who knocked on the ambassador's door and stabbed him to death.'

'Maybe. Does it matter in principle if this nutter is Norwegian, Torhus?'

'What do you mean?'

'Real nutters don't stab a guy and then remove all useful evidence from the crime scene. They leave a series of puzzles so that we can play cops and robbers afterwards. In this case we have a decorative knife, and that's it. Believe me, this was a carefully planned murder by someone not disposed to playfulness, who wanted the job done and the case dropped for lack of evidence. But who knows

– perhaps you need to be just as insane to commit such a murder. And the only nutters I've met so far on this case have been Norwegian.'

22

Tuesday 14 January

AT LENGTH HARRY FOUND THE entrance between two strip bars in Soi 1 in Patpong. He went up the stairs and entered a semi-dark room where a gigantic fan in the ceiling circled lazily. Harry ducked involuntarily under the immense blades; he already had the marks to show that doorways and other domestic constructions were not adapted to his one metre ninety-two.

Hilde Molnes was sitting at a table at the back of the restaurant. Her sunglasses, meant to give her anonymity, had the effect of attracting attention to her, he thought.

'Actually I don't like rice wine,' she said, draining the glass. 'Mekhong is the exception. May I offer you a glass, Officer?'

Harry shook his head. She flicked her fingers and had the glass filled.

'They know me here,' she said. 'They stop when they think I've had enough. And by then as a rule I have had enough.' She laughed huskily. 'I hope it's all right meeting here. Home is . . . a bit sad now. What's the purpose of this consultation, Officer?'

She enunciated the words clearly, the way people who habitually try to hide that they've been drinking do.

'We've just been told that you and Jens Brekke regularly went to the Maradiz Hotel together.'

'There you go!' Hilde Molnes said. 'Finally someone who does his job. If you talk to the waiter here he'd be able to confirm that herr Brekke and I also met here *on a regular basis*.' She spat the words out. 'Dark, anonymous, never any other Norwegians, and on top of that they serve the town's best *plaa lòt*. Do you like eel, Hole? Saltwater eels?'

Harry was reminded of the man they dragged ashore outside Drøbak. He had been in the sea some days, and his pale cadaverous face had looked at them with a child's surprise. Something had eaten his eyelids. But what had caught their attention was the eel. Its tail protruded from the man's mouth and lashed back and forth like a silver whip. Harry could still remember the salty aroma in the air, so it must have been a saltwater eel.

'My grandfather ate almost nothing but eels,' she said. 'From just before the war until he died. Stuffed them down, couldn't get enough.'

'I've also been given some information regarding the will.'

'Do you know why he ate so much eel? Oh, of course you don't. He was a fisherman, but this was before the war and people didn't want to eat eel in Ørsta. Do you know why?'

He saw the same pain flash across her face as he had seen in the garden.

'Fru Molnes—'

'I'm asking if you know why.'

Harry shook his head.

Hilde Molnes lowered her voice and tapped a long red fingernail on the tablecloth as she pronounced every syllable. 'Well, a boat had gone down that winter, it happened in calm weather and only a few hundred metres from land, but it was so cold that not one of the nine men on board survived. There's a channel under where the boat capsized and not a single body was found. Afterwards people claimed that a huge number of eels had come to the fjord. They say eels eat drowned men, you know. Many of the victims were related to people in Ørsta, so the sale of eels took a nosedive. People wouldn't dare be seen returning home with eel in their shopping bags. So Grandad reckoned it was worth his while selling all the other fish and eating the eel himself. Born and bred in Sunnmøre, you know . . .'

She drank from her glass and placed it on the table. A dark ring spread across the cloth.

'Then I suppose he got a taste for it. "There were only nine of them," Grandad said. "That can't have been enough for so many of them. I might have eaten one or two who fed on the poor fellers, but so what? I didn't taste any difference anyway." No difference! That's a good one.'

It sounded like an echo of something.

'What do you think, Hole? Do you think the eels ate the men?'

Harry scratched behind an ear. 'Well, some people claim mackerel eat human flesh too. I don't know. They probably all have a bite, I imagine. Fish, that is.'

Harry let her finish her drink.

'A colleague of mine in Oslo has just spoken to your husband's business lawyer, Bjørn Hardeid, in Ålesund. As you perhaps know, lawyers can revoke client confidentiality when the client has died and in their opinion the information won't harm the client's reputation.'

'I didn't, no.'

'Well, Bjørn Hardeid didn't want to say anything. So my colleague rang Atle's brother, but unfortunately there wasn't a lot to be got out of him, either. He went particularly quiet when my colleague proposed the theory that Atle didn't own as much of the family fortune as many might have thought.'

'What makes you think that?'

'A man who can't pay a gambling debt of 750,000 kroner doesn't necessarily have to be poor, but he is definitely not someone who has a substantial share of a family fortune amounting to two hundred million kroner at his disposal.'

'Where—?'

'My colleague called the Brønnøysund register and got the figures for Molnes Furniture. The capital on the books is less of course, but he discovered that the company is listed on the SMB, so he rang a broker who worked out the stock exchange value for him. The family company Molnes Holding has four shareholders – three brothers and a sister. All the siblings are on the board of Molnes Furniture, and there are no reports of any sales of shares since they were transferred from Molnes Senior to the holding company; so unless your husband sold his part of the holding company to one of the others he should be good for at least . . .' Harry glanced at his notepad where he had written down every word of what was said over the phone. 'Fifty million kroner.'

'They have been thorough, I can see.'

'I didn't understand half of what I just said, I only know it means someone is holding back your husband's money, and I'd like to know why.'

Hilde Molnes peered at him over her glass. 'Do you really want to know?'

'Why not?'

'I'm not so sure that those who sent you imagined they would have to delve so deep into the ambassador's . . . private life.'

'I know too much already, fru Molnes.'

'Do you know about . . .?'

'Yes.'

'Exactly . . .'

She paused while finishing her Mekhong. The waiter came with a top-up, but she waved him away.

'If you also know that the Molnes family has a long tradition as pew warmers at the Inner Mission chapel and members of the Christian Democratic Party, you can perhaps work out the rest.'

'Perhaps. But I would appreciate it if you told me.'

She shivered as if it was only now she could savour the sharp taste of the rice spirit.

'It was Atle's father who decided. When the rumours began to spread in connection with his candidacy for party leader, Atle told his father the truth. A week later his father had rewritten his will. It stated that Atle's share of the family fortune would be in his name, but the right of disposal was transferred to Runa. The right comes into effect when she is twenty-three.'

'And who has the right to the money until then?'

'No one. Which just means it stays in the family business.'

'And what happens now that your husband is dead?'

'Now,' Hilde said, running a finger around the rim of the glass. 'Now Runa will inherit all the money. And the right of disposal is transferred to the person with parental rights until she is twenty-three.'

'So, if I understand you correctly that means the money has been released and is at your disposal.'

'Looks like it, yes. Until Runa is twenty-three.'

'Exactly what does right of disposal entail?'

Hilde Molnes shrugged. 'I really haven't thought about it much. I was only told a few days ago. By Hardeid.'

'So this clause about the right of disposal being transferred to you wasn't something you knew about before?'

'It might have been mentioned. I signed some papers, but this is terribly complicated, don't you think? Anyway, I never paid any attention before.'

'Didn't you?' Harry said airily. 'I thought you said something about people from Sunnmøre . . .'

She smiled wanly. 'I've always been a bad Sunnmøring.'

Harry studied her. Was she pretending she was drunker than she was? He scratched his neck.

'How long have you and Jens Brekke known each other?'

'How long have we been fucking, do you mean?'

'Well, that too.'

'So let's put this in the right sequence. Let me see . . .' Hilde Molnes knitted her brows and squinted up at the ceiling. She tried to support her chin on her hand, but it slipped off, and he knew he was wrong. She was as drunk as a skunk.

'We met at Atle's welcome party two days after arriving in Bangkok. It started at eight, the whole of the Norwegian colony was invited and it took place in the garden in front of the ambassador's residence. He fucked me in the garage, that must have been two or three hours later, I suppose. I say *he* fucked me because I was probably so drunk at that point he hardly needed my cooperation. Or consent. But he had it next time. Or the time after, I don't remember. At any rate, after a few bouts we got to know each other. Was that what you asked? Yes, and since then we've continued to get to know each other. We know each other pretty well now. Is that good enough for you, Officer?'

Harry was annoyed. Perhaps it was the way she made a show of her indifference and self-contempt. Anyway, she gave him no reason to continue treating her with silk gloves.

'You said you were at home the day your husband died. Exactly where were you from five o'clock in the evening until you were told he'd been found dead?'

'I don't remember.'

She screeched with laughter. It sounded like a raven screaming in a quiet forest, and Harry could see they had started to attract attention. For a moment she almost fell off her chair, until she regained her balance.

'Don't look so worried, Officer. I have an *alibi*, you see. Isn't that what it's called? Yes, indeed, a fantastic alibi, I can tell you. I think my daughter will be willing to testify that I was unable to move much that evening. I remember opening a bottle of gin after dinner and my guess is I fell asleep, woke up, had another drink, fell asleep, woke up and so on. You understand, I'm sure.'

Harry understood.

'Anything else you wanted to ask, Hole?'

She drawled the two vowels in his name, not much, but enough to provoke him.

'Just if you killed your husband, fru Molnes.'

In one astonishingly quick, supple movement she grabbed the glass, and before he could stop her he felt it brush against his ear and heard it smash against the wall behind them. She grimaced.

'You might not believe it after that, but I was the top scorer for Ørsta Girls 14–16 Division.' Her voice was calm, as though she had already put what happened behind her. Harry looked at the frightened faces that had turned towards them.

'Sixteen years old, that's an awfully long time ago. I was the best-looking girl in . . . hm, I've probably already told you that. And I had curves, not like now. A girlfriend and I used to go into the referees' changing room accidentally on purpose, wearing tiny towels, and say we'd gone in the wrong door on the way from the shower. All for the team of course. But I don't think it had much effect on the referees. They were probably wondering why we were having a shower *before* the game.'

Suddenly she got up and shouted: '*Ørstagutt hei, Ørstagutt hei, Ørstagutt hei, hei, hei!*' She slumped back down on her chair. The room had gone quiet.

'That was how we cheered. We shouted for Ørsta boys because the word for girls doesn't work, does it. The rhythm's all out. Well, who knows, perhaps we just liked showing off.'

Harry took her by the arm and helped her down the stairs. He gave the taxi driver her address, a five-dollar bill and told him to make sure she got home. He probably didn't understand much of what Harry said, but he seemed to grasp what he meant.

He went into a bar in Soi 2, at the end, towards Silom district. The counter was almost empty and on the stage there were a couple of go-go girls who hadn't been bought for the evening and clearly didn't have much hope of that happening. They might as well have been doing the washing-up as they dutifully shook their legs and their breasts bounced up and down to 'When Susannah Cries'. Harry wasn't sure which he thought was sadder.

Someone put a beer in front of him that he hadn't ordered. He left it untouched, paid and rang the police station from a payphone by the men's toilet. He couldn't see a door for the ladies'.

23

Tuesday 14 January

A LIGHT BREEZE BLEW THROUGH his cropped hair. Harry was standing on a brick overhang at the edge of the roof surveying the city. When he pinched his eyes it was like a carpet of glittering, twinkling lights.

'Get down from there,' a voice said behind him. 'You're making me nervous.'

Liz was sitting in a deckchair with a can of beer in her hand. Harry had gone to the station and found her snowed under piles of reports that had to be read. It was almost midnight, and she had agreed it was time to call it a day. She had locked the office, they had taken the lift up to the eleventh floor, discovered the door to the roof was closed for the night, climbed out of a window, pulled down a fire escape and clambered up.

The blast from a foghorn sounded through the woollen blanket of car traffic.

'Did you hear that?' Liz asked. 'When I was little my father used to say that in Bangkok you could hear elephants calling to each other when they were being freighted by ship. They came from Malaysia because the forests in Borneo had been cut down, and the elephants were chained to the deck on their way to the forests in northern Thailand. For ages after I got here I thought it was the elephants blowing through their trunks.'

The echo died.

'Fru Molnes has a motive, but is it good enough?' Harry said and jumped down. 'Would you kill someone to have the right of disposal over fifty million kroner for six years?'

'Depends on who I had to kill,' Liz said. 'I know a couple of people I would murder for less.'

'I mean: is fifty million kroner for six years the same as five million for sixty years?'

'Negative.'

'Exactly. Shit!'

'Do you wish it was her? Mrs Molnes?'

'I'll tell you what I wish. I wish we could find the bloody murderer so that I could go home.'

Liz belched loudly; it was impressive. She nodded in acknowledgement and put the beer down.

'Poor daughter. Runa's her name, right? '

'She's a tough girl.'

'Are you sure?'

He shrugged and raised an arm to the sky.

'What are you doing?' she asked.

'Thinking.'

'I mean with your hand. What's that?'

'Energy. I'm gathering energy from all the people down there. It's supposed to give eternal life. Do you believe in that kind of thing?'

'I stopped believing in eternal life when I was sixteen, Harry.'

Harry turned, but couldn't see her face in the night.

'Your father?'

He could see the sharp outline of her head nodding.

'Yup. He carried the world on his shoulders, my dad did. Shame it was too heavy.'

'How . . .?' He fell silent.

There was a crunch as she crushed the beer can.

'It's just another sad story about a Vietnam vet, Harry. We found him in the garage, in full dress uniform with his service rifle beside him. He had written a long letter, not to us, but to the US Army. It said he couldn't bear the thought that he'd fled his responsibilities. He'd realised that when he was standing in the doorway of the helicopter taking off from the roof of the American Embassy in Saigon in 1973 and watching the desperate south Vietnamese storming the place to take refuge from the approaching forces. He wrote that he was as responsible as the police who used the butts of their rifles to keep them out, all of them who had promised they would win the war, who had promised democracy. As an officer he saw himself as equally responsible for the US Army's decision to prioritise evacuation at the expense of the Vietnamese who had fought side by side with them. Dad dedicated his military efforts to them and regretted that he had not lived up to his responsibility. Finally, he said goodbye to me and Mom and said we should try to forget him as quickly as possible.'

Harry felt an urge to smoke.

'That's a lot of responsibility to carry,' he said.

'Yeah, but I guess sometimes it's easier to take responsibility for the dead instead of the living. The rest of us have to look after them, Harry. The living. After all, that's the responsibility that drives us.'

Responsibility. If there was one thing he had tried to bury last year, it was responsibility. Whether it was for the living or the dead, himself or others. It only involved guilt and was never rewarded anyway. No, he could not see how responsibility was driving him. Perhaps Torhus had been right, perhaps his motives for wanting to see justice done weren't so noble after all. Perhaps it was just stupid ambition that prevented him from allowing the case to be shelved, that made him so keen to catch someone, no matter who, so long as he could find damning evidence and stamp the file 'Solved'. The newspaper headlines and the back-slapping when he returned from Australia, had they actually meant as little as he liked to believe? This idea that he could trample over everything and everyone because he wanted to get back to Sis's case, perhaps it was just a pretext? Because it had become so, so important for him to *succeed*.

For a second there was silence, it was as though Bangkok was drawing breath. Then the same foghorn rent the air again. A lament. It sounded like a very lonely elephant, Harry thought. And then the cars started honking their horns again.

A note lay on the doormat when he got back to his flat. *I'm in the pool. Runa.*

Harry had noticed that 'pool' was next to the figure 5 on the lift panel, and when he got out on the fifth floor, sure enough, he could smell chlorine. Round the corner was a swimming pool under the open sky with balconies on two sides. The water glittered softly in the moonlight. He crouched down by the edge and stuck out a hand.

'You feel at home here, don't you?'

Runa didn't answer, just kicked out, swam past him and ducked beneath the water. Her clothes and prosthesis lay in a bundle by the sunlounger.

'Do you know what time it is?' he asked.

She appeared from below, grabbed him round the neck and kicked off. He was caught totally unprepared, lost his balance and his hands found naked, smooth skin as he slipped into the water with her. They didn't make a sound, just pushed water to the side like a heavy, warm duvet and sank into it. Bubbles formed in his ears and tickled, and his head felt as if it were expanding. They reached the bottom and he pushed off with his feet and took them to the surface.

'You're crazy!' he spluttered.

She chuckled and swam away with rapid strokes.

He was lying on the side in dripping clothes when she came out of the pool. When he opened his eyes she was holding the pool net trying to catch a large dragonfly floating on the surface of the water.

'That's a miracle,' Harry said. 'I was convinced the only insects that survived in this town were cockroaches.'

'Some of the good ones always survive,' she said, carefully lifting the net. She released the dragonfly and it flew over the pool with a low buzzing noise.

'Aren't cockroaches good?'

'Yuk, they're revolting!'

'They don't have to be bad because they're revolting.'

'Maybe not. But I don't think they're good. It's like they just *exist*.'

'They just *exist*,' Harry repeated, not sarcastically, more reflectively.

'They're made like that. Made for us to want to tread on them. If there weren't so many of them.'

'Interesting theory.'

'Listen,' she whispered. 'Everyone's asleep.'

'Bangkok never sleeps.'

'Yes, it does. Listen. They're sleeping noises.'

The pool net was attached to a hollow aluminium tube, which she blew through. It sounded like a didgeridoo. He listened. She was right.

She followed him down to use the shower.

He was already standing in the corridor and had pressed the lift button when she emerged from his bathroom with a towel around her.

'Your clothes are on the bed,' he said, closing the apartment door.

Afterwards they stood in the corridor waiting for the lift. A red number above the door had started the countdown.

'When are you leaving?' she asked.

'Soon. If nothing turns up.'

'I know you met Mum earlier this evening.'

Harry put his hands in his pockets and looked at his toenails. She had said he ought to cut them. The lift doors opened, and he stood in the doorway.

'Your mother says she was at home the night your father died. And you can testify to that.'

She groaned. 'Honestly, do you want me to answer that?'

'Maybe not,' he said. He took a step back and they looked at each other while waiting for the doors to close.

'Who do you think did it?' he asked at length.

She was still looking at him as the doors slid shut.

24

Wednesday 15 January

IN THE MIDDLE OF JIMI'S guitar solo in 'All Along the Watchtower' the music suddenly stopped and Jim Love gave a start, then realised someone had removed his headphones.

He turned in the chair, and a tall, blond guy who had definitely been a little lax with his sunscreen towered over him in the cramped car-parking booth. Half of the face was hidden behind a pair of pilot sunglasses of dubious quality. Jim had an eye for that kind of thing; his own had cost him a week's pay.

'Hello,' the tall man said. 'I asked if you spoke English.'

The guy spoke with an indefinable accent and Jim answered with a Brooklyn one.

'Better than I speak Thai anyway. How can I help you? Which company do you want?'

'No company today. I want a chat with you.'

'With me? You're not the supervisor from the security company, are you? I can explain the Walkman—'

'No, I'm not. I'm from the police. My name's Hole. My colleague, Nho . . .'

Harry stepped aside, and behind him in the doorway Jim saw a

Thai man with the standard crew cut and freshly ironed white shirt. Which meant that Jim did not doubt for one minute that the badge he held up was genuine. He scrunched up one eye.

'Police, huh? Do you go to the same hairdresser? Ever thought about a new do? Like this?' Jim pointed to his own mop of hair.

The tall man laughed. 'Doesn't look like eighties retro has hit police stations just yet, no.'

'Eighties what?'

'Have you got someone who can take over while we talk?'

Jim explained that he had come to Thailand four years ago on holiday with a few friends. They had hired motorbikes and driven north, and in a little village by the Mekong River on the border with Laos one of them had been foolhardy enough to buy some opium and put it in his backpack. On their way back they were pulled over by the police and searched. On a dusty country road in deepest Thailand they suddenly realised their friend was going to be locked up for an incredibly long time.

'According to the law, they can fucking execute guys smuggling shit. Did you know that? And the three of us who hadn't done nothing thought, oh fuck, we're gonna be in trouble too, accessories or something. Shit, I mean, as a black American, I don't exactly look like a drug smuggler, right? We begged and begged and got nowhere until one of the officers talked about a fine instead. So we scraped together all the dough we had, and they confiscated the opium and let us go. We were so damn happy. The problem was we'd given them the money for our return ticket to the States, right? So . . .'

Jim described with a mass of words and even more gestures how one thing had led to another, that he'd been working as a guide for American tourists, but he'd had trouble with his residence permit and that he'd been lying low, looked after by a Thai girl he'd met, and that when the others were ready to leave he'd decided to stay. After a lot of toing and froing he'd got a residence permit because he'd been offered a job as a car-park attendant, and they needed people who spoke English for the buildings where international gatherings were held.

Jim was talking so much in the end Harry had to stop him.

'Shit, I hope your Thai friend doesn't speak English,' Jim said, glancing nervously at Nho. 'The guys we paid up north—'

'Relax, Jim. We're here to ask about something else. A dark blue Mercedes with a diplomatic number plate was supposed to have been here on the seventh of January, at around four. Does that ring any bells?'

Jim burst out laughing. 'If you asked me which Jimi Hendrix song I was listening to maybe I could answer you, man, but the cars that come in and out of here . . .' He pursed his lips.

'When we were here we were given a ticket. You wouldn't be able to check anything, would you? The registration number or something?'

Jim shook his head. 'We don't worry about that. Most of the parking lot has CCTV, so if anything happens, we can check it out afterwards.'

'Afterwards? Do you mean you record it?'

'Of course.'

'I haven't seen any monitors.'

'That's because there aren't any. This parking garage has six levels, right, so we can't sit and watch it all. Shit, most criminals who see a camera just scram, right? So you're halfway there. And if anyone's dumb enough to sneak in and steal one of the cars, we've got it all on tape for you guys.'

'How long do you keep the videos?'

'Ten days. Most people have worked out if something's missing from their cars by then. Then we record over the tapes.'

'That would mean you've got 4 to 5 p.m. on the seventh of January on tape then?'

Jim peered up at a calendar on the wall. 'You betcha.'

They walked down a staircase and entered a warm, damp basement, where Jim switched on a solitary light bulb and unlocked one of the steel cabinets along the wall. The tapes were stacked neatly in piles.

'There's a lot of tapes to get through if you want to check the whole parking lot.'

'Visitor parking is enough,' Harry said.

Jim searched along the shelves. Obviously every camera had its shelf, and the dates were written on the labels in pencil. Jim pulled out a cassette.

'Bingo.'

He opened another cabinet in which there was a video player and a monitor, inserted the cassette and after a few seconds a black-and-white image appeared on the screen. Harry immediately recognised the visitor parking slots; the recording clearly came from the same camera he had seen the last time they were here. A code at the bottom of the screen showed the day, month and time. They spooled forward to 15.50. No ambassador's car. They waited. It was like watching a freeze-frame; nothing was happening.

'Let's fast-forward,' Jim said.

Apart from the clock in the corner speeding up there was no difference. 17.15. A couple of cars raced by leaving wet marks on the cement. 17.40 and they could see the tracks drying and vanishing, but still no sign of the ambassador's Mercedes. When the clock showed 17.50 Harry told Jim to switch off the video player.

'There should have been an embassy car in one of the visitors' spaces,' Harry said.

'Sorry,' Jim said. 'Looks like someone's given you some bad information.'

'Could it have been parked anywhere else?'

'Of course. Anyone who isn't a regular visitor has to drive past this same camera, we would have seen the car pass.'

'We'd like to see a different video,' Harry said.

'Oh yeah. Which one?'

Nho rummaged through his pockets. 'Do you know where a car with this registration number parks?' he asked, passing him a slip of paper. Jim stared at him suspiciously.

'Shit, man, you speak English after all.'

'It's a red Porsche,' Nho said.

Jim passed back the note. 'I don't need to check. No regulars drive a red Porsche.'

'*Faen!*' Harry said.

'What was that?' Jim asked with a grin.

'A Norwegian word you don't want to learn.'

They walked back into the sunshine.

'I can get you a decent pair cheap,' Jim said, pointing to Harry's sunglasses.

'No, thank you.'

'Anything else you need?' Jim winked and laughed. He had already started clicking his fingers. He was probably looking forward to listening to his Walkman again.

'Hey, Officer!' he shouted after them as they left. Harry turned.

'*Fa-an!*'

They could hear his laughter all the way to the car.

'So what do we know?' Liz asked, putting her feet on the desk.

'We know that Brekke's lying,' Harry said. 'He said that after their meeting he accompanied the ambassador down to where his car was parked in the underground car park.'

'Why would he lie about that?'

'On the phone the ambassador says that he wants confirmation that they're meeting at four o'clock. There's no doubt the ambassador arrived at the office. We've spoken to the receptionist, and she confirmed it. She can also confirm that they left the office together, because Brekke popped by to leave a message. She remembers that because it was around five and she was getting ready to go home.'

'I'm glad someone remembers something.'

'But what Brekke and the ambassador did after that we don't know.'

'Where was the car? I doubt he'd risk parking in the street in that part of Bangkok.'

'They might have agreed to go somewhere else, and the ambassador got someone to look after the car while he was fetching Brekke,' Nho suggested.

Rangsan cleared his throat and turned over a page.

'In a place that's crawling with small-time crooks just waiting for a chance like that?'

'Yeah, I agree,' Liz said. 'It's still weird that he didn't use the underground lot, when it's the easiest and the safest thing to do. He could literally have parked next to the elevator.'

Her little finger rotated in her ear and her expression lit up.

'Where are we actually going with this?' she asked.

Harry threw up his arms in resignation. 'I'd been hoping we could prove Brekke had left the office for the day when he and the ambassador left at five, taking the ambassador's car. And that the recordings would show his Porsche was in the car park overnight. But I didn't consider the possibility that Brekke didn't drive his car to work.'

'Let's forget the cars for now,' Liz said. 'What we do know is that Brekke's lying. So what do we do next?' She flicked Rangsan's newspaper.

'Check alibis,' came the answer from behind.

25

Wednesday 15 January

PEOPLE'S REACTIONS TO BEING ARRESTED are as varied as they are unpredictable.

Harry thought he had seen most variants and was therefore not especially surprised to watch Jens Brekke's suntanned face take on a greyish hue and his eyes wander like those of a hunted animal. Body language changes, and even a tailor-made Armani suit doesn't sit as well any more. Brekke held his head high, but it seemed as though he had shrunk.

Brekke hadn't been arrested, he had just been brought in for questioning, but for someone who had never been picked up by two armed officers who didn't even ask if the time was convenient, the difference was academic. When Harry caught sight of Brekke in the interview room the idea that the man before him had managed to perform a cold-blooded stabbing seemed absurd. However, he'd thought the same before and been wrong.

'I'm afraid we'll have to do this in English,' Harry said, sitting down opposite him. 'It's being recorded.' He pointed to the microphone in front of them.

'I see.' Brekke tried to smile. It looked as if iron hooks were stretching his mouth.

'I had to fight to get this interview,' Harry said. 'As it's being recorded, strictly speaking, a Thai police officer should be doing it, but as you're a Norwegian national, the Chief said it was fine.'

'Thank you.'

'Well, I'm not sure there's much to be grateful for. You've been told you have the right to contact a lawyer, haven't you?'

'Yes.'

Harry was about to ask why he hadn't accepted the offer, but refrained. No reason to give him another chance to deliberate. What he had learned about the Thai legal system was that it was fairly similar to the system in Norway, and hence there was no reason to believe that lawyers were much different either. In which case, the first thing they would do would be to gag their clients. But regulations had been followed and now it was time to get moving.

Harry signalled that the recording could start. Nho came in, read out some formalities as an introduction to the tape and left.

'Is it true that you are having a relationship with Hilde Molnes, the wife of the deceased, Atle Molnes?'

'What?' Two wild, staring eyes met him from across the table.

'I've spoken to Mrs Molnes. I suggest you tell the truth.'

A pause ensued.

'Yes.'

'Bit louder please.'

'Yes!'

'How long has this relationship been going on?'

'I don't know. A long time.'

'Since the ambassador's welcome party eighteen months ago?'

'Well . . .'

'Well?'

'Yes, I think that's correct.'

'Did you know that Mrs Molnes would have the right of disposal over a substantial fortune if her husband died?'

'Fortune?'

'Am I speaking unclearly?'

Brekke gasped like a punctured beach ball. 'It's news to me. I had the impression their capital was relatively limited.'

'Really? The last time I spoke to you, you told me the meeting you and Molnes had in your office on the seventh of January was about investment. We know, furthermore, that Molnes owed a large sum of money. I can't get this to tally.'

A further silence. Brekke was about to say something, then stopped.

'I lied,' he said in the end.

'You have another chance to tell me the truth now.'

'He came to me to discuss my relationship with Hilde . . . with his wife. He wanted it to stop.'

'Not an unreasonable request, perhaps?'

Brekke shrugged. 'I don't know how much you know about Atle Molnes.'

'Assume we know nothing.'

'Let me say that his sexual orientation did not make for much of a marriage.'

He glanced up. Harry nodded for him to go on.

'His keenness for Hilde and me to stop meeting wasn't motivated by jealousy. It was because rumours were apparently circulating in Norway. He said if the relationship became public these rumours would be stoked and that would hurt not only him but also, undeservedly, others in important positions. I tried to delve deeper, but that was all he would say.'

'What did he threaten you with?'

'Threaten? What do you mean?'

'He didn't just say, please, would you mind not meeting a woman I assume you love.'

'Yes, in fact he did. I think that was even the word he used.'

'Which word?'

'Please.' Brekke folded his hands on the table in front of him. 'He was a strange man. "Please."' He smiled weakly.

'Yes, I suppose you don't hear that so often in your business.'

'Nor in yours, I suppose?'

Harry stared at him, but there was no challenge in Brekke's eyes.

'What did you agree to do?'

'Nothing. I said I would give the matter some thought. What could I say? The man was on the verge of tears.'

'Did you consider stopping the relationship?'

Brekke furrowed his brow as if this idea was new to him.

'No. I . . . well, it would have been very difficult for me to stop seeing her.'

'You told me that after the meeting you accompanied the ambassador down to the underground car park where he had his Mercedes. Are you changing that statement now?'

'No . . .' Brekke said in surprise.

'We've checked the CCTV recordings of the date in question between 3.50 and 5.15. The ambassador's Mercedes wasn't parked in the visitors' bay. Would you like to change your statement?'

'Change . . .?' Brekke looked at him in disbelief. 'My God, man, no. I came out of the lift and saw his car. We must have both been on the recording. I even remember we exchanged a few words before he got into the car. I promised the ambassador I wouldn't mention the conversation we'd had to Hilde.'

'We can prove this was not the case. For the last time: Would you like to change your statement?'

'No!'

Harry could hear a firmness in his voice which had not been there before the interview started.

'What did you do after you'd accompanied the ambassador down to the car park, as you maintain?'

Brekke explained that he had gone back up to his office to finish a company analysis report and that he sat there until about midnight, when he took a taxi home. Harry asked if anyone had dropped by or rung him while he was working, but Brekke said that no one could get to his office without the code and that he had blocked his calls so he could work in peace, as he usually did when he was working on reports.

'Is there no one who can give you an alibi? No one who saw you going home, for example?'

'Ben, the caretaker where I live. He may remember. At any rate he usually notices when I come home late wearing a suit.'

'A caretaker who saw you coming home at midnight, is that all?'

Brekke pondered. 'I'm afraid so.'

'OK,' Harry said. 'Someone else will take over now. Would you like something to drink? Coffee, water?'

'No, thank you.'

Harry got up to go.

'Harry?'

He turned. 'It's best if you call me Hole. Or Officer.'

'I see. Am I in trouble?' He said it Norwegian.

Harry pinched his eyes together. Brekke was a sad sight, slumped like a cloth sack.

'I think I'd ring your lawyer now if I were you.'

'I understand. Thank you.'

Harry stopped in the doorway. 'Incidentally, what about the promise you made the ambassador, did you keep it?'

Brekke gave him a sort of apologetic smile. 'Idiotic. I had intended to tell Hilde, of course, I mean, I had to. But when I found out he was dead then . . . well, he was a strange man, and I got it into my head that I should keep the promise even though it had no practical meaning any more.'

'Just a mo. I'll put you on loudspeaker.'

'Hello?'

'We can hear you, Harry. Away you go.'

Bjarne Møller of Crime Squad, Dagfinn Torhus from the Foreign Office and the Police Commissioner for Oslo listened to Harry's telephone report without interrupting him at any point.

Afterwards Torhus spoke up.

'So we have one Norwegian in custody, suspected of murder. The question is: How long can we keep a lid on this?'

The Police Commissioner cleared her throat. 'As the murder is not yet public knowledge, I think we still have a few days, especially since you don't have a great deal on Brekke, other than a false statement and a motive. If you have to let him go it's probably best if no one knows about the arrest.'

'Harry, can you hear me?' It was Møller speaking. There was some atmospheric noise, which Møller took to be confirmation. 'Is the guy guilty, Harry? Did he do it?'

There was some more noise and Møller lifted the Police Commissioner's telephone receiver.

'What did you say, Harry? You . . .? Right. Well, we'll discuss that here and keep in touch.'

Møller rang off.

'What did he say?'

'He didn't know.'

By the time Harry got home it was late. Le Boucheron had been full so he'd eaten at a restaurant in Soi 4 in Patpong, a street full of gay bars. During the main course a man had come over to the table and politely asked if he would like a handjob and then discreetly withdrew when Harry shook his head.

Harry got out on the fifth floor. There was no one around and the lights were off around the pool. He pulled off his clothes and dived in. The water gave him a cooling embrace. He swam a few lengths, felt the resistance in the water. Runa had said that no two pools were identical, that all water had its idiosyncrasies, its special consistency, smell and colour. This pool was vanilla, she had said. Sweet and viscous. He inhaled, but could only smell chlorine and Bangkok. He floated on his back and closed his eyes. The sound of his own breathing underwater made him feel as if he were enclosed in a little room. He opened his eyes. A light went off in one of the flats in the opposite wing. A satellite moved slowly between stars. A motorbike with a broken silencer attempted to move off. Then his gaze went back to the flat. He counted the floors again. He swallowed water. The light had gone off in his flat.

Harry was out of the pool in seconds, pulled on his trousers and looked around in vain for something that could be used as a weapon. He grabbed the pool net leaning against the wall, jogged the few metres to the lift and pressed the button. The doors separated, he stepped in and noticed a faint aroma of curry. It was as if a second had been taken from his life, and when he came to he was lying supine on the cold stone floor of the corridor. Luckily the blow had hit him in the forehead, but a huge figure was standing over him, and Harry knew at once that the odds were not in his favour. He hit out at the lower thigh with the net, but the light aluminium shaft had little effect. He managed to avoid the first kick and staggered to his knees, but the second struck his shoulder and spun him halfway round. His back hurt, but the adrenalin kicked in and he got to his feet with a roar of pain. In the light from the open lift he saw a pigtail jiggling around a shaven skull as a fist was swung, hit him above the eye and knocked him back towards the pool. The figure followed up, and Harry feinted a left before planting a right where he thought the face had to be. It was like punching granite, as though he had hurt himself more than his opponent. Harry stepped back and moved his head to the side, felt a current of air and horror seize his chest. He fumbled at his belt, found the handcuffs, detached them and threaded his fingers inside. He waited until the hulk came closer, took a risk that no uppercut was on its way and ducked. Then he struck, swinging his hip, following with his shoulder, his whole body behind it, and in furious desperation launched his iron-clad knuckles through the darkness until they crunched against flesh and bone, and something gave. He hit again and could feel the iron bore its way through skin. The blood was hot and thick between his fingers; he didn't know if it was his own or his attacker's, but he raised his fist for another blow, shocked that the man was still upright. Then he heard the low, throaty laugh and a trainload of concrete landed on his head, the blackness became blacker and the concept of up and down no longer existed.

26

Thursday 16 January

HARRY WAS BROUGHT ROUND BY the water; instinctively he breathed in and the next moment he was dragged under. He fought, but it made no difference. The water amplified the metallic click of something being locked, and the arm that held him let go. He opened his eyes; everything was turquoise around him and he felt the tiles beneath him. He pushed off, but a jerk on his wrist told him what his brain had been trying to explain and he had refused to accept. He was going to drown. Woo had attached him to the drain at the bottom of the pool with his own handcuffs.

He looked up. The moon was shining down on him through a filter of water. He stretched his free arm up and out of the water. Hell, the pool was only one metre deep here! Harry crouched and tried to stand up, stretched with all his might. The handcuff cut into his thumb, but still his mouth was twenty centimetres below the surface. He noticed the shadow at the edge of the pool moving away. Shit! Don't panic, he thought. Panic uses up oxygen.

He sank to the bottom and examined the grille with his fingers. It was made of steel and was totally immovable, it didn't budge even when he grabbed it with both hands and pulled. How long could he hold his breath? One minute? Two? All his muscles ached, his temples throbbed and red stars were dancing in front of his eyes. He tried to jerk himself loose. His mouth was dry with fear, his brain had started producing images he knew were hallucinations; too little fuel, too little water. An absurd thought struck him – if he drank as much water as he could the water level might sink enough for him to breathe. He banged his free hand against the side of the pool, knowing no one could hear him, for even if the world beneath the water was quiet, the metropolitan clamour of Bangkok continued unabated up above, drowning any other sounds. And if someone had heard him, so what? All they could do was keep him company while he died. A burning heat centred on his head and he prepared to experience what all drowning people have to experience sooner or later: water inhalation. His free hand met metal. The pool net. It was on the edge of the pool. Harry grabbed it and pulled. Runa had been playing didgeridoo. Hollow. Air. He closed his mouth round the end of the aluminium pole and breathed in. He got water in his mouth, swallowed, almost suffocated, tasted dead, dry insects on his tongue and bit round the tube as he fought his cough reflexes. Why was it called oxygen, from the Greek, *oxys*, meaning acid? It isn't acidic, it's sweet, even in Bangkok the air is as sweet as honey. He inhaled loose bits of aluminium and grit that stuck to the mucus in his throat, but he didn't notice. He breathed in and out with a passion, as though he had run a marathon.

The brain was beginning to function again. That was how he knew he had been given merely a postponement of the inevitable. In his blood the oxygen was converted to carbon dioxide, the body's exhaust fumes, and the pole was too long for him to be able to expel the nitrogen completely. So he was inhaling recycled air, again and again, a mixture of ever-decreasing oxygen and increasingly fatal CO_2. This excess of carbon dioxide is called hypercapnia, and he would soon die from it. In fact, because he was breathing so fast, it accelerated the process. After a while he would become sleepy, his brain would lose interest in drawing air, he would breathe less and less and ultimately stop.

So lonely, Harry thought. Chained. Like the elephants on the riverboats. The elephants. He blew down the tube with all the power he could muster.

Anne Verk had lived in Bangkok for three years. Her husband was the CEO of Shell's Thailand office; they were childless, medium unhappy and would stick out a few years together yet. After that she would move back to Holland, finish her studies and search for a new husband. Out of sheer boredom she had applied for a job as an unpaid teacher at Empire and, to her surprise, got it. Empire was an idealistic project whose aim was to offer schooling to the many girls on the game in Bangkok, mainly in English. Anne Verk taught them what they needed in bars; that was why they went. They sat behind their desks, shy, smiling young girls who giggled when she made them repeat after her: 'Can I light your cigarette for you, sir?' Or 'I'm a virgin. You're very bold, sir. Would you like a drink?'

Today one of the girls was wearing a new red dress, which she was clearly proud of and which she had bought at Robinson's department store, she explained to the class in hesitant English. Sometimes it was difficult to imagine that these girls worked as prostitutes in some of the toughest areas of Bangkok.

Like most Dutch people, Anne spoke excellent English and once a week she taught some of the other teachers as well. She got out of the lift on the fifth floor. It had been an especially wearing evening with a lot of arguing about teaching methods, and she was yearning to kick off her shoes in the 200-square-metre apartment when she heard some strange, hoarse trumpeting noises. At first she thought they came from the river, but then she realised they were coming from the swimming pool. She found the light switch and it took her several seconds to take on board and process the sight of a man underwater and the pool net upright in the water. Then she ran.

Harry saw the light come on and saw the figure by the pool. Then it went. It looked like a woman. Had she panicked? Harry had started noticing the first signs of hypercapnia. In theory, it should be bordering on a pleasant feeling, like drifting off under an anaesthetic, but he just felt the terror running through his veins like glacier water. He forced himself to concentrate, breathe calmly, not too much, not too little, but thinking was becoming a challenge.

Accordingly, he didn't notice that the water level was beginning to sink, and when the woman jumped into the pool and lifted him to the surface he was sure an angel had come for him.

PART FOUR

27
Friday 17 January

THE REST OF THE NIGHT was mostly about his headache. Harry sat in a chair in his flat, a doctor came, took a blood sample and said he had been lucky. As though he needed anyone to explain that. Later Liz sat beside him and noted down what had happened.

'What did he want in the apartment?' she asked.

'No idea. To frighten me maybe.'

'Did he take anything?'

He glanced round. 'Not if my toothbrush is still in the bathroom.'

'Clown. How do you feel?'

'Hung-over.'

'We're launching an immediate investigation.'

'Forget it. Go home and get a few hours' shut-eye.'

'You're cheerful all of a sudden.'

'I'm a good actor, aren't I.' He rubbed his face with his hands.

'This isn't a joke, Harry. Do you realise you've been poisoned by CO_2?'

'No more than the average Bangkok citizen, according to the doctor. I mean it, Liz. Go home, I haven't got the energy to talk to you any more. I'll be fine by tomorrow.'

'Take tomorrow off.'

'As you wish. Just go.'

Harry had knocked back the pills the doctor had given him, slept without dreams and didn't wake until late morning when Liz phoned to see how he was. He grunted by way of an answer.

'I don't want to see you today,' she said.

'I love you too,' he said, rang off and got up to dress.

It was the hottest day of the year and at the police station everyone was groaning. Even in Liz's office the air-conditioning system couldn't keep up. Harry's nose had started peeling and he was looking like a rival to Rudolph. He was halfway down his third litre bottle of water.

'If this is the cold season what's the—?'

'All right, Harry.' Liz didn't look as if she thought talking about the heat would make it any more bearable. 'What about Woo, Nho? Any clues?'

'Nothing. I had a serious talk with Mr Sorensen at Thai Indo Travellers. He says he doesn't know where Woo is, he's no longer employed by the firm.'

Liz sighed. 'And we have no idea what he did in Harry's apartment. Nice. What about Brekke?'

Sunthorn had got hold of the caretaker in the block where Brekke lived. In fact, he could remember the Norwegian had come home some time after midnight on the night in question, but he couldn't say precisely when.

Liz informed them that Forensics was already busy combing through Brekke's office and apartment. They were examining his clothes and shoes in particular to see if they could find something – blood, hair, fibres, anything – that could connect Brekke with the murder victim or crime scene.

'Meanwhile,' Rangsan said, 'I have a couple of comments to make about the photos we found in Molnes's briefcase.'

He pinned up three magnified photos on a board beside the door. Even though the images had churned around long enough in Harry's brain for them to lose some of their initial shock effect, he could feel his stomach heave.

'We sent them to the Vice Squad to see what they could make of them. They can't connect the photos with any known distributors of child pornography.' Rangsan turned one of the images. 'Firstly, they were developed on German paper which is not sold in Thailand. Secondly, they're a bit unclear and at first sight reminiscent of private amateur snaps not intended for distribution. Forensics spoke to an expert who stated that they were taken from a distance with a telephoto lens and probably from outside. He thinks this is a window sash.'

Rangsan pointed to a grey shadow at the edge of the picture. 'The fact that the photos are still professional suggests there is a new niche market to be catered for, the peeping Tom segment.'

'So?'

'In America the porn industry earns huge sums selling these so-called private amateur snaps, which are actually created by professional actors and photographers who intentionally make everything look amateur by using simple equipment and avoiding the most dolled-up models. It turns out that people are willing to pay more for what they think are authentic bedroom shots. The same is true for pictures and videos that appear to have been taken from a flat across the street without the subjects' knowledge or agreement. The latter appeals particularly to peeping Toms, people who get off on seeing others while imagining they're unobserved. We think these photos fall into this category.'

'Or,' Harry said. 'Or it could be the photos weren't meant to be distributed; they're taken for blackmail purposes.'

Rangsan shook his head. 'We've considered that, but if so the adults ought to be identifiable in the picture. A typical feature of commercial child pornography is that the abusers' faces are concealed, like here.'

He pointed to the three photos. You could make out the bottom and the lower part of someone's back. The person was naked apart from a red jumper, on which they could see the bottom of a figure 2 and a zero.

'Suppose it was still going to be used for blackmail but the photographer didn't include the face,' Harry said. 'Or he just showed the blackmail target copies where he couldn't be identified.'

'Stop!' Liz waved with one hand. 'What are you saying, Harry? That the man in the photo is Molnes?'

'It's a theory. He was being blackmailed but couldn't pay because of his gambling debts.'

'So?' Rangsan said. 'That doesn't give the blackmailer a motive to murder Molnes.'

'He might have threatened to report the blackmailer to the police.'

'Report the blackmailer and then be convicted for paedophilia?' Rangsan rolled his eyes, and Sunthorn and Nho made poor attempts to conceal their smiles.

Harry hunched his shoulders and raised his hands. 'As I said, it was a theory, and I agree we should drop it. The second theory is that Molnes was the blackmailer—'

'And Brekke is the abuser . . .' Liz rested her chin on her hands, gazing thoughtfully into the air. 'Well, Molnes needed the money, and that gives Brekke a motive for murder. But he already had one, so that doesn't really get us anywhere. What do you think, Rangsan? Is it possible to *rule out* the possibility that it's Brekke in the photos?'

He shook his head. 'The photos are so unclear we can't rule out anyone unless Brekke has any defining features.'

'Who will volunteer to go and check Brekke's ass?' Liz asked to general laughter.

Sunthorn coughed discreetly. 'If Brekke murdered Molnes because of the photos why did he leave them?'

Long silence.

'Is it only me who feels we're wasting our time?' Liz asked at length.

The air conditioning gurgled and it struck Harry that the day was going to be as long as it was hot.

Harry stood in the doorway to the ambassador's garden.

'Harry?' Runa blinked water from her eyes and stepped out of the pool.

'Hi,' he said. 'Your mother's asleep.'

She shrugged.

'We've arrested Jens Brekke.'

He waited for her to say something, ask why, but she said nothing. He sighed. 'I don't mean to pester you with these things, Runa. But I'm sitting in the middle of it, and so are you, so I was wondering if we could help each other.'

'Right,' she said. Harry tried to interpret her tone. He decided to get straight to the point.

'I have to try and find out a bit more about him, what type of person he is, whether he's what he purports to be and so on. I thought I could start with his relationship with your mother. I mean, there's quite a big age gap . . .'

'You suspect he's exploiting her?'

'That sort of thing, yes.'

'My mother might be exploiting *him*, but the other way round . . .?'

Harry sat down in one of the chairs beneath the willow tree, but Runa remained standing.

'Mum doesn't like me being around when they're together, so I've never really got to know him.'

'You know him better than I do.'

'Do I? Hm. He seems smooth, but perhaps that's just the outside. At least he tries to be nice to me. It was his idea, for example, to take me to the boxing. I think he has it in his head that I'm interested in sport because of my diving. Does he exploit her? I don't know. Sorry, this isn't a lot of help, but I don't know how men of that age think. You don't exactly show your feelings . . .'

Harry straightened his sunglasses. 'Thank you, that's great, Runa. Can you ask your mother to ring me when she wakes up?'

She stood beside the pool with her back to the water, launched herself and performed another somersault for him with an arched spine and her head down. He saw the bubbles bursting on the surface as he turned to leave.

After lunch, Harry and Nho took the lift down to the first floor, where Jens Brekke was still being held.

Brekke was wearing the suit he had been arrested in, but he had unbuttoned the shirt and rolled up the sleeves and no longer looked like a broker. A sweaty fringe was stuck to his forehead, and he was staring, as if in surprise, at the hands lying inactive on the table in front of him.

'This is Nho, a colleague of mine,' Harry said.

Brekke looked up, put on a brave face and nodded.

'I have only one question actually,' Nho said. 'Did you accompany the ambassador down to the underground car park where he was parked on Tuesday the seventh of January at five o'clock?'

Brekke looked at Harry, then at Nho.

'I did,' he said.

Nho looked at Harry and nodded.

'Thank you,' Harry said. 'That was all.'

28

Friday 17 January

THE TRAFFIC WAS CRAWLING ALONG, Harry had a headache and the air conditioning was whistling ominously. Nho stopped at the car-park barrier to Barclays Thailand, rolled down the car window and was told by a man in a neatly pressed uniform that Jim Love was not at work.

Nho showed his police ID and explained that they would like to see one of the video cassettes, but the attendant shook his head disapprovingly and said they would have to ring the security company. Nho turned to Harry and shrugged.

'Explain to him that this is a murder investigation,' Harry said.

'I have done.'

'Then we'll have to do some more explaining.'

Harry got out of the car. The heat and the humidity hit him in the face; it was like taking the lid off a saucepan of boiling water. He stretched, ambled round the car, already a bit dizzy. The attendant frowned as almost two metres of red-eyed *farang* approached, and he put his hand on his gun.

Harry stood in front of him, grimaced and grabbed the man's belt with his left hand. The attendant yelled, but he didn't have a chance to react before Harry had undone the belt and stuffed his right hand down the man's trousers. The attendant was raised off the ground as Harry tugged. His underpants gave way with a loud ripping sound. Nho shouted something, but it was too late. Harry was already holding white boxers aloft in triumph. The next moment they were sailing over the attendant's hut and into the bushes. Then he walked slowly round the car and got back in.

'Old school trick,' he said to a wide-eyed Nho. 'You'll have to take over the negotiations from here. Bloody hell, it's hot . . .'

Nho jumped out of the car, and after a short parley he poked his head back in the car, nodded and Harry followed the other two down into the basement, while the attendant kept a glowering eye on, and a suitable distance from Harry.

The video player hummed, and Harry lit a cigarette. He had some notion that nicotine in certain situations stimulated the mental processes. Like when you needed a smoke.

'Right,' Harry said. 'So you think Brekke's telling the truth?'

'You do too,' Nho said. 'Otherwise you wouldn't have brought me down here.'

'Correct.' The smoke made Harry's eyes smart. 'And here you can see why I think that.'

Nho looked at the pictures, gave up and shook his head.

'This cassette is from Monday the thirteenth of January,' Harry said. 'At about ten in the evening.'

'Wrong,' Nho said. 'This is the same recording we saw last time from the day of the murder, the seventh of January. The date's even on the edge of the picture.'

Harry blew out a smoke ring, but there was a draught coming from somewhere and it collapsed at once.

'It's the same recording, but the date's always been wrong. My guess is our pantless friend here can confirm it's easy for them to change the date and the time on the machine and therefore on the picture.'

Nho looked at the attendant, who shrugged and nodded.

'But that doesn't explain how you know when this recording was made,' Nho said.

Harry nodded towards the monitor. 'I realised when I was woken up this morning by the traffic on Taksin Bridge outside the flat where I'm staying,' he said. 'There was too little traffic. This is a six-storey car park in a busy business complex. It's between four and five o'clock and we see *two* cars pass in an hour.'

Harry flicked the ash of his cigarette.

'The next thing I thought about was these.' He got up and pointed at the screen to the black lines on the cement. 'Tracks of wet tyres. From both cars. When were there last wet roads in Bangkok?'

'Two months ago, if not longer.'

'Wrong. Three days ago, the thirteenth of January, between ten and half past, there was a mango shower. I know because most of it went inside my shirt.'

'Yes, that's right,' Nho said. He frowned. 'But these video recorders never stop. If this recording is not the seventh of January but the thirteenth, it must mean the cassette that should be there for that time had been taken out.'

Harry asked the attendant to find the cassette with 13 January on, and thirty seconds later they could see the recording had been stopped at 21.30. Followed by a five-second snowstorm before the picture settled down again.

'The cassette was taken out here,' Harry said. 'The pictures we can see now are what was on the cassette before.' He indicated the date. 'The first of January 05.25.'

Harry asked the attendant to freeze the picture and they sat looking at it while Harry finished his cigarette.

Nho pressed his palms together in front of his mouth. 'So someone here has fixed a cassette so that it looks as if the ambassador's car has never been in the car park. Why?'

Harry didn't answer. He looked at the time. 05.25. Thirty-five minutes before the new year reached Oslo. Where had he been? What had he been doing? Had he been at Schrøder's? No, it must have been closed. He must have been asleep then. At any rate he couldn't remember any fireworks.

The security company was able to confirm that Jim Love had had the night shift on the thirteenth of January, and they gave Nho his address and telephone number without a murmur. Nho rang Love's place, but no one answered.

'Send a patrol car there and check,' Liz said. She seemed elated to have something concrete to go on at last.

Sunthorn came into the office and handed her a file.

'Jim Love doesn't have a record,' he said. 'But Maisan, one of the undercover guys in Narco, recognised the description. If it's the same guy he's been seen at Miss Duyen's several times.'

'What's that supposed to mean?' Harry asked.

'It means he wasn't necessarily as innocent in that opium story as he made out,' Nho said.

'Miss Duyen's is an opium den in Chinatown,' Liz explained.

'Opium den? Isn't that, erm . . . illegal?'

'Of course.'

'Sorry, stupid question,' Harry said. 'But I thought the police were fighting that sort of thing.'

'I don't know what it's like where you come from, Harry, but we try to be practical. If we shut down Miss Duyen's, another opium den would open somewhere else next week. Or those guys just do it in the street. The advantage with Miss Duyen's is that we have control, the undercover guys can come and go as they please and the people who choose to scramble their brains with opium can do so in relatively respectable surroundings.'

There was a cough.

'Plus Miss Duyen probably pays well,' a voice mumbled from behind the *Bangkok Post*.

Liz pretended not to hear.

'Since he hasn't turned up for work today and he's not at home, I bet he's lying on one of Miss Duyen's bamboo mats. Why don't you and Harry take a peek, Nho? Talk to Maisan; he'll be able to give you a hand. Could be good for our tourist to see something.'

29
Friday 17 January

MAISAN AND HARRY WALKED INTO a narrow street where a red-hot breeze blew the litter alongside the fragile house walls. Nho stayed in the car because Maisan thought he stank of cop from miles off. Besides, he was worried they might be suspicious at Miss Duyen's if three people turned up at once.

'Smoking opium is not really a social thing,' Maisan explained in an approximation of an American accent. Harry wondered if the accent and the Doors T-shirt weren't a bit over the top for an undercover narc cop. Maisan stopped in front of an open wrought-iron gate doubling as a door, stamped his cigarette butt into the tarmac with his right boot heel and entered.

Coming in from the bright sunlight, Harry couldn't see anything at first, but he could hear low, muttering voices and followed two backs disappearing into a room.

'Shit!' Harry hit his head on the door frame and turned when he heard familiar laughter. In the darkness by the wall he thought he could discern a huge shape, but he could have been mistaken. Woo was probably keeping a low profile today. He hurried along so as not to lose the two in front. They disappeared down a staircase and Harry jogged after them. Banknotes were changing hands and the door opened enough for them to squeeze in.

Inside it stank of earth, piss, smoke and sweet opium.

Harry's only idea of an opium den came from a Sergio Leone film, in which Robert De Niro was tended to by women wearing silk sarongs, all lying on soft beds with big cushions; everything was lit by a forgiving, yellow light which gave the whole scene a sacred feel. At least that was how he remembered it. Apart from the muted light, there was little that was reminiscent of Hollywood. The dust floating in the air made it hard to breathe, and with the exception of a few bunk beds lining the walls everyone was lying on rugs and bamboo mats on the hard earthen floor.

The darkness and the clammy air which resounded with muffled coughs and throaty rasps led Harry to assume there were only a handful of people inside, but gradually, as his eyes became accustomed to the light, he could see it was a large, open room and there must have been a hundred people, almost all men. Apart from the coughing, it was eerily quiet. Most appeared to be asleep, others barely moved. He saw an old man holding a pipe with both hands while inhaling so hard the creased skin around his cheekbones tightened.

This insanity was organised; they lay in rows, which were divided into squares so that there was room to walk in between, much like in cemeteries. Harry followed Maisan up and down the rows, looking at faces and trying to hold his breath.

'Can you see your guy?' he asked.

Harry shook his head. 'It's too bloody dark.'

Maisan grinned. 'They tried putting up neon lights for a while, to stop all the stealing. But people stopped coming.'

Maisan ventured further into the darkness of the room. Soon he reappeared from the gloom and pointed to the exit. 'I've been told the black kid occasionally goes to Yupa House, down the street.

Some people take their opium away and smoke it there. The owner leaves them in peace.'

Now that Harry's pupils had widened to see in the dark, once again they were subjected to the big dentist's lamp faithfully hanging in the sky outside. He grabbed his sunglasses and put them on.

'Harry, I know a place where I can get you cheap—'

'No thanks. These are fine.'

They collected Nho. Yupa House would demand a Thai police ID for them to be able to see a guest book, and Maisan didn't want to be identified in this neighbourhood.

'Thanks,' Harry said.

'Take care,' Maisan said, merging into the shadows.

The receptionist at Yupa House looked like a thin version of a distorted reflection in a fairground mirror. An oblong face sat on a condor neck above narrow, plunging shoulders. He had thinning hair and a stringy beard. He was formal, courteous and, as he was wearing a black suit, reminded Harry of a funeral director.

He assured Harry and Nho that no one by the name of Jim Love was staying there. When they described him he smiled and he shook his head. Above the reception desk hung a sign declaring the basic house rules: no weapons, no odorous objects and no smoking in bed.

'Excuse us a moment,' Harry said to the receptionist, pulling Nho towards the door. 'Well, you're so good at reading liars . . .'

'Tricky,' Nho said. 'He's Vietnamese.'

'So?'

'Haven't you heard what Nguyen Cao Ky said about his countrymen during the Vietnam War? He said the Vietnamese were born liars. It's in their genes, having learned generation after generation that the truth brings nothing but bad luck.'

'Are you saying he's lying?'

'I'm saying I have no idea. He's good.'

Harry turned, went back to the desk and asked for the master key. The receptionist smiled nervously.

Harry raised his voice a tiny fraction, enunciated 'master key' and smiled back at him through clenched teeth.

'We'd like to go through this hotel room by room. Do you understand? If we find any irregularities we will of course be obliged to close the hotel for further examination, but I doubt there will be a problem.'

The receptionist shook his head and suddenly seemed to have difficulty understanding English.

'I said I doubt it will be a problem. I can see you have a sign expressly forbidding smoking in bed.'

Harry took down the sign and banged it on the desk.

The receptionist stared intently at the sign. Something was stirring beneath his condor neck.

'In room number 304 there's a man called Jones,' he said. 'That might be him.'

Harry turned and smiled to Nho, who shrugged.

'Is Mr Jones in?'

'He's been in his room ever since he checked in.'

The receptionist led them upstairs. They knocked, but no one answered. Nho motioned to the receptionist to open up, and from a calf holster Nho drew a loaded black 35mm Beretta, with the safety catch off. The receptionist's head began to twitch, like a chicken's. He turned the key and took two hasty steps back. Harry carefully pushed the door open. The curtains were pulled tight, and the room was dark. He put a hand inside the door and switched on the light. On the bed lay Jim Love, unmoving with closed eyes and headphones on. A ceiling fan hummed and whirred, ruffling the curtains. The water pipe was on a low table beside his bed.

'Jim!' Harry called, but Jim Love didn't react.

Either he was asleep or he had the Walkman on loud, Harry thought, surveying the room to make sure Jim didn't have company. Then he saw an unhurried fly emerging from Jim's right nostril. Harry walked over to the bed and laid a hand on his forehead. It was like touching cold marble.

30

Friday 17 January

EVERYONE EXCEPT RANGSAN WAS ASSEMBLED in Liz's office later that evening.

'Tell me we've got a lead,' she said menacingly.

'The Forensics people found loads,' Nho said. 'They had three men there and found a stack of fingerprints, hairs and fibres. They said it didn't look as if Yupa House had been cleaned for six months.'

Sunthorn and Harry laughed, but Liz just glared at them.

'Any clues that could actually be linked to the murder?'

'We don't know if it is a murder yet,' Harry said.

'Yes, we do,' Liz snapped. 'Suspected accomplices in murder investigations don't accidentally overdose a few hours before we arrest them.'

'He who is destined for the gallows will not drown, as we say in Norwegian,' Harry said.

'What?'

'I agree.'

Nho added that fatal overdoses were rare among opium smokers. As a rule they lost consciousness before they could inhale too much. The door opened and Rangsan walked in.

'News,' he said, sitting down and picking up a newspaper. 'They've found the cause of death.'

'I didn't think the autopsy result would be through until tomorrow,' Nho said.

'Not necessary. The boys in Forensics found prussic acid on the opium, a thin layer. Guy must have died after the first drag.'

For a moment the table was silent.

'Get hold of Maisan.' Liz was back in the groove. 'We have to find out where Love got his opium.'

'I wouldn't be too optimistic on that score,' Rangsan warned. 'Maisan's talked to Love's main pusher, and he hadn't seen him for a long time.'

'Great,' Harry said. 'But now at any rate we know someone has obviously tried to finger Brekke as the murderer.'

'That doesn't help us,' Liz said.

'I wouldn't be so sure about that,' Harry said. 'We don't know that Brekke was just a scapegoat chosen at random. Perhaps the murderer had a motive for pointing the finger at him, an unresolved grievance.'

'And so?'

'If we let Brekke go something might happen. Perhaps we can entice the murderer out of his corner.'

'Sorry,' Liz said. She stared at the table. 'We're holding on to Brekke.'

'What?' Harry couldn't believe his ears.

'Chief's orders.'

'But—'

'That's the way it is.'

'Besides, we have a new clue which points to Norway,' Rangsan said. 'Forensics sent the results of the tests on the knife grease to their Norwegian colleagues to see what they made of it. They discovered it was reindeer grease, and we don't have a lot of that in

Thailand. Someone in Forensics suggested we should arrest Father Christmas.'

Nho and Sunthorn sniggered.

'But then Oslo said reindeer fat was used by the Sami in Norway to protect their knives.'

'A Thai knife and Norwegian grease. This is getting more and more interesting.' Liz stood up abruptly. 'Goodnight, everyone. I hope you'll all be well rested and ready to go tomorrow.'

Harry stopped her by the lift and asked for an explanation.

'Listen, Harry, this is Thailand and the rules are different. Our Police Chief has got involved and told the Commissioner in Oslo that we've found the murderer. He thinks it's Brekke, and when I informed him of the latest developments he wasn't exactly thrilled, and he insisted that Brekke be held in custody until at least he has an alibi.'

'But—'

'Face, Harry, face. Don't forget that in Thailand you're brought up never to admit a mistake.'

'And when everyone knows who made the mistake?'

'Then everyone helps out and makes sure it doesn't look like a mistake.'

Fortuitously, the lift doors opened and closed behind Liz, thus saving her the benefit of Harry's opinion on the matter. Harry thought about 'All Along the Watchtower'. And now he remembered the line as well that there must be some way out of here.

Was there?

Outside his flat was a letter, and he saw Runa's name on the back.

He unbuttoned his shirt. Sweat lay like a fine layer of oil on his chest and stomach. He tried to remember what it was like being seventeen. Had he been in love? Probably.

He put the letter on the bedside table, unopened, the way he was thinking of returning it. Then he reclined on the bed and half a million cars and an air-conditioning system tried to lull him to sleep.

He thought about Birgitta, the Swedish girl he had met in Australia and who had said she loved him. What was it that Aune had said? That he was 'frightened of committing to other people'? The last thought he remembered was that all redemption comes complete with a hangover. And vice versa.

31

Saturday 18 January

JENS BREKKE LOOKED AS IF he hadn't slept since Harry last saw him. His eyes were bloodshot and his hands fidgeted on the table.

'So you don't remember the car-park attendant with the Afro,' Harry said.

Brekke shook his head. 'As I said, I don't use the car park myself.'

'Let's forget Jim Love for the time being,' Harry said. 'Let's concentrate on who's trying to put you in the slammer.'

'What do you mean?'

'Someone's gone to an awful lot of trouble to destroy your alibi.'

Jens arched his eyebrows so high they almost disappeared into his hairline.

'On the thirteenth of January someone put the seventh of January video cassette into the recorder thereby deleting the hours when we would have seen the ambassador's car and you accompanying him down to the car park.'

Jen's eyebrows came back down and knitted into an 'M'. 'Eh?'

'Think about it.'

'I have enemies, you mean?'

'Maybe. Or maybe it was just convenient to have a scapegoat.'

Jens rubbed the back of his neck. 'Enemies? None that I can think of, not that sort.' His face brightened. 'But that must mean you're letting me go.'

'Sorry, you're still not out of the woods.'

'But you just said that you—'

'The Police Chief won't let you go until we have an alibi. So I'm asking you to rack your brain. Was there anyone, anyone at all, who saw you after you said goodbye to the ambassador and before you arrived home? Was there anyone in reception when you left the office or when you caught the taxi? Did you stop by a kiosk, anything?'

Jens rested his forehead on his fingertips. Harry lit a cigarette.

'Hell, Harry! You've made my mind go blank with all that video stuff. I can't think straight.' He groaned and slapped his hand on the table. 'Do you know what happened last night? I dreamt that I killed the ambassador. That we walked out of the main entrance and drove to a motel where I stabbed him in the back with a big butcher's knife. I tried to stop, but I wasn't in control of my body, it was like I was trapped inside a robot and it kept stabbing, and I . . .'

He paused.

Harry said nothing and let him have all the time he needed.

'The thing is I hate being locked up,' Jens said. 'I've never been able to stand it. My father used to . . .'

He swallowed and clenched his right hand. Harry saw his knuckles whiten. Jens was almost whispering as he went on.

'If someone had come in with a confession saying I could leave if I signed it I'm hard put to know what I would have done.'

Harry got up. 'Keep trying to remember something. Now that we've sorted out the video evidence perhaps you can think a bit more clearly.'

He went towards the door.

'Harry?'

Harry wondered what it was that made people so talkative when you turned your back on them.

'Yeah?'

'Why do you think I'm innocent when all the others appear to think the opposite?'

Harry answered without turning. 'First of all, because we don't have anything like evidence against you, only a threadbare motive and the absence of an alibi.'

'And second?'

Harry smiled and twisted his head. 'Because I thought you were a sack of shit the first time I clapped eyes on you.'

'And?'

'I'm crap at judging people. Have a nice day.'

Bjarne Møller opened one eye, squinted at the clock on the bedside table and wondered who on earth would consider six o'clock in the morning a convenient time to ring.

'I know what the time is,' Harry said before his boss had a chance. 'Listen, there's a guy you have to check out for me. No specifics right now, just gut instinct.'

'Gut instinct?'

'Yes, a hunch. I think we're after a Norwegian, and so the selection is somewhat reduced.'

Møller cleared his throat and brought up a mouthful of mucus. 'Why a Norwegian?'

'Well, on Molnes's jacket and the knife that killed him we found some reindeer fat. And the angle of the stab wound suggests it was a relatively tall person. So not your typical Thai by the looks of things.'

'OK, but couldn't you have waited with this, Hole?'

'Of course,' Harry said. There was a pause.

'So why didn't you?'

'Because there are five detectives and a Police Chief here waiting for you to get your arse in gear, boss.'

Møller rang back two hours later.

'What was it exactly that made you ask us to check out this guy, Hole?'

'Well, I reckoned that someone who used reindeer fat to protect the knife must have been in northern Norway. Then I remembered a couple of pals who came back from military service in Finnmark with these big Sami knives they'd bought themselves. Ivar Løken was in Defence for several years and he was stationed in Vardø. Furthermore, I have an idea he knows how to use a knife.'

'That could be true,' Møller said. 'What else do you know about him?'

'Not a lot. Tonje Wiig thinks he's been shunted into a siding until he retires.'

'Well, there's nothing on him in the criminal database, but . . .' Møller paused.

'But?'

'We had a file on him anyway.'

'What do you mean?'

'His name appeared on the screen, but I couldn't get into his file. An hour later I had a phone call from the Defence High Command in Huseby wondering why I was trying to access his file.'

'Wow.'

'They told me to send a letter if I wanted any information about Ivar Løken.'

'Forget it.'

'I've already forgotten, Harry. We won't get anywhere.'

'Did you talk to Hammervoll in Vice?'

'Yes.'

'What did he say?'

'Needless to say, there were no files on Norwegian paedophiles in Thailand.'

'Thought so. Bloody data protection.'

'It's got nothing to do with that.'

'Oh?'

'We started a database a few years ago, but we didn't have the resources to keep it up to date. Just too many of them.'

When Harry had rung Tonje Wiig to arrange a meeting as swiftly as possible, she had insisted that they meet in the Authors' Lounge at the Oriental Hotel for tea.

'Everyone goes there,' she said.

Harry discovered that 'everyone' was white, wealthy and well dressed.

'Welcome to the best hotel in the world, Harry,' Tonje chirruped from the depths of an armchair in the lobby.

She was wearing a blue cotton skirt and holding a straw hat in her lap, which, along with all the other people in the lobby, lent the place a touch of old, carefree colonialism.

They withdrew to the Authors' Lounge, were served tea and nodded politely to the other white people, who seemed to think that being white was reason enough to greet one another. Harry clinked the porcelain nervously.

'Not your style, Harry?' Tonje sipped her tea while mischievously peering over the top.

'I'm trying to work out why I'm smiling at Americans in golf gear.'

She laughed. 'Oh, a slightly cultivated environment can't hurt.'

'When were checked trousers cultivated?'

'Hm, cultivated people then.'

Harry could hear that the rural town of Frederikstad hadn't done much for the woman sitting opposite him. He thought of Sanphet, the old chauffeur who had changed into an ironed shirt and long trousers and had sat out in the boiling hot sun so that his visitors wouldn't be embarrassed by how simply he lived. That was more cultivated than anything he had seen so far among the foreigners in Bangkok.

Harry asked what Tonje knew about paedophiles in Thailand.

'Only that Thailand attracts a lot of them. As I'm sure you remember, a Norwegian was caught literally with his trousers down in Pattaya last year. Norwegian newspapers published a charmingly arranged photo of three small boys pointing him out for the police. The man's face was blanked out, not the boys' faces though. In the English-language version of *Pattaya Mail* it was the other way round. And they used the man's full name in the leader, after which they consistently called him 'the Norwegian'. Tonje shook her head. 'People here who hadn't heard of Norway before suddenly knew that Oslo was the capital because it said that Norwegian authorities wanted him flown home to Oslo. Everyone wondered why on earth they wanted him back. Here, he would have been locked up for a long time.'

'If the sentences are so strict here, why are there so many paedophiles?'

'The authorities want Thailand to get rid of its reputation as an Eldorado for paedophiles. It damages legitimate tourism. But inside the police force it isn't a high priority because arresting foreigners only brings trouble.'

'So the result is that the authorities work against one another?'

Tonje burst into a beaming smile, which Harry realised was not intended for him but one of the 'everyone' passing behind him.

'Yes and no,' she said. 'Some cooperate. The authorities in Sweden and Denmark have, for example, come to an agreement with the Thai government whereby they can station police officers here to investigate specific cases where Swedes or Danes are involved. They have also passed laws that Swedish and Danish nationals can be convicted in their respective countries for abuse of minors in Thailand.'

'And Norway?'

Tonje shrugged. 'We don't have an agreement yet. I know that Norwegian police have pushed for an equivalent arrangement, but I don't think they quite appreciate the extent of what is going on in Pattaya and Bangkok. Have you seen the children walking around selling chewing gum?'

Harry nodded. The area around the go-go bars in Patpong was teeming with them.

'That's the code. The chewing gum means they're for sale.'

Harry realised with a shudder that he'd bought a packet of Wrigley's off a barefoot, black-eyed boy, who had looked terrified, but Harry had put that down to the crowds and the noise.

'Ivar Løken, the man you pointed out at the funeral reception. Ex-military, you said? Can you tell me any more about his interest in photography? Have you seen any of his pictures?'

'No, but I've seen his equipment and that's impressive enough.'

Her cheeks reddened a touch as it occurred to her why Harry had involuntarily smiled.

'And these trips to Indochina, do you know for certain that's where he went?'

'For certain? Why would he lie?'

'Any idea why he might?'

She folded her arms as if she thought it had turned chilly. 'Not really. How was the tea?'

'I have to ask you a favour, Tonje.'

'And that is?'

'An invitation to dinner.'

She looked up in surprise.

'If you have time,' he added.

She gave a mischievous smile again. 'My appointments book is at your disposal, Harry. Any time at all.'

'Fine.' Harry sucked his teeth. 'I was wondering if you could invite Ivar Løken to dinner tonight between seven and ten.'

She knew how to maintain a mask well enough to avoid too much embarrassment. After he had explained the background, she even agreed. Harry clinked the porcelain a bit more, said he had to be going and made a sudden, clumsy exit.

32
Saturday 18 January

ANYONE CAN BREAK INTO A house – all you do is stick a jemmy in the door frame next to the lock and lean against it until the splinters fly. But breaking in, with the emphasis on 'in' and not 'breaking', in such a way that the occupant is not aware he has had uninvited guests, is an art. An art which Sunthorn had mastered to perfection, it transpired.

Ivar Løken lived in an apartment complex on the other side of Phra Pinklao Bridge, and Sunthorn and Harry had been parked outside for almost an hour when they saw him leave. They waited for ten minutes until they were sure that Løken wouldn't come back for something he had forgotten.

The security was somewhat relaxed. Two uniformed men stood by the garage door chatting; they glanced up, registered a white man and a relatively well-dressed Thai go over to the lift, and resumed their conversation.

When Harry and Sunthorn were in front of Løken's door on the thirteenth floor, or 12B as it said on the lift button, Sunthorn took out two picklocks, one in each hand, which he inserted in the lock. He removed them almost at once.

'Take it easy,' Harry whispered. 'Don't get stressed. We've got all the time in the world. Try some other picklocks.'

'I haven't got any others.'

Sunthorn smiled and pushed the door open.

Harry couldn't believe it. Perhaps Nho hadn't been joking when he hinted darkly about Sunthorn's occupation before he joined the police. But if he hadn't been a lawbreaker before, he certainly was now, Harry thought, as he took off his shoes and stepped into the darkened flat. Liz had explained that to get a search warrant they needed the signature of a lawyer and that would have meant informing the Chief of Police. She thought that might be problematic as he had expressly ordered them to focus all their efforts on Jens Brekke. Harry had pointed out he wasn't under the Chief's jurisdiction and he would hang around Løken's flat to see if there was anything going on. She had got the picture and responded that she wanted to know as little as possible about Harry's plans. However, she commented that Sunthorn was often good company.

'Go down to the car and wait,' Harry whispered. 'If Løken turns up, call his number from the car phone and let it ring three times, no more, OK?'

Sunthorn nodded and was gone.

Harry switched on the light after making sure there were no windows overlooking the street, located the telephone and checked the dial tone. Then he had a look around. It was a bachelor pad, devoid of all ornaments and warmth. Three bare walls, the fourth covered with bookshelves packed with books, both vertical and horizontal, and a modest portable TV. The natural centre in the large room was a wooden table with trestles for legs and an architect's lamp.

In a corner there were two open photographic bags and a camera stand leaning against the wall. The table was covered with strips of paper, presumably offcuts, because there were two pairs of scissors, one large and one small, in the middle.

Two cameras, a Leica and a Nikon F5 with a telephoto lens, stared blindly up at Harry. Beside them were night-vision binoculars. Harry had seen them before; they were an Israeli brand he had used on surveillance jobs. The batteries reinforced all the external light sources and allowed you to see, even in what to the naked eye appeared as total darkness.

A door in the flat led to the bedroom. The bed was unmade, so he assumed Løken belonged to the minority of foreigners in Bangkok who didn't have a house help. It didn't cost much, and Harry had been given to understand that foreigners were almost expected to contribute to employment in the country in this way.

Off the bedroom was an en suite bathroom.

He switched on the light and immediately realised why Løken didn't have a house help.

The bathroom clearly also served as a darkroom. It reeked of chemicals and the walls were plastered with black-and-white photographs. A row of photos had been hung up to dry from a piece of string running across the bath. They showed a man in profile from the chest down and Harry could now see that it wasn't a window sash blocking the shot: the upper part of the window was an intricate glass mosaic with lotus and Buddha motifs.

A boy who could hardly have been more than ten was being forced to perform fellatio, and the camera had zoomed in so close that Harry could see his eyes. They were blank, distant and apparently unseeing.

Apart from a T-shirt, the boy was naked. Harry moved closer to the grainy picture. The man had one hand on his hip, the other on the back of the boy's head. Harry could see the shadow of a profile behind the glass mosaic, but it was impossible to distinguish any features. Suddenly the cramped, stinking bathroom seemed to shrink, and the photos on the wall lurched towards him. Harry gave in to the impulse, tore them down, half in fury, half in despair, the blood pounding in his temples. He glimpsed his face in a mirror before giddily staggering out of the room with a pile of pictures under his arm. He slumped onto a chair.

'Bloody amateur!' he muttered when he was breathing normally again.

This was a flagrant breach of the plan. As they didn't have a search warrant it was agreed they wouldn't leave any traces, just find out what was in the flat and then, if they discovered anything, return with a search warrant later.

Harry looked for a place on the wall to fix his gaze and convince himself it was necessary to take concrete evidence to persuade the stubborn mule of a Police Chief. If they were quick they could get hold of a lawyer that evening and be waiting with the requisite papers when Løken returned from the dinner. While he was debating to and fro, he picked up the night-vision goggles, switched them on and looked through the window. The window looked out onto a backyard, and unconsciously he was searching for a window frame with a glass mosaic like the one in the photos, but all he could see were whitewashed walls swimming in the green shimmer of the goggles.

Harry glanced at his watch. He realised he would need to hang the photos back up. The Police Chief would have to make do with his description. Then his blood froze.

He had heard something. That is, he had heard a thousand things, but one sound among the thousand did not belong to the now familiar cacophony from the streets. And it came from the hall. It was a well-lubricated click. Oil and metal. When the draught told him that someone had opened the door, he thought of Sunthorn, until it struck him that the person who had just entered was trying to be as quiet as possible. Harry held his breath while his brain whirred through his sound archives at a furious pace. A sound expert in Australia had told him that the membrane in your ear can hear the difference in pressure between a million different frequencies. And this had not been the sound of a doorknob being turned but a recently oiled gun being cocked.

Harry was at the back of the room like a living target against the white walls, and the light switch was on the opposite side, by the door. He grabbed the large scissors from the middle of the table, crouched down and followed the cable from the architect's lamp to the socket. He pulled out the plug and rammed the scissors into the hard plastic with all his strength.

A blue light flashed from the socket, after which there was a muffled explosion. Then it was pitch black.

The electric shock numbed his arm, and with the stench of burnt plastic and metal in his nostrils he slid groaning along the wall.

He listened, but all he could hear was traffic and his own heart. It was pounding so hard he could feel it; it was like sitting on a horse at full gallop. He could hear something being carefully laid on the floor and knew the person had removed his shoes. He still had the scissors in his hand. Could he see a shadow moving? It was impossible to say; it was so dark that even the white walls weren't visible. The bedroom door creaked, a click followed. Harry realised the intruder had tried to switch on the light, but the short circuit had obviously blown all the fuses in the flat. That told him at least the person was familiar with the layout. But if it was Løken, Sunthorn would have rung. Or would he? The image of Sunthorn's head leaning against the car window, a little hole above the ear, flickered past him.

Harry wondered whether he should try to crawl towards the front door, but something told him that this was what the other person was waiting for. As he opened the door his silhouette would be like one of the targets at the shooting gallery in Økern. Shit! The man was probably sitting on the floor somewhere with his gun trained on the door right now.

If only he could contact Sunthorn! At that moment he realised he still had the binoculars around his neck. He put them to his eyes, but saw only green fog, as if someone had smeared the lenses with snot. He rotated the focus as far as possible. Everything was still blurred, but he was able to discern the outline of a person standing by the wall on the other side of the table. His arm was bent and the gun was pointing to the ceiling. It was perhaps two metres from the edge of the table to the wall.

Harry launched himself, grabbed the tabletop with both hands and held it in front of him like a battering ram. He heard a groan and the clunk of a gun hitting the floor, then he slid across the table and seized what felt like a head. He tightened his arm around the neck and squeezed.

'*Politiet!*' he shouted and the man froze as Harry pressed the cold steel of the scissor blade against his warm face. For a while they stayed like that, locked around each other, two strangers in the inky darkness, both gasping for breath as if after a marathon.

'Hole?' the other man moaned.

Harry gathered that in his panic he had called out in Norwegian.

'I would appreciate it if you would let me go now. I'm Ivar Løken and I won't try anything.'

33

Saturday 18 January

LØKEN LIT A CANDLE WHILE Harry studied Løken's gun, a specially built Glock 31. He had removed the magazine and put it in his pocket. The gun was heavier than any he had ever held.

'I got the gun when I was serving in Korea,' Løken said.

'I see. Korea. What were you doing there?'

Løken put the matches in a drawer and sat down at the table opposite Harry.

'Norway had a field hospital down there with the UN, and I was a young second lieutenant and thought I liked excitement. After the armistice in 1953 I continued to work for the UN, for the newly established Office of the High Commissioner for Refugees. Refugees streamed across the border from North Korea, and life was a trifle lawless. I slept with it under my pillow.' He pointed to the gun.

'I see. What did you do after that?'

'Bangladesh and Vietnam. Hunger, war and the Boat People. Afterwards life in Norway seemed unbearably trivial, so I was unable to stick it out for more than a couple of years before I had to get out again. You know.'

Harry didn't know. Nor did he know what to believe about this lean individual sitting in front of him. He looked like an old Indian chief, with an aquiline nose and intense, deep-set eyes. His hair was white, his face tanned and wrinkled. In addition, he seemed totally at ease in the situation, which put Harry even more on his guard.

'Why did you come back? And how did you get past my colleague?'

The white-haired Norwegian flashed a lupine grin, and a gold tooth glinted in the flickering candlelight.

'The car you came in doesn't quite fit the neighbourhood. We only have tuk-tuks, taxis and old wrecks parked here. I saw two people in the car, both sitting up a little too straight. So I walked round the corner and into the cafe where I could keep an eye on you. After a while I saw the car light come on and you get out. I reckoned one of you would keep watch and waited until your colleague returned. Then I finished my drink, flagged down a taxi, was driven to the underground car park and got the lift up. Nice little number of yours with the short circuit . . .'

'And normal people don't notice parked cars in the street. Unless they have been trained to do so or are on their guard.'

'Well, first of all, Tonje Wiig is unlikely to win an Oscar for her dinner invitation performance.'

'So what are you *really* doing here?'

Løken reached out for the photos and equipment which were now strewn across the floor.

'Do you live from taking pictures of . . . that?' Harry said.

'Yep.'

Harry felt his pulse race. 'Do you know how many years they'll lock you up for that in Thailand? I've got enough here for ten years, I reckon.'

Løken laughed. A brief, dry laugh. 'Do you think I'm stupid, Detective? You wouldn't have needed to break in if you'd had a search warrant. If I risk being punished for what I have in this flat then what you and your colleague have just done has definitely got me off the hook. Any judge will rule as inadmissible the evidence you have acquired in this way. It's not just irregular, it's absolutely illegal. You might be looking at a prolonged stint inside yourself, Hole.'

Harry struck him with the gun. It was like switching on a tap – the blood poured out of Løken's nose.

Løken didn't move, just looked down at the flowery shirt and the white trousers as they were stained red.

'That's genuine Thai silk, you know,' he said. 'Not cheap.'

The violence should have put the brakes on him, but instead Harry could feel the fury growing.

'You can afford it, you fucking paedophile. I assume they pay you well for this shite.' Harry kicked the photos on the floor.

'Well, I'm not sure about that,' Løken said, holding a white handkerchief to his nose. 'It's in line with the government wage scale. Plus an adjustment for living abroad.'

'What are you talking about?'

The gold tooth glinted again. Harry noticed he was squeezing the gun so hard his hand was beginning to ache. He was glad he'd removed the magazine.

'There are a couple of things you don't know, Hole. You should perhaps have been told, but your Police Commissioner probably thought it unnecessary as this has nothing to do with your murder investigation. But now I've been exposed you may as well know the rest. The Police Commissioner and Dagfinn Torhus from the Foreign Office told me about the photos you found in the ambassador's briefcase and now you know of course that they're mine.' With an outstretched palm, he continued. 'Those and the pictures you can see here are links in a paedophilia investigation which, for a variety of reasons, has been labelled secret until further notice. I've been carrying out surveillance of this person for more than six months. The photos are evidence.'

Harry didn't require a moment to consider; he knew this was the truth. Everything clicked into place, as though deep down he had known all along. The secrecy around Løken's job, the photographic equipment, the night-vision binoculars, the trips to Vietnam and Laos, everything fitted. And the man bleeding from the nose opposite him was suddenly no longer his enemy but a colleague, an ally whose nose he had made a serious attempt to smash.

He nodded slowly and put the gun down on the table.

'Fine, I believe you. Why so secret?'

'Do you know about the agreement Sweden and Denmark have with Thailand to investigate sexual abuse cases here?'

Harry nodded.

'Well, Norway is negotiating with the Thai authorities, and in the meantime, I'm conducting a highly unofficial investigation. We have enough to arrest him, but we have to wait. If we arrest him now we would reveal that we've been looking into the case illegally on Thai territory, and that is politically unacceptable.'

'So who are you working for?'

Løken splayed his palms. 'The embassy.'

'I know that but who do you take orders from? Who's behind all this? What about parliament? Do they know?'

'Are you sure you want to know so much, Hole?'

The intense eyes met Harry's. He was about to say something, but held back and shook his head.

'Tell me who the man in the photo is then.'

'I can't. Sorry, Hole.'

'Is it Atle Molnes?'

Løken stared at the table and smiled. 'No, it isn't the ambassador. He was the prime mover in this case.'

'Is it—?'

'As I said, I don't have any reason to tell you now. If our cases turn out to be connected it may be a matter for discussion, but that's up to our superiors to decide.' He got up. 'I'm tired.'

'How did it go?' Sunthorn asked when Harry was back in the car.

Harry asked him if he could bum a cigarette and hungrily inhaled the smoke into his lungs.

'Didn't find anything. Waste of a trip. My guess is the guy's clean.'

Harry sat in his flat.

Once he'd got back from Løken's apartment, he had spoken to his sister on the phone for almost half an hour. That is, she did most of the talking. It is unbelievable how much can happen in a life in little more than a week. She said she had called their father and that she was going over for dinner. Meatballs. Sis was going to cook, and she hoped her father would open up a bit. Harry hoped so too.

Afterwards he flipped through his notebook and rang another number.

'Hello?' a voice said at the other end.

Harry held his breath.

'Hello?' the voice repeated.

Harry rang off. There had been something verging on pleading in Runa's voice. He really didn't have a clue why he had called her. A few seconds later the telephone peeped. He lifted the receiver and waited to hear her voice. It was Jens Brekke.

'I've got it,' he said. The voice was excited. 'When I took the lift from the car park to the office I bumped into a woman on the ground floor. She got out on the fourth. And I think she'll remember me.'

'Why's that?'

There was a slightly nervous chuckle. 'Because I asked her out.'

'You asked her out?'

'Yes, she's one of the girls who work for McEllis. I've seen her a couple of times before. We were the only two in the lift and her smile was so sweet I couldn't restrain myself.'

There was a pause.

'You remembered that *now*?'

'No, now I remembered *when* it happened, after I'd accompanied the ambassador to his car. For some reason I imagined it had happened the day before. But then it struck me she had got into the lift on the ground floor and that must mean I was coming from lower down. And I don't usually go to the underground car park.'

'So what did she say?'

'She accepted, and I regretted it at once. It was just a flirtation, so I asked for her card and said I'd ring one day so that we could agree on a date. That hasn't materialised of course, but I'm pretty sure she won't have forgotten me.'

'Have you still got her card?'

'Yes, isn't that great?'

Harry deliberated. 'Listen, Jens, that's all well and good, but it isn't that easy. You still don't have an alibi. Theoretically, you could have taken the lift back down. You might have just picked up something you left in your office, right?'

'Oh.' He sounded puzzled. 'But . . .'

Jens stopped and Harry heard a sigh.

'Hell, you're right, Harry.'

Harry hung up.

34

Sunday 19 January

HARRY WOKE WITH A START. Above the monotonous hum coming from Taksin Bridge he heard the roar of a riverboat starting up on Chao Phraya. A whistle sounded and the light made his eyes smart. He sat up in bed, buried his face in his hands and waited for the whistle to stop until he realised it was the telephone. Reluctantly he lifted the receiver.

'Did I wake you?' It was Jens again.

'Never mind,' Harry said.

'I'm an idiot. I'm so stupid I don't know if I dare tell you this.'

'Then don't.'

Silence except for the click of a coin being pressed into a machine.

'I'm joking. Come on.'

'OK, Harry. I've been lying awake all night and thinking, trying to remember what I was doing while I was in the office that night. You know, I can remember to the decimal currency transactions I made several months ago, but I'm not capable of remembering simple, factual things while I'm in prison with a murder sentence hanging over me. Can you understand that?'

'That might be the reason why. Haven't we been through this before?'

'OK, well, this is what happened. You remember I said I'd blocked my calls when I was in the office that night? I was lying there thinking that was Sod's Law. If it had been connected and someone had called I would have had it on the recorder and could have proved where I was. And with this one you can't mess around with the time either, as the park attendant did with the video.'

'What's your point?'

'I remembered, thank God, that I could ring out even if I'd blocked incoming calls. I rang our receptionist and got her to go up and check the recorder. And, you know, she found a call I'd made, and then I remembered the whole thing. At eight I phoned my sister in Oslo. Beat that!'

Harry had no intention of trying.

'Your sister can give you an alibi and you really didn't remember?'

'No. And do you know why? Because she wasn't at home. I just left a message on her answerphone to say that I'd rung.'

'And you didn't remember?' Harry repeated.

'Christ, Harry, you forget that kind of call before you've even put the phone down, don't you. Do you remember all the calls you've made when there was no answer?'

Harry had to concede he was right.

'Have you spoken to your lawyer?'

'Not today. I wanted to tell you first.'

'OK, Jens. Call your lawyer now and I'll send someone up to your office to verify what you've said.'

'This kind of recorder is valid in law, you know.' There was a strained tone to his voice.

'Relax, Jens. Not much longer. They'll have to let you go now.'

The receiver crackled as Brekke breathed out. 'Please say that again, Harry.'

'They'll have to let you go.'

Jens laughed a strangely dry laugh. 'In which case, I'll treat you to a meal, Harry.'

'You'd better not.'

'Why's that?'

'I'm a policeman.'

'Call it an interview.'

'I don't think so, Jens.'

'As you wish.'

A bang came from the street below, perhaps a firework or a puncture.

'I'll think about it.'

Harry cradled the receiver, went into the bathroom and looked in the mirror. He asked himself how it was possible to spend so long in tropical climes and still be so pale. He had never liked the sun particularly, but it hadn't taken this long to tan before. Perhaps his lifestyle over the last year had put paid to his pigment production? He threw cold water in his face, thought of the swarthy drinkers at Schrøder's and looked in the mirror again. Well, at any rate the sun had given him a port wine nose.

35

Sunday 19 January

'WE'RE BACK TO SQUARE ONE,' Liz said. 'Brekke's got an alibi and we have to forget Løken for the moment. Oh, and a giant psychopath who tried to kill a visiting officer is on the loose.' She tipped her chair back and studied the ceiling. 'Any suggestions, folks? If not, this meeting is over, you can do what the hell you like, but I'm still short of a few reports and I'm counting on seeing them by early tomorrow at the latest.'

The officers shuffled out of the door. Harry stayed put.

'Well?'

'Nothing,' he said with an unlit cigarette bobbing up and down in his mouth. The inspector had imposed a smoking ban in her office.

'I can see there's something.'

A faint smile curled the corners of Harry's mouth. 'That was what I wanted to know, Inspector. That you can see there is something.'

She had a serious wrinkle between her eyebrows. 'Let me know when you have something to tell me.'

Harry took out his cigarette and put it back in the packet. 'Yes,' he said, getting up. 'I'll do that.'

*   *   *

Jens leaned back in his chair and smiled, his cheeks flushed, his bow tie glittering. He reminded Harry of a birthday boy.

'I'm almost glad I was locked up for a while. It makes you appreciate the simple things so much more. Like a bottle of Dom Perignon 1985, for example.'

He snapped his fingers at the waiter, who hurried over to the table, lifted the dripping champagne bottle out of the cooler and filled his glass.

'I love it when they do that. Makes you feel like Superman. What do you say, Harry?'

Harry fingered the glass. 'Fair enough. Not my thing actually.'

'We're different, Harry.'

Jens made this declaration with a smile. He seemed to have filled out his suit again. Or else he had just changed into an almost identical one. Harry wasn't sure.

'Some people need luxury like others need air,' Jens said. 'An expensive car, nice clothes and a bit of good service are simply a must for me to feel, well, for me to feel that I exist. Can you understand that?'

Harry shook his head.

'Mmm.' Jens held the champagne glass by the stem. 'I'm the decadent one of the two of us. You should trust your first impressions. I *am* a sack of shit. And for as long as there is room for us sacks of shit in this world I intend to continue being one. *Skål.*'

He savoured the champagne in his mouth before swallowing. Then he grinned and groaned with delight. Harry had to smile and raised his own glass, but Jens gave him a look of disapproval.

'Water? Isn't it time you began to enjoy life, Harry? You really don't have to be so strict with yourself.'

'Sometimes you do.'

'Rubbish. All humans are basically hedonists, some just take longer to realise it. Have you got a woman?'

'No.'

'Isn't it about time?'

'Certainly is. But I can't see what that has to do with enjoying life.'

'True enough.' Jens peered into his glass. 'Have I told you about my sister?'

'The one you rang?'

'Yes. She's single, you know.'

Harry laughed. 'Don't imagine you owe me a debt of gratitude, Jens. I didn't do much, apart from getting you arrested.'

'I'm not joking. Wonderful girl. She's an editor, but I think she works too hard to have time to find herself a man. She also frightens them away. She's like you, strict, a mind of her own. By the way, have you noticed that that's what all Norwegian girls say after they've won some Miss Something-Or-Other award when they have to describe themselves to journalists: that they've got a mind of their own? Minds of their own seem to be two a krone.'

Jens looked pensive.

'My sister took my mother's name when she came of age. And when she came of age, she did it with a vengeance.'

'I'm not so sure your sister and I would be a great match.'

'Why not?'

'Well, I'm a coward. What I'm looking for is a self-effacing woman in a social profession who is so beautiful no one has dared tell her.'

Jens laughed. 'You can marry my sister with a clear conscience. It doesn't matter if you don't like her; she works so hard you won't see much of her anyway.'

'So why did you ring her at home and not at work? It was two in the afternoon when you called?'

Jens shook his head. 'Don't tell anyone, but I can never keep track of the time differences. Whether I have to add or subtract hours, I mean. It's very embarrassing. My father says I'm pre-senile. Says it comes from my mother's side.'

He hastened to add, with an assurance to Harry, that his sister didn't show any signs of the same, more the opposite.

'That's enough, Jens. Tell me more about yourself. Have you begun to think about marriage?'

'Shh, don't say things like that. The word alone gives me palpitations. Marriage . . .' Jens shuddered. 'The problem is that, on the one hand, I'm not cut out for monogamy, but on the other I am a romantic. Once I'm married I can't mess around with other women. Do you know what I mean? And the thought of never having sex with any other women is quite overwhelming, don't you think?'

Harry tried to be empathetic.

'Suppose I do actually go out with the girl from the lift, what do you think would come of it? Utter panic, right? All that just to prove to myself that I'm still capable of taking an interest in another woman. Bit of a failure really. Hilde is . . .' Jens searched for the words. 'She has something I haven't found with anyone else. And believe me, I have looked. I'm not sure I can quite explain what it is, but I don't want to lose it because I know it could be difficult to find again.'

Harry thought that was just as good a reason as any he had heard. Jens rolled the glass between his fingers and gave a lopsided smile.

'Being held on remand must have really got to me because I don't normally talk about these things. Promise you won't tell any of my friends.'

The waiter came over to the table and beckoned to them.

'Come on. It's already started,' Jens said.

'What's already started?'

The waiter led them to the back of the restaurant, through the kitchen and up a narrow staircase. Washtubs stood stacked up on top of one another in the corridor and an old woman in a chair grinned at them with black teeth.

'Betel nuts,' Jens said. 'Dreadful habit. They chew them until the brain rots and their teeth fall out.'

Behind a door Harry heard voices yelling. The waiter opened it, and then they were in a large windowless loft. Twenty to thirty men stood in a cramped circle. Hands were gesticulating and pointing while dog-eared banknotes were counted and passed between them at dizzying speeds. Most of the men were white, some of them in light-coloured linen suits.

'Cockfighting,' Jens explained. 'Private arrangement.'

'Why's that?' Harry had to shout to be heard. 'I mean, I've read that cockfighting is still legal in Thailand.'

'To a certain extent. The authorities have allowed a modified form of cockfighting in which the claw is tied to the back of the foot so that they can't kill each other. And the time is restricted. It's not a fight to the death. This one is run on old rules, so there's no limit to the stakes. Shall we go closer?'

Harry towered over the men in front of them and could easily see into the ring. Two cocks, both brownish-red and orange, strutted around with their heads wagging, apparently uninterested in each other.

'How are they going to make them fight?' Harry asked.

'Don't worry. Those two cocks hate each other more than you and I ever could.'

'Why?'

Jens looked at him. 'They're in the same ring. They're cocks.'

Then, as if at a signal, they went for each other. All Harry could see was fluttering wings and flying straw. Men were screaming in a frenzy, and some of them were jumping up and down. A strange bitter-sweet smell of adrenalin and sweat spread through the room.

'Can you see the one with the comb cut in the middle?' Jens said.

Harry couldn't.

'It's the winner.'

'How can you see that?'

'I can't. I know. I knew before the fight.'

'How . . .?'

'Don't ask.' Jens grinned.

The screams died. One cock was left in the ring. Some men groaned, one man in a grey linen suit had thrown his hat to the ground in frustration. Harry watched the cock dying. A muscle twitched beneath the feathers; then it was motionless. It was absurd; it had looked like a sort of romp, a mass of wings, legs and screaming.

A bloodstained feather sailed past his face. The cock was lifted out of the ring by a man in baggy trousers. He looked as if he was going to burst into tears. The other cock had resumed its strutting. Harry could see the split comb now.

The waiter came over to Jens with a wad of banknotes. Some of the men glanced towards him, some nodded, but no one said anything.

'Don't you ever lose?' Harry asked when they were back in the restaurant again. Jens had lit up a cigar and ordered a cognac, an aged Richard Hennessy 40%. The waiter had to ask for the name twice. It was hard to grasp that this Jens was the same man Harry had comforted on the phone the night before.

'Do you know why gambling is an illness and not a profession, Harry? It's because the gambler loves risk. He lives and breathes for that quivering uncertainty.'

He puffed out the smoke in broad rings.

'With me it's the other way round. I can go to extremes to eliminate risk. What you saw me win today covers my costs and all my effort, and that's no small amount, believe you me.'

'But you never lose?'

'It gives a reasonable return.'

'A reasonable return? You mean enough for gamblers sooner or later to be forced to hock everything they have.'

'Something like that.'

'But isn't some of the charm of gambling lost if you know the result?'

'Charm?' Jens held up the wad of money. 'I think this has enough charm. It can provide me with this.' He spread an open palm around him.

'I'm a simple man.' He studied the glow of his cigar. 'OK, let's call a spade a spade. I'm a bit short on charm.'

He burst into a braying laugh. Harry had to smile along with him.

Jens glanced at his watch and jumped up.

'Lots to do before the USA opens. Things are going mad. See you. Give my sister some thought.'

He was out of the door, and Harry was left sitting and smoking a cigarette and giving the sister some thought. Then he took a taxi to Patpong. He didn't know what he was looking for, but he went into a go-go bar, almost ordered a beer and quickly went out again. He ate frogs' legs at Le Boucheron and the owner came over and explained in very poor English that he was longing to return to la Normandie. Harry told him that his father had been there during D-Day. It wasn't exactly true, but at least it cheered the Frenchman up.

Harry paid and found another bar. A girl in ridiculously high heels perched down beside him, stared at him with her large brown eyes and asked if he wanted a blow job. Of course I bloody do, he thought, and shook his head. He registered that they were showing highlights from a Manchester United match on the TV hanging over the glass shelves in the bar. In the mirror he could see the girls dancing on the small, intimate stage directly behind him. They had stuck tiny gold stars on their breasts to cover the nipples so that the bar wasn't breaking the law against nudity. And each of the girls wore a number on their skimpy panties. The police didn't ask what it was for, but everyone knew it was to avoid misunderstandings when customers wanted to hire girls from the bar. Harry had already seen her. Number 20. Dim was at the back of four girls dancing, and her tired eyes swept over the row of men at the bar like radar. Now and then a fleeting smile crossed her lips, but it didn't rouse any life in her eyes. She appeared to have made contact with a man wearing a kind of tropical uniform. German, Harry guessed, without knowing why. He watched her hips grind lazily from side to side, her shiny black hair flick off her back as she turned, and her smooth, glowing skin that seemed to be illuminated from inside. Had it not been for her eyes, she would have been beautiful, Harry thought.

For a fraction of a second their eyes met in the mirror, and Harry immediately felt uneasy. She showed no signs of recognition, but he shifted his gaze to the TV screen, which showed the back of a player being substituted. Same number. 'Solskjær' it said at the top of the shirt. Harry woke as if from a dream.

'Bloody hell!' he shouted, knocking over his glass and sending Coke into the lap of his devoted courtesan. Harry forced his way out to the sound of indignant shouts behind him: You not my friend!

36
Sunday 19 January

TWO MEN IN GREEN CHARGED through the bushes, one bent low with a wounded comrade over his shoulders. They laid him down under cover, behind a fallen tree trunk, as they raised their rifles, took aim and fired into the undergrowth. A dry voice announced that this was East Timor's hopeless struggle against President Suharto and his brutal regime.

On the podium a man nervously rustled his papers. He had travelled far and wide to talk about his country, and this evening was important. There might not have been many people in the assembly room at the Foreign Correspondents' Club Thailand, only forty to fifty in the audience, but they were vital, together they could carry the message on to millions of readers. He had seen the film that was being shown a hundred times, and he knew that in two minutes he would have to step into the firing line.

Ivar Løken started involuntarily when he felt a hand on his shoulder and a voice whispered: 'We have to talk. Now.'

In the semi-gloom he made out Hole's face. He got up and they left the room together, while a guerrilla with half of his face burnt into a stiff mask explained why he had spent the last eight years of his life in the Indonesian jungle.

'How did you find me?' he asked once they were outside.

'I spoke to Tonje Wiig. Do you come here often?'

'Not sure how often often is, but I like to keep up to date. And I meet useful people here.'

'Like people from the Swedish and Danish embassies?'

The gold tooth glinted. 'As I said, I like to keep up to date. What's up?'

'Everything.'

'Oh yes?'

'I know who you're after. And I know the two cases are connected.'

Løken's smile vanished.

'The funny thing is, when I first got here I found myself a stone's throw from the place you had under surveillance.'

'You don't say.' It was hard to decide if there was any sarcasm in Løken's voice.

'Inspector Crumley took me on a sightseeing trip up the river. She showed me a house belonging to a Norwegian who'd moved a whole temple from Burma to Bangkok. He had a conversation with the ambassador the day he died, but we haven't been able to get hold of him. I met his friend, Bork, at the funeral, and he said he was away on business. But you know Ove Klipra, don't you?'

Løken didn't answer.

'Well, the connection didn't strike me until I was watching a football match earlier on.'

'A football match?'

'The world's most famous Norwegian happens to play for Klipra's favourite club.'

'So?'

'Do you know what Ole Gunnar Solskjær's number is?'

'No, why on earth should I?'

'Well, boys all over the world do, and you can buy his shirt in sports shops from Cape Town to Vancouver. Sometimes adults buy the shirt as well.'

Løken nodded as he stared intently at Harry. 'Number 20,' he said.

'As in the picture. A couple of other things struck me as well. The shaft of the knife we found in Molnes's back had a special glass mosaic and a professor of art history has told us it was a very old knife from northern Thailand, probably made by the Shan people. I spoke to him earlier this evening. He told me the Shan people had also spread to parts of Burma, where among other things they built temples. A characteristic feature of these temples was that the windows and doors were often decorated with the same type of glass mosaic as on the knife. I looked in on the professor on the way here and showed him one of your photos. He had absolutely no doubt that this was a window in a Shan temple, Løken.'

They could hear that the speaker had started. The voice sounded metallic and shrill in the loudspeakers.

'Job well done, Hole. What now?'

'Now you tell me what's going on behind the scenes and I'll take over the rest of the investigation.'

Løken roared with laughter. 'You're joking, aren't you?'

Harry wasn't.

'An interesting suggestion, Hole, but I don't think that will wash. My bosses—'

'I don't think *suggestion* is the right word, Løken. Try *ultimatum*.'

Løken laughed even louder. 'You've got cojones, I'll give you that, Hole. Just what makes you think you're in a position to impose an ultimatum?'

'That you will have an immense problem when I explain to the Bangkok Police Chief what's going on.'

'They'll boot you out, Hole.'

'For what? First of all, my mandate here is to investigate a murder, not to save the arses of some bureaucrats in Oslo. I personally don't have an objection to you trying to haul in a paedophile, but it's not my responsibility. And when parliament gets to hear that they've been kept in the dark about an illegal investigation, my guess is that a few others are in far more danger of being given the sack than me. Way I see it, the chances of unemployment are greater if I become an accessory and keep this to myself. Cigarette?'

Harry held out a newly opened packet of twenty Camel. Løken shook his head, then changed his mind. Harry lit up for both of them, and they sat in two chairs beside the wall. From the hall came the sound of loud applause.

'Why didn't you just let it go, Hole? You've known for a long time that your job here was to tie things up neatly and avoid a fuss, so why couldn't you have bent with the wind and saved yourself and us a whole lot of trouble?'

Harry inhaled deeply and blew out in one long exhalation. Most of the smoke stayed inside.

'I started smoking Camel again this autumn,' Harry said, patting his pocket. 'I had a girlfriend once who smoked Camel. I wasn't allowed to smoke hers; she thought it could become a bad habit. We went InterRailing and on the train between Pamplona and Cannes I ran out of cigarettes. She said that would teach me a lesson. The journey was almost ten hours, and in the end I had to go and bum a cigarette off someone in another compartment while she puffed away on her Camels. Weird, eh?'

He held up the cigarette and blew on the glow.

'Well, I continued bumming smokes off strangers when we arrived in Cannes. To start with, she thought it was funny. When I started to flit from table to table at restaurants in Paris, she thought it was less funny and said I could have one of hers, but I refused. When she met Norwegian friends in Amsterdam and I began to bum fags off them while her packet was on the table, she thought I was being childish. She bought me a packet, and said begging for cigarettes wasn't on, but I left it in the hotel room. When we were back in Oslo and I continued there she said I was sick in the head.'

'Has this story got a point?'

'Yes, she stopped smoking.'

Løken chuckled. 'So there's a happy ending.'

'At about the same time she met a musician from London.'

Løken spluttered. 'You must have gone a bit too far then.'

'Of course.'

'But you didn't learn much from it?'

'No.'

They smoked in silence.

'I see,' Løken said, stubbing out his cigarette. People had started coming out of the room. 'Let's go somewhere and have a beer and I'll give you the whole story.'

'Ove Klipra builds roads. Apart from that, we know very little about him. We know he left for Thailand as a twenty-five-year-old with his engineering degree unfinished and a bad reputation, and that he changed his name from Pedersen to Klipra, which is the name of the area in Ålesund where he grew up.'

They were sitting on a deep leather sofa, and in front of them were a stereo, a TV and a table with one beer, a bottle of water, two microphones and a song book. Harry had at first assumed Løken was joking when he said they were going to a karaoke bar, until he had the reason explained to him. They could hire a soundproof room on an hourly basis, no names, order what they wanted to drink, and beyond that they would be left in peace. Also, there would be the right number of people for them to come and go unnoticed. It was simply the ultimate place for secret meetings, and it appeared it wasn't the first time Løken had been there.

'What kind of bad reputation?'

'When we started to delve deeper into this case it turned out there had been a couple of episodes with underage boys in Ålesund. Nothing was reported, but rumours spread and he found it an opportune moment to move. When he came here he registered an engineering company, had some business cards made, on which he called himself Doctor, and started knocking on doors saying he could build roads. At that time, twenty years ago, there were only two ways to get your hands on road-building projects: either by being related to someone in government or by being rich enough to bribe the same. Klipra was neither and of course the odds were against him. But he learned two things you can be sure formed the basis of the fortune he has today: Thai and flattery. I haven't made up the bit about flattery; he has boasted of it to Norwegians living here. He claims he became so skilled at grinning that even the Thais thought it was too much. In addition, he shared his interest in young boys with a few of the politicians with whom he began to associate. It was perhaps no disadvantage to share vices with them when the contracts for building the so-called Hopewell Bangkok Elevated Road and Train System, BERTS, were handed out.'

'Road and train?'

'Yes. You've probably noticed the big steel pillars they're driving into the ground everywhere in town.'

Harry nodded.

'For the moment there are six thousand pillars, but there will be more. And not just for the motorway because the new train will be above that. We're talking fifty kilometres of ultra-modern motorway and sixty kilometres of rails worth twenty-five billion kroner in order to save this town from suffocating itself. Do you understand? This project must be the grandest road-building project in any city ever, the Messiah of tarmac and sleepers.'

'And Klipra's in on it?'

'No one seems to know who's in or out. What's clear is that the original principal player from Hong Kong has withdrawn and the budget and the schedule are likely to go tits up.'

'A budget overspend? I'm shocked,' Harry commented drily.

'But that means there will definitely be more for the other players, and my guess is Klipra is already well ensconced in the project. If some drop out, the politicians will have to accept that the others adjust their bids. If Klipra has the financial capacity to take a bite of the cake he's been offered, he can soon become one of the region's most powerful entrepreneurs.'

'Yes, but what does this have to do with child abuse?'

'Just that powerful men have a tendency to bend laws in their favour. I have no reason to doubt the present government's integrity, but it hardly increases the chances of an extradition if the man has political influence and an arrest would further delay the whole building programme.'

'So what are you doing?'

'Things are moving. We're waiting for the new extradition agreement to come into effect. Once it's in place, we wait a little, arrest Klipra and explain to the Thai authorities that the photos were taken after the agreement was signed.'

'And convict him for having sex with minors?'

'Plus a murder perhaps.'

Harry recoiled in his chair.

'Did you imagine you were the only person to link the knife with Klipra, Detective?' Løken said, trying to light his pipe.

'What do you know about the knife?' Harry asked.

'I escorted Tonje Wiig to the motel when she identified the ambassador. I took a couple of photos.'

'While there a crowd of police officers standing around watching?'

'Well, it's a very little camera. It can fit in a wristwatch, like this one.' Løken smiled. 'You can't buy them in shops.'

'And then you connected the glass mosaic with Klipra's house?'

'I've been in contact with one of the people involved in the sale of the temple to Klipra, a *pongyi* at the Mahasi Centre in Rangoon. The knife was part of the decorations in the temple and bought by Klipra. According to the monk, these are made in pairs. There should be another knife which is identical.'

'Wait a minute,' Harry said. 'If you contacted this monk you must have had an inkling that the knife was in some way connected to Burmese temples.'

Løken shrugged.

'Come on,' Harry said, 'you're not an art historian as well. We had to use a professor just to establish there was a link with a Shan something or other. You suspected Klipra even before you asked.'

Løken burnt his fingers and threw the match away, annoyed.

'I had reason to believe the murder could have had something to do with Klipra. You see, I was sitting in the flat opposite Klipra's place the day the ambassador was murdered.'

'And?'

'Atle Molnes drove round at about seven. At eight he and Klipra left in the ambassador's car.'

'Are you sure it was them? I've seen the car and as with most embassy cars the windows are tinted, almost impenetrable.'

'I saw Klipra through the camera lens when the car arrived. It parked in the garage and there's a door leading from it into the house, so at first I only saw Klipra getting up and walking to the door. Then I didn't see anyone for a while until I caught sight of the ambassador walking around the sitting room. Then the car left again, and Klipra had gone.'

'You can't be sure it was the ambassador.'

'Why not?'

'Because from where you were sitting you would only have seen the bottom half of him, the rest was hidden by the mosaic.'

Løken laughed. 'Well, that was more than enough,' he said and finally managed to get the pipe lit. He puffed contentedly. 'Because there was only one person who walked around in a bright yellow suit like his.'

In other circumstances Harry might have obliged with a grin, but right now there were too many other things churning round in his head.

'Why haven't Torhus and the Police Commissioner been informed about this?'

'Who says they haven't?'

Harry could feel some pressure behind his eyes. The politicians had kept him completely in the dark. He looked around for something to smash.

37

Sunday 19 January

IT WAS GETTING ON FOR eleven when he got home.

'You have a visitor,' the guard at the gate said.

Harry took the lift up, lay on his back by the pool and listened to the tiny, rhythmical splashes as Runa swam.

'You have to go home,' he said after some time. She didn't answer, and he got up and walked the whole way down to his flat.

Bjarne Møller stood by the window looking out. It was early evening but already pitch black. The cold wasn't going to relinquish its grip in the near future, it seemed. The boys thought it was great fun and came to the table with their fingers frozen and cheeks red while arguing about who had jumped the furthest.

Time went so fast; it wasn't very long since he held them between his skis and ploughed down the hills from Grefsenkollen Ridge. Yesterday he had gone into their bedroom and asked if he should read to them and they had just gave him a funny look.

Trine had said he looked tired. Was he? Maybe. There was a lot to think about, more than he had imagined perhaps when he accepted the job as PAS. If it wasn't reports, meetings and budgets, then one of his officers was banging on the door with a problem Bjarne was unable to solve – a wife who wanted a separation, a mortgage that had grown out of control or nerves that were fraying.

The police work he had been looking forward to when he took the job, leading investigations, had become a subsidiary matter. And still he hadn't got to grips with hidden agendas, reading between the lines or career games. Now and then he wondered if he should still be there, but he knew Trine appreciated the higher salary band. And the boys wanted jump skis. Perhaps it was time they had the computers they had been asking for as well. Tiny snowflakes swirled against the windowpane. He had been such a good policeman.

The telephone rang.

'Møller.'

'Hole. Did you know all the time?'

'Hello? Harry, is that you?'

'Did you know I was chosen especially so that this investigation wouldn't get off the ground?'

Møller lowered his voice. He had forgotten about jump skis and computers. 'I have no idea what you're talking about.'

'I just want to hear you say you didn't know people in Oslo suspected who the murderer was from the word go.'

'OK, Harry. I didn't know . . . By which I mean I don't know what the bloody hell you're talking about.'

'The Police Commissioner and Dagfinn Torhus from the Ministry of Foreign Affairs have known all along that the ambassador and a Norwegian by the name of Ove Klipra drove off in the same car from Klipra's home half an hour before the ambassador arrived at the motel. They also know Klipra had a damn good motive for killing the ambassador.'

Møller sat down heavily. 'And that is?'

'Klipra is one of the richest men in Bangkok. The ambassador was in severe financial difficulties, and he had even taken the initiative to start a highly illegal investigation of Klipra for child abuse. When the ambassador was found dead he had photos in his briefcase of Klipra with a boy. It's not that hard to imagine the reason for his visit to Klipra. Molnes must have managed to convince Klipra that he was solo on this and he had taken the photos himself. Then he must have given him a price for "all copies". Isn't that what they say? Of course it's impossible to check how many copies Molnes had made, but Klipra probably realised that a blackmailer who is also an incurable gambler, like the ambassador, was bound to come knocking again. And again. So Klipra suggested a drive, got out at the bank and told Molnes to go to the motel and wait, he would follow with the money. When Klipra arrived he didn't even have to look for the room, he could see the ambassador's car parked outside, couldn't he. Shit, the guy even managed to trace the knife back to Klipra.'

'Which guy?'

'Løken. Ivar Løken. An old intelligence officer who's been oper-ating here for several years. Employed by the UN, worked with refugees, he says, but what the hell do I know? I reckon he got most of his wages from NATO or something like that. He's been spying on Klipra for months.'

'Didn't the ambassador know that? I thought you said he initi-ated the investigation?'

'What do you mean?'

'You maintain the ambassador went there to blackmail Klipra even though he knew the intelligence guy was watching them.'

'Of course he knew. He got the copies of the photos from Løken, didn't he. So? There's nothing suspicious about the Norwegian ambassador paying a courtesy visit to Bangkok's richest Norwegian, is there.'

'Maybe not. What else did this Løken say?'

'He told me the real reason I was chosen for this job.'

'Which is?'

'The guys who knew about the investigation into Klipra took a risk. If they were caught all hell would break loose; there would be a political outcry, heads would roll, et cetera. So when the ambassador was found murdered and they had a pretty good idea who was responsible they had to ensure the murder inquiry didn't cast any light on their investigations. They had to find a happy medium, do *something*, but not so much that their cover was blown. By sending a Norwegian police officer they couldn't be accused of doing nothing. I was told that they couldn't send a team of officers because the Thai force would take offence.'

Harry's laughter merged with another conversation hurtling somewhere between earth and a satellite.

'Instead they picked a man they reckoned was the least likely to uncover anything at all. Dagfinn Torhus had done his research and found the perfect candidate, someone who definitely wouldn't cause them any problems. Because he would probably spend his nights bent over a crate of beer and his days sleeping off a hangover. Harry Hole was perfect because he barely functions. They could justify the choice, if the question came up, by saying the officer in question had received enthusiastic recommendations after a similar job in Australia. If that wasn't enough PAS Møller had vouched for him, and he should be the best person to judge, shouldn't he.'

Møller didn't like what he heard. Even less because he could see it clearly now, the Police Commissioner's gaze across the table when the question was posed, the imperceptible raised eyebrow. It had been an order.

'But why would Torhus and the Commissioner risk their jobs just to catch a paedophile?'

'Good question.'

Silence. Neither of them dared put into words what they were thinking.

'So what happens now, Harry?'

'Now it's Operation Save Our Arses.'

'Meaning?'

'Meaning that no one wants to be left holding the can. Neither Løken nor I. The deal is he and I keep our gobs shut about this for now and haul in Klipra together. I suppose you'd rather take over the case from there, PAS? Go directly to Storting maybe? You've got an arse to save as well, you know.'

Møller mulled that one over. He wasn't sure he wanted to be saved. The worst that could happen was that they would make him do police work again.

'This is heavy stuff, Harry. I need to think, so I'll ring you back, OK?'

'OK.'

They were receiving faint signals from another conversation in space, which went quiet all of a sudden. They listened to the sound of stars.

'Harry?'

'Yes?'

'To hell with the thinking. I'm with you.'

'Thought you would be, boss.'

'Ring me when you've arrested him.'

'Oh yes, I forgot to say. No one's seen Klipra since the ambassador was murdered.'

38

Monday 20 January

LØKEN PASSED THE NIGHT BINOCULARS to Harry.

'All clear,' he said. 'I know the routines. The guard will go and sit in the hut at the bottom of the drive by the gate. He won't do another round for twenty minutes.'

They were sitting in the loft of a house about a hundred metres from Klipra's property. The window was boarded up, but between two of the planks there was just enough room for binoculars. Or a camera. Between the loft and Klipra's dragonhead-bedecked teak house was a line of low sheds, a road and a high white wall topped with barbed wire.

'The only problem in this town is that there are people everywhere. All the time. So we'll have to walk round and climb over the wall behind that shed over there.'

He pointed and Harry grabbed the binoculars.

Løken had told him to wear discreet, tight-fitting, dark clothes. He chose black jeans and his old black Joy Division T-shirt. He had thought about Kristin when he put on the T-shirt; it was the only one he had managed to make her like, Joy Division. He thought that probably made up for her not liking Camel.

'Let's get going,' Løken said.

The air outside was still, and the dust hovered freely over the gravel path. A group of boys were playing *takraw*, standing in a circle and keeping a little rubber ball in the air with their feet, and they didn't notice the two black-clad *farangs*. Harry and Ivar crossed the street, slipped between the sheds and arrived at the wall undetected. The misty night sky reflected a dirty yellow light coming from millions of bigger and smaller lights, never allowing Bangkok to be completely dark on nights like this. Løken threw his small rucksack over the wall and rolled a thin, narrow rubber mat over the barbed wire.

'You first,' he said, interlacing his fingers to give Harry a foothold.

'What about you?'

'Don't worry about me, come on.'

He hoisted Harry up, so that he could grab a post on top of the wall. Harry placed one foot on the mat and heard the wire tear the rubber underneath as he swung the other foot over. He tried not to think about the story of the boy who had slid down the flagpole at Romsdal Fair without remembering the cleat at the bottom with the rope tied round. His grandad had said the boy's castration cries could be heard right across the fjord.

Next second Løken was standing beside him.

'Jeez, that was quick,' Harry whispered.

'Pensioner's exercise for the day.'

With the pensioner in front they ran with their heads down across the lawn, alongside the house wall and stopped at the corner. Løken took out the binoculars and waited until he was sure the guard was looking in the other direction.

'Now!'

Harry set off, trying to imagine he was invisible. It wasn't far to the garage, but it was lit and there was no cover between them and the guard's hut. Løken followed hard on his heels.

Harry had thought there couldn't be so many ways to break into a house, but Løken had insisted on planning everything down to the last detail. When he had stressed that they had to run close together over the last critical phase Harry had asked if it wouldn't be wiser for one to run while the other kept a lookout.

'What for? We'll know if we've been seen. If we run separately the chances of being seen are double. Don't they teach you anything in the police nowadays?' Harry didn't have any objections to the rest of the plan.

A white Lincoln Continental dominated the garage, from where a side door did indeed lead into the house. Løken had counted on the lock of the side door being easier than the main door, and besides, they couldn't be seen from the gate.

He took out his picklock and got down to work.

'Are you checking the time?' he whispered and Harry nodded. According to the timetable there were sixteen minutes till the guard's next round.

After twelve minutes Harry started to feel his whole body itching.

After thirteen minutes he was wishing Sunthorn would appear in a puff of smoke.

After fourteen minutes he knew they would have to abandon the operation.

'Let's get out of here,' he whispered.

'Bit more,' Løken said, stooped over the lock. 'A few seconds, no more.'

'Now!' Harry hissed between gritted teeth.

Løken didn't answer. Harry breathed in and put an arm around his shoulder. Løken turned to him and their eyes met. The gold tooth glinted. 'Bingo,' Løken whispered.

The door slid open without a sound. They crept in and closed it quietly behind them. At that moment they heard steps in the garage, saw the light from a torch through the window over the door and then the door handle was given a rough shake. They stood with their backs against the wall. Harry held his breath with his heart pounding blood around his body. Then the steps faded.

Harry found it difficult to keep his voice down. 'Twenty minutes you said!'

Løken shrugged. 'Give or take.'

Harry counted, breathing through an open mouth.

They switched on their torches and were about to move into the house when there was a crunch beneath Harry's feet.

'What's that?' He shone the torch downwards. There were small white clumps on the dark parquet floor.

Løken shone his torch on the whitewashed wall.

'Ugh, Klipra's a bodger. This house is supposed to be built of nothing but teak. Well, now I've really lost respect for the guy,' he said. 'Come on, Harry. The clock's ticking!'

They searched the house quickly and systematically according to Løken's instructions. Harry concentrated on doing what he was told, remembering where things had been before he moved them, not leaving fingerprints and checking for bits of tape before opening drawers and cupboards. After a couple of hours they sat down at the kitchen table. Løken had found a few child-porn magazines and a revolver that didn't look as if it had been fired for years. He had taken photos of both.

'The guy's left in a tearing hurry,' he said. 'There are two empty suitcases in his bedroom, the toilet bag's in the bathroom and the wardrobes are crammed full.'

'He might have had a third suitcase,' Harry suggested.

Løken regarded him with a mixture of disgust and indulgence. The way he would have looked at a willing but not exactly bright recruit, Harry thought.

'No man has two toilet bags, Hole.'

Recruit, Harry thought.

'One room left,' Løken said. 'The office on the first floor is locked and the lock is some German monster I can't pick.' He took a jemmy from his rucksack.

'I'd been hoping we wouldn't need this,' he said. 'That door's going to be a mess after we've finished.'

'Doesn't matter,' Harry said. 'I think I put his slippers back on the wrong shelf anyway.'

Løken chuckled.

They used the jemmy on the hinges instead of the lock. Harry reacted too slowly and the heavy door fell into the room with a loud bang. They stood still for a few seconds and waited for the guard's shouts.

'Do you think they heard?' Harry asked.

'Nah. There are so many noises per inhabitant here that one bang more or less won't be noticed.'

Their torchlights ran like yellow cockroaches up and down the walls.

On the wall above the desk hung a red-and-white Manchester United banner over a framed poster of the team. Beneath it was the city coat of arms in red and white with a ship, carved in wood.

The torch stopped at a photograph. It showed a man with a broad, smiling mouth, solid double chin and two slightly bulging eyes sparkling with amusement. Ove Klipra looked like a man who laughed a lot. He had blond curls blowing in the wind. The photo must have been taken on board a boat.

'He doesn't exactly fit the picture of a paedophile,' Harry said.

'Paedophiles seldom do,' Løken said. Harry glanced at him, but he was blinded by the torch. 'What's that?'

Harry turned. Løken shone his torch on a grey metal box in the corner. Harry recognised it at once.

'I can tell you what that is,' he said, happy at last to be able to make a contribution. 'It's a tape recorder worth half a million kroner.

I saw an identical one in Brekke's office. It records phone conversations, and the recording and the time code can't be manipulated, so it can be used in legal disputes. Great if you make deals over the phone to the tune of millions.'

Harry flicked through the documents on the desk. He saw letterheads of Japanese and American companies, agreements, contracts, drafts of agreements and amendments to drafts. The transport project, BERTS, was mentioned in many of them. He noticed a stapled booklet with Barclays Thailand on the front. It was a report on a company called Phuridell. Then he shone the torch upwards. And stopped as the light caught an object on the wall.

'Bingo! Look here, Løken. This must be the other knife you were talking about.'

Løken didn't answer; he had his back to Harry.

'Did you hear what I—?'

'We have to get out, Harry. Now.'

Harry turned and saw Løken's torch pointing at a little box on the wall with a red flashing light. At that moment it felt as if he'd had a knitting needle poked in his ear. The whine was so loud he was immediately semi-deaf.

'Delayed alarm!' Løken shouted, already in mid-stride. 'Turn off the torch!'

Harry staggered down the stairs after him in the darkness. They made for the side door to the garage.

'Wait.' Harry had knelt down, and with his hands he swept up the lumps of plaster on the floor.

Outside, they could hear voices and the rattling of keys. A shaft of moonlight, coloured blue by the glass mosaic in the window over the door, fell onto the parquet floor in front of them.

'What are you doing?'

Harry didn't have time to answer because they heard the bolt turn. They made it to the side door, and the next moment they were running, heads down, across the grass as the hysterical whine of the alarm grew fainter and fainter behind them.

'That was a close call,' Løken said when they were on the other side of the wall. Harry looked at him. The moonlight caught his gold tooth. Løken wasn't even out of breath.

39

Monday 20 January

A CABLE HAD BURNT SOMEWHERE in the wall when Harry had shoved the scissors in the socket, so they sat in the flickering light of a candle again. Løken had just opened a bottle of Jim Beam.

'Why are you wrinkling your nose, Hole? Don't you like the smell?'

'There's nothing wrong with the smell.'

'The taste then?'

'The taste's great. Jim and I are old friends.'

'Ah.' Løken poured himself a generous glass. 'Not such good friends any more perhaps?'

'They say he has a bad influence on me.'

'So who keeps you company now?'

Harry raised the Coke bottle. 'American cultural imperialism.'

'Completely dry now?'

'There was a fair bit of beer in the autumn.'

Løken gave a chuckle.

'So there we have it. I've been pondering why on earth Torhus would choose you.'

Harry knew this was an indirect compliment. Løken thought

that Torhus could have chosen bigger idiots. That there had to be another reason, not that he was an incompetent policeman.

Harry nodded towards the bottle. 'Does that dull the nausea?'

Løken raised his eyebrows.

'Does it allow you to forget the job for a while? I mean the boys. The photos, all the shit?'

Løken knocked back the drink and poured himself another. He took a sip, set down the glass and leaned back in his chair.

'I have special qualifications for this job, Harry.'

Harry had a vague idea what he meant.

'I know what they think, what drives them, what gives them a kick, what temptations they can resist and what they can't.' He produced his pipe. 'I've known them for as long as I can remember.'

Harry didn't know what to say. So he held his tongue.

'Did you say dry? Are you good at it, Harry? At renouncing things? Like in the story about the cigarettes. You just take a decision and stick to it whatever happens?'

'Well, yes, I assume so,' Harry said. 'The problem is that the decisions aren't always good.'

Løken chuckled again. Harry was reminded of an old friend who used to chuckle in the same way. He had buried him in Sydney, but he paid Harry regular visits at night.

'We're the same then,' Løken said. 'I've never laid a hand on a child in my life. I've dreamt about it, fantasised about it and cried about it, but I've never done it. Can you comprehend that?'

Harry swallowed.

'I don't know how old I was the first time my stepfather raped me, but I would guess no more than five. I sank an axe in his thigh when I was thirteen. Hit an artery, he went into shock and almost died. He survived, but ended up in a wheelchair. He said it had been an accident. The axe had slipped out of his hand while he was chopping wood. He probably thought we were quits.'

Løken lifted his glass and glared at the brown liquid.

'Perhaps you think this is an enormous paradox,' he said. 'That children who have been sexually abused are the ones with the greatest statistical chance of becoming abusers themselves?'

Harry pulled a face.

'It's true,' Løken said. 'Paedophiles often know exactly what suffering they are inflicting on the children. Many of the abusers have experienced the fear themselves, the confusion and the guilt. Did you know that several psychologists claim there is a close relationship between sexual arousal and a longing for death?'

Harry shook his head. Løken emptied the glass in one draught and grimaced.

'It's the same with vampire bites. You think you're dead and then you wake up and find you've become a vampire yourself. Immortal, with an unquenchable thirst for blood.'

'And with an eternal longing for death?'

'Exactly.'

'And what makes you so different?'

'Everyone's different, Hole.' Løken finished tamping his pipe and set it down on the table. He had taken off his black roll-neck sweater and the sweat on his naked body glistened. He was sinewy and well built, but loose folds of skin and withered muscles betrayed that he had aged and perhaps one day would die after all.

'When they found a child-porn magazine in my locker in the officers' mess at Vardø I was summoned by the station commander. I was lucky, I assume; they didn't report me. I didn't get a black mark on my record, just a request to resign from the air force. Via my intelligence position I had come into contact with what was once called Special Services, the forerunner of the CIA. They sent me on a course in the States, then I was sent to Korea under the pretext of working for the Norwegian field hospital.'

'And who exactly are you working for now?'

Løken shrugged to indicate it didn't really matter.

'Aren't you ashamed?' Harry asked.

'Of course,' Løken said with a tired smile. 'Every day. It's a weakness I have.'

'So why are you telling me all this?' Harry asked.

'Well, first, I'm too old to run around hiding. Second, because I have others to consider apart from myself. And third, because the shame lies more on an emotional plane than an intellectual one.'

One corner of his mouth rose in a sarcastic grin.

'I used to subscribe to the *Archives of Sexual Behavior* to see if any researchers could specify what sort of monster I was. More out of curiosity than shame. I read an article about a paedophile monk in Switzerland who I'm sure had never done anything at all either, but halfway through the article he'd locked himself in a room and drunk cod liver oil containing fragments of glass, so I never finished reading it. I prefer to see myself as a product of my upbringing and environment, but despite everything a moral person. I manage to live with myself, Hole.'

'But, being a paedophile yourself, how can you work with child prostitution? Does it excite you?'

Løken stared down at the table, rapt in thought. 'Have you ever fantasised about raping a woman, Hole? You don't need to answer, I know you have. It doesn't mean you want to rape someone, does it. Nor does it mean you're unfit to work on rape cases. Even if you can understand how a man can lose his self-control it's actually very simple. It's wrong. It's against the law. The bastard will have to pay.'

The third glass was knocked back. He was down to the label on the bottle.

Harry shook his head. 'Sorry, Løken, I'm struggling to accept that. If you buy child pornography, you're a part of it. Without people like you there wouldn't be a market for this filth.'

'True.' Løken's eyes had glazed over. 'I'm no saint. Yes, I've helped to make the world the vale of woes it is. What can I say? As the song says: If it rains, I'm like everyone else, I get wet.'

Harry suddenly felt old as well. Old and tired.

'So what were the lumps of plaster?' Løken asked.

'Just a wild idea. It struck me it was like the plaster on the screwdriver we found in the boot of Molnes's car. Yellowish. Not completely white like normal whitewash. I'll have the lumps analysed and compared with the plaster in the car.'

'And what would that mean?'

Harry shrugged. 'You never know what anything means. Ninety-nine per cent of the information you gather during a case is worthless. You just have to hope you're alert enough for the one per cent under your nose.'

'True enough.' Løken closed his eyes and settled back in the chair.

Harry walked downstairs to the street and bought some noodle soup with king prawns from a toothless man wearing a Liverpool cap. He ladled it from a black cauldron into a plastic bag, tied a knot and bared his gums. In the kitchen Harry found two soup dishes. Løken woke up with a start when he shook him, and they ate in silence.

'I think I know who gave the order for the investigation,' Harry said.

Løken didn't answer.

'I know you couldn't wait to start the undercover work until the agreement with Thailand was signed and sealed. It was urgent, wasn't it. Getting a result was urgent, that's why you jumped the gun.'

'You don't give in, do you.'

'Is that of any significance now?'

Løken blew on the spoon. 'It can take a long time to gather

evidence,' he said. 'Maybe years. The time aspect was more important than anything else.'

'I'd bet there's nothing in writing to trace back to the prime
mover, that Torhus at the Foreign Office is alone, if it ever came
out. Am I right?'

'Good politicians always make sure to cover their backs, don't
they? They have Secretaries of State to do the dirty work. And
Secretaries of State don't give orders. They just tell Directors what
they have to do to accelerate a stalled career path.'

'Are you by any chance referring to Secretary of State Askildsen?'

Løken slurped a prawn into his mouth and chewed in silence.

'So what was dangled in front of Torhus to lead the operation?
A job as Director General?'

'I don't know. We don't talk about that kind of thing.'

'And what about the Police Commissioner? Isn't she risking quite
a bit?'

'She's probably a good Social Democrat, I suppose.'

'Political ambitions?'

'Maybe. Maybe neither of them is risking as much as you think.
Having an office in the same building as the ambassador doesn't
mean—'

'That you're on their payroll? So who do you work for? Are you
a freelancer?'

Løken smiled at his image in the soup. 'Tell me, what happened
to that woman of yours, Hole?'

Harry looked at him in bewilderment.

'The one who stopped smoking.'

'I told you. She met an English musician and went to London
with him.'

'And after that?'

'Who said anything happened after that?'

'You did. The way you talked about her.' Løken laughed. He had put down his spoon and slumped back in the chair. 'Come on, Hole. Did she really stop smoking? For good?'

'No,' Harry said quietly. 'But now she's stopped. For good.'

He looked at the bottle of Jim Beam, closed his eyes and tried to remember the warmth of only one, the first drink.

Harry sat there until Løken fell asleep. Then he hitched his arms under the older man's shoulders and took him to bed, covered him with a blanket and left.

The porter at River Garden was asleep as well. Harry considered waking him, but decided against it – everyone should get some sleep tonight. A letter had been pushed under Harry's door. Harry left it unopened on the bedside table with the other one, stood by the window and watched a freighter glide beneath Taksin Bridge, black and soundless.

40

Tuesday 21 January

IT WAS GETTING ON FOR ten when Harry arrived at the office. He met Nho on his way out.

'Have you heard?'

'Heard what?' Harry yawned.

'The orders from your Police Commissioner in Oslo.'

Harry shook his head.

'We were told at the meeting this morning. The bigwigs have had a get-together.'

Liz jumped in her chair as Harry burst into her office.

'Good morning, Harry?'

'No, it isn't. I didn't get to bed until five. What's this I hear about scaling down the investigation?'

Liz sighed. 'Looks like our Chiefs have been having another powwow. Your Police Commissioner has been talking about budgets and personnel shortages and she wants you back, and our Police Chief's starting to get twitchy because of all the other murder cases we dropped when this one came up. Of course they're not talking about shelving the case, just downgrading it to normal priority.'

'Which means?'

'It means I've been told to make sure you're sitting on a plane in the next couple of days.'

'And?'

'I told them planes are generally fully booked in January, so it could be at least a week.'

'So we've got a week?'

'No, if economy class is full I was told to book first class.'

Harry laughed. 'Thirty thousand kroner. Tight budgets? They're getting jumpy, Liz.'

As Liz leaned back in her chair it creaked.

'Do you want to talk about it, Harry?'

'Do you?'

'I don't know if I *want* to,' she said. 'Some things are best left in peace, aren't they.'

'So why don't we do that?'

She turned her head, opened the blinds and looked out. Harry sat in such a way that the sunlight gave Liz's shiny pate a kind of white halo.

'Do you know what the average salary of a recruit in the national police force is, Harry? A hundred fifty bucks a month. There are a hundred twenty thousand officers in the force trying to provide for their families, but we can't even pay them enough to provide for themselves. Is it so strange that some of them try to supplement their wages by turning a blind eye?'

'No.'

She sighed. 'Personally, I've never managed to leave things be. God knows, I could have done with a bit extra, but I'm not comfortable with that. It probably sounds a bit like a Girl Scout pledge, but in fact someone has to do the job.'

'Furthermore, it's your—'

'Responsibility, yes.' She gave a weary smile. 'We all have our crosses to bear.'

Harry started to talk. Liz fetched some coffee, told the central switchboard she wasn't taking any incoming calls, made a note, got more coffee, studied the ceiling, cursed and finally told Harry to go out so that she could think.

An hour later she called him in again. She was furious.

'Shit, Harry, do you know what you're asking me to do here?'

'Yes. And I can see you know too.'

'I'm risking my job if I agree to cover you and this Løken.'

'Thanking you.'

'Fuck you!'

Harry grinned.

The woman who answered the telephone at Bangkok's Chamber of Commerce rang off when Harry spoke English. He asked Nho to ring instead, and wrote the name Phuridell, which he'd seen on the front page of the report in Klipra's office. 'Just find out what they do, who owns it and so on.'

Nho went to call, and Harry drummed his fingers on the desk until he picked up the phone and made a call.

'Hole,' came the reply. It was of course his father's name, but Harry knew it was habit and it meant the whole family. He made it sound as if his mother was still in the green sitting-room chair doing embroidery or reading a book. Harry had a suspicion he had started talking to her too.

His father had just got up. Harry asked how he was going to spend the day and was surprised to hear he was going to the cabin in Rauland.

'To chop some wood,' he said. 'I'm running out.'

He rarely went to the cabin.

'How's it going?' his father asked.

'Great. I'll soon be home. How's Sis?'

'She's coping. But she's never going to be a cook.'

They both grinned. Harry could visualise what the kitchen looked like after Sis had made the Sunday lunch.

'Well, you'd better bring her something nice back,' he said.

'I'll find her something. What about you? Anything you fancy?'

The line went silent. Harry cursed himself; he knew that they were both thinking the same thing, that what he wanted Harry couldn't buy in Bangkok. That was how it was every time; whenever he thought he had finally got his father out of himself, he said or did something that reminded his father of her and he was lost again, back into his self-imposed, silent isolation. It was worse for Sis. She was doubly alone when Harry wasn't there.

His father coughed. 'You could . . . you could bring one of those Thai shirts.'

'Yes?'

'Yes, that would be nice. And a pair of proper Nike trainers, they're supposed to be so cheap in Thailand. I took out my old ones yesterday and they're no good any more. How's your jogging by the way? Are you up for a test in Hanekleiva?'

As Harry put the receiver down he felt a strange lump at the top of his chest.

For the rest of the day Harry did nothing.

He doodled and wondered if the doodles resembled anything.

Jens called to ask how the case was going. Harry answered that it was a state secret, and Jens understood, but said he would sleep better if he knew they had another lead suspect. Then Jens told him a joke he had just heard on the phone, about a gynaecologist who said to a colleague that one of his patients had a clitoris like a pickled gherkin. 'That big?' the colleague had asked. 'No,' the gynaecologist had answered. 'That salty.'

Jens apologised for the quality of joke that circulated through the finance world.

Afterwards Harry tried telling the joke to Nho, but either his English or Nho's wasn't up to the task because the situation just became embarrassing.

Then he went into Liz and asked if it was all right if he sat there for a while. After an hour she'd had enough of the silent presence and told him to leave.

He ate dinner at Le Boucheron again. The Frenchman spoke to him in French, and Harry smiled and said something in Norwegian.

Harry dreamt about her again. Red hair spread around and the calm, secure eyes. He waited for what usually followed, the seaweed growing out of her mouth and eye sockets, but it didn't happen.

'It's Jens.'

Harry woke up and realised he had answered the phone in his sleep.

'Jens?' He wondered why his heart had suddenly started beating so fast.

'Sorry, Harry, but this is an emergency. Runa's gone.'

Harry was wide awake.

'Hilde's frantic. Runa should have been home for dinner, and now it's three in the morning. I've called the police, and they've alerted their patrol cars, but I wanted to ask you for help as well.'

'To do what?'

'To do what? I don't know. Could you come over here? Hilde's crying her eyes out.'

Harry could imagine the scene. He had no desire to witness the rest.

'Listen, Jens, there's not a lot I can do right now. Give her a Valium if she isn't too drunk and call all Runa's friends.'

'The police said the same. Hilde says she hasn't got any friends.'

'Shit!'

PART FIVE

41

Wednesday 22 January

HILDE MOLNES WAS DEFINITELY TOO drunk for Valium. She was too drunk for most things, apart from getting even drunker.

Jens didn't appear to notice. He kept running in and out of the kitchen with water and ice looking like a hunted animal.

Harry sat on the sofa half listening to her babble.

'She thinks something terrible has happened,' Jens said.

'Tell her that more than eighty per cent of all missing persons turn up in one piece,' Harry said, as though what he said needed to be translated into her own babblespeak.

'I've told her that. But she thinks someone's done something to Runa. She can feel it in her bones, she says.'

'Nonsense!'

Jens perched on the edge of a chair wringing his hands. He seemed totally incapable of thought or action and looked at Harry imploringly. 'Runa and Hilde have argued a great deal recently. I wondered perhaps . . . if she's run off to punish her mother. It's not beyond the realms of possibility.'

Hilde Molnes coughed, and there was movement from the sofa.

She sat herself up and gulped down some more gin. The tonic was long forgotten.

'She gets like that sometimes,' Jens said, as if she weren't there. And in a way she wasn't, Harry could see. Her jaw had dropped and she was snoring softly. Jens glanced at her.

'The first time I met her she told me she drinks tonic to avoid catching malaria. It contains quinine, you know. But it tastes so boring without gin.' He smiled wanly and lifted the phone again to check the dial tone was there. 'In case she . . .'

'I understand,' Harry said.

They took a seat on the terrace and listened to the town. The sounds of pneumatic drills carried above the hum of the traffic.

'The new elevated motorway,' Jens said. 'They're working on it day and night now. It's going to go straight through the quarter over there.' He pointed.

'I've heard a Norwegian's involved in the project, Ove Klipra. Do you know him?' Harry looked at Jens from the corner of his eye.

'Ove Klipra, yes, of course. We're his biggest broker. I've done quite a few currency deals for him.'

'Oh yes? Do you know what he's up to at the moment?'

'Up to? He's been buying a lot of companies, if that's what you mean.'

'What kind of companies?'

'Mostly smaller entrepreneur-driven companies. He tends to develop capacity to be able to take on a greater share of the BERTS transport contract by buying up subcontractors.'

'Is that wise?'

Jens's spirits rose, obviously relieved to think about something else. 'As long as the buy-outs can be financed, it is. And as long as the companies don't go down the drain before they're awarded the expected commissions.'

'Do you know a company called Phuridell?'

'Certainly do.' Jens laughed. 'Klipra asked us to do some analysis on them and we recommended he should buy. The question, though, is how you know about Phuridell.'

'It wasn't a very lucky recommendation, was it?'

'No, not exactly . . .' Jens seemed perplexed.

'I got someone to sniff around the company yesterday and it turns out that to all intents and purposes it's gone bankrupt,' Harry said.

'That's correct, but what makes you so interested in Phuridell?'

'Let me put it this way: I'm more interested in Klipra. You have a general idea of what he owns. How hard will this hit him?'

Jens shrugged. 'Normally it wouldn't be a problem, but along with BERTS he's financed so many buy-outs on credit that the whole thing is a house of cards. One puff of wind and it could collapse, if you know what I mean. And then Klipra's had it as well.'

'So he bought Phuridell on your company's – or should I say your – recommendation. Only two weeks later it goes bust and now there's a chance that everything he's built up will crash to the ground because of one broker's advice. I don't know much about company analyses, but I do know that three weeks is a very short time. He must have reckoned you'd sold him a second-hand car without an engine. Cowboys like you should be behind bars.'

The direction of Harry's thoughts began to dawn on Jens.

'You don't mean Ove Klipra . . .? You're joking!'

'Well, I have a theory.'

'And that is?'

'Ove Klipra murdered the ambassador at the motel and made sure the finger of suspicion pointed at you.'

Jens stood up. 'Now you're really off beam, Harry.'

'Sit down and listen, Jens.'

Jens dropped back down into the chair with a sigh. Harry leaned across the table.

'Ove Klipra is an aggressive man, isn't he? A so-called man of action?'

Jens hesitated. 'Yes.'

'Suppose Atle Molnes has something on Klipra and demands a large sum of money from him just as Klipra is fighting to keep his head above water.'

'What sort of something?'

'Let's just say that Molnes needs money and he's got his hands on some material that could make Klipra's life very uncomfortable. Normally Klipra might have been able to deal with it, but in this already tight spot the pressure's too much for him. He feels like a cornered rat. Are you with me?'

Jens nodded.

'They leave Klipra's house in the ambassador's car because Klipra insists they should do the handover of the compromising material and the money in a more discreet place. The ambassador has no objections, with good reason. I doubt Klipra has you on his mind when he steps out of the car by his bank and sends the ambassador off to the motel. Which he does so that he can later get into the motel unseen. But then he starts thinking. Perhaps he can kill two birds with one stone. He knows the ambassador had visited you earlier in the afternoon and you would be drawn into the police inquiry anyway. Then he started toying with the idea: perhaps *kind herr* Brekke hasn't got an alibi for the evening?'

'Why on earth would he think that?'

'Because he's requested a company analysis from you for the day after. You've been his broker for so long that he knows a bit about how you work. Perhaps he even rings you from a phone box and has confirmation that you aren't taking calls and no one else can give you an alibi. He has tasted blood, now he wants to go further and persuade the police you're lying.'

'The video recording?'

'As you're Klipra's regular currency adviser he must have visited you several times and knows the system in the car park. Perhaps Molnes mentioned in passing that you had accompanied him down to his car, and he knew you would say that in your statement to the police. And any half-decent detective would check this on the video.'

'So Ove Klipra bribed the attendant and killed him afterwards with prussic acid? Sorry, Harry, but it's asking too much to imagine that Ove Klipra would haggle with a black kid, buy opium and spike it with prussic acid in his kitchen.'

Harry took the last cigarette from his packet; he had been saving it for as long as he could. He glanced at his watch. Actually there was no reason to believe that Runa would phone at five in the morning. Yet he noticed that he made sure the phone was on the periphery of his vision. Jens proffered his lighter before Harry had a chance to find his own.

'Thank you. Do you know anything about Klipra's background, Jens? Did you know he came here as a jack of all trades but in reality he was escaping from Norway amid ugly rumours that had started to spread.'

'I knew he never finished the engineering degree he started in Norway, yes. The rest is news to me.'

'Do you think that a refugee like him, someone who is already an outsider in society, has any scruples about using the means that are necessary to flourish, especially when the means are more or less accepted everywhere? Klipra has been in one of the world's most corrupt industries in one of the world's most corrupt countries for more than thirty years. Have you heard the song, "If it rains, I'm like everyone else, I get wet"?'

Jens shook his head.

'What I'm saying is that as a businessman Klipra plays according to the same rules as everyone else. These people have to make sure they don't get their hands mucky, that's why they hire other people to do their dirty work. I would guess Klipra doesn't even know what Jim Love died of.'

Harry drew on his cigarette. It didn't taste as good as he imagined it would.

'I see,' Jens said at length. 'But there is an explanation for the bankruptcy, so I don't understand why he would blame me. What happened was we bought the company from a multinational concern who hadn't fixed the price of its dollar debt as they had dollars coming in from other daughter companies.'

'What?'

'To cut a long story short – as the company broke away and came into Klipra's possession, the dollar came under incredible pressure. It was like a ticking bomb. I told him to fix the debt instantly by selling dollar futures, but he said he would wait because the dollar was overvalued. With normal currency fluctuations you could say that in the worst-case scenario he was taking a risk. But it was worse than a worst-case scenario. When the dollar almost doubled in value relative to the baht over three weeks, the company's debt doubled as well. The company didn't go bust in the course of the three weeks but three *days!*'

Jens stressed the latter so loudly that Hilde Molnes twitched and mumbled something in her sleep. He looked over with concern and waited until she had rolled onto her side and started to snore again.

'Three days!' he repeated in a whisper, and indicated how short the time was with his thumb and first finger.

'So you think it wouldn't be reasonable of him to blame you?'

Jens shook his head. Harry stubbed out his cigarette; it had been an anticlimax.

'From what I know of Klipra, "reasonable" isn't in his vocabulary. You shouldn't underestimate the streak of irrationality in human nature, Jens.'

'What do you mean?'

'When you bang in a nail and hit your thumb what do you throw at the wall?'

'The hammer?'

'Well, how does it feel to be a hammer, Jens Brekke?'

At half past five Harry called the police station, went through three people before finding someone who could speak acceptable English and she told him they hadn't seen or heard anything.

'She'll turn up,' she said.

'I'm certain she will,' Harry said. 'I imagine she's in some hotel. Before long she'll be ringing for breakfast.'

'What?'

'I imagine . . . never mind. Thanks for your help.'

Jens accompanied him down the staircase. Harry gazed up at the sky; it was getting lighter.

'When all this is over I'd like to ask you a favour,' Jens said. He took a deep breath and smiled sheepishly. 'Hilde has agreed to marry me and I need a best man.'

A couple of seconds passed before Harry realised what he meant. He was so taken aback he didn't know what to say.

Jens was studying the tips of his shoes. 'I know it sounds strange that we're going to get married so soon after the death of her husband, but we have our reasons.'

'Yes, but—'

'You haven't known me long? I know, Harry. However, I wouldn't be a free man now if it weren't for you.' He lifted his chin and smiled. 'Give it some thought anyway.'

As Harry hailed a taxi in the street the sky over the rooftops to the east was lightening. The haze of exhaust fumes, which Harry had presumed disappeared during the night, had just settled between the houses to slumber. Now it was up with the sun and formed part of a magnificent red sunrise. They drove along Silom Road, and the pillars by the road cast long, silent shadows over the blood-drenched tarmac, like sleeping dinosaurs.

Harry sat in bed staring at the bedside table. He'd forgotten all about the letter until now. He picked up the most recent envelope and ripped it open with his key. Perhaps it was because the two envelopes were identical that he had assumed it was from Runa. It was typed, printed on a laser machine, brief and to the point:

> Harry Hole. I can see you. Don't come any closer. She will be returned safe and sound when you are on the plane home. I can find you anywhere. You are alone, very alone. Number 20.

He felt as if someone had gripped him round the throat and he had to stand up to breathe.

This isn't happening, he thought. This *can't* happen – not again.

I can see you . . . Number 20.

He knows what they know.

You are alone.

Somebody had talked. He picked up the phone, but put it down again. Think, think. Woo hadn't taken a thing. He lifted the receiver again and unscrewed the speaking end. Beside the microphone, which was supposed to be there, was a small black object resembling a chip. Harry had seen them before. It was a Russian model, probably better than the bugs the CIA used.

The throbbing of his foot dulled all the other pain as he dealt the bedside table a ferocious kick and sent it flying.

42

Wednesday 22 January

LIZ LIFTED THE COFFEE CUP to her mouth and slurped so loudly that Løken glanced at Harry with one eyebrow raised, as if to ask who this creature was. They were at Millie's Karaoke. From a photo on the wall a platinum-blonde Madonna stared down at them with a hungry gaze while a digitalised sing-back version of 'I Just Called to Say I Love You' blithely limped along. Harry tried to switch off the remote. They had read the letter and no one had responded yet. Harry found the right button and the music stopped abruptly.

'That's what I had to tell you,' Harry said. 'As you can see, we have a leak.'

'What about the bug you say this Woo put in your phone?' Løken asked.

'It doesn't explain how this person knows we're after him. I haven't said much on the phone. Anyway, from now on I suggest we meet here. If we find the informant they might be able to lead us to Klipra, but I don't think we should begin at that end.'

'Why not?' Liz asked.

'I have a feeling the informant is as well disguised as Klipra.'

'Really?'

'By writing that letter Klipra is revealing that he gets information from inside. He would never do that if we had any chance of finding the source.'

'Why not ask the most obvious question?' Løken asked. 'How do you know the informant isn't one of us?'

'I don't. But if it is, we've lost already, so we'll have to take the risk.'

The others nodded.

'Needless to say, time is against us. It's equally needless to say the odds are against the girl. Seventy per cent of kidnaps of this kind end in the victim being killed.' He tried to say this in as neutral a tone as possible, and he avoided their eyes in the sure knowledge that everything he thought and felt was written in his.

'So where do we start?' Liz asked.

'We begin by eliminating,' Harry said. 'Eliminating where she *isn't*.'

'Well, as long as he has the girl they're unlikely to let him cross any international borders,' Løken said. 'Or check in at a hotel.'

Liz agreed. 'He's probably somewhere they can hide for a long time.'

'Is he alone?' Harry asked.

'Klipra isn't associated with any of the crime families,' Liz said. 'The kind of organised crime he's involved in doesn't mess around with kidnapping. Finding someone to take care of an opium slave like Jim Love isn't that hard. But kidnapping a white girl, the daughter of an ambassador . . . Anyone he tried to hire would have checked it all out before agreeing. They would've known the whole police force would be on them if they took the job.'

'So you think he's alone?'

'Like I said, he isn't in one of the families. Inside those families there are loyalties and traditions. But Klipra would employ contractors he could never trust a hundred per cent. Sooner or later they would discover why he wanted the girl and they might use it against him. The fact that he got rid of Jim Love suggests he will stop at nothing to protect his identity.'

'OK, let's assume he's operating solo. Where would he hide her?'

'Loads of places,' Liz said. 'His companies must own a lot of properties, and some of those have to be empty.'

Løken coughed loudly, caught his breath again and swallowed.

'I've suspected for ages that Klipra has a secret love nest. On occasion he's taken a couple of boys with him in the car and has stayed over till the following morning. I've never managed to track down the place; it's certainly not registered anywhere. But it's obvious it must be somewhere he's left in peace, somewhere not too far from Bangkok.'

'Could we find any of the boys and ask them?' Harry said.

Løken shrugged and looked at Liz.

'It's a big city,' she said. 'In our experience these boys disappear like dew in the morning sun the minute we start looking for them. Besides, we'd have to involve lots of other people.'

'OK, forget it,' Harry said. 'We can't risk Klipra getting wind of what we're doing.'

Harry tapped a pen rhythmically against the edge of the table. To his irritation he noticed that 'I Just Called to Say I Love You' was still buzzing round his head.

'So, to summarise, we assume Klipra has carried out this kidnap on his own and that he is in an out-of-the-way place a drive away from Bangkok.'

'What do we do now?' Løken asked.

'I'm off to Pattaya,' Harry said.

He was on the margins of the expat scene. Harry hadn't felt he was very important in the case, just another Norwegian seeking better weather. Roald Bork looked the same as he had at the funeral, same lively blue eyes and gold chain on display. He was standing at the gate as Harry swung round the big Toyota 4×4 in front of his house. The dust settled on the gravel while Harry struggled with the seat belt and the ignition key. As usual, he was unprepared for the heat that hit him as he opened the door and instinctively gasped for breath. There was a salty taste to the air, which told him the sea was right behind the low ridges.

'I heard you coming up the drive,' Bork said. 'Quite a vehicle, that one.'

'I rented the biggest they had,' Harry said. 'I've learned it gives you a kind of priority. You need it with the nutters here driving on the left.'

Bork laughed. 'Did you find the new motorway I told you about?'

'Yes, I did. Except it wasn't quite finished, so they'd closed it with sandbags in a couple of places. But everyone drove over them, and I followed suit.'

'That sounds about right,' Bork said. 'It's not quite legal and not quite illegal. Is it any wonder we fall in love with this country?'

They removed their shoes and went into the house. The cold, cooling stone tiles stung Harry's bare feet. In the living room there were pictures of Fridtjof Nansen, Henrik Ibsen and the Norwegian royal family. In one a boy was sitting on a chest of drawers squinting into the camera. He must have been about ten and had a football under his arm. Documents and newspapers were tidied into neat piles on the dining-room table and piano.

'I've been trying to organise my life a little,' Bork said. 'Find out what happened and why.'

He pointed to one of the piles. 'Those are the divorce papers. I stare at them and try to remember.'

A girl came in carrying a tray. Harry tasted the coffee she poured and looked up at her quizzically when he realised it was ice cold.

'Are you married, Hole?' Bork asked.

Harry shook his head.

'Good. Keep well away. Sooner or later they'll try to get one up on you. I have a wife who ruined me and an adult son who is trying to do the same. And I can't work out what I did to them.'

'How did you end up here?' Harry asked, taking another sip. Actually, it wasn't that bad.

'I was doing a job for Televerket here while they were installing a couple of switchboards for a Thai telephone company. After the third trip I never went back.'

'Never?'

'I was divorced and had everything I needed here. For a while I seriously believed I longed for a Norwegian summer, fjords and the mountains and, well, you know, all that stuff.' He nodded in the direction of the pictures on the wall, as if they could fill in the rest. 'Then I went to Norway twice, but both times I was back within a week. I couldn't stand it, yearned to be here from the moment I set foot on Norwegian soil. I've realised now that I belong here.'

'What do you do?'

'I'm a soon-to-be-retired telecommunications consultant, I take the occasional job, but not too many. I try to work out how long I've got left and how much I'm going to need in that period. I don't want to leave one single øre for the vultures.' He laughed and waved a hand over the divorce papers as if wafting away an evil smell.

'What about Ove Klipra? Why's he still here?'

'Klipra? Hm, I suppose he has a similar tale to tell. Neither of us had very good reasons for returning.'

'Klipra probably had very good reasons not to.'

'All that gossip is absolute rubbish. If Ove had been up to that sort of thing I would never have had anything to do with him.'

'Are you sure?'

Bork's eyes flashed. 'There have been a couple of Norwegians who have come here for the wrong reasons. As you know I'm a kind of senior figure in the Norwegian circle in town, and we feel a certain responsibility for what our compatriots do here. Most of us are decent, and we've done whatever had to be done. These bloody paedophiles have destroyed the reputation of Pattaya to such an extent that when people ask us where we live many have begun to answer with districts like Naklua and Jomtien.'

'What exactly is "whatever had to be done"?'

'Let me put it this way, two have gone back home and one unfortunately never made it.'

'He jumped out of a window?' Harry suggested.

Bork gave a resounding laugh. 'No, we don't go that far. But it's probably the first time the police have received an anonymous tip-off in Thai with a Nordland accent.'

Harry smiled. 'Your son?' He motioned towards the photograph on the chest of drawers.

Bork looked a bit taken aback, but nodded.

'Looks like a nice lad.'

'He was then.' Bork smiled with sad eyes and repeated himself: 'He was.'

Harry looked at his watch. The drive from Bangkok had taken almost three hours, but he had made his way like a learner driver until he had relaxed a little in the final kilometres. Perhaps he would make it back in just over two. He took three photos from his folder and placed them on the table. Løken had blown them up to 24 × 30 centimetres to achieve the full shock effect.

'We think Ove Klipra has a hideaway near Bangkok. Will you help us?'

43

Wednesday 22 January

SIS SOUNDED HAPPY ON THE phone. She had met a boy, Anders. He had just moved into Sogn, in the same corridor, and was one year younger than her.

'He's got glasses too. But that doesn't matter because he's dead good-looking.'

Harry laughed and visualised Sis's new catch.

'He's absolutely crazy. He thinks they'll let us have children together. Just imagine that.'

Harry just imagined that and knew there could be some difficult conversations in the future. But right now he was glad Sis sounded so content.

'Why are you sad?' The question came with an intake of breath, as a natural extension of the news that their father had been to visit her.

'Am I sad?' Harry asked, fully aware that Sis could always diagnose his state of mind better than he could himself.

'Yes, you're sad about something. Is it the Swedish girl?'

'No, it's not Birgitta. There is something that's bothering me now, but it will soon be OK. I'll sort it out.'

'Good.'

There was a rare silence, as Sis wasn't speaking. Harry said they'd better ring off.

'Harry?'

'Yes, Sis?'

He could hear her preparing herself.

'Do you think we could forget all that now?'

'All what?'

'You know, the man. Anders and I, we . . . we're having such a good time. I don't want to think about it any more.'

Harry fell silent. Then he took a deep breath. 'He attacked you, Sis.'

Tears were in her voice at once. 'I know. You don't have to tell me again. I don't want to think about it any more, I'm telling you.'

She sniffed, and Harry felt his chest constrict.

'Please, Harry?'

He could feel he was squeezing the phone. 'Don't think about it. Don't think about it, Sis. Everything's going to be fine.'

They had been lying in the elephant grass for almost two hours and waiting for the sun to set. A hundred metres away, at the edge of a copse, was a small house built in traditional Thai style with bamboo and wood, and featuring an open patio in the middle. There was no gate, only a little gravel path to the main door. Out front was what looked like a colourful birdcage on a pole. It was a *phra phum*, a shrine to the protective spirit of a place.

'The owner has to appease the spirits so that they don't move into the house,' Liz said, stretching her legs. 'So you have to offer them food, incense, cigarettes and so on to keep them happy.'

'And that's enough?'

'Not in this case.'

They hadn't heard or seen any signs of life. Harry tried to think about something else, not about what might be inside. It had only taken them an hour and a half by car from Bangkok, but still it was as though they had arrived in another world. They had managed to park behind a hut by the road, beside a pigpen, and had found a path leading up the steep, tree-clad slope to the plateau where Roald Bork had explained that Klipra's little house was situated. The wood was verdant, the sky blue, and birds of all colours of the rainbow flew over Harry as he lay on his back listening to the silence. At first he had thought he had cotton wool in his ears before realising what it was: he hadn't had any silence around him since he left Oslo.

When darkness fell the silence was over. It had begun with scattered scraping and humming, like a symphony orchestra tuning their instruments. Then the concert started with quacking and cackling and soared in a crescendo when the howling and loud, piercing shrieks from the trees joined the orchestra.

'Have all these animals always been here?' Harry asked.

'Don't ask me,' Liz said. 'I'm a city kid.'

Harry felt something cold brush against his skin and pulled his hand away.

Løken chuckled. 'It's just the frogs out on their evening promenade,' he said. And, sure enough, soon there were frogs all around them apparently jumping wherever the mood took them.

'Well, so long as it's only frogs that's fine,' Harry said.

'Frogs are food too,' Løken said. He pulled a black hood over his head. 'Where there are frogs there are also snakes.'

'You're kidding!'

Løken shrugged.

Harry had no desire to know the truth, but couldn't stop himself from asking. 'What sort of snakes?'

'Five or six different varieties of cobra, a green adder, a Russell's viper plus a good many more. Watch out. They say of the thirty most common varieties in Thailand twenty-six are poisonous.'

'Shit. How do you know if they're poisonous?'

Løken gave him his poor-recruit look again. 'Harry, bearing the odds in mind, I think you should just assume they're all poisonous.'

It was eight o'clock.

'I'm ready,' Liz said impatiently and checked for the third time that her Smith & Wesson 650 was loaded.

'Frightened?' Løken asked.

'Only of the Police Chief finding out what's going on before we get this done,' she said. 'Do you know the average life expectancy of a traffic cop in Bangkok?'

Løken laid a hand on her shoulder.

'OK, let's go.' Liz ran head down through the tall grass and disappeared into the darkness.

Løken studied the house through his binoculars while Harry covered the front with the elephant rifle Liz had requisitioned from the police arms depot, along with a gun, a Ruger SP101. He wasn't used to wearing a calf holster, but shoulder holsters aren't worn where jackets are an impractical item of clothing. A full moon was high in the sky and gave him enough light to make out the contours of the windows and doors.

Liz flashed her torch once, the signal that she was in position under one window.

'Your turn, Harry,' Løken said when he noticed him hesitate.

'Shit, did you have to mention the snakes?' Harry said, checking he had a knife in his belt.

'Don't you like them?'

'Well, the ones I've met made a very bad first impression.'

'If you get bitten, make sure you catch the snake, so you're given the right antidote. Then it doesn't matter if you're bitten a second time.'

Harry couldn't see if Løken was smiling in the darkness, but guessed he was.

Harry ran towards the house that loomed out of the night. Because he was running, it looked as if the silhouette of the fierce dragonhead on the roof ridge was moving. Yet the house looked very dead. The shaft of the sledgehammer in his rucksack banged against his back. He had stopped thinking about snakes.

He arrived at the second window, signalled to Løken and crouched down. It was a while since he had run so far; that was probably why his heart was pounding so hard. He heard light breathing next to him. It was Løken.

Harry had suggested tear gas, but Løken had rejected the idea point-blank. The gas would prevent them from seeing anything, and they had no reason to believe that Klipra was waiting for them with a knife to Runa's throat.

Løken raised a fist to Harry as a signal.

Harry nodded and could feel his mouth was dry, a sure sign that adrenalin was pumping through his veins in the right quantities. The butt of the gun was clammy in his hands. He checked that the door opened inwards before Løken swung the sledgehammer.

The moonshine was reflected on the iron, and for a brief second he resembled a tennis player serving before the hammer came down with immense power and smashed the lock with a bang.

The next moment Harry was inside, and his torchlight was circling the room. He saw her immediately, but the light moved on, as if acting off its own instructions. Kitchen shelves, a fridge, a bench, a crucifix. He couldn't hear the animal noises any more. He was transported back to Sydney, and heard only the sound of chains, waves smacking against the side of a boat in a marina, and the gulls screaming, perhaps because Birgitta was lying on the deck and forever dead.

A table with four chairs, a cupboard, two beer bottles, a man on the floor, not moving, blood under his head, his hand hidden by her hair, a gun under the chair, a painting of a dish of fruit and an empty vase. *Stilleben. Nature morte.* Still life. The torchlight swept over her and he saw it again: the hand, pointing upwards against the table leg. He heard Runa's voice: 'Can you feel it? You can have eternal life!' As though she was trying to summon energy for a final protest against death. A door, a freezer, a mirror. Before he was blinded he saw himself for a brief instant – a figure in black clothes with a hood over his head. He looked like an executioner. Harry dropped the torch.

'Are you OK?' Liz asked, laying a hand on his shoulder. He intended to answer, opened his mouth, but nothing came out.

'This is Ove Klipra, yes,' Løken said. He crouched down by the dead man, the scene lit by a bare bulb in the ceiling. 'How odd. I've been watching this guy for months.' He placed his hand on the man's forehead.

'Don't touch!'

Harry grabbed Løken's collar and pulled him up. 'Don't . . . !' He let go as fast. 'Sorry, I . . . Just don't touch anything. Not yet.'

Løken said nothing, and stared at him. Liz had her deep wrinkle between her non-existent eyebrows again.

'Harry?'

He slumped down on a chair.

'It's over now, Harry. I'm sorry, we're all sorry, but it's over.'

Harry shook his head.

She leaned over him and laid a big, warm hand on his neck. The way his mother used to do. Shit, shit, shit.

He got up, pushed her away and went outside. He could hear Liz and Løken's whispers from inside the house. He looked up at the sky, searched for a star, but couldn't find one.

It was almost midnight when Harry went to the door. Hilde Molnes opened it. He looked down; he hadn't phoned in advance and could hear from her breathing that soon she would be in tears.

They sat opposite each other in the living room. He couldn't see anything left in the gin bottle, and she seemed clear-headed enough. She wiped away the tears. 'She was going to be a diver, you know?'

He nodded.

'But they wouldn't let her take part in normal competitions. They said the judges wouldn't know how to assess her. Some people said it was unfair. Diving with only one arm gave you an advantage.'

'I'm sorry,' he said. It was the first thing he had said since he arrived.

'She didn't know,' she said. 'Had she known she wouldn't have spoken to me in that way.' Her face contorted, she sobbed and the tears ran down the wrinkles by her mouth like small streams.

'Didn't know what, fru Molnes?'

'That I'm ill!' she shouted, and buried her face in her hands.

'Ill?'

'Why else would I anaesthetise myself like this? My body will have been eaten up soon. It's just rotten, just dead cells.'

Harry said nothing.

'I meant to tell her,' she whispered between her fingers. 'The doctors told me six months. But I wanted to tell her on a good day.' Her voice was barely audible. 'But there weren't any good days.'

Harry, unable to sit, got to his feet. He walked over to the large window overlooking the garden, avoided the family photographs on the wall because he knew who his eyes would meet there. The moon was reflected in the swimming pool.

'Have they rung back, the men your husband owed money?'

She lowered her hands. Her eyes were red from crying and ugly.

'They rang, but Jens was here and he spoke to them. Since then I've heard nothing.'

'So he takes care of you, does he?'

Harry wondered why he had asked her that of all questions.

Perhaps it had been a clumsy attempt to console her, to remind her she still had someone.

She nodded mutely.

'And now you're going to get married?'

'Do you object?'

Harry turned to her. 'No, why should I?'

'Runa . . .' She didn't get any further, and the tears began to roll down her cheeks again. 'I haven't experienced much love in my life, Hole. Is it asking too much to want a few months' happiness before the end? Couldn't she allow me that?'

Harry watched a little petal floating into the pool. He was reminded of the freighters from Malaysia.

'Do you love him, fru Molnes?'

In the ensuing silence he listened for a fanfare.

'Love him? What does that matter? I'm capable of imagining I love him. I think I could love anyone who loves me. Do you under-stand?'

Harry glanced towards the bar. It was three steps away. Three steps, two ice cubes and a glass. He closed his eyes and could hear the ice cubes clink in the glass, the gurgle of the bottle as he poured the brown liquid over and finally the hiss as the soda mixed with the alcohol.

44

Thursday 23 January

IT WAS SEVEN O'CLOCK IN the morning when Harry returned to the crime scene. At five he had given up trying to sleep, dressed and got into the hire car in the car park. There was no one else around, the forensics team had finished for the night and wouldn't appear for another hour at least. He pushed the orange police tape aside and went in.

It looked quite different in the daylight: peaceful and well kept. Only the blood and the chalk outlines of two bodies on the rough wooden floor were testimony to the fact that it was the same room he had been in the night before.

They hadn't found a letter, yet no one had been in any doubt as to what had happened. The question was more why Ove Klipra had shot her and then himself. Had he known the game was up? In which case, why not just let her go? Perhaps it hadn't been planned, perhaps he had shot her while she was trying to escape or because she had said something that had sent him over the edge? And then he had shot himself? Harry scratched his scalp.

He studied the chalk outline of her body and the blood that hadn't been washed clean. Klipra had shot her in the neck with the gun they had found, a Dan Wesson. The bullet had passed straight through her, tearing the main artery, which had managed to pump out so much blood it ran over to the kitchen sink before the heart stopped beating. The doctor said she had lost consciousness at once because her brain didn't get enough oxygen and she died after three or four pumps of the heart. A hole in the window showed where Klipra had been standing when he shot her. Harry stood inside the chalk silhouette of Klipra's body. The angle was right.

He looked at the floor.

The blood formed a coagulated black halo where his head had been. That was all. He had shot himself through the mouth. Harry saw that the crime scene people had chalked the spot where the bullet had entered the double bamboo wall. He imagined how Klipra would have lain down, twisted his head and looked at her, perhaps wondering where she was before pulling the trigger.

He went outside and found where the bullet exited. He peered through the aperture and looked straight at the painting on the opposite wall. Still life. Strange, he had thought he would be looking down at the silhouette of Klipra. He continued towards the place where they had been lying in the grass the day before, stamping hard so as not to bump into reptiles, and stopped by the house of spirits. A small, smiling Buddha figure with a globular stomach took up most of the space, along with some withered flowers in a vase, four filter cigarettes and a couple of used candles. A little white cavity at the back of the ceramic figure showed where the bullet had struck. Harry took out his Swiss army knife and prised out a deformed lump of lead. He looked back at the house. The bullet had travelled in a straight horizontal line. Klipra had of course been standing when he shot himself. Why had he thought he had been lying down?

He walked back to the house. Something wasn't right. Everything seemed so nice and tidy. He opened the fridge. Empty, nothing to keep two people alive. A vacuum cleaner fell out and hit his big toe when he opened the kitchen cupboard. He swore and heaved it back in, but it rolled out again before he could close the door. Looking closer, he saw a hook for storing the vacuum.

A system, he thought. There is a system here. But someone has been meddling with it.

He removed the beer bottles from the top of the freezer and opened it. Pale, red meat shone up towards him. It wasn't wrapped, just stowed in large pieces, and in some places the blood had frozen into a black membrane. He lifted a piece out, examined it before cursing his own morbid imagination and putting it back. It looked like standard, straightforward pork.

Harry heard a sound and whirled round. A figure froze in the doorway. It was Løken.

'Jesus, you startled me, Harry. I was sure the place was empty. What are you doing here?'

'Nothing. Sniffing around. And you?'

'Just wanted to see if there were any papers we could use on the paedophile case here.'

'Why's that? That case must be done and dusted now he's dead, isn't it?'

Løken shrugged. 'We need solid evidence that we did the right thing as there's no doubt our surveillance will come under the spotlight now.'

Harry looked at Løken. Did he seem a touch tense?

'For Christ's sake, you've got the photos. What better evidence could you find?'

Løken smiled, but not enough for Harry to see his gold tooth. 'You may be right, Harry. I'm probably just a nervous old man who wants to be absolutely sure. Have you found anything?'

'This,' Harry said, holding up the lead bullet.

'Hm.' Løken, inspected it. 'Where did you find it?'

'In the spirit house over there. And I can't work out why.'

'Why not?'

'It means Klipra must have been standing when he shot himself.'

'So?'

'Then blood would have been spurting all over the kitchen floor. But there's no blood coming from him except for where he was lying. And even there there's not a lot.'

Løken held the bullet between his fingertips. 'Haven't you heard of the vacuum effect in suicide cases?'

'Explain.'

'When a victim lets the air out of his lungs and closes his mouth around a gun barrel there will be a vacuum, which means the blood will run into the mouth instead of out of the exit wound. From there it runs into the stomach and leaves behind these small mysteries.'

Harry looked at Løken. 'That's news to me.'

'It would be boring if you knew everything at the age of thirty-something,' Løken said.

Tonje Wiig had rung to say that all the big Norwegian newspapers had phoned and the more bloodthirsty of them had announced their imminent arrival in Bangkok. In Norway, the headlines were focusing for the moment on the daughter of the recently deceased ambassador. Ove Klipra was, despite his status in Bangkok, an unknown name at home. It was true that *Kapital* had interviewed him a couple of years ago, but as neither Per Ståle Lønning nor Anne Grosvold had had him as a guest on their shows, he had escaped public attention.

'The Ambassador's Daughter' and the 'Unknown Norwegian Magnate' had both been reported shot dead, most probably by intruders or prowlers.

In Thailand, however, photos of Klipra were plastered across the newspapers. The *Bangkok Post* journalist questioned the police's theory about a prowler. He wrote that you couldn't rule out the possibility that Klipra had murdered Runa Molnes and afterwards committed suicide. The newspaper also speculated freely on what consequences this might have for the BERTS transport project. Harry was impressed.

However, both countries emphasised that information released by the Thai police had been very sparing.

Harry drove up to the gate of Klipra's residence and sounded his horn. He had to admit that he had begun to like the big Toyota Jeep. The guard came out and Harry rolled down the window.

'Police. I rang you,' he said.

The guard gave him the obligatory guard's look before opening the gate.

'Could you unlock the front door for me?' Harry asked.

The guard jumped onto the running board and Harry felt his eyes examining him. Harry parked in the garage. The guard rattled his bunch of keys.

'The main door's on the other side,' he said, and Harry almost let slip that he already knew. As the guard inserted the key into the lock and was about to twist it, he turned to Harry. 'Haven't I seen you before, sir?'

Harry smiled. What could it have been? The aftershave? The soap he used? Smell is said to be the sense the brain remembers best.

'Very unlikely.'

The guard returned the smile. 'Sorry, sir. Must have been someone else. I can't tell the difference between *farangs*.'

Harry rolled his eyes, but then he stopped in mid-roll. 'Tell me, do you remember a blue embassy car coming here just before Klipra left?'

The guard nodded. 'No problem remembering cars. That was a *farang* as well.'

'What did he look like?'

The guard laughed. 'As I said . . .'

'What was he wearing?'

He shook his head.

'A suit?'

'I think so.'

'A yellow suit. Yellow, like a chicken?'

The guard frowned and fixed him with a stare. 'Chicken? No one has a suit like a chicken.'

Harry shrugged. 'Well, some people do.'

He stood in the hall where Løken and he had entered and studied a small, round circle in the wall. It looked as if someone had been trying to hang a picture but had given up trying to put in a screw.

He went up to the office, leafed through the documents, mostly at random, switched on the computer, and was asked for a password. He tried 'MAN U'. Incorrect.

Polite language, English.

'OLD TRAFFORD'. Incorrect again.

One final attempt before being automatically locked out. He glanced around as if to find a clue in the room. What was his? He chuckled. Of course. The most common password in Norway. He carefully typed in the letters P-A-S-S-W-O-R-D, then pressed enter.

The machine seemed to hesitate for a second. Then it switched itself off and he received a not quite so polite message, black on white, that he had been refused access.

'Shit.'

He tried switching the machine off and on, but there was only a white screen.

He flicked through more papers, found a recent shareholders' list for Phuridell. A new shareholder, Ellem Ltd, was listed with three per cent of the shares. Ellem. A crazy idea struck Harry, but he rejected it.

At the bottom of a drawer he found the manual for the recording device. He looked at his watch and sighed. He would have to start reading. After half an hour, he was playing the tape. Klipra's voice babbling in Thai for the most part, but he heard Phuridell mentioned a couple of times. After three hours he gave up. The conversation with the ambassador on the day of the murder simply wasn't on any of the tapes. For that matter, there were no others from that day, either. He stuffed one of the tapes in his pocket, switched off the machine and made sure to give the computer a kick on the way out.

45

Friday 24 January

HE DIDN'T FEEL MUCH. ATTENDING the funeral was like watching a TV repeat. Same place, same priest, same urn, same shock to your eyes when you emerge in the sun afterwards, and the same people standing at the top of the stairs and looking at one another in doubt. Almost the same people. Harry said hello to Roald Bork.

'You found them, yes?' was all he said. There was a grey veil over his alert eyes; he seemed changed, as though what had happened had added years to his age.

'We found them.'

'She was so young.' It sounded like a question. As though he wanted someone to explain to him how this kind of thing could happen.

'Hot,' Harry said, to change the subject.

'It's hotter where Ove is.' He said it casually, but his voice had a hard, bitter tone. He wiped his brow with a handkerchief. 'By the way, I've realised I need a break from this heat. I've booked a flight home.'

'Home?'

'Yes, to Norway. Asap. I rang my lad and said I wanted to meet him. Quite a while passed before I clicked that it wasn't him on the phone but his son. Heh-heh. I'm getting senile. A senile grandfather, that'll be something.'

In the shade of the church, Sanphet and Miss Ao stood together, away from the others. Harry went over to them and reciprocated their *wai*.

'Could I ask you a quick question, Miss Ao?'

Her gaze flitted to Sanphet before nodding.

'You sort the post at the embassy. Can you remember if you've received anything from a company called Phuridell?'

She considered the question before responding with an apologetic smile. 'I don't remember. There are so many letters. I can look through the ambassador's office tomorrow if you'd like. It might take a bit of time. He wasn't exactly tidy.'

'It's not the ambassador I'm thinking about.'

She gave him an uncomprehending look.

Harry sighed. 'I don't even know if this is important, but would you contact me if you find anything?' he asked.

She locked eyes with Sanphet.

'She will, Officer,' Sanphet said.

Harry was sitting in her office waiting when Liz rushed in completely out of breath. There were beads of sweat on her forehead.

'Oh my God,' she said. 'You can feel the tarmac through your shoes out there.'

'How did the briefing go?'

'Fine, I guess. The bosses congratulated us on solving the case and didn't ask any detailed questions about the report. They even bought our story about anonymous tip-offs leading us to Klipra. If the Chief thought something was fishy he decided not to kick up a fuss.'

'I didn't think he would. After all, he has nothing to gain.'

'Is that cynicism, Mr Hole?'

'Not at all, Miss Crumley. Just a naive, young officer beginning to understand the rules of the game.'

'Maybe. But in their heart of hearts everyone's probably glad Klipra's dead. There would have been some very unpleasant revelations if the case had gone to court, not just for a couple of Police Chiefs but for the authorities in our two countries as well.'

Liz kicked off her shoes and leaned back contentedly. The springs in the chair creaked while the unmistakable aroma of sweaty feet spread through the room.

'Yes, it's conspicuously handy for a number of people, don't you think?' Harry said.

'What do you mean?'

'I don't know. I think it stinks.'

Liz glanced at her toes and then looked at Harry.

'Has anyone ever told you you're paranoid, Harry?'

'Yeah, of course. But that doesn't mean the little green men *aren't* after you, does it.'

She seemed nonplussed. 'Relax, Harry.'

'I'll try.'

'So when are you going?'

'As soon as I've spoken to the pathologist and Forensics.'

'Why do you need to talk to them?'

'Just to rid myself of the paranoia. You know . . . a few mad ideas I've had.'

'All right,' Liz said. 'Have you eaten?'

'Yes,' Harry lied.

'Oh, I hate eating on my own. Can't you just keep me company?'

'Another time?'

Harry got to his feet and left the office.

*   *   *

The young pathologist cleaned his glasses as he spoke. The pauses were sometimes so long that Harry wondered if the slow-moving flow of words had come to a complete halt. But then another word came, then another, the cork freed itself and he continued. It sounded as though he was afraid Harry would criticise his English.

'The man had been lying there for a maximum of two days,' the doctor said. 'Any longer in this heat and his body . . .' He puffed out his cheeks and demonstrated with his arms. '. . . would have been like a huge gas balloon. And you would have noticed the smell. As far as the girl is concerned . . .' He looked at Harry and puffed out his cheeks again. 'Ditto.'

'How quickly did Klipra die from the shot?'

The doctor moistened his lips and Harry had the sense he could actually feel time passing.

'Quickly.'

'And her?'

The police doctor stuffed his handkerchief into his pocket.

'Instantly.'

'I mean, could either of them have moved after the shot, had convulsions or something like that?'

The doctor put on his glasses, ensured they were straight and removed them again.

'No.'

'I've read that during the French Revolution, before the guillotine, when executions were still performed by hand, the condemned were told that sometimes the executioner missed and that if they could stand up and leave the scaffold afterwards they could go free. Apparently some tried to stand up without a head and walk several steps, but then they fell, to tremendous cheers from the crowd, of course. If I remember correctly, a scientist explained that the brain may be to a certain degree preprogrammed and muscles may work overtime as great amounts of adrenalin are pumped into the heart before the head is cut off. That's what happens when chickens are decapitated.'

The doctor smirked. 'Very amusing, Officer. But I'm afraid they're cock and bull stories.'

'So how do you explain this?'

He passed the doctor a photo showing Klipra and Runa lying on the floor. The doctor looked at the photo, then put on his glasses and examined it in detail.

'Explain what?'

Harry pointed to the picture. 'See there. His hand is covered by her hair.'

The doctor blinked, as if a speck of dust in his eye was preventing him from seeing what Harry meant.

Harry waved away a fly. 'Listen, you know how your subconscious can instinctively draw conclusions, don't you?'

The doctor shrugged.

'Well, without being aware of it, mine concluded that Klipra must have been lying there when he shot himself, because that's the only way he could already have had his hand under her hair. But the angle of the shot shows that he was standing. How could he have shot her and then himself and yet have her hair on top of and not under his hand?'

The doctor took off his glasses and resumed his cleaning.

'Perhaps she shot them both,' he said, but by then Harry had gone.

Harry took off his sunglasses and squinted with smarting eyes into the shadowy restaurant. A hand waved in the air and he headed for a table under a palm tree. A stripe of sun caused the steel frames of his glasses to flash as the man stood up.

'You got the message, I can see,' Dagfinn Torhus said. His shirt had large, dark rings under the armpits and a jacket hung over the back of his chair.

'Inspector Crumley said you'd rung. What brings you here?' Harry asked, holding out a hand.

'Administrative duties at the embassy. I arrived this morning to clear up some paperwork. And we have to appoint a new ambassador.'

'Tonje Wiig?'

Torhus smiled weakly. 'We'll have to see. There are lots of things to take into consideration. What can you eat here?'

A waiter was already at their table, and Harry looked up enquiringly.

'Eel,' the waiter said. 'Vietnamese speciality. With Vietnamese rosé wine and—'

'No, thank you,' Harry said, peering at the menu and pointing to the coconut-milk soup. 'With mineral water please.'

Torhus shrugged and nodded the same.

'Congratulations.' Torhus poked a toothpick between his teeth. 'When are you off?'

'Thank you, but I'm afraid the congratulations are a little premature, Torhus. There are still a couple of loose threads to tidy up.'

The toothpick stopped. 'Loose threads? It's not your job to deal with those. You pack your things and get on home.'

'That's not so easy.'

The hard, blue bureaucrat eyes glinted. 'It's over, do you understand? The case has been cracked. It was all over the front pages in Oslo yesterday that Klipra killed the ambassador and his daughter. But we'll survive, Hole. I suppose you're referring to the Police Chief in Bangkok, who says that they can't see any motive for it and that Klipra may have been insane. So simple and so totally incomprehensible. But the important thing is that people buy it. And they are buying it.'

'So the scandal is a matter of record?'

'Both yes and no. We've managed to keep a lid on the motel stuff. The nub is that the Prime Minister hasn't been embroiled in the scandal. Now we have other matters on our minds. The press has been ringing us here to ask why news of the ambassador's murder wasn't made public earlier.'

'What do you say in response?'

'What the hell can I say? Language problems, misunderstandings, the Thai police sending us flawed information initially, that sort of thing.'

'And they buy it?'

'No, they don't. But they can't accuse us of misinforming them, either. In the press release it says the ambassador was found dead in a hotel and that is correct. What did you say when you found the daughter and Klipra, Hole?'

'I didn't.' Harry took some deep breaths. 'Listen, Torhus, I found a couple of porn magazines at Klipra's house which suggest he was a paedophile. That hasn't been mentioned in any of the police reports.'

'Really? Well, well.' The voice didn't betray for an instant that he was covering anything up. 'Anyway, you no longer have an assignment here in Thailand, and Møller wants you back as soon as possible.'

Boiling hot coconut-milk soup was placed on the table, and Torhus stared sceptically at his bowl. His glasses steamed up.

'*Verdens Gang* is bound to take a nice photo of you when you arrive at Fornebu Airport,' he said acidly.

'Try one of the red ones,' Harry said, pointing.

46

Friday 24 January

ACCORDING TO LIZ, SUPAWADEE WAS the person who solved most of the murder cases in Thailand. His most important instruments were a microscope, some test tubes and litmus paper. Sitting opposite Harry, he was beaming like a sun.

'That is correct, Harry. The bits of lime plaster you gave us contain the same limewash solution as the dust on the screwdriver in the boot of the ambassador's car.'

Instead of contenting himself with answering yes or no to Harry's enquiry, he repeated the whole question so that there would be no misunderstandings. Supawadee had an excellent grasp of linguistics; he knew that in English questions and answers can be complicated for a Thai. If Harry had got on the wrong bus in Thailand, started doubting himself and said to another passenger: 'This *isn't* the bus to Hua Lamphong, *is* it.' with the correct stress and intonation, the Thai might have answered 'yes', in the sense of 'yes, you're right, this isn't the bus to Hua Lamphong'. *Farangs* know this happens. Supawadee's experience was that most farangs, being less intelligent, weren't aware of how questions worked, so he had come to the conclusion that it was best to answer the questions in full.

'That's also correct, Harry. The contents of the vacuum cleaner bag at Klipra's cabin were very interesting. It contained carpet fibres from the boot of the ambassador's car, the ambassador's suit and also from Klipra's jacket.'

Harry noted this with mounting excitement. 'What about the two tapes I sent you? Did you send them to Sydney?'

Supawadee beamed even more, if at all possible, for this was the bit that pleased him most.

'This is the twentieth century, Officer, we don't *send* tapes. They would have taken at least four days. We recorded them onto a DAT tape and emailed the recordings to this sound expert of yours.'

'Jeez, can you do that?' Harry asked, half to make Supawadee happy and half resigned. Computer freaks always made him feel old. 'And what did Jésus Marguez say?'

'At first I told him it was absolutely impossible to tell what kind of room someone was phoning from, based on an answerphone message. But your friend was extremely persuasive. He talked a lot about frequency domains and hertz, which was very educational. Did you know, for example, that in one microsecond the ear can distinguish between a million different sounds? I think he and I could—'

'Conclusion, Supawadee?'

'His conclusion was that the two recordings are from two different people, but it is very likely they were recorded in the same room.'

Harry could feel his heart racing.

'What about the meat in the freezer?'

'You're correct again, Harry. The meat in the freezer was pork.'

Supawadee blinked and laughed with sheer elation. Harry knew there was more to come.

'And?'

'But the blood wasn't just pig blood. Some of it was human.'

'Do you know who from?'

'Well, it'll take a few days before I get the definitive answer from the DNA test, so provisionally I can give you only an answer with ninety per cent accuracy.'

If Supawadee had had a trumpet Harry was sure he would have played a fanfare first.

'The blood comes from our friend, *nai* Klipra.'

At last Harry got through to Jens in his office.

'How's it going, Jens?'

'OK.'

'Are you sure?'

'What do you mean?'

'You sound . . .' Harry couldn't find a word for how he sounded. 'You sound a bit sad,' he said.

'Yes. No. It's not so easy to say. She's lost all her family and . . .' The voice trailed off.

'And you?'

'Don't start.'

'Come on, Jens.'

'It's just that if I'd ever wanted to pull out of this marriage, it's absolutely impossible now.'

'Why's that?'

'My God, I'm the only person she has, Harry. So I know I should be thinking about her and all she's been through, but instead I'm thinking about myself and what I'm getting myself into. I'm obviously a bad person, but the whole thing frightens me. Do you understand?'

'I think so.'

'Hell, if only this were just about money . . . at least that's something I understand. But these . . .' He searched for the word.

'Feelings?' Harry suggested.

'Right. It's such shit.' He laughed mirthlessly. 'Anyway, I've made up my mind that for once in my life I'm going to do something that's not just about me. And I want you to be there and kick me up the arse if you detect the slightest sign of resistance. Hilde needs to think about other things, so we've already set the date. The fourth of April. Easter in Bangkok – how does that sound? She's already looking on the brighter side and has half decided to cut down on her drinking. I'll send you your ticket in the post, Harry. Don't forget I'm counting on you, so you're not bloody pulling out.'

'If I'm the most suitable candidate for best man I can't imagine what your social life is like, Jens.'

'I've conned everyone I know at least once. I don't want any stories of that sort in the best man's speech, all right?'

Harry laughed. 'OK, give me a few days to mull it over. I was ringing, though, to ask you for a favour. I'm trying to find out something about one of the owners of Phuridell, a company known as Ellem Ltd, but all I can find in the company register is a PO box in Bangkok and confirmation that the share capital has been paid.'

'It must be a relatively new owner. I haven't heard the name. I'll do a bit of ringing round and see if I can dig up something. I'll call you back.'

'No, Jens. This is strictly confidential. Only Liz, Løken and I know anything about it, so you mustn't mention it to anyone. Not even anyone else in the police knows. The three of us are meeting in secret this evening, so it would be great if you had anything by then. I'll ring you, OK?'

'All right. This sounds heavy. I thought the case was done and dusted.'

'It will be this evening.'

*　　*　　*

322

The sound of pneumatic drills on rock was deafening.

'Are you George Walters?' Harry shouted into the ear of the man wearing the yellow helmet who the men in overalls had pointed out to him.

He turned to Harry. 'Yes, who are you?'

Twenty metres beneath them the traffic was crawling at a snail's pace. It was going to be another afternoon of gridlock.

'Detective Officer Hole. Norwegian police.'

Walters rolled up a technical drawing and gave it to one of the two men beside him.

'Oh, yes.'

He made a timeout signal to the man drilling and the relative silence settled like a filter on the eardrums as the machine was turned off.

'A Wacker,' Harry said. 'LHV5.'

'Oh, met it before, have you?'

'I had a summer job on a building site years ago. Shook my kidneys up with one of them.'

Walters nodded. His eyebrows had been bleached white by the sun, and he looked tired. Wrinkles had already formed deep into the middle-aged face.

Harry pointed down the concrete road running like a Roman aqueduct through a stony wilderness of houses and skyscrapers. 'So this is BERTS, Bangkok's salvation?'

'Yes,' Walters said, looking in the same direction as Harry. 'You're standing on it now.'

The reverence in his voice, plus the fact that he was here and not in an office, told Harry that the boss of Phuridell was happier with engineering than with accounts. It was more exciting to see how the project was taking shape than to get too involved with solving the company's dollar debt.

'Reminds you of the Great Wall of China,' Harry said.

'This will bring people together, not keep them out.'

'I've come here to ask about Klipra and this project. And Phuridell.'

'Tragic,' Walters said, without specifying which particular element he was referring to.

'Did you know Klipra, Mr Walters?'

'I wouldn't put it that strongly. We met at several board meetings and he called me a couple of times.' Walters put on some sunglasses. 'That was all.'

'Called you a couple of times? Isn't Phuridell a pretty big company?'

'More than eight hundred employees.'

'You're the boss here, and you hardly spoke to the owner of the company you work for?'

'Welcome to the world of business.' Walters surveyed the road and city as though all the rest was nothing that concerned him.

'He invested quite a lot of money into Phuridell. Are you trying to say he didn't care?'

'He obviously didn't have any objections to the way the company was being run.'

'Do you know anything about a company called Ellem Ltd?'

'I've seen the name on the list of shareholders. We've had other matters on our minds lately.'

'Like how to solve the problem of the dollar debt?'

Walters turned to Harry again. He saw a distorted version of himself in the sunglasses.

'What do you know about that?'

'I know that your company needs refinancing if you're going to keep going. You have no obligation to give any information as you're not listed on the stock exchange any more, so you can hide your problems from the outside world for a while, hoping a saviour will appear with new capital. It would be frustrating to throw in the towel now that you're in a position to get more contracts from BERTS, wouldn't it?'

Walters signalled to the engineers that they could take a break.

'My guess is that this saviour is going to turn up,' Harry continued. 'He'll buy the company for a song and will probably become very wealthy when the contracts start rolling in. How many people know about the company's plight?'

'Listen here, mate—'

'Hole. The board, of course. Anyone else?'

'We inform all the owners. Apart from that, we see no reason to tell everyone about affairs that don't concern them.'

'Who do you think is going to buy the company, Mr Walters?'

'I'm the administrative director,' Walters snapped. 'I'm employed by shareholders. I don't get mixed up in owner issues.'

'Even if it might mean the sack for you and eight hundred others? Even if you won't be allowed to continue with this any longer?' Harry nodded towards the concrete disappearing into the mist.

Walters didn't answer.

'Actually, maybe it's more like the Yellow Brick Road. In *The Wizard of Oz*, you know?'

George Walters nodded slowly.

'Listen, Mr Walters, I've called Klipra's solicitor and a couple of the returning small-time shareholders. In the last few days Ellem Ltd has bought up your shares in Phuridell. None of the others would be able to refinance Phuridell, so they're just happy they've left a company but haven't lost all of their investment. You say you're not interested in the owners, Mr Walters, but you look like a responsible man. And Ellem is your new owner.'

Walters took off his sunglasses and rubbed his eyes with the back of his hand.

'Will you tell me who's behind Ellem Ltd, Mr Walters?'

The drills started again, and Harry had to move closer to him to hear.

Harry nodded. 'I just wanted to hear you say that,' he shouted back.

47

Friday 24 January

IVAR LØKEN KNEW IT WAS over. Not a fibre in his body had given up, but it was over. The panic came in waves, washed over him and retreated. And all the time he knew he was going to die. It was a wholly intellectual conclusion, but the certainty trickled through him like ice melting. The time he had walked into the booby trap at My Lai and stood there with a bamboo stake stinking of shit through his thigh and another through his foot up to the knee he hadn't for one second thought he was going to die. When he lay shaking with fever in Japan and they said his foot would have to be amputated he had said he would rather die, but he knew that death was not an alternative, it was impossible. When they had brought an anaesthetic, he had knocked the syringe out of the nurse's hand.

Idiotic. Then they had let him keep his foot. *As long as there's pain there's life* he had scratched into the wall above the bed. He had been at the hospital in Okabe for almost a year before he won his fight against his own infected blood.

He told himself he had lived a long life. Long. That was something after all. And he had seen others who had gone through worse.

So why resist? His body said no, the way he had said no all his life. Had said no to crossing the line when desire was driving him, said no to letting them crack him when the military dismissed him, said no to feeling sorry for himself when humiliation lashed him and reopened sores. Primarily, though, he had said no to closing his eyes. For that reason he had absorbed everything: wars, suffering, brutality, courage and humanity. So much that he could say without fear of contradiction that he had lived a long life. Not even now did he close his eyes; he barely blinked. Løken knew he was going to die. If he'd had tears he would have cried.

Liz looked at her watch. It was half past eight, and she and Harry had been sitting in Millie's Karaoke for close on an hour. Even Madonna was beginning to look impatient rather than hungry in the photo.

'Where is he?' she said.

'Løken will come,' Harry said. He was standing by the window; he had pulled up the blind and saw his own reflection run through by car headlights crawling past on Silom Road.

'When did you talk to him?'

'Straight after talking to you. He was at home, tidying up the photos and camera equipment. Løken will come.'

He pressed the backs of his hands against his eyes. They had been irritated and red when he woke up today.

'Let's make a start,' he said.

'What do you mean?'

'We have to go through everything,' Harry said. 'One last reconstruction.'

'OK. But why?'

'Liz, we've been on the wrong track the whole time.'

He let go of the cord, the blind crashed down and it sounded as if something was falling through thick foliage.

*   *   *

Løken was sitting in a chair. A line of knives lay on the table in front of him. Each one of them was capable of killing a man in seconds. Indeed it was strange how easy it was to kill another human being. So easy that now and then it seemed incredible that most people got as old as they did. One circular movement, like peeling an orange, and the throat was cut. Blood pumped out at such a rate that death occurred in seconds, at least if the murder was carried out by someone who knew their trade.

A stab to the back required greater precision. You could strike twenty to thirty times without hitting anything in particular; you were just hacking away harmlessly at human flesh. But if you knew your anatomy, knew how to puncture a lung or the heart, it was child's play. If you stabbed from the front it was best to aim low and pull upwards so that you got under the ribcage and reached the vital organs. But it was easier from behind, as long as you aimed to the side of the spine.

How easy was it to shoot someone? Very easy. The first time he had killed was with a semi-automatic in Korea. He had taken aim, pulled the trigger and seen a man fall. That was it. Never any pangs of conscience, nightmares or nervous breakdowns. Perhaps because it was war, but he didn't believe that was the whole explanation. Perhaps he lacked empathy? A psychologist had explained to him that he was a paedophile because he had a damaged soul. He might just as well have said evil.

'OK, listen carefully now.' Harry had taken a seat opposite Liz. 'On the day of the murder the ambassador's car went to Ove Klipra's house at seven o'clock, but the ambassador wasn't driving.'

'He wasn't?'

'No. The guard doesn't remember seeing anyone in a yellow suit.'

'So?'

'You've seen the suit, Liz. It would make a petrol-pump attendant seem discreet. Do you think you would forget a suit like that?'

She shook her head, and Harry continued.

'The driver parked the car in the garage, rang the bell by the side door and when Klipra opened up he was probably looking straight down a gun muzzle. The visitor went inside, closed the door and politely asked Klipra to open his mouth.'

'Politely?'

'I'm trying to give the story a bit of colour. OK?'

Liz pursed her lips and placed a finger over them.

'Then he inserted the gun barrel, ordered Klipra to bite and fired, cold-blooded, ruthless. The bullet went through the back of Klipra's head and into the wall. The murderer wiped up the blood and . . . well, you know what a mess that makes.'

Liz nodded and waved him on.

'In short: the mystery person removed all the traces. At the end, he fetched the screwdriver from the boot and used it to lever the bullet out of the wall.'

'How do you know that?'

'I found plaster on the floor in the hall and a hole left by the bullet. Forensics has proved it's the same limewash solution we found on the screwdriver in the boot.'

'And then?'

'Then the murderer left again in the car and moved the ambassador's body so that he could put the screwdriver back in its place.'

'So he'd already killed the ambassador?'

'I'll come back to that later. The murderer changed into the ambassador's suit, then he entered Klipra's office, took one of the two Shan knives and the keys to the hideaway. He also made a quick call from Klipra's office and took along the tape of the conversation. Then he dumped Klipra's body in the boot and drove off at around eight.'

'This is pretty hard to follow, Harry.'

'At half past eight he checked into Wang Lee's.'

'Come on, Harry. Wang Lee identified the ambassador as the person who'd checked in.'

'Wang Lee had no grounds to suspect that the dead man on the bed was not the same person who had checked in. All he saw was a *farang* in a yellow suit hidden behind a pair of sunglasses. And remember the ambassador had a very distracting knife sticking out of his back when Wang Lee had to identify him.'

'Yes, what about the knife?'

'The ambassador was killed with a knife, yes, but long before they came to the motel. A Sami knife, I imagine, since it was greased with reindeer fat. You can buy that kind of knife anywhere in Finnmark, in Norway.'

'But the doctor said the stab wound matched the Shan knife.'

'Well, it would. The Shan knife is longer and broader than the Sami knife, so it's impossible to see that another knife was used first. Keep up with me now. The murderer came to the hotel with two dead bodies in the boot, asked for a room as far away from reception as possible so that he could reverse the car and carry Molnes the few metres into the room. He also asked not to be disturbed until he said he was ready. In the room he changed again and put the ambassador in the suit. But he was under pressure and messed up. Do you remember I commented that the ambassador was obviously going to meet a woman because his belt was a notch tighter than usual?'

Liz clicked her tongue against her palate. 'The murderer didn't notice the worn notch when he was tightening the belt.'

'An insignificant mistake, nothing that would give him away, but one of the many trivial points that mean this murder does not add up. While Molnes was on the bed he carefully pushed the Shan knife in the old wound before wiping the handle and removing any traces.'

'That also explains why there wasn't much blood in the motel room. He was killed somewhere else. Why didn't the doctor notice that?'

'It's always difficult to say how much a knife wound is going to bleed. It depends on which arteries are severed and how far the blade stops the flow. Nothing is obviously out of the ordinary. At around nine he left the motel with Klipra in the boot and drove to Klipra's hideaway.'

'He knew where that house was? Then he must have known Klipra.'

'He knew him well.'

A shadow fell over the table, and a man sat down opposite Løken. The balcony was open to the deafening traffic noise outside and the whole room reeked of exhaust fumes.

'Are you ready?' Løken asked.

The giant with the plait looked at him, clearly surprised that he spoke Thai.

'I'm ready,' he answered.

Løken, pallid, smiled. He felt very weary. 'So what are you waiting for? Get on with it.'

'When he got to Klipra's hideaway, he unlocked the door and dumped Klipra in the freezer. Then he washed and hoovered the boot so that we wouldn't be able to find any traces of the bodies.'

'OK, but how do you *know* this?'

'Forensics found Ove Klipra's blood in the freezer and fibres from the boot and from the two dead men's clothing in the vacuum cleaner.'

'Jesus. So the ambassador wasn't a neat freak, as you claimed when we examined the car?'

Harry smiled. 'I knew the ambassador wasn't a neat and tidy type when I saw his office.'

'Did I hear you correctly? Did you say you made a *mistake?*'

'Yes, you did.' Harry raised an index finger. 'But Klipra was neat and tidy. Everything in the cabin seemed so clean, so organised, do you remember? There was even a hook in the cupboard to keep the vacuum cleaner in place. But when I opened the cupboard door, it rolled out. As if the person who had used it last didn't know their way around. That was what made me send the vacuum cleaner bag to Forensics.'

Liz slowly shook her head as Harry carried on.

'When I saw all the meat in the freezer I realised you could easily keep a dead man there for weeks without the body . . .' Harry puffed out his cheeks and demonstrated with his hands.

'There's something wrong with you,' Liz said. 'You should see a doctor.'

'Do you want to hear the rest or not?'

She did.

'Afterwards he drove to the motel, parked the car and entered the room where he put the car key in Molnes's pocket. Then he vanished into the night without a trace. Literally.'

'Hang on! When we drove to the cabin it took us ninety minutes one way, right? It's about the same distance from here. Our friend Dim found him at half past eleven, so two and a half hours after you're saying the murderer left the motel. He couldn't have possibly have made it back to the motel before Molnes's body was found. Or have you forgotten that?'

'Not at all. I've even driven the stretch. I started at nine o'clock, waited at the cabin for half an hour and drove back.'

'And?'

'I was back at a quarter past twelve.'

'See. It doesn't add up.'

'Do you remember what Dim said about the car when we questioned her?'

Liz bit her top lip.

'She didn't remember any car,' Harry said. 'Because it wasn't there. At a quarter past twelve they were in reception waiting for the police and didn't notice the ambassador's car sneak in.'

'Christ, I thought we were dealing with a careful murderer. The police might have been waiting for him when he got back.'

'He was careful, but he couldn't anticipate that the murder would have been discovered before his return. The agreement was that Dim wouldn't go to the room until he rang her, wasn't it. But Wang Lee became impatient and almost ruined the whole plan. The murderer can't have suspected anything when he was replacing the car keys.'

'So blind luck then?'

'This man doesn't base anything on luck.'

He must be a Manchurian, Løken thought. From Jilin province perhaps. During the Korean War he had been told that the Red Army recruited many of its soldiers from there because they were so tall. Whatever the logic of that was, they sank deeper into the mud and were bigger targets. The other person in the room stood behind him humming a song. Løken couldn't swear to it, but it sounded like 'I Wanna Hold Your Hand'.

The Chinese man had picked up a knife from the table, if you can call a seventy-centimetre curved sabre a knife. He weighed it in his hands, like a baseball player choosing a bat, then raised it above his head without a word. Løken clenched his teeth. At the same time the pleasant drowsiness of his barbiturate sedation wore off, the blood froze in his veins and he lost his self-control. As he screamed and tugged at the leather straps binding his hands to the table, the humming approached from behind. A hand grabbed his hair, yanked his head back, and a tennis ball was stuffed into his mouth. He could feel the hairy surface on his tongue and palate;

it attracted saliva to it like blotting paper and his screams became feeble groans.

The tourniquet around his forearm had been pulled so tight that he had long lost any feeling in his hand, and when the sabre came down with a dull thud and he didn't feel anything he thought for a moment it had missed him. Then he saw his right hand on the other side of the blade. It had been clenched and now it was slowly opening. The cut was clean. He could see two severed white bones protruding. The radius and the ulna. He had seen them in other people, but never his own. Because of the tourniquet, there wasn't a lot of blood. It wasn't true what people say, that sudden amputations don't hurt. The pain was unbearable. He waited for the shock, the paralysing state of nothingness, but that avenue was closed at once. The man who had been humming stuck a syringe in his upper arm, through his shirt, not even attempting to find a vein. That was what was so great about morphine. It worked wherever you put it. He was aware that he could survive this. For quite a long time. As long as they wanted.

'What about Runa Molnes?' Liz was cleaning her teeth with a matchstick.

'He could have picked her up whenever he wanted,' Harry said.

'And then he took her up to Klipra's hideaway. What happened after that?'

'The blood and bullet hole in the window suggest that she was shot inside the cabin. Probably as soon as they arrived.'

It was almost easy when he talked about her like this, as a murder victim.

'I don't understand that,' Liz said. 'Why would he kidnap her and kill her right away? I thought the whole point was to use her to stop your investigation. He could only do that if Runa Molnes was alive. You might have wanted proof that she was safe before submitting to his demands.'

'And how would I submit to his demands?' Harry asked. 'Go back to Norway – and then Runa would run home smiling? And the kidnapper could breathe a sigh of relief just because I had promised he would be left in peace, even though he had no other means of applying pressure? Was that how you saw events unfolding? Did you think he would just let her . . .?'

Harry noticed Liz's eyes and realised he had raised his voice. He shut up.

'I didn't, no. I'm talking about what the murderer was thinking,' Liz said, still with her gaze fixed on him. The worried frown between her eyebrows was back again.

'Sorry, Liz.' He pressed his fingertips against his jawbone. 'I must be tired.'

He got up and walked to the window again. The cold on the inside and the hot, humid air on the outside of the pane had combined to produce a fine, grey layer of condensation on the glass.

'He didn't kidnap her because he was frightened I was finding out more than I should. He had no reason to believe that; I couldn't see further than the end of my own nose.'

'So what was the motive for the kidnap? To confirm our theory: that it was Klipra who was behind the murder of the ambassador and Jim Love?'

'That was the secondary motive,' he said into his glass. 'The primary one was that he had to kill her as well. When I . . .'

They could hear the faint sounds of a bass in the next-door room.

'Yes, Harry?'

'When I saw her she was already doomed.'

Liz breathed in. 'It's almost nine, Harry. Perhaps you should tell me who the murderer is before Løken comes?'

Løken had locked the door to his flat at seven and walked down the street to catch a taxi to Millie's Karaoke. He had seen the car at once. It was a Toyota Corolla, and the man behind the wheel seemed to fill the whole vehicle. In the passenger seat he saw the outline of another person. He wondered whether he should go over to the car and find out what they wanted, but decided to test them first. He thought he knew what they were after and who had sent them.

Løken hailed a taxi, and after it had gone a few blocks he could see that the Corolla was indeed following them.

The taxi driver noticed that the *farang* at the back wasn't a tourist and dropped the offer of massage. But when Løken asked him to take a few detours the driver apparently revised his opinion. Løken met his eyes in the mirror.

'Sightseeing, sir?'

'Yes, some sightseeing.'

After ten minutes there was no longer any doubt. The plan was clearly that Løken should lead the two policemen to the secret meeting place. Løken wondered how the Police Chief had caught wind of their meetings. And why he took it so amiss that one of his inspectors should be involved in a bit of irregular cooperation with foreigners. It might not have been totally by the book, but it had produced results in the end.

On Sua Pa Road the traffic came to a standstill. The driver squeezed into a gap between two buses and pointed to the pillars being built. A steel girder had fallen and killed a motorist last week. He had read about it. They had published the photos as well. The driver shook his head, took out a cloth and wiped the dashboard, the windows, the Buddha figure and the photo of the royal family before spreading out a copy of *Thai Rath* over the wheel with a sigh and opening it at the sports section.

Løken looked through the rear window. There were just two cars between them and the Toyota Corolla. He looked at his watch. Half past seven. He was going to be late, even if he couldn't shake off these two idiots. Løken made up his mind and tapped on the driver's shoulder.

'I can see someone I know,' he said in English and gesticulated behind him.

The driver was sceptical, suspicious that the *farang* was going to run off without paying.

'Back in a minute,' Løken said, squeezing out of the door.

One day less to live, he thought as he breathed in enough CO_2 to knock out a family of rats, and walked calmly through the traffic towards the Toyota. One headlamp must have hit something because the light shone straight into his face. He prepared his speech, already looking forward to seeing their surprised faces. Løken was only a couple of metres away and could make out the two people in the car. Suddenly he was unsure of himself. There was something about their appearance that wasn't right. Even taking into account that policemen were not generally the smartest, they did at least know that discretion was the first commandment when you were tailing someone. The man in the passenger seat was wearing sunglasses despite the fact that the sun had set some time ago, and the giant in the driver's seat was very conspicuous. Løken was about to turn back when the car door opened.

'Hey, mister,' a soft voice said. This was a mess. Løken tried to get back to the taxi, but a car had squeezed in and blocked the way. He looked back at the Corolla. The Chinese man was coming towards him. 'Hey, mister,' he repeated as cars in the opposite lane began to move. It sounded like whispering in a hurricane.

Løken had once killed a man with his bare hands. He had smashed his larynx with a rabbit chop, the precise way they had been taught at the training camp in Wisconsin. But that was a long time ago, he had been young. And terrified. Now he wasn't, he was only angry.

It probably wouldn't make any difference.

When he felt the two arms around him and his feet were off the ground he knew it wouldn't make any difference. He tried to shout, but the air his vocal cords needed to vibrate had been squeezed out of him. He saw the starry sky rotating slowly before it was hidden by an upholstered car ceiling.

He felt hot, tingling breath on his neck and looked through the Corolla windscreen. The man with the sunglasses was standing by the taxi and passing some notes through the driver's window. The grip on Løken loosened and in one long, trembling breath he inhaled the filthy air as if it were spring water.

The taxi driver rolled up the window and the man with the sunglasses was on his way back towards them. He had just removed his sunglasses, and as he stepped into the light from the damaged headlamp, Løken recognised him.

'Jens Brekke?' he whispered in astonishment.

48
Friday 24 January

'JENS BREKKE?' LIZ BURST OUT.

Harry nodded.

'Impossible! What about his alibi, the goddamn foolproof tape showing he called his sister at eight?'

'Yes, he *did* call her, but not from his office. I asked why on earth he would ring his workaholic sister at home during work hours. He said he'd forgotten what time it was in Norway.'

'And?'

'Have you ever heard of a currency broker who *forgets* what time it is in another country?'

'I don't understand.'

'Everything became clear when I saw that Klipra had a similar machine to Brekke's. After shooting Klipra he called his sister's answerphone, knowing there was no one there, from Klipra's office and took the tape with him. It shows when he rang, but not where from. We never considered the possibility that the tape may be from another recorder. But I can prove a tape was removed from Klipra's office.'

'How?'

'Do you remember that early on the afternoon of the seventh of January a call was made to Klipra on the ambassador's mobile phone? It's not on any of the tapes in his office.'

Liz laughed. 'That asshole fabricated a watertight alibi and sat in prison waiting to play the trump card so it would look as convincing as possible?'

'I think I can hear admiration in your voice, Inspector.'

'It's purely professional. Do you think he planned it all from the beginning?'

Harry looked at his watch. His brain had begun to Morse through a message that something was wrong.

'If there's one thing I'm confident of it's that everything Brekke has done was planned. He hasn't left a single detail to chance.'

'How can you be so sure?'

'Well,' he said, placing an empty glass against his face, 'he told me. He hates risks. He won't play unless he knows he's going to win.'

'I guess you've worked out how he killed the ambassador too, then?'

'First of all, he followed the ambassador down into the underground car park. The receptionist can vouch for that. Then, he took the lift back up. The girl who he asked out in the lift can vouch for that. Probably he killed the ambassador in the car park, stabbed him in the back with the Sami knife as the ambassador was getting into the car, took his keys and dumped him in the boot. Then he locked the car, went over to the lift and waited until someone pressed the button so that he could be sure to have another witness on his way back up.'

'He even asked her out so that she would remember him.'

'Right. If someone else had appeared he would have concocted some other plan. Then he blocked all incoming calls to make it look as if he was busy, took the lift down again and drove to Klipra's in the ambassador's car.'

'But if he killed the ambassador in the parking lot he would have been caught on camera.'

'Why do you think that CCTV tape went missing? Of course no one had tried to sabotage Brekke's alibi. He made Jim Love give him the tape. The evening we met him at the boxing match he was in a rush to get back to the office. Not to talk to American clients but to meet Jim Love so that he could get in and record over him killing the ambassador. And reprogramme the timer so that it would look as if someone was trying to sabotage his alibi.'

'Why didn't he just remove the original tape?'

'He's a perfectionist. He knew some bright young detective would realise sooner or later that the recording and the time didn't match.'

'How?'

'Because he used another evening's tape to record over the scene in question. Sooner or later the police would talk to employees in the building who could testify that they had driven past the camera between five o'clock and half past on the seventh of January. The proof that the tape has been tampered with is of course that they're *not* on the recording. The rain and the wet tyre tracks meant we clicked faster than we would otherwise have done.'

'So you were no smarter than he wanted you to be?'

Harry shrugged. 'Nope. But I can live with that. Jim Love couldn't. He received his payment in poisoned opium.'

'Because he was a witness?'

'As I said, Brekke doesn't like taking risks.'

'But what about the motive?'

Harry puffed out his cheeks. It sounded like a juggernaut braking.

'Do you remember us wondering if the right to dispose of over fifty million kroner for six years was a good enough motive for killing the ambassador? It wasn't. But to have it for the rest of his life was a good enough motive for Jens Brekke to kill three people. According to the will, Runa would inherit the money when she was of age, but as it doesn't say anything about what happens if she dies, the money will obviously follow the line of inheritance. That is, the fortune will belong to Hilde Molnes. The will doesn't prevent her from gaining access now.'

'How's Brekke going to make her give him the money?'

'He doesn't have to do a thing. Hilde Molnes has six months left to live. Long enough for her to marry him, and just long enough for Brekke to play the perfect gentleman.'

'So he got rid of the husband and the daughter so he can inherit the fortune when she dies?'

'Not only that,' Harry said. 'He's spent the money already.'

Liz furrowed her brow.

'He's taken over an almost bankrupt company called Phuridell. If what Barclays Thailand thinks will happen happens, the company could be worth twenty times what he paid.'

'So why would the others sell?'

'According to George Walters, the boss of Phuridell, "the others" are a couple of small-time shareholders who refused to sell their block of shares to Ove Klipra when he became the majority share-holder because they knew something big was brewing. But after Klipra disappeared off the scene they were informed the dollar debt could crack the company, so they happily accepted Brekke's offer. The same is true of the firm of solicitors administering Klipra's estate. The total purchase price is around a hundred million kroner.'

'But Brekke hasn't got the money yet.'

'Walters says that half of the money is due on signature, the other half in six months. How he's going to pay the first half, I don't know. He must have scraped together the money some other way.'

'And what happens if she doesn't die within six months?'

'For some reason I believe Brekke's going to make sure it happens. He mixes her drinks . . .'

Liz gazed into the air thoughtfully. 'Didn't he think it would seem suspicious if he turned up as the new owner of Phuridell at this exact moment?'

'Yes, that's why he bought the shares in the name of a company called Ellem Ltd.'

'Someone could have found out he was behind it.'

'He isn't, on the surface. The company's been set up in Hilde's name. But of course he inherits it when she dies.'

Liz shaped her lips into a soundless 'O'. 'How did you work all this out?'

'With the help of Walters. But I had a suspicion when I saw Phuridell's list of shareholders at Klipra's house.'

'Really?'

'Ellem.' Harry smiled. 'At first it made me suspect Ivar Løken. His nickname from the Vietnam War was LM. But the solution was even more banal.'

'I give up.'

'If you reverse Ellem it's Melle. Hilde Molnes's maiden name.'

Liz looked at Harry as if he were an attraction in the zoo.

'You're not real,' she mumbled.

Jens looked at the papaya he was holding in his hand.

'Do you know what, Løken? When you take a bite from a papaya it tastes of vomit. Have you noticed that?'

He sank his teeth into the flesh. The juice ran down his cheek.

'And then it tastes of cunt.'

He leaned back and laughed.

'You know, a papaya costs five baht here in Chinatown – as good as nothing. Everyone can afford it. Eating a papaya is one of the so-called simple pleasures. And as with other simple pleasures you don't appreciate them until they're gone. It's like . . .' Jens gesticulated as if he was searching for a suitable analogy. 'Like being able to wipe your arse. Or have a wank. All that's required is at least one hand.'

He lifted Løken's severed hand by the middle finger and held it in front of his face.

'You've still got one. Think about it. And think about *all* the things you can't do without hands. I've already given it some thought, so let me help. You can't peel an orange, you can't thread bait onto a fish hook, you can't caress a woman's body or button up your own trousers. Yes, you can't even shoot yourself, in case you should be tempted to do that. You'll need someone to help you with everything. Everything. Give it some thought.'

Blood dripped from the hand, bounced on the edge of the table and spattered Løken's shirt with small red dots. Jens put the hand down. The fingers pointed to the ceiling.

'On the other hand, with both hands intact there is no limit to what one can do. You can strangle a person, roll a joint and hold a golf club. Do you know how far medical science has advanced today?'

Jens waited until he was sure Løken wasn't going to answer.

'They can sew a hand back on without damaging so much as a nerve. They go up into your arm and pull down nerves like rubber bands. Within six months you'll barely know that once it had been severed. Of course that depends on whether you can get to a doctor fast enough and you remember to take the hand with you.'

He passed behind Løken's chair, rested his chin on his shoulder and whispered in his ear:

'Look what a nice hand. Beautiful, isn't it? Almost like the hand in the Michelangelo painting. What's it called?'

Løken didn't answer.

'You know, the one they used in the Levi's ad.'

Løken had fixed his gaze on a point in the air above him. Jens sighed.

'Obviously neither of us is an art connoisseur, eh? Well, perhaps I'll buy a few famous pictures when this is over, see if that can stimulate some interest. By the way, how much time do you think we have before it's too late to sew on the hand? Half an hour? An hour? Perhaps longer if we'd put it in ice, but I'm afraid we've run out today. Fortunately for you, it's only a fifteen-minute drive from here to Answut Hospital.'

He took a deep breath, put his mouth close to Løken's ear and yelled:

'WHERE ARE HOLE AND THE WOMAN?'

Løken gave a start and bared his teeth in a painful grin.

'Sorry,' Jens said. He picked a bit of papaya off Løken's cheek. 'It's just that it's rather important for me to get hold of them.'

A hoarse whisper stirred Løken's lips. 'You're right . . .'

'What?' Jens said. He leaned close to his mouth. 'What did you say? Speak up, man!'

'You're right about papayas. They do stink of vomit.'

Liz folded her hands on top of her head.

'The Jim Love stuff. I can't quite picture Brekke in the kitchen mixing prussic acid into opium.'

Harry smirked. 'Brekke said the same about Klipra. You're right. He had someone to help him, a pro.'

'You don't exactly put out a want ad for people like that, do you.'

'Nope.'

'Maybe someone he just happened to meet? He goes to some pretty shady places. Or . . .' She paused when she saw him watching her. 'Yes?' she said. 'What is it?'

'Isn't it obvious? It's our old friend Woo. He and Jens have been working together all along. It was Jens who ordered him to bug my phone.'

'It seems like too much of a coincidence that the same guy

who was working for Molnes's creditors was also working for Brekke.'

'That's because it's not a coincidence. Hilde Molnes told me the loan shark's thugs who had rung her after the ambassador's death immediately stopped calling after she had spoken to Brekke on the phone. I doubt that he scared them, let's put it like that. When we visited Thai Indo Travellers, Mr Sorensen said they had no scores to settle with Molnes. He may have been telling the truth. My guess is Brekke paid off the ambassador's debts. In exchange for other services, naturally.'

'Woo's services.'

'Exactly.' Harry looked at his watch. 'Bloody hell, what's happened to Løken?'

Liz got up with a sigh. 'Let's try calling him. Maybe he's fallen asleep.'

Harry scratched his chin, lost in thought. 'Maybe.'

Løken felt a pain in his chest. He'd never had heart problems, but knew a little about the symptoms. If it was a heart attack he hoped it was powerful enough to kill him. He was going to die anyway, so it would be good if he could cheat Brekke of the pleasure. Although who knows, perhaps he didn't get any pleasure out of it. Perhaps it was for Brekke as it had been for him – a job that had to be done. One shot, a man falls and that's that. He looked at Brekke. He watched his mouth move and realised to his surprise that he couldn't hear anything.

'So when Ove Klipra asked me to sort out Phuridell's dollar debt he did it over lunch instead of on the phone,' Jens said. 'I couldn't believe my ears. An order of around half a billion and he gives it to me verbally without any traceable record! That's the kind of chance you can wait half your life for in vain.'

Jens wiped his mouth with a serviette.

347

'When I returned to the office I did the dollar dealings in my own name. If the dollar went down I could just transfer the deal to Phuridell and say I was fixing the price of the dollar debt as we'd discussed. If it went up I could pocket the gain and flatly deny Klipra had asked me to buy the dollar rates. He couldn't prove a thing. Guess what happened, Ivar. Is it all right if I call you Ivar?'

He scrunched up the serviette and aimed at a litter bin by the door.

'Yes, Klipra threatened to go to the management of Barclays Thailand with the case. I explained to him that if Barclays Thailand endorsed him, they would have to replace his loss. Plus they would lose their best broker. Put simply: they couldn't afford to do anything but support me. So he threatened to use his political connections. You know what? He never got that far. I realised I could get rid of a problem, Ove Klipra, and at that same time take over his company, Phuridell, one that was going to take off like a rocket. And when I say that, it's not because I hope and believe that, the way these pathetic share speculators do. I *know* it will. I'll make sure it happens.' Jens's eyes shone. 'Just as I know this Harry Hole and the bald-headed woman are going to die tonight. It will happen.' He looked at his watch. 'I apologise for the melodrama, but *tempus fugit*, Ivar. It's time to consider your best interests, isn't it?'

Løken started at him with vacant eyes.

'Not afraid, eh? The hard nut?' Slightly bemused, Brekke pulled a loose thread from a buttonhole. 'Shall I tell you how they'll be found, Ivar? Each tied to a post, somewhere in the river with a bullet in the bodies and faces like dropped meat pies. Heard that expression before, have you, Ivar? No? Perhaps they didn't use it when you were young, eh? I'd never been able to picture it. Until my friend Woo here told me that a boat propeller can literally rip the skin off a man and show the flesh underneath. Do you get me? It's a neat trick Woo picked up from the local mafia. Of course people might ask what the two of them had done to make the mafia so mad, but they'll never find out, will they. Especially not from you, as you'll be getting a free operation and five million dollars to tell me where they are. You've had a lot of practice disappearing, creating a new identity and all that, haven't you.'

Ivar Løken watched Jens's lips move and heard the echo of a voice in the distance. Words like boat propeller, five million and a new identity fluttered past. He had never been a hero in his own eyes and had never had an inordinate desire to die as one. But he knew the difference between right and wrong, and within reasonable bounds he had striven to do what was right. No one else but Brekke and Woo would ever know if he had met his death with his head held high or not, no one would talk about old Løken over a beer among vets in the intelligence service or at the Ministry of Foreign Affairs, and Løken wouldn't have cared one way or the other anyhow. He didn't need a reputation after his death. His life had been a well-kept secret, and so it was probably natural that his death would be the same. But if this situation was not the place for a grand gesture he also knew that all he would gain from giving Brekke what he wanted was a quicker death. And he no longer felt any pain. So it wasn't worth it. If Løken had heard the details of Brekke's suggestion it wouldn't have made any difference. Nothing would make any difference. For at that moment the mobile phone attached to his belt began to beep.

49

Friday 24 January

AS HARRY WAS ABOUT TO hang up he heard a click and a new tone, and he realised his call was being transferred from Løken's home number to his mobile. He waited, let it ring seven times before he gave up and thanked the girl with the plaits behind the desk for letting him use the phone.

'We've got a problem,' he said as he returned to the room. Liz had taken off her shoes to inspect some dry skin.

'The traffic,' she said. 'It's always the traffic.'

'I was transferred to his mobile phone, but he didn't answer that, either. I don't like it.'

'Relax. What could happen to him here in peaceful Bangkok? He must have left his cellphone at home.'

'I made a mistake,' Harry said. 'I told Brekke we were meeting tonight and asked him to find out who was behind Ellem Ltd.'

'You did what?' Liz took her feet off the table.

Harry thumped the table with his fist making the coffee cups jump. 'Fuck, fuck, fuck! I wanted to see how he would react.'

'React? Harry, this isn't a game!'

'I'm not playing a game. I arranged to ring him from the meeting so that we could catch up with him somewhere. My plan had been Lemon Grass.'

'The restaurant we went to before?'

'It's close by and better than risking an ambush at his place. There are three of us, so I imagined an arrest à la Woo.'

'But then you scared him off by mentioning Ellem?' Liz groaned.

'Brekke's not stupid. He could smell a rat long before then. He talked about the best-man nonsense again, to test me, to check if I had him in my sights.'

Liz snorted. 'What a load of macho bullshit! If you two have anything personal invested in this, get it out of your system. For Christ's sake, Harry, I thought you were too professional for that.'

Harry didn't answer. He knew she was right: he'd behaved like an amateur. Why on earth had he mentioned Ellem Ltd? He could have invented a hundred other pretexts to meet. Perhaps there was something in what Jens had said, that some people like risk for risk's sake. Perhaps he was one of the gamblers Brekke considered so pathetic. No, it wasn't that. Not just that at any rate. His grandfather had once explained why he never shot grouse when they were on the ground: it's not nice.

Was that why? A kind of inherited hunting ethic: you frightened the prey to shoot them in flight, to give them a symbolic chance of getting away.

Liz interrupted his train of thought.

'So what do we do now, Detective?'

'Wait,' Harry said. 'We'll give Løken half an hour. If he hasn't turned up I'll phone Brekke.'

'And if Brekke doesn't answer?'

Harry drew a deep breath. 'Then we phone the Chief of Police and mobilise the whole force.'

Liz swore through gritted teeth. 'Did I tell you what it's like to be a traffic cop?'

Jens looked at the display on Løken's phone and chuckled. It had stopped beeping.

'Great phone you've got, Ivar,' he said. 'Ericsson's done a fine job, don't you agree? You can see the caller's number. So if it's someone you don't want to talk to, you don't have to. Unless I'm much mistaken someone's wondering why you haven't turned up. Because you don't have a lot of friends ringing you at this time of day, do you, Ivar.'

He threw the phone over his shoulder and Woo nimbly stepped to the side and caught it.

'Find out whose number that is and where. Now.'

Jens sat down next to Løken.

'This operation is beginning to get rather urgent, Ivar.'

Holding his nose, he looked down at the floor where a pool had formed around his chair.

'I mean, really, Ivar.'

'Millie's Karaoke,' Woo said in staccato English. 'I know where it is.'

Jens patted Løken on the shoulder.

'Sorry, but we've got to be off now, Ivar. We'll have to go to the hospital when we're back.'

Løken was aware of the vibration of steps fading in the distance and waited for the air pressure from the slamming of the door. It didn't come. Instead he heard the distant echo of a voice by his ear.

'Oh yes, I almost forgot, Ivar.'

He felt hot breath on his temple.

'We need something to tie them to the poles with. Could I borrow this tourniquet? You'll get it back. I promise.'

Løken opened his mouth and felt the mucus in his throat loosen as he roared. Someone else had taken over command in his brain, and he didn't feel the jerk on the leather straps as he saw the blood wash over the table and the shirtsleeves absorb it all until they were red. He didn't notice the door close.

Harry jumped up at the light tap on the door.

Involuntarily he grimaced when it wasn't Løken but the girl from reception.

'You Harry, mister?'

He nodded.

'Telephone.'

'What did I say?' Liz said. 'Hundred baht it's the traffic.'

He followed the girl to reception, noting in his subconscious that she had the same raven-black hair and the same slim neck as Runa. He stared at the tiny black hairs at the nape of her neck. She turned, flashed a quick smile and stretched out her hand. He nodded and took the receiver.

'Yes?'

'Harry? It's me.'

Harry thought he sensed his blood vessels widening as his heart began to pump blood faster round his body. He took a couple of breaths before speaking calmly and clearly.

'Where's Løken, Jens?'

'Ivar? He's got his hands full and can't make it.'

Harry could hear from his voice that the masquerade was over; this was Jens Brekke speaking now, the same person he had spoken to in the office the first time. The same teasing, provocative tone of a man who knows he is going to win, but wants to enjoy it before delivering the *coup de grâce*. Harry tried to grasp what it was that could have swung the odds against him.

'I've been waiting for you to call, Harry.' This was not the voice of a desperate man, but one who was in the driving seat, with one nonchalant hand on the wheel.

'Well, you're ahead of the game, Jens.'

Jens laughed. 'It seems I always am, Harry. How does it feel?'

'Wearing. Where's Løken?'

'Would you like to know what Runa said before she died?'

Harry felt a tingling sensation underneath the skin on his forehead. 'No,' he heard himself say. 'I just want to know where Løken is, what you've done to him and where we can find you.'

'Harry, that's three wishes at once!'

The membrane in the telephone microphone vibrated with his laughter. But there was something else struggling to capture Harry's attention, something he couldn't quite identify. The laughter stopped abruptly.

'Do you know how much self-sacrifice is required to execute a plan like this, Harry? To check and double-check, to follow all the little detours to make it infallible? Not to mention the physical discomfort. Killing is one thing, but do you think I enjoyed sitting in prison all that time? You might not believe me, but what I said about being locked up is true.'

'So why did you bother with all the detours?'

'I've told you before, eliminating risks has a cost, but it's worth it, it's always worth it. Framing Klipra required painstaking work.'

'So why didn't you make it simple? Mow them all down and blame the mafia?'

'You think like one of the losers you usually chase, Harry. You're like gamblers, you forget the whole picture, the consequences. Of course I could have killed Molnes, Klipra and Runa in simpler ways and made sure I didn't leave any traces. But that wouldn't have been enough. Because when I took over the Molnes fortune and Phuridell it would have been pretty obvious I had a motive for killing all three of them, wouldn't it? Three murders and one person with a motive for all of them. Even the police would have been able to suss that one, don't you think? Even if you hadn't found any damning evidence you could have made life fairly unpleasant for me. So I had to create an alternative scenario for you. Where one of the victims was the perpetrator. A solution that wasn't so difficult that you couldn't sort it out or so easy that you wouldn't be happy with it. You ought to thank me, Harry. I made you look good when you were on Klipra's trail, didn't I.'

Harry was only half listening; he had gone back in time. Then he'd had a murderer's voice in his ear as well. Then it had been the water in the background that had given him away, but now all Harry could hear was the faint hum of music that could have been anywhere at all.

'What do you want, Jens?'

'What do I want? Well, what do I want? Just a chat, I suppose.'

To keep me on the line, Harry thought. He wants to keep me on the line. Why? Synthetic drums splashed and a clarinet warbled.

'But if you'd like to know precisely, I was just ringing to say . . .'

Harry could hear 'I Just Called to Say I Love You' playing.

'. . . that your colleague could do with a facelift. What do you think, Harry? Harry?'

The receiver swung to and fro in an arc just above the floor.

Harry felt the sweet rush of adrenalin as though it had been injected into him while he ran down the corridor. The girl with the plaits had backed up against the wall in fear as he dropped the receiver, pulled out his borrowed Ruger SP101 from his calf holster and loaded it in one smooth movement. Had she understood when he shouted to her to call the police? No time to wonder about that now, he was there. Harry kicked open the first door and squinted straight into four shocked faces above the gunsights.

355

'Sorry.'

In the next room he almost fired a shot out of sheer fright. In the middle of the floor stood a tiny, dark-skinned Thai with his legs akimbo wearing a glittering silver suit and porno-style sunglasses. It took Harry a couple of seconds to realise what he was doing, but by then the rest of 'Hound Dog' was stuck in the Thai Elvis's throat.

Harry stared down the corridor. There had to be at least fifty rooms in all. An alarm bell had been sounding somewhere in his head, but his brain had been so overloaded already that he had tried to shut it out. Now he could hear it loud and clear. Liz! Shit, shit, shit. Jens *had* kept him on the line.

He sprinted down the corridor, and as he rounded the corner he saw the door to their room was open. He didn't think any more, didn't fear, didn't hope, just ran, knowing he had crossed the reluctant-to-kill boundary. It wasn't like a bad dream any more, it wasn't like running through water up to your waist. He burst through the door and saw Liz huddled up behind the sofa. He swung his gun round, but too late. Something hit him under the kidneys, knocked the air out of him, and the next moment he felt a grip tightening around his neck, and glimpsed a coiled microphone cable, and the smell of his breath was overwhelming.

Harry thrust his elbow backwards; it met something and he heard a groan.

'*Tay*,' a voice said, and a fist came from behind and struck him under the ear, making him go dizzy. He felt something serious had happened to his jaw. Then the cable round his neck tightened again. He tried to insert a finger, but it was no use. His tongue, inert, was being squeezed out of his mouth as though someone was kissing him from inside. Perhaps he wouldn't have to pay his dentist's bill, everything was already going black.

Harry's brain was fizzing. He couldn't take any more, he tried to make up his mind to die, but his body wouldn't obey. He instinctively thrust an arm in the air, but there was no pool net to save him now. There was only prayer, as if he were standing on the bridge in Siam Square begging for eternal life.

'Stop!'

The cable around his neck slackened and oxygen cascaded into his lungs. More, he had to have more! There didn't seem to be enough air in the room, and his lungs felt as if they were going to explode out of his chest.

'Let him go!' Liz had struggled to her knees and was pointing her Smith & Wesson 650 at Harry.

Harry could feel Woo crouching behind him as he tightened the cable again, but now Harry had his left hand between the cable and his neck.

'Shoot him,' Harry croaked in a Donald Duck voice.

'Let go! Now!' Liz's pupils were black with fear and anger. A line of blood ran from her ear, over a collarbone and into her neckline.

'He won't let go. You'll have to shoot him,' Harry whispered hoarsely.

'Now!' Liz shouted.

'Shoot!' Harry yelled.

'Shut up!' Liz's gun hand wavered as she tried to keep her balance.

Harry leaned back towards Woo. It was like propping yourself up against a wall. Liz had tears in her eyes, and her head was tipped forward. Harry had seen it before. She had serious concussion, and they had very little time.

'Liz, listen to me now!'

The cable was tightened, and Harry heard the skin on the edge of his hand split.

'Your pupils are wide open, you're about to go into shock, Liz! Listen! You have to shoot now before it's too late! You'll lose consciousness soon, Liz!'

A sob emerged from her lips. 'Fuck you, Harry! I can't. I . . .'

The cable was cutting through his flesh as if it were butter. He tried to clench his fist, but some nerves must have been torn.

'Liz! Look at me, Liz!'

Liz blinked and blinked again and looked at him through blurry eyes.

'That's great, Liz. If you can manage to miss me you're bloody bound to hit him!'

She watched him open-mouthed, then she lowered the gun and burst into laughter. Harry tried to hold Woo back, he had started moving forward, but it was like standing in front of a locomotive. They were above her when something exploded in Harry's face. A smarting pain travelled through his nerve channels, a new pain, burning this time. He smelt her perfume, he felt her body give way under the weight of Woo pinning all three of them to the floor. The echo of thunder rolled out through the open door and down the corridor. Then there was silence.

Harry was breathing. He lay trapped between Liz and Woo, but his chest was rising and falling. That could only mean he was alive. Something kept dripping. He tried to repress the memory; there was no time for it now, the wet rope, the cold, salty drops on the deck. This wasn't Sydney. They fell on Liz's forehead, her eyelids. Then he heard her laughter again. Her eyes opened and were two black windows with white frames in a red wall. Grandad was wielding his axe, dull, muffled blows, the thud as the wood landed on the hard, stamped earth. The sky was blue, the grass tickled his ears, a seagull flew in and out of his vision. He wanted to sleep, but his face was ablaze, he could smell his own flesh from the gunpowder that had burnt his pores.

With a groan he rolled out from inside the human sandwich. Liz was still laughing, her eyes were wide open, and he let her continue.

He rolled Woo onto his back. His face had frozen in a surprised expression; his jaw hung open in protest against the black entry wound in his forehead. He had moved Woo, but he could still hear the dripping. He turned to the wall behind them and saw that it wasn't his imagination. Madonna had changed hair colour again. Woo's plait had attached itself to the top of the picture frame and given her a black, punky hairstyle, dripping something that looked like a mixture of egg nog and red fruit juice. It fell onto the thick carpet with a soft splash.

Liz was still laughing.

'Having a party?' he heard a voice say from the doorway. 'And you haven't invited Jens? And there was me thinking we were friends . . .'

Harry didn't turn; his eyes ransacked the floor in a desperate search for the gun. It must have fallen under the table or behind the chair when Woo punched him in the back.

'Is this what you're looking for, Harry?'

Of course. He turned slowly and stared down the muzzle of his own Ruger SP101. He was about to open his mouth and utter something when he saw Jens was about to shoot. He was holding the gun with both hands and had already leaned forward a fraction to absorb the recoil.

Harry saw the police officer who had rocked back on the chair at Schrøder's, his moist lips, the scornful smile he didn't smile, but it was there anyway. The same invisible smile when the Police Commissioner would ask for a moment's silence.

'The game's up, Jens,' he heard himself say. 'You won't get away with this.'

'The game's up? Who actually says that?' Jens sighed and shook his head. 'You've been watching too many shit action movies, Harry.'

His finger curled around the trigger.

'But, well, OK, this is over now. You've just made this look even better than I'd planned. Who do you think will get the blame when they find a mafia henchman and two police officers killed by one another's bullets?'

Jens squeezed one eye shut, hardly necessary at a distance of three metres. Not a gambler, Harry thought, closing his eyes and subconsciously breathing in, ready to be on the receiving end.

His eardrums were shattered. Three times. Not a gambler. Harry felt his back hit the wall, the floor, he didn't know what, and the smell of cordite stung his nostrils. The smell of cordite. He understood nothing. Hadn't Jens fired three times? Shouldn't he have stopped smelling?

'Shit!' It sounded like someone shouting from under a duvet.

The smoke drifted away and he saw Liz, sitting with her back to the wall, one hand gripping a smoking gun, the other holding her stomach.

'Jesus, he hit me! Are you there, Harry?'

Am I? Harry wondered. He vaguely remembered the kick to the hip that had half spun him round.

'What happened?' Harry shouted, still deaf.

'I fired first. I hit him. I know I hit him, Harry. How did he get away?'

Harry got up, knocked the cups off the table and finally steadied himself on his feet. His left leg had gone to sleep. Sleep? He put his hand on his hip and his trousers were drenched. He didn't want to look. Stuck out a hand.

'Give me the gun, Liz.'

His eyes were fixed on the doorway. Blood. There was blood on the linoleum. That way. That way, Hole. Just follow the path that has been marked out for you. He looked at Liz. A red rose was growing between her fingers on her blue shirt. Fuck, fuck, fuck!

She groaned and passed him her Smith & Wesson 650.

'Bring him back, Harry.'

He hesitated.

'And that's an order!'

50
Friday 24 January

EVERY TIME HE TOOK A step he thrust his leg forward, hoping it wouldn't give way beneath him. Everything swam before his eyes and he knew it was his brain trying to flee the pain. He limped past the girl in reception, who seemed to be stuck in a pose for *The Scream*, not a sound passed her lips.

'Ring for an ambulance!' Harry yelled, and she woke up. 'A doctor!'

Then he was outside. The wind had dropped; it was just hot, oppressively hot. A car had careered at an angle across the road, there were skid marks on the tarmac, the door was open and the driver was outside waving his arms. He pointed up in the air. Harry held up his arms and ran across the road without looking, knowing that if they saw that he couldn't give a toss they might stop. There was a shriek of rubber. He stared up at where the man had pointed. A caravan of grey elephant silhouettes towered above him. His brain cut in and out like a badly functioning car radio, and a lone trumpet blast filled the night. To the brim. Harry felt the draught of the hooting juggernaut almost tear his shirt off as it thundered past his heels.

He was back again, his eyes searching up the concrete pillars. The elevated Yellow Brick Road. BERTS transport. Yes, why not? In a way it seemed logical.

An iron ladder led to an opening in the concrete directly above him, fifteen, twenty metres up. He could see a segment of the moon through the gap. He put the gun handle between his teeth, noticed that his belt was hanging down, tried not to think what a bullet that had sheared his belt could have done to his hip and hoisted himself up the ladder with his arms. The iron pressed into the cut he had received from the microphone cable.

Can't feel a thing, Harry thought, and swore as the blood that had covered his hand like a red washing-up glove caused him to lose his grip. He angled his right foot onto the rung and pushed off, climbed onto the next one and pushed off again. Better now. So long as he didn't pass out. He looked down. Ten metres? He'd definitely better not pass out. Onwards and upwards. Everything went dark. At first he thought it was his eyes and stopped, but when he looked down he could see cars below and hear a police siren cutting through the air like a saw blade. He looked up again. The opening at the top of the ladder was black; he couldn't see the moon any more. Had the sky clouded over? A drop splashed onto the gun barrel. Another mango shower? Harry went for the next rung, his heart throbbed, missed a couple of beats and then continued, it was doing the best it could.

What's the point? he thought, looking down. Soon the first police car would be there. Jens had probably run down the ghost road howling with laughter, already down a ladder two blocks away and then, hey presto, lost in the crowds. The fucking Wizard of Oz.

The drop ran down the handle and into Harry's clenched teeth.

Three thoughts struck him at once. The first was that if Jens had seen him coming out of Millie's Karaoke alive he probably wouldn't run off. He had no choice; he would have to finish the job.

The second was that raindrops don't taste sweet and metallic.

The third was that it hadn't clouded over, someone was blocking the opening, someone who was bleeding.

Then things began to happen very fast again.

He hoped there were still enough nerves in his left hand to keep it wrapped around the rung. Harry grabbed the gun from his mouth with his right, saw sparks flying off the rung above and heard the hiss of the ricochet, felt something catch his trouser leg before he aimed the gun at the black circle and felt the recoil in his damaged jaw as he fired. A muzzle flared and Harry emptied the magazine. Kept pressing. Click, click, click. Bloody amateur.

He could see the moon again, dropped the gun and before it hit the ground he was already climbing the ladder. Then he was up. The road, toolboxes and heavy construction equipment were bathed in the yellow light from a ridiculously big balloon someone had tied above them. Jens was sitting on a pile of sand, arms crossed over his stomach, rocking backwards and forwards, roaring with laughter.

'Shit, Harry, you've really messed things up. Look.'

He unfolded his arms. Blood bubbled out, thick and gleaming.

'Black blood. That means you hit the liver, Harry. There's a chance my doctor is going to impose an alcohol ban on me. Not good.'

The police sirens had grown louder and louder. Harry tried to control his breathing.

'I wouldn't take it to heart, Jens. I've heard the brandy they serve in Thai prisons is terrible.'

He limped towards Jens, who was pointing a gun at him.

'Now, now, Harry, don't overdo it, it just hurts a bit. Nothing that can't be fixed for money.'

'You've run out of bullets,' Harry said, continuing to walk.

Jens laughed and coughed. 'Good try, Harry, but you're the one who's run out of bullets, I'm afraid. You see, I can count.'

'Can you?'

'Ha ha. I thought I'd told you. Numbers. Knowing that kind of thing is how I make my living.'

He showed Harry with the fingers of his free hand.

'Two at you and the dyke in the karaoke dive and three at the ladder. That's one left for you, Harry. Worth putting a bit aside for a rainy day, you know.'

Harry was only two steps away.

'You've been watching too many shit action movies, Jens.'

'Famous last words.'

Jens sat up with an apologetic expression on his face and pulled the trigger. The click was deafening. Jens's moue was replaced with disbelief.

'It's only in shit action movies that all the guns have six bullets, Jens. That one's a Ruger SP101. Five.'

'Five?' Jens glared at the gun. 'Five? How do you know?'

'Knowing that kind of thing is how I make my living.'

Harry could see the blue lights on the road beneath them. 'Best if you give it to me, Jens. The police have a tendency to shoot on sight if they see a gun.'

Confusion was written all over Jens's face as he passed the gun to Harry, who stuffed it into his waistband. Perhaps it was because the belt wasn't there and the gun fell down his trouser leg, perhaps it was because he was tired, perhaps it was because he relaxed when he saw what he thought was capitulation in Jens's eyes. He lurched backwards as the punch struck him, caught unawares by how fast Jens moved. He felt his left leg buckle beneath him, then his head hit the concrete with a crunch.

He was out for a second. Mustn't lose consciousness. The radio searched desperately for the station. The first thing he saw was a gold tooth glinting. Harry blinked. It wasn't a gold tooth; it was the moon reflecting on the blade of a Sami knife. Then the hungry steel arced down towards him.

Harry would never know if he had acted instinctively or if there had been a mental process behind what he did. His left hand rose with fingers spread, straight towards the shiny steel. The knife breached his palm with consummate ease. When the knife was through to the handle, Harry pulled his hand away and kicked with his good leg. He hit his target somewhere in the black blood, Jens folded, groaned and fell sideways into the sand. Harry struggled to his knees. Jens had crawled into the foetal position and was holding both hands to his stomach. He was screaming. With laughter or pain, it was hard to say.

'Fuck, Harry. It hurts so much it's just fantastic.' He gasped, grunted and laughed in turn.

Harry got to his feet. He looked at the knife protruding through both sides of his hand, unsure what the wisest course of action would be: pull it out or leave it in to stop the blood? He heard something shouted through a megaphone from the street below.

'Do you know what's going to happen now, Harry?' Jens had closed his eyes.

'Not really.'

Jens paused to collect himself. 'Let me explain then. This is going to be a big pay day for a whole stack of policemen, lawyers and judges. You bastard, Harry, this is going to cost me.'

'What do you mean?'

'What do I mean? Are you playing the Norwegian Boy Scout again now? Everything can be bought. If you have money. I've got money. Besides . . .' He coughed. 'There are a couple of politicians with vested interests in the building industry who do not want to see BERTS go down the pan.'

Harry shook his head. 'Not this time, Jens. Not this time.'

Jens bared his teeth in a pained blend of a smile and a grimace. 'Want to bet?'

Come on, Harry thought. Don't do anything you'll regret, Hole.

He looked at his watch, a reflex action in his profession. Time of arrest for the report.

'There's one thing I was wondering about, Jens. Inspector Crumley thought I was giving too much away when I asked you about Ellem Ltd. Perhaps I was. But you've known for a long time that I knew it was you, haven't you?'

Jens tried to focus on Harry. 'A while. That's why I never understood why you worked so hard to release me from remand. Why, Harry?'

Harry felt dizzy and sat down on one of the toolboxes.

'Well, perhaps it hadn't occurred to me yet that I knew it was you. Perhaps I wanted to see what card you were going to play next. Perhaps I just wanted to flush you out. I don't know. What made you think I knew?'

'Someone said.'

'Impossible. I haven't said a word about it until tonight.'

'Someone knew without you saying.'

'Runa?'

Jens's cheek was trembling and he had white saliva at the corners of his mouth. 'Do you know what, Harry? Runa had what some call intuition. I call it observational prowess. You have to learn to hide your thoughts better, Harry. Don't open up to the enemy. It's incredible what a woman is willing to tell you if you threaten to cut off what makes her a woman. You—'

'How did you threaten her?'

'Nipples. I threatened to cut off her nipples. What do you think about that, Harry?'

Harry had lifted his face to the sky and closed his eyes, as though expecting rain.

'Did I say something wrong, Harry?'

Harry felt hot air streaming through his nostrils.

'She was waiting for you, Harry.'

'Which hotel do you stay at when you're in Oslo?' Harry whispered.

'Runa said you would come and save her, she said you knew who had kidnapped her. She cried like a baby and hit out with her prosthesis. It was quite funny. So—'

The sound of vibrating metal. Clang, clang, clang. They were on their way up the ladder. Harry looked at the knife still in his hand. No. He glanced around. Jens's voice grated in his ear. A sweet tingle started somewhere down in his stomach, a light hiss in his head, like getting drunk on champagne. Don't do it, Hole, hold on tight. But he could already feel the ecstasy of free fall. He let go.

The lock on the toolbox gave at the second kick. The pneumatic drill was a Wacker, light, probably no more than twenty kilos, and started at the first press of the button. Jens shut his mouth at once and his eyes widened as his brain gradually grasped what was going to happen.

'Harry, you can't—'

'Open wide,' Harry said.

The roar of the juddering machine drowned the traffic beneath them, the yapping megaphone and the sound of the vibrating iron ladder. Harry leaned over Jens with his legs apart, his face still raised towards the sky and his eyes closed. It was raining.

Harry slumped into the sand. Lay on his back and gazed up at the sky; he was on the beach, she asked if he would put some cream on her back, she had such sensitive skin. Didn't want to get burnt. Not burnt. Then they were there, loud voices, boots on the concrete and the greased click of guns being cocked. He opened his eyes and was blinded by a light on his face. Then the torch moved on and he glimpsed the outline of Rangsan.

Harry caught the smell of his own gall before the contents of his stomach filled his mouth and nose.

EPILOGUE

51

LIZ WOKE UP KNOWING SHE would see the yellow ceiling with the T-shaped crack in the plaster. For two weeks she had been staring at it. She wasn't allowed to read or watch TV because of a fractured skull, only listen to the radio. The bullet wound would heal quickly, they said, no vital organs had been damaged.

Not vital to her anyway.

A doctor had been to see her and asked if she had any plans to have children. She had shaken her head and didn't want to hear the rest, and he had acquiesced. There was time enough for bad news later; now she was trying to concentrate on the good news. Such as not having to direct the traffic for the next few years. And the Police Chief dropping by to say she could have a few weeks off.

Her eyes wandered to the windowsill. She tried to turn her head, but they had built an apparatus like an oil rig over her head, making it impossible to move.

She didn't like being alone, had never liked it. Tonje Wiig had visited her the day before and asked if she knew what had happened to Harry. As though he had contacted her telepathically while she had been lying in a coma. But Liz had realised that Wiig's concern wasn't merely professional and she hadn't commented. She only said he would turn up soon enough.

Tonje Wiig had looked so lonely and dejected. Well, she would survive. She was the type. She had been informed that she was the new ambassador, taking up the post in May.

Someone coughed. She opened her eyes.

'How's it going?' a hoarse voice said.

'Harry?'

A lighter clicked and she smelt cigarette smoke.

'You're back then?' she said.

'Just keeping my head above water.'

'What are you doing?'

'Experimenting,' he said. 'Trying to find the ultimate way of losing consciousness.'

'They say you walked out of the hospital.'

'There wasn't any more they could do for me.'

She laughed carefully, letting the air out in small bursts.

'What did he say?' Harry asked.

'Bjarne Møller? It's raining in Oslo. Looks like spring will be early this year. Otherwise nothing new. Told me to say hello and tell you everyone's sighing with relief on both sides. Director General Torhus popped by with flowers and asked after you. He told me to congratulate you.'

'What did Møller say?' Harry repeated.

Liz sighed. 'OK, I gave him your message and he checked it out.'

'And?'

'You know how unlikely it is that Brekke would've had anything to do with your sister's assault, don't you.'

'Yes.'

She could hear the crackle of the tobacco as he inhaled.

'Perhaps you should let it go, Harry.'

'Why?'

'Brekke's ex-wife didn't understand the questions. She'd dumped him because she thought he was *boring*, not for any other reason. And . . .' She breathed in. 'And he wasn't even in Oslo when your sister was assaulted.'

She tried to hear how he was taking this.

'Sorry,' she said.

She heard the cigarette fall and a rubber heel grind it into the stone tiles.

'Well, I just wanted to see how you were,' he said. Chair legs scraped on the floor.

'Harry?'

'I'm here.'

'Just one thing. Come back. Promise me you will. Don't stay out there.'

She could hear his breathing.

'I'll come back,' he said without any intonation, as though sick of this refrain.

52

HE WATCHED THE DUST DANCE in a solitary beam of light intruding
through a crack in the wooden floor above them. His shirt clung to
him like a terrified woman, the sweat smarted on his lips and the
stench of the earth floor made him feel sick. But then he was passed
the pipe, one hand gripped the needle and spread the black tar over
the hole; he held the pipe still over the flame and life was mellow
again. After the second drag they appeared: Ivar Løken, Jim Love
and Hilde Molnes. After the third, the rest appeared. Apart from
one. He drew the smoke down into his lungs, held it there until he
thought he would explode and then at last she was there. She was
standing in the veranda doorway with the sun on one side of her
face. Two steps, then she floated through the air, black and arched
from the soles of her feet to the tips of her fingers, a gentle arc,
endlessly slow, breaking the surface with a soft kiss, diving deeper
and deeper into the water until it closed behind her. It bubbled; a
wave lapped against the side of the pool. Then it was still, and the
green water reflected the sky again as though she had never existed.
He inhaled for a last time, lay back on the bamboo mat and closed
his eyes. Then he heard the soft splashes of swimming strokes.

Now read on for the first chapter from the next
Harry Hole thriller.

The Redbreast

Available now in paperback

1

Toll Barrier at Alnabru
1 November 1999

A GREY BIRD GLIDED IN and out of Harry's field of vision. He drummed his fingers on the steering wheel. Slow time. Somebody had been talking about 'slow time' on TV yesterday. This was slow time. Like on Christmas Eve before Father Christmas came. Or sitting in the electric chair before the current was turned on.

He drummed harder.

They were parked in the open area behind the ticket booths at the toll gate. Ellen turned up the radio a notch. The commentator spoke with reverence and solemnity.

'The plane landed fifty minutes ago, and at exactly 6.38 a.m. the President set foot on Norwegian soil. He was welcomed by the Mayor of Ullensaker. It is a wonderful autumn day here in Oslo: a splendid Norwegian backdrop to this summit meeting. Let us hear again what the President said at the press conference half an hour ago.'

It was the third time. Again Harry saw the screaming press corps thronging against the barrier. The men in grey suits on the other side, who made only a half-hearted attempt not to look like Secret Service agents, hunched their shoulders and then relaxed them as they scanned the crowd, checked for the twelfth time that their earpieces were correctly positioned, scanned the crowd, dwelled for a few seconds on a photographer whose telephoto lens was a little too long, continued scanning, checked for the thirteenth time that their earpieces were in position. Someone welcomed the President in English, everything went quiet. Then a scratching noise in a microphone.

'First, let me say I'm delighted to be here . . .' the President said for the fourth time in husky, broad American-English.

'I read that a well-known American psychologist thinks the President has an MPD,' Ellen said.

'MPD?'

'Multiple Personality Disorder. Dr Jekyll and Mr Hyde. The psychologist thought his normal personality was not aware that the other one, the sex beast, was having relations with all these women. And that was why a Court of Impeachment couldn't accuse him of having lied under oath about it.'

'Jesus,' Harry said, looking up at the helicopter hovering high above them.

On the radio, someone speaking with a Norwegian accent asked, 'Mr President, this is the fourth visit to Norway by a sitting US President. How does it feel?'

Pause.

'It's really nice to be back here. And I see it as even more important that the leaders of the state of Israel and of the Palestinian people can meet here. The key to—'

'Can you remember anything from your previous visit to Norway, Mr President?'

'Yes, of course. In today's talks I hope that we can—'

'What significance have Oslo and Norway had for world peace, Mr President?'

'Norway has played an important role.'

A voice without a Norwegian accent: 'What concrete results does the President consider to be realistic?'

The recording was cut and someone from the studio took over.

'We heard there the President saying that Norway has had a crucial role in . . . er, the Middle Eastern peace process. Right now the President is on his way to—'

Harry groaned and switched off the radio. 'What is it with this country, Ellen?'

She shrugged her shoulders.

'Passed Post 27,' the walkie-talkie on the dashboard crackled.

He looked at her.

'Everyone ready at their posts?' he asked. She nodded.

'Here we go,' he said. She rolled her eyes. It was the fifth time he had said that since the procession set off from Gardemoen Airport. From where they were parked they could see the empty motorway stretch out from the toll barrier up towards Trosterud and Furuset. The blue light on the roof rotated sluggishly. Harry rolled down the car window to stick out his hand and remove a withered yellow leaf caught under the windscreen wiper.

'A robin redbreast,' Ellen said, pointing. 'Rare to see one so late in autumn.'

'Where?'

'There. On the roof of the toll booth.'

Harry lowered his head and peered through the windscreen.

'Oh yes. So that's a robin redbreast?'

'Yep. But you probably can't tell the difference between that and a redwing, I imagine?'

'Right.' Harry shaded his eyes. Was he becoming short-sighted?

'It's a rare bird, the redbreast,' Ellen said, screwing the top back on the thermos.

'Is that a fact?' Harry said.

'Ninety per cent of them migrate south. A few take the risk, as it were, and stay here.'

'*As it were?*'

Another crackle on the radio: 'Post 62 to HQ. There's an unmarked car parked by the road two hundred metres before the turn-off for Lørenskog.'

A deep voice with a Bergen accent answered from HQ: 'One moment, 62. We'll look into it.'

Silence.

'Did you check the toilets?' Harry asked, nodding towards the Esso station.

'Yes, the petrol station has been cleared of all customers and employees. Everyone except the boss. We've locked him in his office.'

'Toll booths as well?'

'Done. Relax, Harry, all the checks have been done. Yes, the ones that stay do so in the hope that it will be a mild winter, right? That may be OK, but if they're wrong, they die. So why not head south, just in case, you might be wondering. Are they just lazy, the birds that stay?'

Harry looked in the mirror and saw the guards on either side of the railway bridge. Dressed in black with helmets and MP5 machine guns hanging around their necks. Even from where he was he could see the tension in their body language.

'The point is that if it's a mild winter, they can choose the best nesting places before the others return,' Ellen said, while trying to stuff the thermos into the already full glove compartment. 'It's a calculated risk, you see. You're either laughing all over your face or you're in deep, deep shit. Whether to take the risk or not. If you take the gamble, you may fall off the twig frozen stiff one night and not thaw out till spring. Bottle it and you might not have anywhere to nest when you return. These are, as it were, the eternal dilemmas you're confronted with.'

'You've got body armour on, haven't you?' Harry twisted round to check. 'Have you or haven't you?'

She tapped her chest with her knuckles by way of reply.

'Lightweight?'

She nodded.

'For fuck's sake, Ellen! I gave the order for ballistic vests to be worn. Not those Mickey Mouse vests.'

'Do you know what the Secret Service guys use?'

'Let me guess. Lightweight vests?'

'That's right.'

'Do you know what I don't give a shit about?'

'Let me guess. The Secret Service?'

'That's right.'

She laughed. Harry managed a smile too. There was a crackle from the radio.

'HQ to post 62. The Secret Service say it's their car parked on the turn-off to Lørenskog.'

'Post 62. Message received.'

'You see,' Harry said, banging the steering wheel in irritation, 'no communication. The Secret Service people do their own thing. What's that car doing up there without our knowledge? Eh?'

'Checking that we're doing our job,' Ellen said.

'According to the instructions *they* gave us.'

'You'll be allowed to make *some* decisions, so stop grumbling,' she said. 'And stop that drumming on the wheel.'

Harry's hands obediently leapt into his lap. She smiled. He let out one long stream of air: 'Yeah, yeah, yeah.'

His fingers found the butt of his service revolver, a .38 calibre Smith & Wesson, six shots. In his belt he had two additional speed loaders, each holding six shots. He patted the revolver, knowing that, strictly speaking, he wasn't actually authorised to carry a weapon. Perhaps he really was becoming short-sighted; after the forty-hour course last winter he had failed the shooting test. Although that was not so unusual, it was the first time it had happened to Harry and he didn't like it at all. All he had to do was take the test again – many had to take it four or five times – but for one reason or another Harry continued to put it off.

More crackling noises: 'Passed point 28.'

'One more point to go in the Romerike police district,' Harry said. 'The next one is Karihaugen and then it's us.'

'Why can't they do it how we used to? Just say where the motorcade is instead of all these stupid numbers,' Ellen asked in a grumbling tone.

'Guess.'

They answered in unison: 'The Secret Service!' And laughed.

'Passed point 29.'

He looked at his watch.

'OK, they'll be here in three minutes. I'll change the frequency on the walkie-talkie to Oslo police district. Run the final checks.'

Ellen closed her eyes to concentrate on the positive checks that came back one after the other. She put the microphone back into position. 'Everything in place and ready.'

'Thanks. Put your helmet on.'

'Eh? Honestly, Harry.'

'You heard what I said.'

'Put your helmet on yourself!'

'Mine's too small.'

A new voice. 'Passed point 1.'

'Oh shit, sometimes you're just so . . . unprofessional.' Ellen pulled the helmet over her head, fastened the chin strap and made faces in the driving mirror.

'Love you too,' said Harry, studying the road in front of them through binoculars. 'I can see them.'

At the top of the incline leading to Karihaugen the sun glinted off metal. For the moment Harry could only see the first car in the motorcade, but he knew the order: six motorcycles from the Norwegian police escort department, two Norwegian police escort cars, a Secret Service car, then two identical Cadillac Fleetwoods (special Secret Service cars flown in from the US) and the President sitting in one of them. Which one was kept secret. Or perhaps he was sitting in both, Harry thought. One for Jekyll and one for Hyde. Then came the bigger vehicles: ambulance, communications car and several Secret Service cars.

'Everything seems quiet enough,' Harry said. His binoculars moved slowly from right to left. The air quivered above the tarmac even though it was a cool November morning.

Ellen could see the outline of the first car. In thirty seconds they would have passed the toll gates and half the job would be over. And in two days' time, when the same cars had passed the toll going in the opposite direction, she and Harry could go back to their usual work. She preferred dealing with dead people in the Serious Crime Unit to getting up at three in the morning to sit in a cold Volvo with an irritable Harry, who was clearly burdened by the responsibility he had been given.

Apart from Harry's regular breathing, there was total quiet in the car. She checked that the light indicators on both radios were green. The motorcade was almost at the bottom of the hill. She decided she would go to Tørst and get drunk after the job. There was a guy there she had exchanged looks with; he had black curls and brown, slightly dangerous eyes. Lean. Looked a bit bohemian, intellectual. Perhaps . . .

'What the—'

Harry had already grabbed the microphone. 'There's someone in the third booth from the left. Can anyone identify this individual?'

The radio answered with a crackling silence as Ellen's gaze raced from one booth to the next in the row. There! She saw a man's back behind the brown glass of the box – only forty or fifty metres away. The silhouette of the figure was clear in the light from behind, as was the short barrel with the sights protruding over his shoulder.

'Weapon!' she shouted. 'He's got a machine gun.'

'Fuck!' Harry kicked open the car door, took hold of the frame and swung out. Ellen stared at the motorcade. It couldn't be more than a few hundred metres off. Harry stuck his head inside the car.

'He's not one of ours, but he could be Secret Service,' he said. 'Call HQ.' He already had the revolver in his hand.

'Harry . . .'

'Now! And give a blast on the horn if HQ say it's one of theirs.'

Harry started to run towards the toll booth and the back of the man dressed in a suit. From the barrel, Harry guessed the gun was an Uzi. The raw early morning air smarted in his lungs.

'Police!' he shouted in Norwegian, then in English.

No reaction. The thick glass of the box was manufactured to deaden the traffic noise outside. The man had turned his head towards the motorcade now and Harry could see his dark Ray-Bans. Secret Service. Or someone who wanted to give that impression.

Twenty metres now.

How did he get inside a locked booth if he wasn't one of theirs? Damn! Harry could already hear the motorcycles. He wouldn't make it to the box.

He released the safety catch and took aim, praying that the car horn would shatter the stillness of this strange morning on a closed motorway he had never wanted at any time to be anywhere near. The instructions were clear, but he was unable to shut out his thoughts: *Thin vest. No communication. Shoot, it is not your fault. Has he got a family?*

The motorcade was coming from directly behind the toll booth, and it was coming fast. In a couple of seconds the Cadillacs would be level with the booths. From the corner of his left eye he noticed a movement, a little bird taking off from the roof.

Whether to take the risk or not . . . the eternal dilemma.

He thought about the low neck on the vest, lowered the revolver half an inch. The roar of the motorcycles was deafening.